UNHOLY TERROR

"I know you," the zealot priest rasped. "The barbarian who preferred the company of Vaspurakaners to mine." Zemarkhos' stabbing finger darted at the Vaspurakaners his magic had slain. "There they lie, given over to death by Phos' just judgment."

"Any evil wizard could work the same, without taking Phos' mantle for himself," Marcus shouted, and the crowd gasped. "Come on, show everyone here Phos' power—strike *me* dead with it."

"No need to beg," Zemarkhos said, his voice an eager whisper. "I will give you what you want." The priest's arm shot toward the tribune, and Marcus stumbled under the immaterial blow. His ears roared; his sight grew dark; agony filled his mind like the kiss of molten lead.

Dimly he heard Zemarkhos' cackle of cruel, vaunting laughter.

By Harry Turtledove
Published by Ballantine Books:

The Videssos Cycle:

THE MISPLACED LEGION

AN EMPEROR FOR THE LEGION

THE LEGION OF VIDESSOS

SWORDS OF THE LEGION

NONINTERFERENCE

Book Four of *The Videssos Cycle*

Swords of the Legion

Harry Turtledove

A Del Rey Book

BALLANTINE BOOKS • NEW YORK

A Del Rey Book
Published by Ballantine Books

Copyright © 1987 by Harry Turtledove

All rights reserved under International and Pan-American Copyright Conventions. Published in the United States of America by Ballantine Books, a division of Random House, Inc., New York, and simultaneously in Canada by Random House of Canada Limited, Toronto.

Library of Congress Catalog Card Number: 87-91490

ISBN 0-345-33070-6

Manufactured in the United States of America

First Edition: October 1987
Fourth Printing: December 1989

Cover Art by Romas
Map by Shelly Shapiro

For Alison, Rachel, and Laura again

WHAT HAS GONE BEFORE:

THREE COHORTS OF A ROMAN LEGION, LED BY MILITARY TRI-
bune Marcus Aemilius Scaurus and senior centurion Gaius
Philippus, were ambushed by Gauls. The Gallic leader Viridovix
challenged Marcus to single combat. Both bore druids' swords.
When the blades crossed, a dome of light surrounded Viridovix
and the Romans. Suddenly they were in the world of the Empire
of Videssos, a land where the priests of Phos could work real
magic. There they were hired as mercenaries by the Empire.

In Videssos the city, capital of the Empire, Marcus was
presented to the soldier-Emperor Mavrikios Gavras and his
brother Thorisin. Later, at a banquet, he met Mavrikios'
daughter Alypia and the sorcerer Avshar. Avshar forced a
duel, but when the druids' sword neutralized Avshar's spells,
Marcus won. Avshar sought revenge by magic. It failed, and
Avshar fled to his homeland Yezd, western enemy of Videssos. Videssos declared war on Yezd.

Troops flooded into the capital, and tension arose between
the mercenaries from the island Duchy of Namedalen and the
native Videssians over a small matter of religion. Each regarded the other as heretical. The Videssian patriarch Balsamon preached tolerance, but fanatic monks soon started a riot.
Marcus led the Romans to quell that. As the riot was ending,
Marcus saved the Namdalener woman Helvis. Soon she and
her young son joined him in the Roman barracks.

Finally Videssos' army moved west against Yezd, accompanied by women and children. Marcus was pleased that
Helvis had become pregnant, but shocked to learn that the left
wing was commanded by young and inexperienced Ortaias

1

Sphrantzes, son of the prime minister, Vardanes Sphrantzes.

Three Vaspurakaners joined later—Senpat Sviodo and his wife Nevrat to act as guides, and the general Gagik Bagratouni. When the fanatic priest Zemarkhos cursed him, Bagratouni threw the priest and his dog into a sack and beat them. Marcus finally intervened.

At last the two armies met. The battle seemed a draw, until a spell from the sorcerer Avshar panicked Ortaias, who fled. As the left wing collapsed, the Emperor was killed and the army routed.

The Romans retreated eastward in order, rescuing the teacher-priest Nepos and being joined by Laon Pakhymer and his mounted Katrishers as cavalry support. They wintered in a friendly town, learning that Ortaias had declared himself Emperor and forced Alypia to marry him.

Thorisin Gavras had wintered in a nearby town with twenty-five hundred troops. In the spring, the legion joined him to march on Videssos the city. The gates were barred, but a group inside the city opened them. As the defenders fled, Avshar, disguised as Ortaias' commander Rhavas, tried foul magic, but was foiled by the swords of Viridovix and Marcus. Avshar retreated, then suddenly vanished.

Thorisin was crowned Emperor. He annulled Alypia's marriage and banished Ortaias to serve as a humble monk. But he was handicapped by lack of funds. He sent Marcus to supervise the accounting "pen-pushing" bureaucrats, and Marcus discovered that many rich landowners did not pay their taxes. The worst offender was a general, Onomagoulos, a former friend of Mavrikios Gavras. Learning this, Thorisin sent Namdaleni under count Drax to deal with Onomagoulos.

He also sent a group north to seek help from the Arshaum. The Greek physician Gorgidas, disgusted at being unable to learn healing magic, joined, as did Viridovix, fleeing a wrathful lover.

Drax overcame and killed Onomagoulos, then declared the western region Namdalener territory under him. Thorisin sent Marcus and the legion to defeat him.

In the north, Viridovix was kidnapped by outlaws working for Avshar. He escaped to a nomad village, which was soon destroyed by the outlaws. Viridovix and young Batbaian fled into a raging blizzard. Meantime, Gorgidas and the others reached the Arshaum leader Arghun. Gorgidas managed to save Arghun when the Yezda envoy tried to poison him, and

Arghun mustered an army to help Videssos by striking Yezd. On the march, they found the almost-frozen Viridovix. Gorgidas saved him, using the healing magic which he had given up on before.

Meantime, Marcus moved against count Drax and his Namdaleni. After a difficult campaign, he defeated them and took the leaders as prisoners. Among them was Soteric, brother of Helvis. She used wine and her body to put Marcus into a sound sleep, then stole out to free the prisoners and go with them, taking Marcus' children. With mixed sadness and shame, Marcus returned to report to Thorisin.

His brief account was not enough for the Emperor. With Alypia watching, Thorisin ordered Nepos to prepare a drug to make Marcus talk freely and truthfully, then inquired all details, even the personal ones. At the end, Thorisin admitted, "I have raped an innocent man."

Marcus returned to his job supervising the pen-pushers, but tried like a hermit to shut the world away. Alypia, however, sympathized deeply with him. Greeting him at a festival, she got him to take her to dinner. And dinner led to other things. . . .

I

"I'D LIKE TO HAVE A BETTER LOOK AT THAT ONE, IF I COULD,"
Marcus Aemilius Scaurus said, pointing to a necklace.

"Which?" asked the jeweler, a fat, bald little man with a
curly black beard. The Roman pointed again. A grin flashed
across the craftsman's face; he bobbed a quick bow. "You
have good taste, my master—that is a piece fit for a princess."

The military tribune grinned, too, at the unintended truth
in the jeweler's sales talk. I intend it for one, he thought.
That he did not say; what he did came out in a growl:
"With a price to match, no doubt." Best to start beating the
fellow down before he named a figure, for Scaurus intended
to have the necklace.

The jeweler, who had played this game many times, assumed a look of injured innocence. "Who spoke of money?
Here," he said, pressing the chain into Marcus' hands, "take
it over to the window; see if it is not as fine as I say. Once
you are satisfied of that, we can speak further, if you like."

The shop had its shutters flung wide. The sun shone bravely, though every so often the northerly breeze would send a
patch of cloud in front of it, dimming for a moment the
hundreds of gilded spheres that topped Phos' temples, large
and small, all through Videssos the city. It was still winter, but
spring was in the air. Gulls scrawked high overhead; they
lived in the Videssian Empire's capital the year around. Closer
by, the tribune heard a chiffchaff, an early arrival, whistle
from a rooftop.

He hefted the necklace. The thick, intricately worked

4

chain had the massy, sensuous feel of pure gold. He held it close to his face; months of work with tax receipts in the imperial chancery were making him a trifle nearsighted. The nine square-cut emeralds were perfectly matched in size and color, a deep, luminous green. They would play up Alypia Gavra's eyes, he thought, smiling again. Between them were eight oval beads of mother-of-pearl. In the shifting light their elusive color shimmered and danced, as if seen underwater.

"I've seen worse," Marcus said grudgingly as he walked back to the jeweler behind his counter, and the bargaining began in earnest. Both of them were sweating by the time they agreed on a price.

"Whew!" said the artisan, dabbing at his forehead with a linen rag and eyeing the tribune with new respect. "From your fairness and accent I took you for a Haloga, and Phos the lord of the great and good mind knows how free the northerners are with their gold. But you, sir, you haggle like a city man."

"I'll take that for a compliment," Scaurus said. Videssians often mistook the tribune for one of the big, towheaded northmen who served the Empire as mercenaries. Most of his Romans were short, olive-skinned, and dark of hair and eye, like the folk into whose land they had been swept three and a half years before, but he sprang from the north Italian town of Mediolanum. Some long-forgotten Celtic strain gave him extra inches and yellow hair, though his features were aquiline rather than Gallic sharp or blunt like a German's—or, in this world, a Haloga's.

The jeweler was wrapping the necklace in wool batting to protect the stones. Marcus counted out goldpieces to pay him. The artisan, taking no chances, counted them again, nodded, and opened a stout iron strongbox. He dropped them in, say-ing, "And I owe you a sixth. Would you like it in gold or silver?"

"Silver, I think." Videssian sixth-goldpieces were shoddy things, stamped from the same dies as the one-third coins but only half as thick. They were fairly scarce, and for good rea-son. In a purse they bent and even broke, and they were more likely to be of short weight or debased metal than more com-mon money.

Marcus put the four silver coins in his belt-pouch and tucked the necklace away inside his tunic. He would have to cross the plaza of Palamas to get back to his room in the palace complex, and light-fingered men flocked to the great square no less than honest merchants. The jeweler tipped him a wink, understanding perfectly. "You're a careful one. You wouldn't want to lose your pretty so soon after you get it."

"No indeed."

The jeweler bowed, and held the bow until Scaurus left his shop. He waved as the tribune walked past the window. Well pleased, the Roman returned the salute.

He walked west along Middle Street toward the plaza of Palamas. Videssians bustled all around him, paying him no mind. Most of the men wore thick, plainly cut tunics and baggy woolen trousers like his own. Despite the chilly weather, a few favored the long brocaded robes that were more often used as ceremonial garb than street wear. Town toughs swaggered along in their own costume: tunics with great billowing sleeves pulled tight at the wrists and clinging hose dyed in as many bright colors as they could get. Some of them shaved the backs of their heads. The Namdaleni—sometimes mercenaries, sometimes deadly foes for Videssos—had that style, too, but with them it served a purpose: to let their heads fit their helmets more snugly. For Videssos' ruffians it was simply a fad.

The tribune jumped when one of the roughnecks shouted his name and came up to him, hand outstretched. Then he recognized the fellow, more by his bad teeth than anything else. "Hello, Arsaber," he said, clasping hands. The bravo had been one of the men who threw open the gates to the city when Thorisin Gavras took the imperial throne from the usurper Ortaias Sphrantzes, and had fought bravely enough on the Romans' side.

"Good to see you, Ronam," Arsaber boomed, and Marcus gritted his teeth—that idiot usher's mispronunciation at a long-ago banquet looked to be immortal. Cheerfully oblivious, the Videssian went on, "Meet my woman, Zenonis, and these three lads are my sons: Tzetzes, Stotzas, and Boethios. Love, boys, this is the famous Scaurus, the one who beat the Namdaleni and the bureaucrats both." He winked at the tribune. "My bet is, the pen-pushers're tougher."

"Some ways," Marcus admitted. He nodded to Zenonis, a small, happy-looking woman of about thirty in flowered silk headscarf, rabbit-fur jacket, and long wool skirt; gravely shook hands with Tzetzes, who was about six. The other two boys were too young to pay much attention to him—Stotzas was two or so, while Zenonis carried Boethios, a tiny babe swaddled in a blanket.

Arsaber stood by, beaming, as the tribune made small talk with his family. The ruffian would have been the very picture of domesticity but for his outlandish clothes and the stout bludgeon that hung on his belt. After a while he said, "Come on, dear, we'll be late to cousin Dryos'. Roast quails," he explained to Scaurus, pumping his hand again.

The tribune caught himself looking down at his fingers; it was a good idea to count them after shaking hands with Arsaber. He surreptitiously patted his chest to make sure the smiling rogue had not managed to filch away his necklace.

The chance meeting saddened him; it took a while to figure out why. Then he realized that Arsaber's family reminded him achingly of the one he had built up until Helvis found her native Namdalener ties more important than the ones that bound her to him and deserted him, helping her brother Soteric and several other important prisoners escape in the process. The child they had been expecting would only be a little younger than Boethios—but Helvis was in Namdalen now, and Scaurus did not know if it was boy or girl.

In vanished Italy, in a youth he would never see again, he had trained in the Stoic school of philosophy, had been taught to stay untroubled in the face of sickness, death, slander, and intrigue. The sentiment was noble, but, he feared, past his attainment after her betrayal of their love.

The thought of Italy brought to mind the remaining Romans, the survivors of everything this world could throw at them. In many ways he missed them more even than Helvis and his children. They alone shared with him a language, indeed an entire past that was alien to Videssos and all its neighbors. He knew they had spent an easy winter at their garrison duty in the western town of Garsavra; that much Gaius Philippus' three or four brief notes had made clear. But the senior centurion, though a soldier without peer, was only sketchily literate, and his scrawled words did not call up the feeling of being with the legionaries that Scaurus needed in his semi-exile in the capital.

Boots squelching through dirty, half-melted snow, he walked past the block-long red granite pile of a building that housed the imperial archives, various government ministries, and the city prison. His somber mood lifted; he smiled and reached inside his tunic to touch the necklace once more. For all he knew, Alypia Gavra might be going through the archives now, looking for material to add to her history. So she had been doing on Midwinter's Day a few months past, when she happened to encounter the tribune as she left the government offices.

That night a friendship had become much more. Their meetings since, though, were far fewer than Marcus would have wanted. As Thorisin's niece, Alypia was hemmed round with the elaborate ceremonial of an ancient empire, the more so since the Emperor had no legitimate heir.

The Roman tried not to think of the danger he courted along with her. If discovered, he could expect scant mercy. Thorisin sat none too secure on his throne. The Emperor would only see him as an ambitious mercenary captain seeking to improve his own position through an affair with the princess. Scaurus had done great service for him, but he had also flouted Thorisin's will more than once—and, worse perhaps, proved right in doing so.

The plaza of Palamas drove such worries from his head. If Videssos the city was a microcosm of the polyglot Empire of Videssos, then its great square made a miniature of a miniature. Goods from every corner of the world appeared there, and merchants from every corner of the world to sell them. A few nomadic Khamorth crossed the Videssian Sea from the imperial outpost at Prista to hawk the products of the Pardrayan steppe—tallow, honey, wax—at the capital. A couple of huge Halogai, their hair in yellow braids, had set up a booth for the furs and amber of their northern home. Despite the war with Yezd, caravans still reached Videssos from the west with silks and spices, slaves and sugar. A Namdalener trader spat at the feet of a bored-looking Videssian who had offered him a poor price for his cargo of ale; another was displaying a table of knives. A Khatrisher, a lithe little man who looked like a Khamorth but acted like an imperial, dickered with a factor over what he could get for the load of timber he had brought to the city.

And along with the foreigners were the Videssians themselves: proud, clever, vivid, loud, quick to take offense, and as quick to give it. Minstrels strolled through the surging crowds, singing and accompanying themselves on drums, lutes, or pandouras, which had a more plangent, mournful tone. Marcus, who had no ear for music, ignored them as best he could. Some of the locals were not so kind. "Why don't you drown that poor cat and have done?" somebody shouted, whereupon the maligned musician broke his lute over the critic's head. The people around them pulled them apart.

Shaven-headed priests and monks of Phos moved here and there in their blue robes, some exhorting the faithful to pray to the good god, others, on some mission from temple or monastery, haggling with as much vigor and skill as any secular. Scribes stood behind little portable podiums, each with stylus or quill poised to write for folk who had money but no letters. A juggler cursed a skinny carpenter who had bumped him and made him drop a plate. "And to Skotos' ice with *you*," the other returned. "If you were any good, you would have caught it." Courtesans of every description and price strutted and pranced, wearing bright, hard smiles. Touts sidled up to strangers, praising this horse or sneering at that.

Venders, some in stalls, others wanderers themselves, cried their wares: squid, tunny, eels, prawns—as a port, the city ate great quantities of seafood. There was bread from wheat, rye, barley; ripe cheeses; porridge; oranges and lemons from the westlands; olives and olive oil; garlic and onions; fermented fish sauce. Wine was offered, most of it too sweet for Scaurus' taste, though that did not stop him from drinking it. Spoons, goblets, plates of iron, brass, wood, or solid silver were offered; drugs and potions allegedly medicinal, others allegedly aphrodisiacal; perfumes; icons, amulets, and books of spells. The tribune was cautious even toward small-time wizards here in Videssos, where magic was realer than it had been in Rome. Boots, sandals, tooled-leather belts; hats of straw, leather, linen, cloth-of-gold; and scores more whose yells Marcus could not catch because they drowned each other out.

A shout like the roar of a god came from the Amphitheater, the huge oval of limestone and marble that formed the plaza of Palamas' southern border. A seller of dried figs grinned at Scaurus. "A long shot came in," he said knowingly.

"I'd bet you're right." The tribune bought a handful of fruit. He was popping them into his mouth one at a time when he nearly ran into an imperial cavalry officer, Provhos Mourtzouphlos.

Mourtzouphlos lifted an eyebrow; scorn spread across his handsome, aristocratic features. "Enjoying yourself, outlander?" he asked ironically. He brushed long hair back from his forehead and scratched his thickly bearded chin.

"Yes, thanks," Marcus answered with as much aplomb as he could muster, but he felt himself flushing under the Videssian's sardonic eye. Even though he had ten years on the brash young horseman, who was probably not yet thirty, Mourtzouphlos was native-born, which more than canceled the advantage of age. And acting like a barbarian bumpkin in front of him did not help either. Mourtzouphlos was one of the many imperials with a fine contempt for foreigners under any circumstances; that the Roman was a successful captain only made him doubly suspicious to the other.

"Thorisin tells me we'll be moving against the Yezda in the Arandos valley after the roads west dry," the Videssian said, carefully scoring a couple of more points against Scaurus. His casual use of the Emperor's given name bespoke the renown he had won in the campaign with Gavras against Namdalener invaders around Opsikion in the east, while the tribune toiled unseen in the westlands against the great count Drax and more Namdaleni. And his news was from some council to which the Roman, in disfavor for letting Drax get away in the escape Helvis had devised, had not been invited.

But Marcus had a comeback ready. "I'm sure we'll do well against them," he said. "After all, my legionaries have held the plug of the Arandos at Garsavra the winter long."

Mourtzouphlos scowled, not caring to be reminded of that. "Well, yes," he grudged. "A good day to you, I'm sure." With a flick of his cloak, he turned on his heel and was gone.

The tribune smiled at his stiff retreating back. There's one for you, you arrogant dandy, he thought. Mourtzouphlos' imitation of the Emperor's shaggy beard and unkempt hair annoyed Scaurus every time he saw him. Thorisin's carelessness about such things was part of a genuine dislike for formality, elegance, or ceremony of any sort. With the cavalryman it was pure pose, to curry favor with his master. That cape he had flourished was thick maroon samite trimmed in ermine, while he wore a belt of gold links and spurred jackboots whose leather was soft and supple enough for gloves.

When Marcus came on a vender with a tray of smoked

sardines, he bought several of those and ate them, too, hoping
Mourtzouphlos was watching.

Rather apprehensively, the tribune broke the sky-blue wax
seal on the little roll of parchment. The note inside was in a
thin, spidery hand that he knew at once, though he had not
seen it for a couple of years: "I should be honored if you
would attend me at my residence tomorrow afternoon." With
that seal and that script, the signature was hardly necessary:
"Balsamon, ecumenical Patriarch of the Videssians."

"What does *he* want?" Scaurus muttered. He came up with
no good answer. True, he did not follow Phos, which would
have been enough to set off almost any ecclesiastic in the
Empire. Balsamon, though, was not typical of the breed. A
scholar before he was made into a prelate, he brought quite
un-Videssian tolerance to the patriarchal office.

All of which, Marcus thought, leaves me no closer to
what he wants with me. The tribune did not flatter himself
that the invitation was for the pleasure of his company; the
patriarch, he was uneasily aware, was a good deal more
clever than he.

His Stoic training did let him stop worrying about what he
could not help; soon enough he would find out. He tucked
Balsamon's summons into his beltpouch.

The patriarchal residence was by Phos' High Temple in the
northern part of the city, not far from the Neorhesian harbor. It
was a fairly modest old stucco building with a domed roof of
red tiles. No one would have looked at it twice anywhere in
the city; alongside the High Temple's opulence it was doubly
invisible.

The pine trees set in front of it were twisted with age, but
green despite the season. Scaurus always thought of the antiq-
uity of Videssos itself when he saw them. The rest of the
shrubbery and the hedgerows to either side had not yet come
into leaf and were still brown and bare.

The tribune knocked on the stout oak door. He heard foot-
steps inside; a tall, solidly made priest swung the door wide.
"Yes? How may I serve you?" he asked, eyeing Marcus' man-
ifestly foreign figure with curiosity.

The Roman gave his name and handed the cleric Balsamon's summons, watched him all but stiffen to attention as he
read it. "This way, please," the fellow said, new respect in his
voice. He made a smart about-turn and led the tribune down a

hallway filled with ivory figurines, icons to Phos, and other antiquities.

From his walk, his crisp manner, and the scar that furrowed his shaved pate, Marcus would have given long odds that the other had been a soldier before he became a priest. Likely he served as Thorisin Gavras' watchdog over Balsamon as well as servant. Any Emperor with an ounce of sense kept an eye on his patriarch; politics and religion mixed inextricably in Videssos.

The priest tapped at the open door. "What is it, Saborios?" came Balsamon's reedy voice, an old man's tenor.

"The outlander is here to see you, your Sanctity, at your command," Saborios said, as if reporting to a superior officer.

"Is he? Well, I'm delighted. We'll be talking a while, you know, so why don't you run along and sharpen your spears?" Along with having his guess confirmed, the tribune saw that Balsamon had not changed much—he had baited his last companion the same way.

But instead of scowling, as Gennadios would have done, Saborios just said, "They're every one of them gleaming, your Sanctity. Maybe I'll hone a dagger instead." He nodded to Scaurus. "Go on in." As the Roman did, the priest shut the door behind him.

"Can't get a rise out of that man," Balsamon grumbled, but he was chuckling, too. "Sit anywhere," he told the tribune, waving expansively; the order was easier given than obeyed. Scrolls, codices, and writing tablets lined every wall of his study and were stacked in untidy piles on the battered couch the patriarch was using, on several tables, and on both the elderly chairs in the room.

Trying not to disturb the order they were in—if there was any—Marcus moved a stack of books from one of the chairs to the stone floor and sat down. The chair gave an alarming groan under his weight, but held.

"Wine?" Balsamon asked.

"Please."

With a grunt of effort, Balsamon rose from the low couch, uncorked the bottle, and rummaged through the chaos around him for a couple of cups. Seen from behind, the fat old graybeard in his shabby blue robe—a good deal less splendid than Saborios', to say nothing of less clean—looked more like a retired cook than a prelate.

But when he turned round to hand Scaurus his wine—

the cup was chipped—there was no mistaking the force of character stamped on his engagingly ugly features. When one looked at his eyes, the pug nose and wide, plump cheeks were forgotten. Wisdom dwelt in this man, try though he sometimes did to disguise it with a quirk of bushy, still-black brows.

Under his eyes, though, were dark pouches of puffy flesh; his skin was pale, with a faint sheen of sweat on his high forehead. "Are you well?" Marcus said in some alarm.

"You're still young, to ask that question," the patriarch said. "When a man reaches my age, either he is well or he is dead." But his droll smile could not hide the relief with which he sank back onto the couch.

He raised his hands above his head, quickly spoke his faith's creed: "We bless thee, Phos, Lord with the right and good mind, by thy grace our protector, watchful beforehand that the great test of life may be decided in our favor." Then he spat on the floor in rejection of the good god's foe Skotos. The Videssian formula over food or drink completed, he drained his cup. "Drink," he urged the Roman.

He cocked an eyebrow when Marcus failed to go through the ritual. "Heathen," he said. In most priests' mouths, it would have been a word to start a pogrom; from Balsamon it was simply a label, and perhaps a way to get a sly dig in at the tribune.

Of its kind, the wine was good, though as usual Scaurus longed for something less cloying. He beat Balsamon to his feet and poured a second cup for both of them. The patriarch nodded and tossed it down; settling cautiously back into his seat, Marcus worked at his more slowly.

Balsamon was studying him hard enough to make him fidget. Age might have left the patriarch's eyes red-tracked with veins, but they were none the less piercing for that. He was one of the few people who gave the tribune the uncomfortable feeling that they could read his thoughts. "How can I help your Sanctity?" he asked, attempting briskness.

"I'm not *your* Sanctity, as we both know," the patriarch retorted, but again no fanatic's zeal was in his voice. When he spoke again, it was with what sounded like real admiration. "You don't say a lot, do you? We Videssians talk too bloody much."

"What would you have me say?"

" 'What would you have me say?' " Balsamon mimicked.

His laugh set his soft paunch quivering. "You sit there like a natural-born innocent, and anyone who hadn't seen you in action would take you for just another blond barbarian to be fooled like a Haloga. Yet somehow you prosper. This silence must be a useful tool."

Without a word, Marcus spread his hands and shrugged. Balsamon laughed harder; he had a good laugh, one that invited everyone who heard it to share the joke. The tribune found himself smiling in response to it. But when he said, "Truly, I don't call this past winter prospering," his smile slipped.

"Some ways, no," the patriarch said. "We're none of us perfect, nor lucky all the time either. But some ways..." He paused, scratching his chin. His voice was musing as he went on. "What do you suppose she sees in you, anyway?"

It was a good thing Marcus' cup was on the arm of his chair; had it been in his hand, he would have dropped it. "She?" he echoed, hoping he only sounded foolish and not frightened.

"Alypia Gavra, of course. Why did you think I sent for you?" Balsamon said matter-of-factly. Then he saw Scaurus' face, and concern replaced the amusement on his own. "I didn't mean to make you go so white. Finish your wine, get some wind back in your sails. She asked me to ask you here."

Mechanically, the tribune drank. Too much was happening too fast, alarm and relief jangling together like discordant lute strings. "I think you'd best tell me more," he said. Another fear was in there, too; had she had enough of him, and tried to pick an impersonal way to let him know?

He straightened in his chair. No—were it that, Alypia had the decency, and the courage, to tell him to his face. His memories were whispering to him; that was all. Having been abandoned by one woman he had trusted and loved, it was hard to be sure of another.

The twinkle was back in Balsamon's eyes, a good sign. He said blandly, "She said you might be interested to learn that she had scheduled an afternoon appointment with me three days from now, to pick my brains for what I recall of Ioannakis III, the poor fool who was Avtokrator for a couple of unhappy years before Strobilos Sphrantzes."

"And so?" Alypia had been working on her history long before the Romans came to Videssos.

"Why, only that if she happened to go someplace else when

she was supposed to be here, in my senility and decrepitude I don't think I'd know the difference, and I'd babble on about Ioannakis all the same."

The tribune's jaw fell; amazed gladness shouted in him. Balsamon watched, all innocence. "I must say this senility and decrepitude of yours are moderately hard to see," Marcus said.

Did one of the patriarch's eyelids dip? "Oh, they come and go. For instance, I suspect I shan't remember much of this little talk of ours tomorrow. Sad, is it not?"

"A pity," Scaurus agreed gravely.

Then Balsamon was serious once more, passing an age-spotted hand in front of his face. "You had better deserve her and the risk she runs for your sake." He looked the Roman up and down. "You just may. I hope you do, for your sake as well as hers. She always was a good judge of such things, but with what she suffered she cannot afford to be wrong."

Marcus nodded, biting his lip. After Alypia's father—Thorisin's older brother Mavrikios—was killed at Maragha, young Ortaias Sphrantzes had claimed the throne and gone through the forms of marriage with her to help cement his place. But Ortaias' uncle Vardanes was the true power in that brief, unhappy reign and took her from his nephew as a plaything. The tribune's hands tightened into fists whenever he thought of those months. He said, "That once, I wished I were a Yezda, to give Vardanes the requital he deserved."

Balsamon's mobile features grew grave as he studied Scaurus. "You'll do, I think." He stayed somber. "You hazard yourself in this, too," he said. The tribune began a shrug, but Balsamon's eyes held him still. "If you persist, greater danger will spring from it than any you have ever known, and only Phos can guess if you will win free in the end."

The patriarch's gaze seemed to pierce the tribune; his voice went slow and deep. Marcus felt the hair prickle on his arms and at the nape of his neck. Videssian priests had strange abilities, many of them—healing and all sorts of magery. The Roman had never thought Balsamon more than an uncommonly wise and clever man, but suddenly he was not so sure. His words sounded like foretelling, not mere warning.

"What else do you see?" Marcus demanded harshly.

The patriarch jerked as if stung. The uncanny concentration faded from his face. "Eh? Nothing," he said in his normal voice, and Scaurus cursed his own abruptness.

After that, the talk turned to inconsequential things. Marcus found himself forgetting to be annoyed that he had not learned more. Balsamon was an endlessly absorbing talker, whether dissecting another priest's foibles, discoursing on his collection of ivory figurines from Makuran—"Another reason to hate the Yezda. Not only are they robbers and murderous Skotos-lovers, but they've cut off trade since they began infesting the place." And he swelled up in what looked like righteous wrath—or laughing at himself.

He picked at a bit of dried eggyolk on the threadbare sleeve of his robe, commenting, "You see, there is a point to my untidiness after all. Had I been wearing that—" He pointed to a surplice of cloth-of-gold and blue silk, ornamented with rows of gleaming seed pearls. "—when I was at breakfast the other day, I might have been liable to excommunication for soiling it."

"Another reason for Zemarkhos," Scaurus said. The fanatic priest, holding Amorion in the westlands in defiance of Yezda and Empire alike, had hurled anathemas at Balsamon and Thorisin both for refusing to acclaim his pogrom against the Vaspurakaners driven into his territory by Yezda raiders— their crime was not worshiping Phos the same way the Videssians did.

"Don't twit me over that one," Balsamon said, wincing. "The man is a wolf in priest's clothing, and a rabid wolf at that. I tried to persuade the local synod that chose him to reconsider, but they would not. 'Unwarranted interference from the capital,' they called it. He reminds me of the tailor's cat that fell into a vat of blue dye. The mice thought he'd become a monk and given up eating meat."

Marcus chuckled, but the patriarch's stubby fingers drummed on his knee; his mouth twisted in frustration. "I wonder how many he's burned since power fell into his lap— and what more I could have done to stop him." He sighed, shaking his head.

In an odd way, his gloom reassured the tribune. After his own failures, it did not hurt to be reminded that even as keen a man as Balsamon could sometimes come up short.

Saborios, certainly as efficient as a soldier if he was not one, had the door open for Scaurus even as he reached for the latch.

* * *

Alypia Gavra sat up in the narrow bed and poked Marcus in the ribs. He yelped. She touched the heavy gold of the necklace. "You are a madman for this," she said. "It's so beautiful I'll want to wear it, and how can I? Where will I say it came from? Why won't anyone have seen it before?"

"A pox on practicality," Scaurus said.

She laughed at him. "Coming from you, that's the next thing to blasphemy."

"Hrmmp." The Roman leaned back lazily. "I thought it would look good on you and I was right—the more so," he smiled, "when it's all you're wearing."

He watched a slow flush of pleasure rise from her breasts to her face. It showed plainly; she was fairer of skin than most Videssian women. He sometimes wondered if her dead mother had a touch of Haloga blood. Her features were not as sharply sculpted as those of her father or uncle, and her eyes were a clear green, rare among the imperials.

Mischief danced in them. "Beast," she said, and tried to poke him again. He jerked away. Once he had made the mistake of grabbing her instead and seen her go rigid in unreasoning panic; after Vardanes, she could not stand being restrained in any way.

The sudden motion nearly tumbled both of them out of bed. "There, you see," the tribune said. "That poking is a habit of mine you never should have picked up. Look what it brings on."

"I like doing things as you do," she said seriously. That brought him up short, as such remarks of hers always did. Helvis had tried to push him toward her own ways, which only made him more stubborn in clinging to his. It was strange, hearing from a woman that those were worth something.

He gave a sober nod, one suited to acknowledging something a legionary might have said, then grunted in annoyance, feeling very much a fool. He sat up himself and kissed her thoroughly. "That's better," she said.

Chickens clucked and scratched below the second-story window, whose shutters were flung wide to let in the mild air. Marcus could see the ponderous bulk of Phos' High Temple pushing into the sky not far away. He and Alypia had managed one meeting at this inn during the winter, so had it become a natural trysting place when she was supposed to be visiting Balsamon.

The innkeeper, a stout, middle-aged man named Aetios, shouted at a stableboy for forgetting to curry a mule. The fellow's eyes had sparked with recognition when Scaurus and the princess asked for a room, but the tribune was sure it was only because he had seen them before, not that he knew Alypia by sight. And in any case, with him, silver was better than wine for washing unpleasant memories away. His lumpish face came alive at the sweet sound of coins jingling in his palm.

Alypia made as if to get up, saying, "I really should go see Balsamon, if only for a little while. That way neither he nor I can be caught in a lie."

"If you must," Marcus said grumpily. With the ceremony that surrounded her as niece and closest kin of the Avtokrator, she could steal away but rarely, and the chance she took in doing so hung like a storm cloud over their meetings. He savored every moment with her, never sure it would not be the last.

As if reading his thoughts, she clung to him, crying, "What will we do? Thorisin is bound to find out, and then—" She came to a ragged stop, not wanting to think about "and then." In his short-tempered way, Thorisin Gavras was a decent man, but quick to lash out at anything he saw as a threat to his throne. After the strife he had already faced in his two and a half years on it, the tribune found it hard to blame him.

Or he would have, had the Emperor's suspicions affected anyone but him. "I wish," he said with illogical resentment, "your uncle would marry and get himself an heir. Then he'd have less reason to worry about you."

Alypia shook her head violently. "Oh, aye, I'd be safe then—safe to be married off to one of his cronies. He dares not now, for fear whoever had me would use me against him. Let his own line be set, though, and I become an asset to bind someone to him."

She stared at nothing; her nails bit his shoulder. Through clenched teeth she said, as much to herself as to him, "I will die before I lie again with a man not of my choosing."

Scaurus did not doubt she meant exactly that. He ran a slow hand up the smooth column of her back, trying to gentle her. "If only I were a Videssian," he said. That a princess of the blood could be given to an outland mercenary captain, even one more perfectly trusted than himself, was past thinking of in haughty Videssos.

"Wishes, wishes, wishes!" Alypia said. "What good are they? All we can truly count on is our danger growing worse the longer we go on, and only Phos knows when we will be free of it."

The tribune stared; in Videssos he was never sure where coincidence stopped and the uncanny began. "Balsamon told me something much like that," he said slowly, and at Alypia's inquiring glance recounted the strange moment when the patriarch had seemed to prophesy.

When he was done, he was startled to see her pale and shaken. She did not want to explain herself, but sat silent beside him. But he pressed her, and at last she said, "I have known him thus before. He gazed at you as if to read your soul, and there was none of his usual sport in his words." It was statement, not question.

"You have it," Scaurus acknowledged. "When did you see him so?"

"Only once, though I know the fit has taken him more often than that. 'Phos' gift,' he calls it, but I think curse would be a better name. He has spoken of it to me a few times; that he trusts me to share such a burden is the finest compliment I've ever had. You guessed well, dear Marcus," she said, touching his hand: "He sometimes has the prescient gift. But all he ever learns with it is of destruction and despair."

The Roman whistled tunelessly between his teeth. "It is a curse." He shook his head. "And how much more bitter for a joyful man like him. To see only the coming trouble, and to have to stay steady in the teeth of it . . . He's braver than I could be."

Alypia's face reflected the same distress the tribune felt.

"When was it you saw him?" he asked her again.

"He was visiting my father, just before he set out for Maragha. They were arguing and trading insults—you remember how the two of them used to carry on, neither meaning a word of what he said. Finally they ran out of darts to throw, and Balsamon got up to leave. You could see it coming over him, like the weight of the world. He stood there for a few seconds; my father and I started to ease him back down to a chair, thinking he'd been taken ill. But he shrugged us away and turned to my father and said one word in that—certain—voice."

"I know what you mean," Scaurus said. "What was it?"

" 'Good-bye.' " Alypia was a good mimic; the doom she packed into the word froze the Roman for a moment. She shivered herself at the memory. "No use pretending it was just an ordinary leave-taking, though my father and Balsamon did their best. Neither believed it; I've never seen Balsamon so flat in a sermon as he was at the High Temple the next day."

"I remember that!" Marcus said. "I was there, along with the rest of the officers. It troubled me at the time; I thought we deserved a better farewell than we got. I guess we were lucky to have any."

"Was that luck, as it turned out?" she asked, her voice low. She did not wait for a reply, but rushed on, "And now he sees peril to you. I'll leave you, I swear it, before I let you come to harm because of me." But instead of leaving, she clung to him with something close to desperation.

"Nothing the old man said made me think separating would matter," said Scaurus. "Whatever happens will happen as it should." The Stoic maxim did nothing to ease her; his lips on hers were a better cure. They sank back together onto the bed. The bedding sighed as their weight pressed the straw flat.

Some time later she reached up to touch his cheek and smiled, as she often did, at the faint rasp of newly shaved whiskers under her fingers. "You are a stubborn man," she said fondly; in a land of beards, the tribune still held to the smooth-faced Roman style. She took his head between her palms. "Oh, how could I think to leave you? But how can I stay?"

"I love you," he said, hugging her until she gave a startled gasp. It was true but, he knew too well, not an answer.

"I know, and I you. How much safer it would be for both of us if we did not." She glanced out the window, exclaimed in dismay when she saw how long the shadows had grown. "Let me up, dearest. Now I really must go."

Marcus rolled away; she scrambled to her feet. He admired her slim body for a last few seconds as she raised her arms over her head to slide on the long dress of deep gold wool; geometrically decorated insets of silk accented her narrow waist and the swell of her hips. "It suits you well," he said.

"Quite the courtier today, aren't you?" She smiled, slipping on sandals. She patted at her hair, which she wore short and straight. With a woman's practicality, she said, "It's lucky I don't fancy those piled-up heads of curls that are all the rage these days. They couldn't be repaired so easily."

She wrapped an orange linen shawl embroidered with flowers and butterflies around her shoulders and started for the door. "The necklace," Marcus said reluctantly. He was out of bed himself, fastening his tunic closed.

Her hand flew to her throat, but then she let it drop once more. "Balsamon can see it before I tuck it into my bag. After all, what other chance will I have to show it, and to show how thoughtful—to say nothing of daft—you were to give it to me?"

He felt himself glow with her praise; he had not heard much—nor, to be fair, given much—as he and Helvis quarreled toward their disastrous parting. Alypia gasped at the kiss he gave her. "Well!" she said, eyes glowing. "A bit more of that, sirrah, and Balsamon will get no look at my bauble today."

The tribune stepped back. "Too dangerous," he said with what tatters of Roman hardheadedness he had left. Alypia nodded and turned to go. As she did, something rattled inside her purse. Marcus laughed. "I know that noise, I'll wager: stylus and waxed tablet. Who was it the patriarch said, Ioannakis II?"

"The third; the second is three hundred years dead." She spoke with perfect seriousness; the history she was composing occupied a good deal of her time. When Scaurus caught her eye, she said, "There are pleasures and pleasures, you know."

"No need to apologize to me," he said quickly, and meant it. Were it not for her active wit and sense of detail, the two of them could not have met even half so often as they did, and likely would have been discovered long since.

"Apologize? I wasn't." Her voice turned frosty on the instant; she would not stand being taken lightly over her work.

"All right," he said mildly, and saw her relax. He went on, "You might want to compare notes with my friend Gorgidas when the embassy to the Arshaum comes back from the steppe." With a sudden stab of loneliness, he wondered how the Greek physician was faring; despite his acerbic front, he was what Homer called "a friend to mankind."

Many Videssians would have raised an eyebrow at the idea of learning anything from outlanders, but Alypia said eagerly, "Yes, you've told me how the folk in the world you came from write history, too. How valuable it will be for me to have such a different view of the art—we've been copying each other for too long, I fear."

She looked out the window again, grimaced in annoyance. "And now for a third time I'll try and go. No, say not one word more; I really must be gone." She stepped into his arms, kissed him firmly but quickly, and slipped out the door.

Marcus stayed behind for a few minutes; they chanced being seen together as little as they could. Meeting more than once at the same place was a risk in itself, but the inn's convenience to the patriarchal residence weighed against the danger —and Aetios, once paid, asked no questions.

To spin out the time, the tribune went downstairs to the taproom and ordered a jack of ale; sometimes he preferred it to the sweet Videssian wine. Aetios handed him the tall tarred-leather mug with a knowing smirk, then grunted when the Roman stared back stonily, refusing to rise to the bait. Muttering to himself, the innkeeper went off to serve someone else.

The taproom, almost empty when Scaurus had come to the inn early in the afternoon, was filling as day drew to a close. The crowd was mostly workingmen: painters smeared with paint; bakers with flour; carpenters; tailors; a barber, his mustaches and the end of his beard waxed to points; bootmakers; an effeminate-looking fellow who was probably a bathhouse attendant. Many of them seemed regulars and called greetings to each other as they saw faces they knew. A barmaid squeaked indignantly when the barber pinched her behind. One of the painters, who was guzzling down wine, started a song, and half the tavern joined him. Even Marcus knew the chorus: "The wine gets drunk, but you get drunker."

He finished his ale and picked his way out through the growing crowd. He heard someone say to a tablemate, "What's the dirty foreigner doing here, anyway?" but his size —to say nothing of the yard-long Gallic sword that swung on his hip—let him pass unchallenged.

He bore the blade wherever he went. He might have

laughed at the power of the druids when he was serving with Caesar's army, but their enchantments, wrapped in his sword and Viridovix', had swept the legionaries from Gaul to Videssos. And in Videssos, with sorcery a fact of life, the two enchanted weapons showed still greater power. Not only were they unnaturally strong in the attack, cleaving mail and plate, but the druids' marks stamped into the blades turned aside harmful magic.

The great golden globes on spires above the High Temple glowed ruddily in the light of the setting sun. After a brief glance their way, Marcus turned his back and walked south toward Middle Street. His progress was slow; traffic clogged Videssos' twisting lanes: people afoot; women on donkeys or in litters; men riding mules and horses; and carts and wagons, some drawn by as many as half a dozen beasts, full of vegetables, fruits, and grain to keep the ever-hungry city fed. Animals brayed; teamsters clapped hands to belt-knives as they wrangled over a narrow right-of-way, ungreased axles screeched.

"Well, go ahead, walk right past me. I'll pretend I don't know you either," said an indignant voice at the tribune's elbow.

He spun around. "Oh, hello, Taso. I'm sorry; I really didn't see you."

"A likely story, with this mat of fuzz on my chin." The ambassador from Khatrish sniffed. A small, birdlike man, Taso Vones would have looked perfectly Videssian except that, instead of trimming his beard as did all imperials save priests, he let it tumble in bushy splendor halfway down his chest. He loathed the style, but his sovereign the khagan insisted on it as a reminder that the Khatrisher ruling class ultimately sprang from Khamorth stock. That they had been intermarrying with their once-Videssian subjects for something close to eight hundred years now was not allowed to interfere with the warrior tradition.

Vones cocked his head to one side, reminding Scaurus more than ever of a sparrow: bright, perky, unendingly curious. "You haven't been out and about much, have you? Thorisin finally let you off the string, eh?" he guessed shrewdly.

"You might say so," the Roman answered, casting about for a story that would cover him. Whatever it was going to be, he knew he would have to work it into the conversation naturally; just throwing it out would make the envoy take it for a lie and, being gleefully cynical about such things, call him on it at once.

But Vones did not seem much interested in Marcus' answer; he was full of news of his own. "Had we not met this way, I'd have come to see you in the next day or two."

"Always a pleasure."

"Always a nuisance, you mean," the Khatrisher chuckled. Marcus' denials were, on the whole, sincere; Taso's breezy frankness was a refreshing relief from the Videssian style, which raised innuendo to a high art. Even Vones, though, hesitated before going on. "I've news from Metepont, if you care to hear it."

Scaurus stiffened. "Do you?" he said in as neutral a tone as he could manage. Metepont lay on the west coast of the island Duchy of Namdalen; more to the point, it was Helvis' town. Sighing, the tribune said, "You'd best give it to me. I'd sooner have it from you than most other people I could think of."

"For which praise I thank you." Vones looked faintly embarrassed, an expression the Roman had not seen on him before. At last he said, "You have a daughter there. My news must be weeks old by now, but from all I know, mother and child were both doing well. She named it Emilia. That's not a Namdalener name; does it come from your people?"

"Hmm? Yes, it's one of ours," Marcus said absently. No reason to expect the Khatrisher to remember his gentile name, not when he'd only heard it a couple of times years ago. He wondered whether Helvis was twisting the knife further, or thought of it as some sort of apology. He shook his head. A child he would never see... "How did you learn about it?"

"As you might expect—from the great count Drax. He's hiring mercenaries again, to replace the regiment you broke up for him last year. He had a message of his own for you, too—said he'd like to have you on his side for a change, and he'd make it worth your while to switch."

With studied deliberation, Scaurus spat into the dirt between two flagstones. "He's a fool to want me. Any man who'd turn his coat once'll turn it twice."

Vones laughed at his grimness. "He also said he knew you'd tell him to go to the ice, so get your chin off your chest."

Marcus stayed somber. He could think of a way for Drax to have a chance of prying him away from Videssos: send Thorisin the same message he'd given Taso, and let the Emperor's suspicion do the rest. He wondered if that would occur to the Namdalener. It might; Drax had the mind of a snake. While many islanders aped Videssian ways, the great count could match the imperials at their own intrigues.

Scaurus shook his head again, slowly, like a man bedeviled by bees. The past, it was clear, was not done stinging him yet.

"Hello, look who's coming up behind you," Taso Vones said, snapping his reverie. "Everyone's favorite Videssian officer." The tribune turned to see who had earned that sardonic compliment. He gave a grunt of laughter when he spotted Provhos Mourtzouphlos halfway down the block, almost hidden behind a cart piled high with apples.

The cavalryman looked for a moment as though he would spurn their company, but came up when Taso waved to him. The little Khatrisher bowed from the waist, a paradigm of politeness. "Good evening to you, your excellency. Out slumming, I see." Instead of his usual coxcomb's clothes, Mourtzouphlos was in an ill-fitting homespun tunic, with baggy, mud-colored trousers tucked into torn boots.

He had lost none of his arrogance, though. Looking down his long nose at Vones, he said, "If you must know, easterner, I was hoping a show of poverty would help beat a knave down on the price of a filly." That showed more wit than Marcus would have expected from him.

"And what of you two?" the Videssian went on. "Hatching plots?" He did not bother hiding his disdain.

"Foiling them, if I can," Scaurus said. He gave Mourtzouphlos Taso's news of Drax, adding, "Since you see so much of the Avtokrator these days, best you pass the warning on."

The sarcasm rolled off Mourtzouphlos without sticking, though Taso Vones suffered a sudden coughing fit and had to be slapped on the back. Watching the cavalryman trying to be gracious in his thanks was satisfaction enough for Marcus, though he recovered too quickly to suit the Roman. He had hoped for several minutes of awkwardness, but got only a few sentences' worth.

"Will there be anything more?" Mourtzouphlos asked, for all the world as if Scaurus and Vones had approached him rather than the other way round. When they were silent, he jerked his head in a single short nod. "A pleasant evening to you both, then." He started down the street as though they did not exist.

He actually jumped when Vones called after him, "Did you buy that filly, my lord?"

"Eh?" Mourtzouphlos blinked, collected himself, and said with a scowl, "No; I found some ne'er-do-well's been riding her hard. She's of no value jaded so." He chuckled unpleasantly. "An interesting experience, all the same." And he was off again, swaggering in his shabby boots.

"Self-satisfied bastard," Marcus said as soon as he was out of earshot.

"Isn't he, though?" Taso did a wicked imitation of the officer's nasty laugh. "Like most of that sort, he's satisfied with very little." He plucked at Scaurus' sleeve. "Come with me, why don't you, if you have some gold in your pouch? Come anyway; I'll stake you. I'm for a dice game at a Namdalener tin-merchant's house—you know how the islanders love to gamble. And old Frednis sets a rare table, too. Just wait till you taste the smoked oysters—ah! And the asparagus and crabmeat..." He ran his tongue over his lips, like a cat that scents cream.

The Roman patted guiltily at his midriff; these long dull weeks hunched over a desk were putting weight on him. Well, he told himself, you don't *have* to eat much. "Why not?" he said.

Stumbling in the darkness, Scaurus climbed the stone stairs to his small chamber in the bureaucrat's wing of the Grand Court. The hallways, full of the bustle of imperial business during the day, echoed to the slap of his boots. He could still hear Taso Vones singing, faint in the distance, as the Khatrisher lurched off toward his quarters in the Hall of the Ambassadors.

He had not lied, the tribune thought muzzily. Frednis the Namdalener did not stint his guests, not with food nor drink. And the dice were hot; new gold clinked in Scaurus' belt pouch. At any Roman game he would have been skinned, but to the Videssians a double one was a good throw, not a loser: "Phos' suns," they called it.

Pale shafts of moonlight from narrow outer windows guided him down the corridor. He carefully counted doorways as he passed them; the chambers to either side of his own were mere storerooms.

Then his hand was on his sword hilt, for a line of light from a lamp, yellow as butter, slipped out from beneath the bottom of his door. He slid the blade free as quietly as he could. Whoever was inside—sneak thief? spy? assassin?—would regret it. His first thought was of Avshar and wizardry, but the druids' marks on his blade did not glow as they did when magic was near. Only a man, then.

He seized the latch and threw the door wide as he sprang into the room. "Who the—?" he started to roar, and then half choked as his shout was swallowed in a gurgle of amazement.

Gaius Philippus stood in a wary fencer's crouch beside the tribune's bed, *gladius* at guard position; the senior centurion had not lived to grow gray by taking chances. When he saw it was Scaurus coming through the doorway, he swung the shortsword up in salute. "Took you long enough," he remarked. "Must be past midnight."

"What are you *doing* here?" Marcus said, stepping forward to clasp his hand. Not until he felt the other's callused palm against his own did he wholly believe Frednis' wine had not left him seeing things.

"Cooling my heels, till now," the stocky veteran replied, grinning at the tribune's confusion. That was literally true; he was barefoot, his unlaced *caligae* kicked into a corner, one with its hobnailed sole flipped over. He had made himself comfortable during his wait in other ways as well, if the empty jug of wine not far away was any indication.

"And beyond that?" Marcus was smiling, too, mainly at the pleasure of feeling sonorous Latin roll off his tongue; he had not used his birthspeech all winter long. And Gaius Philippus was a Roman's Roman: brave, practical, without much imagination, but stubborn enough to bull ahead on any course he set himself.

His presence was a marker of that last trait, for he explained: "Your bloody damn fool pen-pushers here, sir, haven't sent our lads a single goldpiece the last two months. If they don't see some money pretty fornicating quick they'll start plundering the countryside round Garsavra, and then it's Hades out to lunch for discipline, as well you know. That we can't have."

Scaurus nodded; the legionaries took more delicate handling as mercenaries for Videssos than they had with the full weight of Roman military tradition on them. It was what remained of that tradition that made them as effective as they were in the Empire, where most infantry was no better than rabble. But with their pay in arrears they were tinder waiting for a spark.

The tribune asked, "Why didn't you write me?"

"For one thing, these cursed dirt roads the Videssians insist on using for the sake of their precious horses were arse-deep in mud till a couple of weeks ago, and what were the odds of a letter getting through? For another, I'm not sure I could write that much. It doesn't come easy to me, you know.

"Besides—" Gaius Philippus set his jaw as he came to the meat of things. "—you want something done right, do it yourself. I want you to find me the seal-stamper who bungled this business so I can tell him where to head in. If the damned imperials are going to hire troops to do their fighting for 'em, they'd best treat 'em right. And one of 'em's going to remember it from now on."

Scaurus already knew who the guilty bureaucrat was; the picture of the senior centurion chewing him out in his best parade-ground bellow was irresistible delightful. "I'll do it," he said. "I want to watch: it'll be like throwing a hiveful of wasps on a desk and then whacking it with a stick."

"Aye, won't it just?" Gaius Philippus said with no less anticipation. He gave a satisfied nod. Not for the first time, Marcus thought his features belonged on a sestertius or denarius—his neat, short cap of iron-gray hair; scarred, jutting chin; angular cheekbones; and proud aquiline nose made him ideal for the starkly realistic portraiture of a Roman coin.

The veteran waved round the bare little room, which held no furniture save Scaurus' mattress, a chair that doubled as lampstand, and a much-battered pine wardrobe with a Videssian obscenity carved into one side.

"I thought you lived softer than this," he said. "If this is all Thorisin's giving you, you'd do better coming back to us. When will you, anyway?"

Marcus spread his hands helplessly. "It's not that simple. I'm not in good odor here, after letting Drax go."

"Oh. That," Gaius Philippus said with distaste. Of course he knew the story; the legionaries Scaurus had sent back after the great count escaped would have brought it with them. The senior centurion hesitated, then went on in what was meant for sympathy, "A plague take the scheming bitch." Anger and rough contempt filled his voice; beyond his body's pleasure, he had scant use for women.

Caught between gratitude and the irrational urge to spring to Helvis' defense, the tribune said nothing. After an awkward few seconds Gaius Philippus changed the subject. "The lads miss you, sir, and asked me to give you their best."

"Did they?" Marcus said, touched. "That's good of them." A thought struck him. "Who's in charge there, with you in the city?"

"Well, with you not there after Junius Blaesus, uh, died—" Gaius Philippus got through that as quickly as he could; Helvis had knifed the junior centurion. "—I bumped Sextus Minucius up to his spot." Seeing Marcus raise an eyebrow, he said, "I know he's young for it, but he's shaping well. He's a worker, that one, and nobody's fool. He's tough enough to flatten anyone who talks back, too."

"All right. You know best, I'm sure." With more than thirty years in the legions, the senior centurion made a better judge of soldiers than Scaurus himself, and the tribune was wise enough to realize it. He did ask, though, "How do the outlanders take to him?" Since coming to Videssos, the legionaries had had a good many local recruits to help fill out their ranks; in his Romanness, Gaius Philippus might not even have seen their acceptance of Minucius as a problem.

But his answer showed he had. "Gagik gets on with him fine." Bagratouni headed a two-hundred-man contingent of Vaspurakaners, organized as an oversize maniple; driven from their homeland by the Yezda and then caught in Zemarkhos' pogrom, they fought with a dour, savage valor under their canny *nakharar*. Gaius Philippus' next sentence further reassured Scaurus: "Minucius isn't too proud to ask Bagratouni what he thinks, either."

"That's fine," the tribune said. "I'm glad I had the sense to do the same, with you." He had learned the warrior's trade now, but when he joined Caesar in Gaul, he had been a raw political appointee, very much dependent on his senior centurion. Gaius Philippus grunted at the praise. Marcus asked, "How's Zeprin the Red faring?"

The veteran grunted again, but with a different intonation "He still just wants to be a common trooper, worse luck."

Marcus shook his head. "Too bad. There's a good man

wasting himself." The burly Haloga had been a marshal in Mavrikios Gavras' Imperial Guards, but after he survived Maragha when the Emperor and the rest of the guards regiment were slain he blamed himself and turned his back on officer's rank. Soldiering was all he knew, but he refused to endanger anyone but himself by his actions.

"And Pakhymer?" Scaurus asked.

This time it was a snort from Gaius Philippus. "Pakhymer is—Pakhymer." The two Romans grinned at each other. Laon Pakhymer's brigade of light cavalry from Khatrish was not strictly a part of their command, but the two forces had served side by side since the Maragha campaign. Pakhymer's easy going, catch-as-catch-can style had driven the methodical senior centurion quietly mad all that time. However he did it, though, he generally got results.

"What else do I need to tell you?" Gaius Philippus said to himself, absently scratching at one of the puckered scars on his right forearm; his left, protected by his *scutum*, was almost unmarked. He brightened. "Oh, yes—a pair of new underofficers: Pullo and Vorenus."

"Both at once, eh?" Marcus asked slyly.

"Aye, both at once," Gaius Philippus said, not rising to the tribune's teasing. "You think I had the ballocks to promote one and not the other?" The two legionaries had fought for years over which made the better soldier, a feud that ended only when they saved each other's lives in a skirmish with Drax' Namdaleni.

"No quarrel, no quarrel," Scaurus said in some haste. He sighed; the wine he had drunk at Frednis' was making him low. "Seems you've done a splendid job, Gaius. I don't know why anyone would miss me; you've managed everything just as I would have."

"Don't say that, sir!" Gaius Philippus cried, real alarm in his voice. "Begging your pardon, but I wouldn't have your bloody job on a bet. Oh, I can handle this end of it: who to promote, who to slap down, which march route to pick, how to dress my line. But the rest of it, especially in this mercenary's game—picking your way through the factions as Thorisin and the pen-pushers square off against each other, knowing when to keep your mouth shut, keeping some shriveled old turd of an officer happy so he doesn't bugger you the minute you turn your back . . . Thank the gods the road from the city to Garsavra's been all over mud what with winter and all, so the damned Videssians weren't able to pull me eight ways at once." He threw up his hands. "Take it back, please. We need you for it!"

It was probably the longest speech Marcus had ever heard him make. Moved, he reached out and clasped the senior centurion's hand. "Thanks, old friend," he said softly.

"For what? The truth?" Gaius Philippus said, outwardly as scornful as ever of any show of emotion. But his hard features could not quite hide his pleasure, and he shuffled his feet awkwardly. He fetched up against the empty jug of wine, which rolled away, bumping on the slightly uneven floor. The veteran followed it with his eyes. "You know," he said, "that wasn't nearly enough. We should have more."

Marcus swallowed a groan. He was already expecting a thick head, but he could not turn the senior centurion down. Gamely he said, "Why not?" for the second time that evening. Come morning, he knew, he would have his answer, but he went out even so.

II

THE ARSHAUM CAMP WOKE WITH THE SUN. SWORDS flashed in the morning light outside one of the beehive-shaped felt tents; steel rang sweetly against steel. One of the fencers whooped and gave a great roundhouse slash. The other, a smaller man, ducked under it and stepped smartly forward. He stopped his thrust bare inches from his opponent's chest.

"To the afterworld with you, you kern," Viridovix panted, stumbling back and throwing his arms wide in surrender. The Gaul wiped the sweat from his face with a freckled forearm and brushed long coppery hair out of his eyes. "Sure and you must ha' been practicing on the sly."

Gorgidas studied him narrowly. "Are you sure you did not give me that opening?" Physician by training, historian by avocation, the Greek was no skilled swordsman. He had seen too much of war in his medical service with the Roman legions for it to draw him as it did Viridovix. But, having been forced to see he needed a warrior's skills to survive on the steppe, he set about acquiring them with the same dogged persistence he gave to medical lore.

The big Celt grinned at him, green eyes crinkling with mirth. "And what if I did? You were after having the wit to take it, which was the point. Not bad, for a man so old and all," he added, to see Gorgidas fume. Save for the beard the Greek had lately grown, which was streaked all through with white, he might have been any age from twenty-five to sixty; his lean body was full of a surprising spare strength, while his face did not carry much loose flesh to sag with the years.

"You don't have to be so bloody proud. You're no younger than I am," Gorgidas snapped. Viridovix' grin got wider. He preened, stroking the luxuriant red mustaches that hung almost to his shoulders. They were still unsilvered. He had scraped off the beard he grew earlier in the winter, but no gray had lurked there either.

"Boast over what you may," the Greek said sourly, "but both of us wake up to piss oftener of nights then we did a few years ago, when we were on the lazy side of forty. Deny it if you can."

"Och, a hit and no mistake," Viridovix said. "And here's another for you!" He sprang at Gorgidas. The physician got his *gladius* up in time to turn the Gaul's blow, but it sent the shortsword—a gift from Gaius Philippus, and one he had never thought he'd use—spinning from his hand.

"Still not bad," the Celt said, picking it up for him. "I'd meant to spank your ribs with the flat o' my blade that time."

"Bah! I should have held on." Gorgidas opened and closed his fist several times, working flexibility into his numbed fingers. "You have a heavy arm there, you hulking savage." He was too honest not to give praise where it was due, though his sharp tongue diluted it in the giving.

"Well, may you be staked out for the corbies, scoffer of a Greekling." Viridovix swelled with mock indignation. Between themselves they spoke a bastard mix of Latin and Videssian. Each was the only representative of his people in this new world and each felt the pain of his own language slowly dying in him for want of anyone with whom to speak it. Gorgidas kept Greek alive by composing his history in that tongue. But only druids wrote the Celtic speech, so Viridovix was denied even that relief.

Around them the camp was coming to life. Some nomads were tending to their small, shaggy horses while others knocked down tents and rolled the fabric up around the sticks that formed their frameworks. Still more crouched round fires as they breakfasted; the morning was chilly. They mixed water with dry curds and spooned up the thick, soupy, tasteless mix; gnawed at slabs of salted and dried beef, mutton, goat, or venison; or speared horsegut-cased sausages on sticks and roasted them over the flames. Many of them did not have as much as they wanted; supplies were running low.

Mounted sentries trotted in from the perimeter, rubbing at eyes red and tired from their sleepless duty. Others rode out to take their place. The Arshaum grumbled at the tight watch their khagan Arghun kept. What if they were on the plains of Pardraya, east of the river Shaum, instead of in their own steppelands to the west? Their ancestors had smashed the Khamorth over the river to Pardraya half a century before; few believed the rival nomad folk would dare contest their passage.

For all that, though, the Arshaum were men who enjoyed fighting for its own sake, and Gorgidas and Viridovix were not alone in weapons play. Plainsmen thrust light lances and flung javelins both afoot and mounted. They fired arrows at wadded balls of cloth tossed into the air and at shields propped upright on the ground. Their double-curved bows, reinforced with sinew, sent barbed shafts smashing through the small, round targets—shafts that could pierce a corselet of boiled leather or chain mail afterwards.

A bowstring snapped just as an archer let fly, sending his arrow spinning crazily through the air. "Heads up!" the Arshaum yelled, and all around him nomads dove for cover.

"Why does he go shouting that, the which would do a man no good at all?" Viridovix said. "Riddle it out for me, Gorgidas dear."

"He must have meant it especially for you, you unruly Celt," the physician replied with relish, "knowing you always do the opposite of whatever you're told."

"Honh! See if I'm fool enough to be asking for another explanation from you any time soon."

Not far away, a plainsman thudded into the dirt, flung over his wrestling partner's shoulder; the Arshaum were highly skilled at unarmed combat. Their swordplay was less expert. Several pairs slashed away at each other with the medium-length curved blades they favored. The yataghans, heavy at the point, were all very well for quick cuts from horseback, but did not lend themselves to scientific fencing.

"Had enough?" Gorgidas asked, sheathing his sword.

"Aye, for the now."

They wandered over to watch one of the dueling pairs, perhaps the unlikeliest match in the camp. Arghun's son Arigh was going at it furiously with Batbaian, the son of Targitaus, their blades a silvery glitter as they met each other stroke for stroke.

They were both khagans' sons, but there their resemblance ended. For looks, Arigh was a typical enough Arshaum: slender, lithe, and swarthy, with a wide, high-cheekboned face, short, almost flat nose, and slanted eyes. Only a few black hairs grew on his upper lip and straggled down from the point of his chin. But Batbaian was a Khamorth, with his people's broad-shouldered frame, thick curly beard half hiding his heavy features, and a strong, fleshy beak in the center of his face. He would have been handsome but for the red ruin of a socket where his left eye had been.

The eye he still had was the "mercy" of Avshar and Varatesh the bandit chief. They had taken a thousand prisoners when they crushed the army Targitaus raised against them, and then given those prisoners back to Batbaian's father ... all but fifty of them with both eyes burned away, the rest left with one to guide their comrades home. Seeing them so ravaged, Targitaus died of a stroke on the spot. Varatesh fell on his devastated clan three days later. As far as Viridovix knew, Batbaian was the only clansman left alive—save himself, whom Targitaus had adopted into the Wolves after he escaped Varatesh and his henchmen. The bandits missed them only because they were attending an outlying herd; they rode in at day's end to find massacre laid out before them.

The Gaul's features, usually merry, grew grim and tight as he fell into memory's grip. Batbaian had had a sister—but Seirem was dead now, and perhaps that was as well, with what she met before she died. Part of Viridovix' heart was dead with her; a tomcat by nature, he had come late to love and lost it too early.

The past winter he and Batbaian had lived the outlaw's life, revenge their only goal. At last he thought to cross west into Shaumkhiil and seek aid from the Arshaum against Varatesh and Avshar, his puppet-master. Batbaian's hate burned away his fear of the western nomads; where the Arshaum despised the Khamorth, the latter had almost a superstitious dread for the folk who had harried them east over the steppe.

Having traveled with the Arshaum force for weeks, though, Batbaian saw that they were men, too, not the near-demons he had thought. And he had earned their respect as well, for the hardships he had borne and for his skill with his hands. His burly build let him shoot farther than most of them, and if he was now giving ground to Arigh, his foe was fast and deceptive as a striking snake.

"The wind-spirits take it!" he cursed in his own guttural tongue, falling back again. In a mixture of bad Videssian—which Arigh understood, having served his father as envoy to the Empire—and worse Arshaum, he went on, "With only eye one, not able to tell how away far you are."

Arigh's grin was predatory, his teeth very white. "My friend, Varatesh's men would not heed your whining, and I will not either."

He pressed his attack, his slashes coming from every direction at once. Then he was staring at his empty hand; his sword lay on the ground at his feet. Batbaian leaped forward and planted a boot on it. He tapped Arigh on the chest with his blade. The watchers whooped at the sudden reversal.

"Why you dirty son of a flop-eared goat," Arigh said without much rancor. "You suckered me into that, didn't you?"

Batbaian only grunted. The summer before he had been hardly more than a boy, full of a boy's chatter and bubbling enthusiasm for everything around him. These days he was a man, and a driven one. He spoke seldom, and his smile, which was rarer, never reached past his lips.

"Puir lad," Viridovix murmured to Gorgidas. "A pity you canna unfreeze the spirit of him, as you did wi' this carcass o' mine."

"I know no gift for that, save it come from within a man's own soul," the physician answered. Then he spread his hands and admitted, "For that matter, when I found you I thought I would have to watch you die, too."

"A good thing you didn't. My ghost'd bewail you for it."

"Hmm. No doubt, if it takes after you in the flesh." But the Greek could not stay flippant long, not where the healing he had worked on Viridovix was concerned.

Ever since he was swept into Videssos with the legionaries, he had studied its healing art, an art that relied not so much on herbs and scalpels as on mustering and unleashing the power of the mind to beat back disease and injury—call it magic, for lack of a better word. He had seen Phos' healer-priests work cures on men he had given up for doomed, and chased after their skill like a hunter trailing some elusive beast.

But the stubborn rationality on which he prided himself would not let him truly accept that curing by mind alone was possible; it ran too much against all his training, all his deepest beliefs. And so for years he tried and, not genuinely believing he could succeed, never did. Only the lash of desperation at finding Viridovix freezing in a fierce steppe blizzard made him transcend his doubts and channel the healing energies through himself and into the Gaul.

He had healed again afterwards, closing and cleansing the bites an Arshaum took from a wolf that would not die with three arrows in its chest. Knowing he could heal made the second time easy. The nomad's gratitude was wine-sweet, and the Greek accepted as a badge of honor the tearing weariness that always followed healing.

"Why for we standing round?" Batbaian demanded. "We should riding be." Without waiting for an answer, he turned away from Arigh and went off to his string of horses to pick a mount for the day's ride.

Behind him, Arigh shook his head. "That one would ride through fire for his revenge."

The Arshaum around him nodded, sympathizing with Batbaian's blood feud. But Viridovix started in alarm, whipping his head round to make sure the Khamorth had not heard the remark. "Dinna say that to him, ever," he warned. " 'Twas Avshar's fires trapped him in the shindy, and all the rest, too." The Gaul shuddered as he remembered those tall, arrow-straight lines of flame darting like serpents over the steppe at the evil wizard's will.

There was compassion under the unfeeling veneer Arigh cultivated, though he often did not let it out. Even when he did, it was usually with a self-deprecating, "All that time in Videssos has left me soft." But now he bit his lip, admitting, "I'd forgotten."

A last delay held up the army's departure a few minutes more. All the tents were down and stowed on horseback save the one shared by Lankinos Skylitzes and Pikridios Goudeles, Thorisin's envoys to Arghun. Skylitzes was long since out and about; the tall imperial officer looked with dour amusement at the sign of his tentmate's sleepiness.

He stuck his head inside the tent and roared, "Up, slugabed! Is this a holy day, for you to spend it all between the sheets?"

Goudeles emerged in short order, but mightily rumpled,

tunic on back-to-front, and belt out of half its loops. Rubbing sleep from his eyes, the pen-pusher winced at the ironic cheer that greeted his appearance. "Oh, very well, here I am," he said testily. He glowered at Skylitzes; the two of them were as cat and dog. "Mightn't you have picked a less drastic way to rouse me?"

"No," Skylitzes said. He was that rarity, a short-spoken Videssian.

Still grumbling, Goudeles began to knock down the tent, but made such a slow, clumsy job of it that Skylitzes, with an exasperated grunt, finally pitched in to help. "You bungler," he said, almost kindly, as he tied the roll of tent fabric and sticks onto a packsaddle.

"Bungler? I?" Goudeles drew himself up to his full height, which was not imposing. "No need to mock me merely because I was not cut out for life in the field." He caught Gorgidas' eye. "These soldiers have a narrow view of life's priorities, do they not?"

"No doubt," the Greek answered. As he was already mounted, he sounded a trifle smug. Goudeles looked hurt, one of his more artful expressions. In truth, the bureaucrat was a carpet knight, infinitely more at home in the elaborate double-dealing of Videssos the city than here on the vast empty steppe. But his gift for intrigue made him a sly, subtle diplomat, and he had done well in helping persuade Arghun to favor the Empire over Yezd.

He spent a few seconds trying to restore the point to his beard, but gave it up as a bad job. "Hopeless," he said sadly. He climbed onto his own horse and patted his belly, still ample after close to a year on the plains. "Am I too late to break my fast?"

Skylitzes rolled his eyes, but Viridovix handed Goudeles a chunk of meat. The pen-pusher eyed it skeptically. "What, ah, delicacy have we here?"

"Sure and it's half a roast marmot," the Celt told him, grinning. "Begging your honor's pardon and all, but I was after eating the last of my sausage today."

Goudeles turned a pale green. "Somehow I find my appetite is less hearty than it was, though my thanks, of course, for your generosity." He gave the ground squirrel back to Viridovix.

"Ride, then," Skylitzes snapped. As Goudeles clucked to his horse, though, the officer admitted to Gorgidas, "I'm low myself; we should stop for a hunt soon."

The Greek dipped his head in his people's gesture of agreement. "So am I." He shuddered slightly. "We could go on the nomad way for a while, living off our horses' blood." He did not intend to be taken seriously. The idea revolted him.

Not so Skylitzes; all he said was, "That's for emergencies only. It runs the animals down too badly." He had traveled the steppes before and was at home with the customs of the plainsmen, speaking both the Arshaum and Khamorth tongues fluently.

The Arshaum moved steadily over the Pardrayan plain, their course a bit east of south. Alternately walking and trotting, their ponies ate up the miles. The rough-coated little beasts were not much for looks, but there was iron endurance in them. Gorgidas blessed the wet ground and thick grass cover of approaching spring; later in the year the army would have kicked up great choking clouds of dust.

When afternoon came, the sun sparkled off the waters of the inland Mylasa Sea on the western horizon. Other than that, the steppe was all but featureless, an endless, gently rolling sea of grass that stretched from the borders of Videssos further west than any man knew. As a landscape, Gorgidas found it dull. He had grown up with the endless variety of terrain Greece offers: seacoast, mountains, carved valleys kissed by the Mediterranean sun or dark under forest, and flatlands narrow enough to walk across in half a day.

To Viridovix the limitless vistas of the steppe were not so much boring as actively oppressive. His Gallic woods cut down the sweep of vision, left a man always close to something he could reach out and touch. The plains made him feel tiny and insignificant, an insect crawling across a tray. He fought his unreasoning fear as best he could, riding near the center of the army to use the nomads around him as a shield against the vastness beyond.

Each day he looked south in the hope of seeing the mountains of Erzerum—the peaks that separated Pardraya from Yezd—shoulder their way up over the edge of the world. So far he had been disappointed. "One morning they'll be peeping up, though, and none too soon for me," he said to Batbaian. "It does a body good, knowing there's an end to all this flat."

"Why?" Batbaian demanded, as used to open space as Viridovix was to his narrow forest tracks. His companions also shook their heads at the Celt's strange ways. As he usually did, Batbaian rode with the ten-man guard squad that had accompanied the Videssian embassy out from Prista. Except for Viridovix and Skylitzes, the troopers were the only ones with the army who spoke his tongue, and most of them had Khamorth blood.

The squad leader, Agathias Psoes, was a Videssian, but years at the edge of Pardraya had left him as at home in the language of its people as in the imperial tongue. "Country doesn't matter one way or the other," he said with an old soldier's cynicism. "It's the bastards who live on it that cause the trouble."

Viridovix burst out laughing. "Here and I thought I was rid o' Gaius Philippus for good and all, and up springs his shadow." Psoes, who knew next to nothing of the Romans, blinked in incomprehension.

"What are the lot of you grunting about there?" an Arshaum asked. Viridovix turned his head to see Arghun the khagan and his younger son Dizabul coming up alongside the guardsmen. The men from Shaumkhiil spoke a smooth, sibilant tongue; the harsh gutturals of the Khamorth speech grated on their ears.

With Arghun, though, the teasing was good-natured. He led the Gray Horse clan, the largest contingent of the Arshaum army, more by guile and persuasion than by the bluff bluster Viridovix had used as a chief among the Lexovii back in Gaul.

The Celt translated as well as he could; he was beginning to understand the Arshaum language fairly well, but speaking it was harder. "And what do you think of that, red whiskers?" Arghun asked. Viridovix' exotic coloring fascinated him, as did the Celt's luxuriant mustaches. The khagan grew only a few gray hairs on his upper lip and frankly envied the other's splendid ornament.

"Me? I puts it the other way round. People is people anywheres, but the—how you be saying?—scenery, it change a lot."

"Something to that," Arghun nodded, an instinctively shrewd politician for all his barbaric trappings.

"How can you tell, father?" Dizabul said, his regular features twisting into a sneer. "He talks so poorly it's next to impossible to make out what he says." With a supercilious smile, he turned to Viridovix, "That should be 'I would put,' outlander, and 'people are people,' and 'scenery changes.' "

"I thank your honor," the Gaul said—not at all what he was thinking. Dizabul struck him as Arghun's mistake; the lad had grown up having his every whim indulged, with predictable results. He also loathed his brother and everyone connected with him, which added venom to the tone he took with Viridovix. "Spoiled as a salmon a week out of water," the Gaul muttered in his own speech.

Arghun shook his head at Dizabul in mild reproof. "I'd sooner hear good sense wearing words of old sheepskin than numskullery or wickedness decked out in sable."

"Listen to him and welcome, then," Dizabul snarled, bristling at even the suggestion of criticism. "I shan't waste my time." He flicked his horse's reins and ostentatiously trotted away.

Gorgidas, who was deep in conversation with Tolui the shaman, glanced up as Dizabul rode past. His eyes followed the comely youth as another man's might a likely wench. He was only too aware of the young princeling's petulance and vile temper, but the sheer physical magnetism he exerted almost made them forgettable. He realized he had missed Tolui's last couple of sentences. "I'm sorry. What were you saying?"

"When spring is far enough for the frogs to come out," Tolui repeated, "there is a potion I intend to try on Arghun's lameness. It should be only days now."

"Ah?" said the Greek, interested again as soon as medicine was mentioned. His own knowledge had been enough to save the khagan's life from a draft of hemlock Bogoraz of Yezd had given him when Arghun decided for Videssos, but the paralyzing drug left Arghun's legs permanently weakened. Gorgidas had not been able to work the Videssian styly of healing then, and it did no good against longestablished infirmities.

"I need nine frogs," the shaman explained. "Their heads are pithed, and the yellow fluid that comes out is mixed with melted goat fat in a pot. The pot is sealed and left in the sun for a day and in a fire overnight. Then the oil that is left is dabbed on the afflicted joints with a feather. Most times it works well."

"I'd not heard of that one before," Gorgidas admitted, intrigued and a little nauseated. He thought of something else.

"Lucky for you Arghun is no Khamorth, or you'd never get near him with that medicine."

Tolui barked laughter. "True. Just another proof the Hairies—" He used his people's contemptuous nickname for the heavily bearded natives of Pardraya. "—hardly rate being called men at all."

"Tomorrow we will hunt," Arghun declared, sitting by the campfire and spooning up the last of his miserable meal of curds and water. A few of his men still hoarded a bit of sausage or smoked meat, while others had knocked over hares or other small game while they traveled; but most were reduced to the same iron rations he carried, or to blood.

"About time. This Pardraya is a paltry place," said Irnek, a tall nomad who led the Arshaum of the Black Sheep clan, next most numerous after the Gray Horses of Arghun and sometimes rivals to them. Puzzlement dwelt in the Arshaum's eyes; he was a clever man, confused by what he was finding. He went on, "It should not be so. This land draws more rain than our Shaumkhiil and ought to support rich flocks. Not from what we've seen, though; I begin to forget the very look of a cow or sheep."

Angry growls of agreement rose from the plainsmen who heard him. They had counted on raiding the herds of the Khamorth as they traversed Pardraya on their way to Yezd, but since they crossed the Shaum those herds were nowhere to be found. They took the occasional stray cow, goat, fat-tailed sheep, but came across none of the great flocks that were as vital to the nomads as a farmer's crops to him.

For that matter, they had seen few Khamorth, not even scouts dogging their trail. The Arshaum took that as but another sign of cowardice, and joked about it. "What do the Hairies do when they see us coming?" to which the answer was, "Who knows? We never get the chance to find out."

The men who traveled with them worried more. Viridovix knew from bitter experience that Avshar could track him by his blade. No magic would bite on it, but that very blankness made it detectable to the wizard-prince. "Sure and it's no happen-so we've not had greetings from the spalpeen. Belike he's brewing somewhat against us."

"A greater concern," Pikridios Goudeles said, "is why no great number of Khamorth have gone over to us. Living under Avshar can scarcely be pleasant."

"A good point," said Gorgidas, who had wondered the same thing.

"Two reasons," Batbaian answered in his labored Videssian. "One, he rules through Varatesh, who is outlaw, yes, but from family of a khagan. He makes a good dog." The plainsman's eye narrowed in contempt.

"That one's more than Avshar's hound," Viridovix disagreed. The time he had spent in Varatesh's clutches made him thoroughly respect the outlaw chieftain's talents.

"I say what I say," Batbaian declared flatly. He stared at the Gaul, challenging him to argue further. Viridovix shrugged and waved for him to go on. "All right. Other reason is that most Khamorth worse afraid of Arshaum than of wizard. I was, so much I did not think of them till you say they might be help in revenge. May be lots of rebels hate Avshar but fear us here, too."

"Something to that," Skylitzes said. "He's also had the winter to deal with uprisings. A lesson or two from him would make anyone thoughtful."

"Thoughtful, forsooth!" Goudeles said. "Are you in a contest of understatement with me, Lankinos? Shall we go on to style this hateful winter just past 'cool,' Phos' High Temple 'large,' and Erzerum 'hilly'?"

Skylitzes' mouth twitched in the grimace he used for a smile. "Fair enough. We could call you 'gassy,' while we were about it."

The bureaucrat spluttered while his comrades laughed. Gorgidas made them serious once more when he asked, "If Avshar does assail us, how are we going to be able to resist him?"

"Fight him, crush him, kill him," Batbaian growled. "Stake him out on plains for vultures to eat. Why else did V'rid'rish bring me here to join you?"

"Crush him, aye, but how?" the Greek persisted. "Many have tried, but none succeeded yet."

Batbaian glared at him as he would have at anyone who questioned the certainty of vengeance. Skylitzes said, "These Arshaum are better warriors than the Khamorth, Gorgidas—and both sides think that's true, which helps make it so."

"What of it?" Gorgidas said. "Avshar need not have the finest soldiers to win. Look at Maragha, look at the battle on the steppe here last fall against Batbaian's father. In both of them it was his magic that made his victory for him, not the quality of his troops."

A gloomy silence fell. There was no denying the physician was right; he usually was. At last Viridovix said, "Very good, your generalship, sir, you've gone and named the problem for us. Are you after having somewhat in mind for solving it, or is it you want the rest of us grumpy as your ain self?"

"To the crows with you," Gorgidas said, nettled at the teasing. "What do I know of ordering battles and such? You were the great war-chieftain back there in Gaul—what would *you* do?"

Viridovix suddenly grew bleak. "Whatever the unriddling may be, I dinna ken it. For fighting the whoreson straight up, I was, and see how well that worked."

Cursing his clumsy tongue, Gorgidas started an apology, but Viridovix waved it away. "It was a question fairly put. The now, the best I know to do is find my bedroll and hope some good fairy'll whisper me my answer whilst I sleep."

"Fair enough." The Greek's eyes were getting sandy, too.

When morning came Viridovix was still without his solution. "Och, it's no luck the puir fairies ha'. They must wear out the wings of 'em or ever they get to this wretched world, the which is so far away and all," he said sadly.

His disappointment was quickly forgotten, though, in amazement over the Arshaum hunt. "Not ones to do things by halves, are they now?" he said to Gorgidas.

"Hardly." The entire Videssian embassy party made up a small part of one wing of the Arshaum army which, led by Arghun, spread out in a long east-west line across the steppe. The other half of the force, under Irnek's command, rode south. Sometime near noon they would also spread out, and then move north as Arghun's followers came down to meet them, the two lines trapping all the game between them.

The Khamorth did not stage such elaborate hunts; Batbaian was astonished to watch the Arshaum deployment. "This might as well war be," he said to Arigh.

"Why not?" the other returned. "What harder foe than hunger? Or do you enjoy the feel of your belly cozying up to your backbone?" It took a good deal to make the grim young Khamorth smile, but his lips parted for a moment.

When Arghun saw his line in position and judged Irnek had taken the rest of the nomads far enough south to shut in a good bag of game, he raised the army's standard high above his head. Fluttering on the end of a lance was Bogoraz's long wool caftan, all that was left of the treacherous ambassador. Like the Videssian party, he had sworn an oath to Arghun's shamans that he meant the khagan no harm and walked through their magic fire as surety for it. When he broke his pledge, the fire claimed him.

With the lifting of the standard, the line rolled forward. The Arshaum who had them pounded on drums, tooted pipes and bone whistles, winded horns. The rest yelled at the top of their lungs to scare beasts from cover.

Trotting along with the rest, Viridovix threw back his head and let out the unearthly wailing shriek of a Gallic war cry. "I don't know about the bloody animals," Gorgidas said with a shudder, "but you certainly frighten me."

"And what good is that, when you're nobbut skin and bones? Och, look, there goes a hare!" An Arshaum shot the little creature at the top of its leap. Backed by his potent bow, the arrow knocked it sideways. It kicked a couple of times and lay still. The plainsman leaned down from his saddle, grabbed it by the ears, and tossed it into a sack.

Viridovix howled again. "Something worthwhile for me to do, then; it's no dab hand at the bow I make, not next to these lads."

"Nor I," the Greek replied. He flapped his arms, bawled out snatches of Homer and Aiskhylos. Whether or not it was his antics that flushed it, another rabbit broke cover in front of him. Instead of running away, the panicked little beast darted straight past his horse. He cut at it with his sword, far too late. The nomad next to him shook his head derisively, mimed drawing a bow. He spread his hands in rueful agreement and apology.

Something went "Honk! Ho-onkk!" a couple of hundred feet down the line. Gorgidas saw a shape running through the grass, a couple of plainsmen in hot pursuit. Then it suddenly bounded into the air, flying strongly on short, stubby wings. The sun shone, metallic, off bronze tail feathers and head of iridescent red and green. "Pheasant!" Viridovix whooped. A storm of arrows brought the bird down. The Gaul fairly drooled. "Age him right, braise him with mushrooms, wild thyme, and a bit o' wormwood to cut the grease—"

"Remember where you are," Gorgidas said. "You'll be lucky if he gets cooked." Crestfallen, Viridovix gave a regretful nod.

A nomad shouted and his horse screamed in terror as a furiously spitting wildcat sprang at them. It clawed the horse's flank, sank its teeth into the Arshaum's calf, and was gone before anyone could do anything about it. The cursing plainsman bound up his leg and rode on, ignoring his comrades' jeers. Gorgidas reminded himself to look at the wound when the hunt was gone. Untended animal bites were almost sure to fester.

More arrows leaped into the sky as the hunters splashed through a small, chilly stream and sent geese and ducks up in desperate flight. Viridovix greedily snatched up a fat goose that had tumbled to earth with an arrow through its neck. "I'll not let anyone botch this," he said, as if challenging the world. "All dark meat it is, and all toothsome, too. O' course," he went on with a pointed glance Gorgidas' way, "I might enjoy the sharing of it, at least with them as dinna mock me."

"I'm plainly doomed to starve, then," the Greek said. Viridovix made a rude noise.

Goudeles said, "If it's praises you seek, outlander, I'll gladly compose a panegyric for you in exchange for a leg of that succulent fowl." He struck a pose—not an easy thing to do on horseback for such an indifferent rider—declaiming, "Behold the Phos-fostered foreigner, magnificent man of deeds of dought—"

"Oh, stifle it, Pikridios," Skylitzes said. "You're still fatter than the damned bird is, and slipperier than goose grease ever was." Not a bit offended, the bureaucrat went right on, the course best calculated to annoy Skylitzes.

"I wish we could bag more of these birds," Gorgidas said. "Too many are getting away."

"We will," Arigh promised, "but there aren't enough to be worthwhile this time." He pointed. "See? Tolui is ready when we come on a big flock."

The shaman was not wearing his usual garb, which differed not at all from that of the rest of the plainsmen: fur cap with ear flaps, tunic of sueded leather, heavy sheepskin jacket—some wore wolf, fox, or otter—leather trousers, and soft-soled boots. Instead, he had donned the fantastic regalia of his calling. Long fringes, some knotted to trap spirits and others dyed bright colors, hung from every inch of his robe and streamed behind him as he rode. A lurid, leering mask of hide stretched over a wooden framework hid his face. Only the sword that swung at his belt said he was human, not some demon's spawn.

Skylitzes followed Arigh's pointing finger, too. The Videssian officer made Phos' sun-sign against evil, muttering a prayer as he did so. Gorgidas caught part of it: ". . . and keep me safe from heathen wizardry." Unafraid of worldly dangers, Skylitzes had all his faith's pious suspicion of other beliefs.

Gorgidas gave a wry laugh; he was in no position to sneer at the soldier. He mistrusted magic, too, of every sort, for it flew straight against the logical set of mind with which he had faced the world since he was a beardless youth. That he worked it himself made him no more easy with it.

He must have been thinking aloud, for Viridovix turned his head and said, "Sure and this is a new world, or had your honor never noticed, being so busy scribbling about it and all? Me, now, I take things as they come, the which is more restful nor worrying anent the wherefore of 'em."

"If you're pleased to be a cabbage, then be one," the Greek snapped. "As for me, I'd sooner try to understand."

"A cabbage, is it? Och, well, at the least you credit me for a head, which is kindlier than you've sometimes been, I'm thinking." Viridovix grinned impishly; just as Goudeles' bombast made Skylitzes growl, his own blithe unconcern irritated Gorgidas more than any angry comeback.

A herd of onagers galloped away from the oncoming riders. The small-eared wild asses could almost have been miniature horses, but for their sparsely haired tails and short, stiff, brushy manes. Three wolves coursed beside them, not hunters now but hunted, fleeing before the Arshaum as from a fire on the steppe.

However hardened they had grown to the saddle, neither Viridovix nor Gorgidas could endure with the Arshaum, who rode as soon as they could walk. The long, hard ride chafed the physician's thighs raw and left the Celt's fundament sore as if he had been kicked. They both groaned as their horses jounced over a low rise and pounded toward another stream.

The drumming thunder of hoofbeats sent a cloud of waterfowl flapping skyward—ducks, geese, and orange-billed swans, whose great wings made a thunder of their own. Birds fell as the nomads started shooting at long range, but again it seemed almost all would evade the arrows.

Gorgidas saw Tolui's devil-masked face turn toward Arghun. The khagan made a short, chopping motion with his right hand. The shaman began to chant; both arms moved in quick passes. He guided his horse with the pressure of his knees alone. A rider in the Greek's world would have been hard-pressed to stay in the saddle thus, but stirrups made it easy for the Arshaum.

Black clouds boiled up over the stream as soon as his spell began, come from nowhere out of a clear sky. A squall of rain, a veritable curtain of water, pelted the escaping birds. It had been only seconds since they took flight, now the sudden deluge smashed them back to earth. Gorgidas heard squawks of terror through the sorcerous storm's hiss.

As quickly as it had blown up, the rain stopped. Water birds lay all along the banks of the stream, some with broken wings, others half drowned, still others simply too stunned to fly. Raising a cheer for Tolui, the plainsmen swooped down on them. They clubbed and shot and slashed, grabbing up bird after bird.

"Roast duck!" Goudeles cried with glee as he bagged a green-winged teal. He thumbed his nose at Viridovix. "You'll not hear that panegyric now!"

"No, nor miss it either," the Gaul retorted. Skylitzes gave a single sharp snort of laughter.

They splashed through the muck Tolui's storm had made. With a glance at the westering sun, Arghun picked up the pace. "We will need daylight for the final killing," he called. His riders passed the word along.

Then Gorgidas heard cheers from the far left end of the line, where scouts stretched out ahead of the main band of hunters. A few minutes later they sounded from the right as well—Irnek's half of the army was in sight. Moving with the smooth precision experience brings, the horsemen on the flanks galloped forward from both parties to enclose the space between and finally trap all the animals in it.

That space grew smaller and smaller as the two lines approached. The beasts within were pressed ever more tightly: wolves, foxes, wildcats, rabbits bouncing underfoot, deer, wild asses, sheep, a few cows, goats. The nomads relentlessly plied them with arrows, pulling one quiverload after another from their saddlebags. The din, with the yelps and screeches and brays of wounded animals mixed with the frightened howls and lowing of those not yet hit and with the hunters' cries, was indescribable.

Driven, hunted, and jammed together as they were, the terrified creatures' reactions were nothing like they would have been in more normal circumstances. They ran this way and that in confused waves, seeking an escape they could not find. And some were desperate enough to surge out against the yelling, waving riders who ringed them all around.

A stag sprang between Gorgidas and Viridovix and was gone, bounding over the plain in great frightened leaps. Arigh whirled in the saddle to fire after it, but missed. Then he and everyone around him cursed in fury as a hundred panicked onagers made a shambles of the hunting line. Other animals of every sort swarmed through the gap.

Agathias Psoes' horse was bowled over when a fleeing wild ass ran headlong into it. The Videssian underofficer sprang free as his mount crashed to the ground, then leaped for his life to dodge another onager. Only the knowledge he had earned with years on the steppe saved him. He frantically laid about him, yelling as loud as he could to make the stampeding beasts take him for an obstacle to be avoided and not a mere man ripe for the trampling. It worked, they streamed past him on either side. When an Arshaum rode close, he clambered up behind the nomad.

Guiding his pony with a skill he had not thought he owned, Gorgidas managed to evade the onagers. He was congratulating himself when Batbaian shouted a warning. The Greek turned his head to find a wolf, a huge shaggy pack leader, bounding his way. It sprang straight for him, jaws agape.

His months of weapon drill proved their worth; before he had time to think, he was thrusting at the snarling beast's face. But his horse could not endure the wolf's onset. It bucked in terror, ruining his stroke. Instead of stabbing through the wolf's palate and into its brain, his *gladius* scored a bloody line down its muzzle, just missing a blazing yellow eye.

The wolf bayed horribly and leaped again. An arrow whistled past Gorgidas' cheek, so close he felt the wind of its passage. It sank between the wolf's ribs. The beast twisted in midair, snapping at the protruding shaft. Bloody foam started from its mouth and nostrils. Two more arrows pierced it as it writhed on the ground; it jerked and died.

"Good shot!" Gorgidas called, looking round to see who had loosed the first arrow. Dizabul waved back at him; he too was busy fighting to keep his mount under control. The Greek tried to read the expression on the prince's too-handsome face, and failed. Then Dizabul caught sight of a gray fox darting away and spurred after it, reaching behind him for another arrow to fit to his bow.

"Well, what about it?" Goudeles asked the physician a few minutes later, when the breakout was contained. The bureaucrat somehow managed to look jaunty even though his face was gray-brown with dust and tracked by streams of sweat. He gave Gorgidas a conspiratorial wink.

"What about what?" the Greek said, his mind back on the hunt.

"You don't play the innocent well," Goudeles told him; he had the Videssian gift for spotting duplicity whether it was there or not. But when he said, "Tell me you weren't wondering whether that shaft was meant for the wolf or you," Gorgidas had to toss his head in a Hellenic no. Dizabul had no reason to love him. He had backed Bogoraz until Gorgidas foiled the Yezda's try at poisoning his father; his pride suffered for finding himself so drastically in the wrong. Then, too, he might well have become khagan if the poisoning had succeeded. . . .

"You're not wrong," Gorgidas admitted. The pen-pusher wet his finger and drew a tally-mark in the air, pleased at his own cleverness.

As the light began to fail, the nomads opened their lines and let the trapped beasts they had not slain escape. They dismounted, drove off the gathering carrion birds, and set about butchering their kills. "Faugh!" said Viridovix, wrinkling his nose. The slaughterhouse stench oppressed Gorgidas, too, but it was hardly worse than battlefields he had known.

The Arshaum set fires blazing in long straight trenches and began to smoke as much of the meat as they could. Arghun hobbled from one to the next with Irnek, supervising the job. "A pity our women and yurts aren't here," Gorgidas heard him say.

"Aye, it is," the younger plainsman agreed. "So many hides, so much bone and sinew wasted because we haven't time to deal with them as we should." Steppe life was harsh; not making the greatest possible use of everything they came across went against the nomads' grain.

While the sweaty work went on, the hunters carved off choice gobbets and roasted them for their day's meal. "Not a bit peckish, are they now?" Viridovix said, between bites of the plump goose he'd taken.

"You do pretty well yourself," Gorgidas replied, gnawing on a leg from the same bird; the Celt had a good-sized pile of bones in front of him. But he was right; the nomads out-ate him without effort. Used to privation, they made the most of plenty when they had it. Seeing them somehow gulp down huge chunks of half-cooked meat reminded the Greek of a time when, as a boy, he had watched a small snake engulfing a large mouse.

Batbaian ate by himself, his back to the fires. As Gorgidas' emptiness faded and he began to be able to think of other things than food, he got up to invite the Khamorth over to talk. When Viridovix saw where he was going, he reached out and held the physician back. "Let the lad be," he said quietly.

Irritated, Gorgidas growled, "What's your trouble? He'll be happier here than brooding all alone."

"That's not so at all, I'm thinking. Unless I miss my guess, the blazes are after reminding him o' the ones Avshar used to snare him. That they do me, and I wasna caught by 'em. If he has somewhat to say, he'll be by, and never you fret over that."

The Greek sat down again. "You may be right. You said something of the same thing to Arigh a few days ago, didn't you?" He eyed Viridovix curiously. "I wouldn't have expected you to be so careful of another's feelings."

Viridovix toyed with his mustaches, as if wondering whether his manhood was questioned. He finally said, "Hurting a body without call is Avshar's sport, and after a bit o' him, why, I've fair lost the stomach for it."

"You're growing up at last," Gorgidas said, to which the Celt only snorted in derision. The physician thought of something else. "If Avshar somehow does not know how large an army has crossed into Pardraya, these fires will give us away."

"He knows," Viridovix said with gloomy certainty. "He knows."

* * *

Coincidence or not, two days later a Khamorth rode into the Arshaum camp under sign of truce, a white-painted shield hung from a lance. As he was brought before Arghun and his councilors, he looked about with an odd blend of arrogance laid over fear. He would flinch when the Arshaum scowled at him, then suddenly straighten and glower back, seeming to remember the might he himself represented.

Certainly his bow before the khagan was perfunctory enough to fetch black looks from the plainsmen. He ignored them, asking in his own language, "Does anyone here speak this tongue and yours both?"

"I do." Skylitzes took a long step forward.

The Khamorth blinked at finding an imperial at Arghun's side, but recovered well. He was perhaps forty-five, not handsome but shrewd-looking, with eyes that darted every which way. Half of one of his ears was missing. By steppe standards, he wore finery; his cap was sable, his wolfskin jacket trimmed with the same fur, his fringed trousers of softest buckskin. A red stone glittered in the heavy gold ring on his right forefinger; his horse's trappings were ornamented with polished jet.

"Well, farmer," he said, putting Skylitzes in his place with the nomad's easy contempt for folk who lived a settled life, "tell the Arshaum I am Rodak son of Papak, and I come to him from Varatesh, grand khagan of the Royal Clan and master of all the clans of Pardraya."

The Videssian officer frowned at the insult, but began to translate. Batbaian broke in, shouting, "You filthy bandit, you drop dung through your mouth when you call Varatesh a khagan, or his renegades a clan!" He would have sprung for Rodak, but a couple of Arshaum grabbed him by the shoulders and held him back.

Rodak had presence; he looked down his prominent nose at Batbaian, as if noticing him for the first time. Turning back to Arghun, he said, "So you have one of the outlaws along, do you? Well, I will make nothing of it; he's been marked as he deserves."

"Outlaw, is it?" Batbaian said, twisting in the grip of the Arshaum. "What did your clan, your *real* clan, outlaw *you* for, Rodak? Was is manslaying, or stealing from your friends, or just buggering a goat?"

"What I was is of no account," Rodak said coolly; Skylitzes translated both sides of the exchange. "What I am now counts."

"Yes, and what are you?" Batbaian cried. "A puffed-up piece of sheep turd, making the air stink for your betters. Without Avshar's black wizardry, you'd still be the starving brigand you ought to be, you vulture, you snake-hearted lizard-gutted cur, you green, hopping, slimy frog!"

That was the deadliest affront one Khamorth could throw at another; the men of Pardraya loathed and feared frogs. Rodak's hand flashed toward his saber. Then he froze with it still untouched, for two dozen arrows were aimed at him. Moving very slowly and carefully, he drew his hand away.

"Better," Arghun said dryly. "We have experience with treacherous envoys; they do not go well with weapons."

"Or with insults," Rodak returned. His lips were pale, but from anger this time, Gorgidas thought, not fear.

"Insult?" Batbaian said. "How could I make you out fouler than you are?"

"That is enough," Arghun said. "I will settle what he is." Batbaian held his tongue; Arghun framed his orders mildly, but expected them to be obeyed. The khagan returned to Rodak. "What does your Varatesh want with us?"

"He warns you to turn round at once and go back to your own side of the river Shaum, or face the anger of all the clans of Pardraya."

"Unless your khagan makes a quarrel with me, I have none with him," Arghun said. At that, Batbaian cried out again. "Be silent," Arghun told him, then turned to Rodak once more. "My quarrel is with Yezd—this is but the shortest road to Mashiz. Tell that to Varatesh very plainly, yes, and to your Avshar as well. So long as I am not attacked, I will not look for trouble with you Khamorth. If I am . . ." He let the sentence trail away.

Rodak licked his lips. The wars with the Arshaum were burned into the memory of his people. "Avshar comes from Yezd, they say, and is adopted into the Royal Clan; indeed, he stands next to Varatesh there."

"What is that to me?" Arghun's voice was bland. Batbaian suddenly smiled, not a pleasant sight; Viridovix was reminded of a wolf scenting blood. Arghun continued, "You have my answer. I will not turn back, but I make war on Yezd, not on you, unless you would have it so. Take that word to your master."

Skylitzes hesitated before he rendered the khagan's last sentence into the Khamorth speech. "How would you have me translate that?"

"Exactly as I said it," Argun said.

"Very well." The word the Videssian used for "master" meant "owner of a dog."

Rodak glowered at him and Arghun from under heavy brows. "When my chief—" He came down hard on the proper term. "—hears of this, we will see how funny he finds your little joke. Think on one-eye here; before long you may be envying his fate."

He wheeled his horse and rode away. Behind him, Arigh yipped like a puppy. A chorus of laughing Arshaum took up the call, yapping and baying Rodak out of camp. He roweled his horse savagely as he galloped northeast. Batbaian walked over to Arigh and slapped him on the back in wordless gratitude. Chuckling nomads kept barking at each other until it was full dark.

But back at the tent he shared with Viridovix, Gorgidas was less cheerful. He scrawled down what had happened at Rodak's embassy, noting, "The Khamorth are caught between two dreads, the ancient fear of their western neighbors and the new terror raised by Avshar. As the one is but the memory of a fright and the other all too immediate, the force of the latter, I think, shall prevail among them."

As he sometimes did, Viridovix asked the Greek what he'd written. "You're after thinking the shindy's coming, then?"

"Very much so. Why should Avshar let Yezd be ravaged if he can block the attack with these plainsmen, who are but tools in his hand? And I have no doubt he will be able to move them against us."

"Nobbut a tomnoddy'd say you're wrong," Viridovix nodded. He drew his sword, checked the blade carefully for rust, and honed away a couple of tiny nicks in the edge—as tame a reaction to the prospect of a fight as Gorgidas had seen from him. Since Seirem had perished in the massacre of Targitaus' camp, the big Gaul saw war's horror as well as its excitement and glory.

When he was satisfied with the state of the blade, he sheathed it again and stared moodily into the fire. At last he said, "We should thrash them, I'm thinking."

"Then sound as if you believed it, not like a funeral dirge!"

Gorgidas exclaimed in some alarm. The mercurial Celt seemed sunk in despair.

"You ha' me, for in my heart I dinna," he said. "Indeed and we're the better fighters, but what's the use in that? Yourself said it a few days ago: it's Avshar's witchering wins his battles for him, not his soldiers."

Gorgidas pursed his lips, as at a bad taste. All Avshar's troops needed to do was hold fast, draw their foes in until they were fully engaged, and the wizard-prince's magic would find a weakness or make one. To hold fast . . . his head jerked up. "*Autò ékhō!*" he shouted. "I have it!"

Viridovix jumped, grumbling crossly, "Talk a language a man can understand, not your fool Greek."

"Sorry." Words poured from the physician, a torrent of them. He forgot himself again once or twice and had to backtrack so the Gaul could follow him. As Viridovix listened, his eyes went wide.

"Aren't you the trickiest one, now," he breathed. He let out a great war whoop, then fell back on his wolfskin sleeping blanket, choking with laughter. "Puddocks!" he got out between wheezes. "Puddocks!" He dissolved all over again.

Gorgidas paid no attention to him. He was already sticking his head out the tent flap. "Tolui!" he yelled.

III

"THAT'S THE ONE," MARCUS SAID, POINTING. "HIS NAME'S Iatzoulinos."

"Third from the back on the left, is it?" Gaius Philippus growled. The tribune nodded, then regretted it. There was a dull, pounding ache in his head, from too much wine and not enough sleep. The senior centurion strode forward, saying, "His name doesn't matter a fart to me and it'll be so much dog dung to him, too, when I'm through with him."

He stamped down the narrow aisleway between the rows of desks. His high-crested helm nearly brushed the ceiling; his scarlet cloak of rank billowed about his shoulders; his shirt of mail clanked at every step. Scaurus leaned against the doorpost, watching bureaucrats look up in horror from their tax rolls, memoranda, and counting boards at the warlike apparition loosed in their midst.

Intently bent over his book of accounts, Iatzoulinos did not notice the Roman's approach even when Gaius Philippus loomed over his desk like a thundercloud. The secretary kept transferring numbers from one column to another, checking each entry twice. Though hardly past thirty, he had an older man's pallor and fussy precision.

Gaius Philippus scowled at him for a few seconds, but he remained oblivious. The senior centurion rasped his *gladius* free. Marcus sprang toward him—he had not brought him here to see murder done.

But Gaius Philippus brought the flat of the blade crashing down on Iatzoulinos' desk. The bureaucrat's ink pot leaped into the air and overturned; beads flew from his counting board.

He leaped himself, staring about wildly like a man waking to a nightmare. With a cry of dismay, he snatched his ledger away from the spreading puddle of ink. "What is the meaning of this madness?" he exclaimed, voice cracking in alarm.

"You shut your sniveling gob, you worthless sack of moldy tripes." Gaius Philippus' bass roar, trained to be heard through battlefield din, was fearsome in an enclosed space. "And sit down!" he added, slamming the pen-pusher back into his chair when he tried to scuttle away. "You're bloody well going to listen to me."

He spat into the ink spot. Iatzoulinos shriveled under his glare. No shame there, Marcus thought. That glower was made for turning hard-bitten legionaries to mush. "So you're the fornicating cabbagehead's been screwing over my men, eh?" the senior centurion barked, curling his lip in contempt.

Iatzoulinos actually blushed; the red was easy to see on his thin, sallow features. "It may possibly be the case that, due to some, ah unfortunate, ah, oversight, disbursement has experienced, ah, a few purely temporary delays—"

"Cut the garbage," Gaius Philippus ordered. Likely he had not understood half the pen-pusher's jargon. He noticed he was still holding his sword and sheathed it so he could poke a grimy-nailed finger in Iatzoulinos' face. The bureaucrat's eyes crossed as he regarded it fearfully.

"Now you listen and you listen good, understand me?" the veteran said. Iatzoulinos nodded, still watching the finger as though he did not dare look at the man behind it. Gaius Philippus went on, "It was you god-despised seal-stampers first took to hiring mercenaries because you decided you couldn't trust your own troops any more, 'cause they liked their local nobles better than you. Right?" He shook the secretary. "Right?"

"I, ah, believe something of that sort may have been the case, though this policy was, ah, implemented prior to the commencement of my tenure here."

"Mars' prick, you talk that way all the time!" The Roman clapped his hand to his forehead. He took a few seconds to pick up his chain of thought. "For my money, you were thinking with your heads up your backsides when you came up with that one, but forget that for now. Listen, you mud-brained bastard son of an illegitimate bepoxed she-goat, if you have to have troops that fight for money, what in the name of a bald-arsed bureaucrat do you think they'll do if there's no bloody money?" His voice rose another couple of notches, something Scaurus would not have guessed possible. "If they weren't kind and gentle like me, they'd tear your fornicating head off and piss in the hole, that's what! You'd probably remember better that way anyhow."

Iatzoulinos looked about ready to faint. Deciding things had gone far enough, Marcus called, "Since you are kind and gentle, Gaius, what will you do instead?"

"Eh? Oh. Hrrm." The centurion was thrown off stride for a second, but recovered brilliantly. Shoving his face within a couple of inches of the pen-pusher's, he hissed, "I give you four days to round up every goldpiece we're owed—and in old coin, too, none of this debased trash from Ortaias' mint—or I start saving up piss. Understand me?"

It took three tries, but Iatzoulinos got a "Yes" out.

"Good." Gaius Philippus glared round the room. "Well, why aren't the rest of you lazy sods working?" he snarled, and tramped out.

"A very good day to you all, gentlemen," Marcus said to the stunned bureaucrats, and followed him. He had an afterthought and stuck his head back in. "Don't you wish you were dealing with the nobles again?"

Alypia Gavra laughed when the tribune told her the story. "And did he get the pay for your soldiers?" she asked.

"Every bit of it. It went off to Garsavra by courier, let me see, ten days ago. He's staying in the city until the receipt comes back from Minucius. If it's not here pretty soon, or if it's even a copper short, I would not care to be wearing Iatzoulinos' sandals."

"Rocking the bureaucrats every so often is not a bad thing," Alypia said seriously. "They're needed to keep the Empire running on an even keel, but they are trained in the city and they serve here and begin to think that everything comes down to entries in a ledger. Bumping up against reality has to be healthy for them."

Marcus chuckled. "I think Gaius Philippus was rather realer than Iatzoulinos cared for."

"From what I've seen of him, I'd say you're right." Alypia got out of bed. It was only a few steps to the jug of wine on the table against the far wall. She poured for both of them. The wine was the best this inn offered, but none too good. Compared even to Aetios' tavern, the place was dingy and cramped. The din of hammers on copperware of every sort came unceasingly through the narrow window.

When the tribune put down his cup—yellow-brown unglazed clay, ugly but functional—he caught Alypia watching him curiously. He arched his eyebrows. She hesitated, then asked, "Have you told him about us?"

"No," Scaurus said at once. "The fewer who know, the better."

She nodded. "That's so. Yet surely, if half what you and my uncle have said of him is true, he would never violate your trust. And I know the two of you are close; it shows in the way you work together." She looked the question at him.

"You're right, he'd never betray us," the tribune said. "But telling him would not make me easier and would just make him nervous. He'd see only the risk, and never understand that for you it was worth taking."

"Never say you were not born a courtier, dear Marcus," she murmured, her eyes glowing. He hugged her close; her skin was like warm satin against his.

"Gangway there!" The rough shout came through the window, accompanied by the clatter of iron-shod hooves on paving-stones. With Alypia in his arms, the tribune did not pay the noise much attention, but it registered. The coppersmiths' district was a poor quarter of the city, with horses few and far between.

A few minutes later the inn's whole second floor shook as several men in heavy boots pounded up the wooden stairs. Marcus frowned. "What nonsense is this?" he muttered, more annoyed than alarmed. Better safe, he decided. He climbed to his feet, slid his sword free of its sheath, and wrapped his tunic round his arm for a makeshift shield.

The door came crashing in. Alypia screamed. Scaurus started to spring forward, then froze in his tracks. Four armored archers were in the hallway, bows drawn and aimed at his belly. Half a dozen spearmen crowded after them. And Provhos Mourtzouphlos, a wide smile of invitation on his face, said, "Take another step, outlander, why don't you?"

Wits numb in disaster, the tribune lowered his blade. "No?" Mourtzouphlos said, seeing he would not charge. "Too bad." His voice cracked like a whip. "Then back off!"

The Roman obeyed. "Jove," he said. "Jove, Jove, Jove." It was neither prayer nor curse, simply the first noise he happened to make.

The Videssian bowmen followed. Three kept arrows trained on him while the fourth turned his weapon toward Alypia, who was sitting rigidly upright in bed, the coverlet drawn to her chin to hide her nakedness. Her eyes were wide and staring, like those of a trapped animal.

"No need to aim at her," Marcus said softly. The archer, a young man with a hooked nose and liquid brown eyes that told of Vaspurakaner blood, nodded and lowered his bow.

"You be silent," Mortzouphlos said from the doorway. He suddenly seemed to notice the tribune was still holding his sword. "Drop it!" he ordered, then snapped at the last bowman, "Gather that up, Artavasdos, if you have nothing better to do."

Mourtzouphlos looked Scaurus' unclad frame up and down. "Damned foreign foolishness, scraping your face every day," he said, stroking his own whiskers. His grin grew most unpleasant. "When Thorisin's done with you, you'll likely be able to keep your cheeks smooth without needing to shave." His voice went falsetto; he grabbed at his crotch in an unmistakable gesture.

Marcus' blood ran cold; of themselves, his hands made a protective cup. One of the troopers behind Mourtzouphlos laughed. Alypia came out of her terrified paralysis. "No!" she cried in horror. "Blame me, not him!"

"No one asked your advice, slut," Mourtzouphlos said coldly. "A fine one you make to talk, whoring with the Sphrantzai and then spreading yourself for this barbarian."

Alypia went white. "Shut your foul mouth, Mourtzouphlos," Scaurus said. "You'll pay for that, I promise."

"What are your promises worth?" The Videssian cavalry officer stepped up and slapped him in the face.

Ears ringing, Marcus shook his head to clear it. "Do what you like with me, but have a care how you treat her Majesty the Princess. You'll get no thanks from Thorisin for tormenting her."

"Will I not?" Mourtzouphlos retorted, but with a touch of doubt; his men, reminded of Alypia's title, looked at each other for a moment. Mourtzouphlos pulled himself together. "As for doing what I'd like with you—there's no time for that now, worse luck. Get your trousers on, Ronam," he barked. Scaurus had to swallow a startled laugh; if he began, he did not think he would be able to stop.

Mourtzouphlos rounded on Alypia. "And you, my lady," he said, speaking the honorific like a curse. "Come on, out of there. D'you think I'll leave you to wait for your next customer?" His men leered in anticipation.

"Damn you, Provhos," Scaurus said. Alypia stayed motionless beneath the blanket, dread on her face. After her treatment at the hands of Vardanes Sphrantzes, Marcus knew the humiliation Mourtzouphlos was piling on her might break her forever. When the cavalryman reached out to tear the cover away, he shouted, "Wait!"

"And why should I?"

"Because she is still the Emperor's niece and last living relative. No matter what he may do to me, do you think he'll thank you for making his scandal worse?" That was a keen shot; the Roman could see calculation start behind Mourtzouphlos' eyes. He pressed his tiny advantage: "Give her leave to dress in peace; where will she go?"

Mourtzouphlos rubbed his chin as he thought. At last he jerked a thumb at Scaurus. "Take him out into the hall." As the archers obeyed, he said to Alypia, "I'm warning you, be quick."

"Thank you," she said, to him and Marcus both.

"Bah!" Mourtzouphlos slammed the door. He growled at his troopers, "Well, what are you standing around for? Tie this whoreson up." One of the spearmen jerked the tribune's hands behind him, while a second lashed his wrists together with rawhide thongs.

Before the last knot was tied, Alypia emerged from the cubicle, still tugging at the sleeves of her dark-gold linen dress. She wore her usual dispassionate air like a shield against enemies, but Marcus saw how her hand trembled when she shut the door behind her. Her voice, though, was steady if toneless as she said to Mourtzouphlos, "Do what you must."

"Move, then," he said brusquely. Scaurus stumbled on the stairs; he would have fallen had the archer carrying his sword not grabbed his shoulder. The drinkers in the taproom below stared as the soldiers led their prisoners out. In high spirits once more, Mourtzouphlos tossed a couple of silverpieces to the innkeeper. "This for the custom I may have scared off."

The taverner, a lean-faced bald fellow who looked to have no use for on-duty troopers in his place, made the coins disappear.

Two more spearmen were outside keeping an eye on the squad's horses. "Mount up," Mourtzouphlos said. He bowed mockingly to Scaurus. "Here's a gelding for you to ride, instead of your filly. Think on that, outlander."

"You knew!" Marcus blurted in dismay.

"So I did," Mourtzouphlos said smugly. "Saborios has sharp ears, and making sure he was right was worth the time I spent in those cheap, scratchy clothes."

"Saborios!" Scaurus and Alypia said together, exchanging an appalled glance. The princess burst out, "Phos, what will my uncle do to Balsamon?"

"Not a damned thing," Mourtzouphlos answered in disgust. "It would cost him riots, more's the pity." He turned that nasty grin on the tribune again. "The same doesn't apply to you, of course. I only wish I could rout every other greedy mercenary from Videssos so easily. Now ride!"

One of the cavalryman's soldiers had to help Scaurus into the saddle; no horseman, he could not mount without his hands. His mind was whirling as Mourtzouphlos tied a lead to his horse's reins. In principle, ironically, he agreed with the imperial—Videssos would have done better with all native troops.

But Alypia said, "So you would free the Empire of mercenaries, would you, Mourtzouphlos? Tell me, then, you've never made peasants on your estates into personal retainers. Tell me you've never held back tax monies from the fisc." Her voice dripped scorn. Cat-graceful, she swung herself up onto the horse by Scaurus'.

The aristocrat flushed, but he came back, "Why should I give the cursed pen-pushers the gold to spend on more hired troops?" With the provincial nobles converting the Empire's freeholders to private armies and the bureaucrats taxing them into serfdom, no wonder Videssos was short of soldiers. Its manpower pool had been drying up for more than a hundred years.

"Ride!" Mourtzouphlos repeated. He dug spurs into his mount's flank. It bounded forward, and so, perforce, did Marcus' animal. He almost went over its tail; only a quick clutch with his knees saved him. He did not think Mourtzouphlos would mind if he got trampled.

"Make way, in the Emperor's name!" the Videssian officer shouted again and again, trying to hurry through the city's crowded streets. Some of the traffic did move aside to let his troopers pass, but as many riders and folk afoot stopped and turned to gape at him. He would have made better progress keeping quiet, but he crowed out his victory like a rooster.

Marcus endured the journey, distracted from the full mortification of it by his struggle to hold his seat. That so occupied him that he had little chance to turn his head Alypia's way. She rode steadily on, eyes set straight ahead, as if neither the crowd nor her guards had any meaning to her. Once, though, her glance met Scaurus', and she sent him a quick, frightened smile. His horse missed a step, jouncing him in the saddle before he could return it.

After the hurly-burly and close-pressing swarm of humanity in the plaza of Palamas, the palace compound's wide uncrowded lanes were a relief to the tribune, or would have been had not Mourtzouphlos stepped up his squadron's pace to nearly a gallop. A fat eunuch carrying a silver tray scurried onto the edge of the grass as the horsemen thundered by. His head whipped round, and he dropped his platter with a clang when he recognized their prisoners.

They pounded through a grove of cherry trees just beginning to come into fragrant pink blossom and pulled to a halt before a single-story building of stucco trimmed with gleaming marble that was the imperial family's private quarters. Sentries sprang to attention on seeing Mourtzouphlos—or was it for Alypia Gavra? Another eunuch, a steward in a robe of dark red silk embroidered with golden birds, appeared in the entranceway. Mourtzouphlos called, "His Majesty expects us."

"Bide a moment." The chamberlain vanished inside. Mourtzouphlos and his men dismounted, as did Alypia and Scaurus; the tribune managed to slide off his horse without stumbling. Some of the sentries knew him and exclaimed in surprise to see him bound. But before he could answer, the steward returned and beckoned Mourtzouphlos and his unwilling companions forward. "Bring two or three of your guards," he said, indicating the cavalrymen, "but leave the rest here. His Imperial Majesty does not feel they will be required."

Marcus paid no attention to the splendid antiquities he

was hurried past, relics of a millenium and a half of Videssian history. The guards frogmarched him along; they did not quite dare mete out the same treatment to Alypia, who walked beside him free of restraint. Prisoner she might be, but, as the tribune had reminded them, she was also the Emperor's niece.

The eunuch chamberlain ducked into a doorway. He started to speak, but Thorisin Gavras irritably broke in, "I know who they are, you bloody twit! Go on, get out of here." Blank-faced, the steward withdrew. Mourtzouphlos led Scaurus and Alypia in to the Avtokrator of the Videssians.

Gavras spun round at their entrance. The motion was lithe, but the Emperor's shoulder sagged just a little, and his eyes were trimmed with red. He looks tired, was Marcus' first thought, followed a moment later by, he looks more like Mavrikios than ever. The burden Avtokrators carried aged them quickly.

But Thorisin remained more impetuous than his older brother had been. "Oh, send your lads back outside, Provhos," he said impatiently. "If we can't handle a girl and a tied man, Phos have pity on us." He slapped the hilt of his saber, an unadorned, much-used weapon in a plain leather sheath.

That seemed to give him an idea. "Artavasdos!" he called after the guards—any Emperor who wanted a long rule knew as many of his men's names as he could. The soldier stood in the doorway. "Is that this wretch's sword you have there?" He jerked a thumb at the Roman. When Artavasdos nodded, he went on, "Well, why don't you fetch it over to Nepos, the sorcerer-priest at the Academy? He's been panting for a long look at it since he found out about it." Artavasdos nodded again, saluted, and disappeared.

Marcus winced as the sword was taken away and felt more naked than he had when Mourtzouphlos and his men surprised him. That druid-enchanted blade, with its twin that Viridovix carried, had swept the Romans from Gaul to Videssos and in the Empire it had proved potent in its own right. He never willingly let himself be separated from it; now his will mattered nothing.

He was dismayed enough to miss Thorisin's words to him. Mourtzouphlos sharply prodded him in the ribs. A frown on his long face, the Emperor repeated, "Still no proskynesis, eh, even for your head's sake? You're a stiff-necked bastard,

Roman, and no mistake, but not stiff enough for the axe to bounce off."

"What good would a prostration do?" the tribune said. "You won't spare me on account of it." The proskynesis had not even occurred to him; the custom of republican Rome was to bend the knee to no man.

"Too proud, are you?" Thorisin said. "But not too proud, I see, to sneak out and sleep with my brother's daughter."

"Well said!" Mourtzouphlos exclaimed. Scaurus felt his cheeks go hot; he had no answer for the Emperor.

Alypia said, "It was not as you think, uncle. If anything, I sought him out rather than he me."

"A harlot whoring with a lumpish heathen," Mourtzouphlos fleered. "That makes neither you nor him better, strumpet."

"Provhos," the Emperor said sharply, "I will handle this with no help from you." The cavalryman opened his mouth and closed it again with a snap. Thorisin Gavras' anger was nothing to risk.

"And I love him," Alypia said.

"And I her," Marcus echoed.

Mourtzouphlos seemed about to explode. Thorisin shouted, "What in Skotos' name difference does that make?" He turned to his niece. "I thought you had better sense than to drag the name of our clan through the bathhouses."

"Me?" she said, her voice wild and dangerous. "Me? What of your oh-so-sweet doxy Komitta Rhangavve, who straddled anything that wasn't dead like a bitch in heat, and had you lampooned for it last Midwinter's Day in the Amphitheater in front of half the city?"

Thorisin stopped in his tracks, as if clubbed. He went red, then white. Provhos Mourtzouphlos looked as though he wished he were somewhere else; listening to a family feud in the imperial family could prove unhealthy.

Even more loudly, Alypia went on, "And if you're so concerned to keep us from reproaches, dear uncle, why didn't you put your precious mistress aside when you became Avtokrator, and marry and get yourself an heir?"

In her fury and gallantry she reminded Marcus of an outmatched fencer throwing everything into a last desperate attack, win or die. Thorisin flinched, but growled, "This is not about me, but about you and how what you've done touches me." His voice went up to a roar: "Bizoulinos! Domentziolos!

Konon!" The chamberlain who had conducted Mourtzouphlos'
party to the Emperor hurried in, along with two other eunuchs. Gavras ordered them, "Take Alypia to her quarters
here. See she stays there till I command otherwise; your lives
are answer for it."

"That's right!" she cried. "If you have no answer, hide the
question away so you need not think about it anymore." The
stewards led her away. She cast a last backward look at
Scaurus but, not wanting to make his position more hopeless
than it already was, said nothing.

"Whew!" said the Emperor, wiping his forehead. "You
must be a sorcerer yourself, Roman; I've never seen her so
fierce." He laughed humorlessly. "She has the Gavras temper,
under all that calm she usually puts on." His stare grew sharp
again. "Now—what do we do with you?"

"I am loyal to your Majesty," Marcus said.

"Ha!" That was Mourtzouphlos, but he subsided like a
scolded small boy when Thorisin turned his eye on him; all
their long past had trained the Videssians to quail before the
imperial office's power.

Gavras turned back to the tribune. "Loyal, are you? You
have a bloody odd way of showing it, then." He stroked his
chin; year by year, his beard was going grayer. "If you were
a Videssian, you'd be deadly dangerous to me. You're a
good soldier and halfway decent bureaucrat; you might be
able to line up both factions behind you. Bad enough as
is—tell me to my face you're not an ambitious man."

It was the very word he had known the Emperor would tax
him with. "Is that a sin?" he said.

"In a mercenary captain it's a sin past forgiving. Ask
Drax."

Scaurus backtracked. "It has nothing to do with my feelings about Alypia. You must know her well enough to know
she would recognize advances that came from self-interest for
what they were."

"What does an assotted wench know?" Mourtzouphlos
sneered, but Thorisin paused for a moment. If his officer did
not, he respected Alypia's clear thinking.

"If I had been a traitor," Marcus pressed on, "would I have
stayed with you in the civil war against Ortaias and Vardanes?
Would I have warned you against Drax when you sent him out
to fight Baanes Onomagoulos? Would I have fought against

him last year when he tried to set up his new Namdalen in the westlands?"

"Consorting with an imperial princess without the leave of the Avtokrator is treason for a Videssian, let alone an outlander," Thorisin said flatly, and the tribune's heart sank. "And if you were as pure of heart as you claim, why would you have met with the Namdaleni and plotted abandoning me when it seemed I could not take Videssos from the Sphrantzai? What does your tattling against Drax prove? Any officer will score off his rival if he can. If you despised and suspected him so, why did you let him get away to scheme new mischiefs against me?"

"You know how that happened," Scaurus said, but weakly; it was plain Thorisin would hear no defense. The irony galled the tribune, for he genuinely favored Thorisin's reign. In the troubled times Videssos faced, he could see no chance for a better ruler. And the Empire itself he heartily admired. Despite its flaws, it had given generations union, peace, and, on the whole, good government—ideals republican Rome professed, but failed to live up to.

"What I know," Gavras said, "is that I cannot trust you. That suffices." The tribune heard the finality in his voice. After three civil wars and foreign invasions from west and east, the Emperor would not take chances that touched his safety. With reversed positions, Scaurus likely would have felt the same.

"His head—or any other part you care to take—would be an ornament on the Milestone," Mourtzouphlos suggested. The red granite column in the plaza of Palamas was the point from which all distances were measured in the Empire, and also served to display the remains of miscreants.

"No doubt," Thorisin said. "But I fear his damned regiment would rise if I execute him, and they're dangerous men holding an important position. This needs more thought. He'll be safe enough for the time being locked in gaol, don't you think?"

Mourtzouphlos still seemed disappointed, but managed a nod. "As you say, your Majesty."

"Scaurus and the princess? I can't believe it," Senpat Sviodo said, gesturing theatrically to show his astonishment.

His sweeping wave almost upset his wife's cup of wine. Nevrat Sviodo rescued it with a quick grab. "Tell us more, cousin," she urged. She brushed her thick, black, curly hair back from her face.

"Not much to tell," Artavasdos replied. His eyes flicked this way and that. The three Vaspurakaners were sitting at a corner table in an uncrowded tavern and speaking their own language, but he still looked nervous. Nevrat did not blame him. His news was too inflammatory to be easy with.

"Well, how did you get to be one of the ones who took them?" Senpat asked. He played with the pointed end of his beard, close-trimmed in the imperial fashion to accent his swarthy good looks.

"About the way you'd expect," Artavasdos said. "Mourtzouphlos came to the barracks and ordered my squad out—he said he had a job for us With his rank, no one argued. He didn't tell us who we were after until we were almost at the inn where they were."

"The princess, though." Senpat was still shaking his head.

"Mourtzouphlos said they'd been at it for a couple of months he was sure of, and maybe longer than that. The way they acted when we broke in on them makes me believe it. They seemed more worried about each other than themselves, if you know what I mean."

"That sounds like Marcus," Nevrat said.

"I knew you and your husband were friends of his, cousin, so I thought you'd better know." Artavasdos hesitated. "Being friends with him might not be a good idea right now. Maybe you should get out of the city for a while."

"So bad as that, Artavasdos?" Nevrat said, alarmed.

The soldier considered. "Well, maybe not. Thorisin is too shrewd to massacre people who know people who've fallen foul of him, I think."

"I hope so," Nevrat said, "or with his temper there'd not be many folk for him to rule." She was not really worried about herself or Senpat; she thought her cousin had gauged the Emperor's common sense well. But that would not help Scaurus. He was guilty in fact, not by association.

"I can't believe it," Senpat said again.

Nevrat had trouble, too, but for reasons different from her husband's. Senpat did not know that Marcus, in his desperation after Helvis left him, had made a tentative approach to her this past fall. She saw no reason ever to mention it; the tribune had understood she meant the no she gave him.

But now this! She wondered how long the attraction had grown between Scaurus and Alypia Gavra. And, despite wanting no one but Senpat herself, she felt a tiny touch of pique that Marcus should have found someone else so soon after she turned him down.

"What are you laughing at, dear?" Senpat asked her.

She felt herself flushing. She was glad she was as dark as her husband; in the dim tavern, no one could tell. "Me," she said, and did not explain.

The barred door at the far end of the corridor opened with the groan of a rusty hinge. Two guards pushed a creaking handcart through. Another flanked them on either side, with arrows nocked in their bows. All four men looked bored.

"Up, you lags!" one of the archers called unnecessarily. The prisoners were already crowding to the front of their cells; feeding time marked the high point of their day.

Marcus hurried forward with the rest, his belly growling in anticipation. Out of reach on the wall above his head, a torch sputtered and almost went out. He coughed on noxious smoke. Torches gave the prison such light as it had; it was underground, a basement level of the sprawling imperial offices on Middle Street.

A hidden ventilation system carried off enough smoke to keep the air breathable, but only just. Along with the torches, the gaol reeked of moldering straw, unwashed humanity, and full chamber pots. When Mourtzouphlos' troopers had thrown Scaurus into one of the little cells, the stench all but drove him mad. Now, after what he thought was four or five days, he took it for granted.

The cart squeaked down the long, narrow passageway, stopping in front of the cells on either side. One of the guards pushing it handed an earthen jug of water to the prisoner on the left, while the other gave the prisoner on the right a small loaf and a bowl of thin stew. Then they traded sides and pushed the handcart down another few feet.

The tribune passed yesterday's empty jug and bowl back to the guard and took his rations in exchange. The water tasted stale; the bread, of barley and oats, was full of husks and of grit from the millstone. The bits of fish in the stew might have been fresh once, but not any time recently. He spooned it up with a bit of crust, then licked the bowl. There was never enough to satisfy. He paid little attention to his belly's constant grumbling. He was not a good enough Stoic to keep a tight rein on his emotions, but mere bodily discomfort did not matter to him.

After the guards had finished their rounds, there was nothing to do but talk. Marcus did not contribute much; he had got howls of derision when he answered, "Treason," to the fellow who asked him why he had been jailed. The ordinary criminals who made up most of the prison population sneered at "politicals," as they called his kind. Besides, he had nothing new to teach them.

A thief was holding forth on ways to beat locks. "If you have plenty of time, you can work sand down into the bolt hole a few grains at a time until the pin comes up high enough for you to lift it out. It's quiet, but slow. Or, if the lock is in a dark place, you can make a net of fine mesh and attach it to a bit of thread, then push it down into the bolt hole. When the pin gets dropped in, all you have to do is lift and you're home free.

"For quick work, though, a pincer's the thing. Cut a groove in one half and leave the other flat, so you can get a good grip on the pin—it's a cylinder, you see, dropped down into its hole so that half of it's in the doorjamb and ther other half in the bar. Look at the cells across from you, you dips. It's the very same setup they use here, but they're canny enough to keep the locks too far away for us to reach. By Skotos, I'd be out of here in a minute if that weren't so."

Scaurus believed him; he had the matter-of-fact confidence of a man who knew his trade. When he was through, a pompous voice a long way down the corridor began explaining how to color glass paste to counterfeit fine gems. "Ha!" someone else called. "If you're so good, what're you doing here?" His only answer was injured silence.

After that the talk turned to women, the other subject on which the prisoners would go on all through the day. The tribune had a story that would have astonished them—and no intention of telling it.

He slept two or three more times, waking up after each one with new bites. Lice and fleas had a paradise in the filthy straw bedding; he lost count of how many roaches he killed as they skittered across the brick floor. Some of the convicts ate them. He was not hungry enough for that.

His belly told him it was not long before feeding time when a squad of Videssian regular troops came clattering down into the gaol. Their leader showed his pass to the guard captain, who walked along the row of cells until he came to the one that held the tribune. "This him?"

"Let me look," the soldier said. "Aye, that's the fellow."

"He's yours then." The guard produced a key, drew up the bolt, and slid out the bar that held Scaurus' door closed. "Come on, you," he snapped at the Roman.

Marcus stumbled out, then pulled himself to attention as he faced the squad leader. As well go down with the eagle high, his legionary training said, as yield it and go down regardless. "Where are you taking me?" he asked crisply.

"To the Emperor," the Videssian replied. If Scaurus' bearing impressed him, he did a good job of hiding it. He made a sour face. "No—to the bathhouse first. You stink." His men grabbed the tribune by the elbows and hustled him away.

In fresh clothes, even ones that did not fit him well, with his still-damp hair slicked back from his eyes, Marcus felt a new man. The soldiers had finally had to drag him out of the warm pool at the bathhouse. He had soaped twice and scraped himself with a strigil till his skin turned red. He still wore the red-gold beginnings of a beard; razors were hard to come by in Videssos. The whiskers itched and made him look scruffy, constantly reminding him of his time in prison.

He felt a small flicker of relief when his captors took him, not to the Grand Courtroom, but to the Emperor's residence. Whatever lay ahead did not include one of the formal public condemnations the Videssians staged with such pomp and ceremony.

He knew he could not expect to see Alypia with her uncle, but her absence forcibly brought his predicament back to him. Thorisin Gavras wore full imperial regalia, a bad sign; he only donned the red boots, the gem-encrusted purple robe, and the domed crown to emphasize the power of his office. But for the guards, the only soul with Scaurus and the Emperor in the little audience chamber was one of the imperial stewards—Konon, it was—with a scribe's waxed tablet and stylus.

Gavras inspected the Roman. "Are you ready to hear my judgment?" he asked sternly.

"Have I a choice?"

The scribbling steward looked shocked; the Emperor gave a grunt of laughter. "No," he said, and turned forbidding again. "Know that you are convicted of treachery against the imperial house."

Marcus stood mute, hoping the ice he felt in his belly did not show on his face. His sentence rolled down on him like an avalanche: "As traitor, you are dismissed from your post as *epoptes* in the imperial chancery." Though that office had been a plum for Scaurus, whose hopes ran beyond the army life, losing it did not cast him into despair.

But Thorisin was continuing: "Having forfeited our trust, you are also stripped of your command over your Romans and shall be prevented from any intercourse with them, the better to prevent future acts of sedition or rebellion. Your lieutenant Gaius Philippus assumes your rank and its perquisites, effective at once."

Permanent exile from all that was left of his own people, his own world . . . the tribune hung his head; his nails bit into his palms. Low-voiced, he said, "He's a fine soldier. Have you told him of this yet?"

"I shall, but we are not finished here, you and I," the Emperor said. "There is only one standard penalty for treason, as well you know. In addition to such trivia as loss of ranks and titles, you also stand liable to the headman's axe."

After the prospect of exile, the axe seemed a small terror; at least it was quickly done. Marcus blurted, "If you plan on killing me, why did you bother with the rest of that rigmarole?"

Gavras did not answer him directly. Instead he said, "That will do, Konon." The fat beardless chamberlain bowed and left. Then the Emperor turned back to the Roman, a sour smile on his face. "You would be flattered to know there are people who would sooner I did not execute the sentence—to say nothing of you."

"Are there?" Scaurus echoed.

"Oh, indeed, and a bloody noisy flock they are, too. Alypia, of course, though if you were as innocent as she makes you out, you'd still be a virgin and not in your mess at all. She almost makes me believe it—but not quite.

"And there's Leimmokheir the drungarios of the fleet, a fine, upstanding sort if ever there was one." Gavras cocked an eyebrow at the admiral's unflinching rectitude. "But then, he owes you one. If it weren't for your stubbornness he'd still be jailed, or short a head himself for treason. So how much is his advice worth?"

"You are the only judge of that," Marcus said, but he was warmed to learn Leimmokheir had not forgotten him.

"Those, and a couple more like them, are pleas I can understand." Thorisin looked him up and down. "But how in Phos' name did Iatzoulinos come to send me a good word for you?"

"Did he?" the tribune said, amazed. Then he squelched a laugh; one taste of Gaius Philippus had probably made the pen-pusher hope Scaurus would live forever.

"Aye, he did." Gavras' mouth twisted. "Mistake me not, outlander. There's no doubt of your guilt. But I admit I am forced to wonder just a hair at your motives, and so I will give you a hairsbreadth chance to redeem yourself."

Marcus started to lean forward, but the clutch of the guards brought him up short. "What would you, then?"

"This: put an end to Zemarkhos' rebellion in Amorion. His lying anathemas raise trouble for me all through the Empire, from narrow-minded priests and over-religious laymen alike. Bring that off, and I'd say you'd earned yourself a pardon. More, in fact—if you can do it, I'll make you a noble, and not one with small estates, either. That I pledge to you. I will take oath on it at the High Temple to any priest you name save Balsamon—nay, even to him—if you doubt me."

"No need. I agree," Marcus said at once. Thorisin was short-tempered and suspicious, but the tribune knew he kept his promises. His mind began to buzz with schemes: straight-out conquest, bribery . . . "What force will I have at my disposal?"

"I can spare you a good cavalry horse," the Emperor said. Scaurus started to smile, then checked himself; Thorisin's face was hard, his eyes deadly serious. "Aye, I mean it, Roman. Win your own salvation, if you can. You get no help from me."

One man, against the zealots with whom the fanatic priest had even held the Yezda at bay since Maragha? "It salves your conscience, does it, to send me off to suicide instead of killing me yourself?" The tribune nodded bitterly, no longer caring what he said.

"You are a proved traitor, and mine to do with as I

wish," Gavras reminded him. He folded his arms across his chest. "Call it what you will, Scaurus. I need not argue with you."

"As you say. Give me back my sword, then. If I'm to 'win my own salvation,' " Marcus made that a taunt, "let me do it with what is mine."

Thorisin considered. "That is a fair request." He found a scrap of parchment, inked a reed pen, wrote furiously. "Here, Spektas," he said, handing the note to one of Scaurus' guards, "take this to Nepos. When he gives you the blade, bring it back here. The Roman can carry it to his ship."

"Ship?" the tribune said as Spektas hurried away.

"Yes, ship. Did you expect me to send you by road, and maybe find you going off to your Romans and stirring up who knows how much mischief? Thank you, no. Moreover," and the Emperor unbent very slightly, "sea travel's faster than land. If you put in at Nakoleia on the coast north of Amorion, you'll only have a short run inland through Yezda-held territory. And you should get into town in time for the *panegyris*—the trade-fair—dedicated to the holy Moikheios. It draws merchants and customers from far and wide, and should be your best chance to slip in without being spotted."

Scaurus grudged him a nod. Whether Gavras saw it so or not, that was help of a sort. "One more thing," he said to the Emperor.

"What now?" Thorisin growled. "You are in no position to bargain, sirrah."

With the freedom perfect weakness brings, Marcus retorted, "Why not? The worst you can do is take my head, and you can do that anyhow."

The Emperor blinked, then grinned crookedly. "True enough. Say on."

"If I bring Zemarkhos down, you will make a noble of me?"

"I said so once. What of it?"

Scaurus took a deep breath, more than half expecting to die in the next minute. "Should I somehow come back from Amorion, I think I will have shown my loyalty well enough to suit even you. Give me a noble's privilege, then. If I come back, give me leave to court your niece openly, as any noble might hope to do."

"Why, you insolent son of a whore! You dare ask me that, hied here for treason?" Gavras seemed to grow taller in his regalia. One of the guardsmen cursed. Marcus felt the grip on him tighten, heard a sword slide out of its scabbard. He nodded, though he felt fresh sweat prickle at his armpits.

"To the ice with you!" the Emperor exclaimed, and Scaurus thought it was the end. But Thorisin was glaring at him with reluctant respect. "Skotos chill you, I owe Alypia half a hundred goldpieces. She told me you would say that. I didn't think there could be so much brass in any man."

"Well?" Marcus said, but his knees sagged with relief. Had the answer been no, it would have been over already.

"If you return, I will not kill you out of hand for it," the Emperor ground out, word by word. He turned to the guards' squad leader, gestured imperiously. "Take him away!"

"My sword is not here yet," Marcus reminded him.

"Are you trying to find out how close to the edge you can walk, Roman?" Gavras slammed his fist down on the tabletop. "I begin to see why your folk has no kings—who would want the job?" To the guards again: "Let him have whatever gear he wants, but get him out of my sight—wait for his cursed sword outside." And finally to Scaurus once more, it being the Emperor's prerogative to have the last word: "Shall I wish you success, or not?"

The *Seafoam* was a naval auxiliary, an oared cargo-carrier about seventy feet long, with sharp bows and a full stern. She had ten oarports on either side of her hull, as well as a single broad, square-rigged sail, brailed up now that she was in harbor.

Staggering a little under the weight of the heavy kit he carried, Marcus paused at the top of the gangplank. The squad of imperial guards watched him from the dock.

"Permission to come aboard?" he called, recognizing an officer by the knee-length tunic he wore and the shortsword on his hip. Most of his sailors were naked or nearly so, with perhaps a loincloth or leather belt on which to sling a knife.

"Keep at it," the man told his crew, who were stowing pointed wine jars and rounder ones full of pickled fish, along with bales of raw wool and woolen cloth, in the hold. Then he gave his attention to the tribune. "You're our special passenger, eh? Aye, drop down and join us. Give him a hand with his pack, there, Ousiakos!"

The sailor helped ease it to the deck. Rather awkwardly, Scaurus came after it; a true Roman, he was not used to ships. The officer walked up to shake his hand. "I'm Stylianos Zautzes, master of this wallowing tub." The Videssian was in his early forties, whipcord lean, with a grizzled beard, thick bushy eyebrows that met about his nose, and a skin turned to dark leather by years in the sun. When he shed his black, low-crowned cap to scratch his head, the tribune saw he was nearly bald.

Taron Leimmokheir jumped down beside Marcus. The men on deck stiffened to attention, giving him the Videssian salute with right fists over their hearts. "As you were," he said in his raspy bass. The drungarios of the fleet turned to Zautzes. "You take care of this one, Styl," he told the *Seafoam*'s captain, putting an arm round the tribune. "He's a good fellow, for all he's fallen foul of his Majesty. That's not hard to do, as I should know." He flicked his head back to get his mane of silver hair out of his eyes; he had left it long after Thorisin released him from prison.

Zautzes saluted again. "I would anyway, for my own pride's sake. But wasn't he to have a horse? It's not shown up."

"Landsmen!" Leimmokheir said contemptuously. On board ship, things had to be on time and right the first time; there was no room for sloppiness. "I should be able to waste so much time. As is, I can't even stay; I'm off to finish fitting out a squadron for coast patrol. Phos with you, outlander." He squeezed Scaurus' shoulder, pounded Zautzes on the back, and then took a tall step up onto the gangplank and hurried away.

The loading of the *Seafoam* went on. Marcus watched bales of hay tossed into the hold as fodder for his horse. Of the horse itself there was no sign. He shouted a question to the Videssian guardsmen still standing about on the pier. Their leader spread his hands and shrugged.

Zautzes said, "Sorry, Scaurus, but if the beast doesn't turn up by mid-afternoon we'll have to sail without it. I have dispatches to carry that won't keep. Maybe you'll be able to find some sort of animal in Nakoleia."

"Maybe," the tribune said dubiously. The minutes dragged on. He kept one eye on the pier, the other on the sailors to see how close they were to finishing loading.

Two of them dropped a wine jar. Zautzes swore as they swabbed the sticky stuff from the deck and threw the jar's fragments over the rail into the sea. One cut his foot on a shard and limped over to bandage it. Zautzes rolled his eyes in disgust. "You belong behind a plow, Ailouros." The luckless seaman's crewmates promptly took to calling him "Farmer."

Watching the mishap, Marcus forgot about the pier. He jumped at a shout from the gangplank: "Ahoy, or whatever it is you sailor bastards say! Can I get on your bloody boat?"

The tribune whirled. "Gaius! What are you doing here?"

"You know this lubber?" Zautzes demanded, bristling at hearing his beloved *Seafoam* called a boat. When Marcus had explained, the Videssian captain grudgingly called to Gaius Philippus, "Aye, board if you will."

The senior centurion did, grunting as he landed on the deck. He stumbled when he hit, being in full armor—transverse-crested helm, mail shirt, metal-studded leather kilt, and greaves, all polished till they gleamed—with a heavy pack slung on his back. Marcus caught his elbow and steadied him. "Thanks."

"It's nothing." The tribune studied him curiously. "Are you here to see me off? You're overdressed, I'd say."

"To Hades with seeing you off." Gaius Philippus hawked phlegm, but under Zautzes' warning eye spat over the rail. "I'm with you."

"What?" Scenting betrayal from the Emperor, Scaurus reached for his sword hilt. "Thorisin promised you'd take my place once I was gone."

"Oh, he offered it to me. I told him to put it where a catamite would enjoy it." Zautzes' jaw fell; no one spoke thus to the Avtokrator of the Videssians. Gaius Philippus flicked a glance his way and dropped into Latin. "You can nail me on a cross, sir," he said to the tribune, "before I take a post from the man who robbed you of yours."

"He had his reasons," Scaurus said, also in Latin, and clumsily told the senior centurion what they were. He finished, "So if you want to change your mind, Gavras will likely give you the command no matter what you said to him. He thinks well of you; he's told me so, many times."

Hearing of the tribune's involvement with Alypia for the first time, Gaius Philippus reacted as Marcus had been sure he would. "You must've been balmy, playing with fire like that." He gave his own verdict: "Women bring more trouble than they're worth. I've said it before, and more than once, too."

Not having a good answer, Marcus kept quiet.

"But treason?" the senior centurion went on. "Not a chance. What would you want to throw over Gavras for? Whoever came next'd only be worse."

"So I thought, exactly."

"Of course—you're no thickhead. And I'll not go back, either. I'd sooner be your man than his suspicious Majesty's." He chuckled. "I've finally turned true mercenary, haven't I, when commander counts for more than country?"

"I'm glad," Marcus said simply, adding, "Not that you have much to look forward to, coming with me."

"Zemarkhos, you mean? But there's two of us now, and that doubles our chances, or maybe better. Aye," the veteran said to Scaurus' unspoken question, "Gavras told me where he was sending you." He scratched his head. "Far as I can see, you're lucky. With his temper up, I'm surprised he didn't just kill you and have done."

"Truth to tell, so was I, though I wasn't about to tell him that," Marcus said. "But while I was gathering my gear I thought it over. If Zemarkhos nails me, Thorisin's no worse off than if he'd shortened me himself. If I deal with him in Amorion, well, Thorisin's still stuck with me, but he's rid of his madman priest, who's more dangerous to him than I'd ever be, whether he admits it or not. And if we somehow do each other in, why then Gavras has two hares in the same net."

Gaius Philippus pursed his lips. "Hangs together," he admitted. "It's a good piece of Videssian double-dealing, right enough. They're slicker than Greeks, I swear. Three setups, and he wins them all." He cocked an eyebrow at the tribune. "Only trouble is, in two of 'em you—or rather, we—don't."

If the prevailing winds held, Nakoleia was about a week's sail from Videssos. As long as they did, Zautzes let his crew rest easy at the oars and traveled under sailpower alone. The blue-dyed sheet would flutter and flap as the breeze shifted. Scaurus' horse, which had finally arrived, was tethered to the stempost. It twitched its ears nervously at the strange noises behind it for the first few hours out of port, then decided they were harmless and ignored them.

Knowing he would never master the big roan gelding by equestrian skill alone, the tribune did his best to get it used to him and, if he could, well-disposed, too. He curried its glossy coat, stroked its muzzle, and fed it dried apricots and apples begged from the *Seafoam*'s cook. The beast, which had an admirably even disposition, accepted his attentions with an air of deserving no less.

Scaurus proved a good sailor and easily adapted to shipboard routine, stripping down to light tunic and sword belt in the mild spring air. Gaius Philippus had a sound enough stomach, but stayed in trousers and kept on wearing his nail-soled *caligae*. "Give me something with some bite to it," he said, eyeing the tribune's bare feet with disapproval.

"Whatever suits you," Marcus answered mildly. "I thought it best to follow the sailors' lead. They know more about this business than I do."

"If they were all that smart, they'd stay on land." Gaius Philippus drew his *gladius*, tested the edge with his thumb. "Care for some work?" he asked. "No doubt you could use it, after a winter of seal-stamping."

"You're right there," the tribune said. He started to unsheath his own sword, stopped in surprise. A long sheet of parchment was wrapped several times round the blade, held in place with a dab of gum.

"What do you have there?" Gaius Philippus said, seeing him pause.

"I don't know, yet." Scaurus freed his sword from its brass scabbard. He worked the parchment loose, slid it down over the point, and scraped the gum off his blade with his thumbnail.

He unrolled the note. "What does it say? Who sent it?" Gaius Philippus demanded as he came up to peer at the curlicues of Videssian script. Unlike the tribune, he had never learned to read or write the Empire's language, having enough trouble with Latin.

"It's from Nepos," Marcus said. He did not read it aloud, but went through it quickly so he could give Gaius Philippus the gist in Latin.

"Phos prosper you, outlander," the tubby priest and mage had written. "I am glad to have had at last the opportunity to examine this remarkable weapon of yours and only regret the circumstances which made my examination possible. This brief scrawl will summarize what I have learned; the iron-clad ruffian who will return your blade to you is clumping about outside my door even as I write."

Marcus had to smile; he could see Nepos scribbling frantically while Spektas glowered in at him from the corridor. He was sure the guardsman had not managed to hurry Nepos very much.

The tribune read on: "The spells with which your sword is wrapped are of a potency I confess I have not seen. I attribute this to the extremely weak and uncertain nature of magic in your native world, upon which you and your comrades have often remarked. Only charms of extravagant force, it is my guess, would function there at all. Here, however, it is easier to unleash enchantments. As a result, those on your blade, made for harsher circumstances, become wonderfully powerful indeed.

"They are, in fact, so strong I have had great difficulty in evaluating their nature. Testing-spells are subtle things, and the crude strength of your sword's enchantments is too much for them, just as one would not measure the ocean with a spoon. But forgive me; you want what I *do* know.

"Two separate spells, then, are laid on your blade. The first wards the sword and its bearer from opposing magics. This you have seen for yourself, of course, many times. I will only say that it far surpasses in force any such spells I have previously encontered. I wish I could determine how it was cast.

"Because of the warding spell's power, the other cantrip had to be investigated by indirect means, and I fear my results with it are not altogether satisfactory. It is in any case a more subtle enchantment. As far as I can tell, it is a charm somehow intended to protect not merely the individual who carries the sword, but his entire people as well. No Videssian sorcerer could begin to create such a spell, but I hazard that you were brought to Videssos through its agency.

"If I had your red-haired friend's blade to test along with yours, I might have more definite information to offer you—or I might be utterly destroyed. The enchantments are of that magnitude.

"My apologies for not being able to tell you more. I do not think you came here by chance alone, but that is a feeling for which I can offer no proof. I may say, however, that a certain historian with whom we are both acquainted shares my belief. We both wish you success in your trials;

the Lord of the great and good mind willing, we shall see you again. Nepos."

The tribune did not translate that last paragraph for Gaius Philippus, but felt a warm glow as he read it. Though Alypia had not had any chance to communicate with him directly, she was clever enough to realize his sword would probably come back to him and somehow got a message where it would do the most good.

He wadded up the parchment and tossed it into the sea.

Gaius Philippus asked a typical, bluntly pragmatic question: "What good does it do you to know how your sword's magicked? You're no wizard, to spell with it."

"Too true. I wish I could, and singe Zemarkhos' beard for him."

"Well, you can't," Gaius Philippus said, "and if you don't pay attention to using it as it should be used, you won't live to face him anyway. So watch yourself!" He lunged at the tribune's chest. Marcus sprang backward as he parried the veteran's next thrust. Seamen crowded around to watch them fence.

IV

THE STANDARD FLYING FROM THE UPTHRUST LANCE WAS black as soot, an outlaws' standard once, but now one to make all Pardraya tremble. More than bandits rode in Varatesh's fighting tail now; even the most birth-proud khagans acknowledged him as head of the newly risen Royal Clan and sent their contingents to war at his side. Worse would befall them if they said him nay, and they knew it.

Scowling, Varatesh dug spurs into his pony's flanks. The shaggy little horse squealed and sprang ahead. The great black stallion at its side paced it without effort. Varatesh's frown grew deeper as his glance flicked to the white-robed rider atop the huge horse. Head of the Royal Clan—Royal Khagan— master of the steppe! So everyone proclaimed him, Avshar loud among them, but he and the wizard-prince knew the lie for what it was.

Puppet! The word rang inside his head, sour as milk gone bad. Without Avshar, he would still be a chieflet of renegades, a skulker, a raider—a flea, biting and hopping away before a hand came down to crush him. There were times he wished it were so. He was a killer many times over before Avshar found him, but he had not had any idea of what evil was.

He knew now. These days he never slept without seeing irons heating in the fires, without smelling burned flesh, without hearing men shriek as their eyes were seared away. And he had consented to it, had wielded an iron himself— his skin crept when he thought of it. But through that horror he had become Royal Khagan, had made his name one with fear.

Avshar chuckled beside him, a sound that reminded him of ice crackling on a winter stream. The wizard-prince's mantlings streamed out behind him as his horse trotted southwest. He swaddled himself from head to foot.

"We shall shatter them," the sorcerer said, and chuckled again at the prospect. He spoke the Khamorth tongue with no trace of accent, though not a plainsman. As for what he was —alone on all the steppe, Varatesh had seen beneath his robes, and wished he had not.

"Shatter them," Avshar repeated. "They will rue the insult they gave to Rodak and thus to you as well, my lord." The wizard's terrible voice held no sardonic overtone as he granted Varatesh the title, but the nomad was undeceived. Avshar went on, "Your brave warriors—and a sorcery I have devised for the occasion—shall break the fable of Arshaum invincibility once for all."

Varatesh shivered at the cruel greediness in the wizard-prince's manner, but could find no fault with what he said. The Arshaum were traversing Pardraya without his let—was he a lamb or a kid, for them to ignore as they pleased? "Do the omens promise success?" he asked.

Avshar turned his dreadful unseen stare on the plainsman. Varatesh flinched under it. With a freezing laugh, the wizard-prince replied, "What care I for omens? I am no *enaree*, Varatesh, no puling, effeminate tribesman peering timidly into the future. The future shall be as I make it."

"Do the omens promise success?" Gorgidas asked Tolui. A longtime skeptic, he had scant belief in foretelling, but in this world he was coming to doubt his doubts.

"We will know soon," the shaman said, his voice echoing and unearthly behind the madman's smile of his devil-mask. He reached out for a thin wand of willow-wood; the welter of fringes on the arm of his robe dragged through the dust.

The Arshaum leaders leaned forward in their circle round him. He drew a dagger from his belt and sliced the wand in half lengthwise. "Give me your hand," he said to Arghun. The khagan obeyed without question, and did not draw back when the shaman cut his forefinger. Tolui smeared Arghun's blood on one half of the split willow wand, saying, "This will stand for our army." He stabbed the other half into the soil of Pardraya, so that it came up black with mud. "This serves for the Khamorth."

"I would have my blood you given," Batbaian said.

Even amusement sounded eerie through the mask's unmoving lips. "The Khamorth who are our enemies, I should have said," Tolui explained. Batbaian flushed. Tolui went on: "Enough now. Let us see what knowledge the spirits will grant, if they see fit to answer me."

The shaman picked up a drum with an oval head; its sides were as heavily fringed as his robe. He rose, tapping the drum softly. Its tone was deep and hollow, a fitting accompaniment to the wordless, crooning chant he began. He danced round the two wands, his steps at first slow and mincing, then higher, faster, more abandoned as he darted now this way, now that, paying no heed to the officers and princes who scattered before him.

A hoarse voice cried out in a nameless tongue ten feet above his head. Another answered, high and girlish. Gorgidas jumped; Lankinos Skylitzes, pale round the mouth, drew Phos' sun-circle on his breast. Gorgidas thought of ventriloquism, but then both voices shouted at once—no trickster could have worked that.

Tolui was dancing furiously. "Show me!" he cried. Drumbeats boomed like thunder. "Show me!" He shouted again and again. The second voice shouted with him, pleading, demanding. The first voice answered, but roughly, in rejection.

"Show me! Show me!" Now a whole chorus of voices joined the shaman's. "Show me!" Then came an angry bellow that all but deafened Gorgidas, and sudden silence after.

"Ah!" said Irnek, and at the same time, Viridovix: "Will you look at that, now!"

The two wands, one red with Arghun's blood, the other dark and dirty, were stirring on the ground like live things. They rose slowly into the air until they reached waist height. All the Arshaum watched them tensely. Viridovix gaped in awe.

Like a striking snake, the muddy wand darted at the one that symbolized Arghun and his men. That one attacked in turn; they both hovered as if uncertain. Then they slowly sank together, still making small lunges at each other. The bloodstained one came to rest atop the other. The Arshaum shouted in triumph, then abruptly checked themselves as it rolled off.

They cried out again, this time in confusion and dismay, as the blood suddenly vanished from the red-smeared wand, which split into three pieces. Their eyes were wide and staring; Gorgidas guessed this was no ordinary divination. Then the wand representing the Khamorth broke into a dozen fragments. Several of those burst into flame; after perhaps half a minute, the largest disappeared.

Tolui pitched forward in a faint.

Gorgidas dashed to his side, catching him before he hit the ground. He pulled the mask from the shaman's head and gently slapped his cheeks. Tolui moaned and stirred. Arigh stooped beside the two of them. He thrust a skin of kavass into Tolui's mouth. The shaman choked as the fermented mare's milk went down his throat, spraying it over Gorgidas and Arigh. His eyes came open. "More," he wheezed. This time he kept it down.

"Well?" Irnek said. "You gave us a foretelling the likes of which we've never seen, but what does it mean?"

Tolui passed a hand over his face, wiped sweat away. He was pale beneath his swarthiness. He tried to sit, and did at the second try. "You must interpret it for yourself," he said, shaken to the core. "Beyond what you saw, I offer no meanings. More magic than mine, and stronger, is being brewed; it clouds my vision and all but struck me sightless. I feel like a ferret who set out after mice and didn't notice a bear till he stumbled over its foot."

"Avshar!" Gorgidas said it first, but he was only half the name ahead of Viridovix and Batbaian.

"I do not know. I do not think the magician sensed me; if he had, you would be propping up a corpse. It was like no wizardry I have touched before, like black, icy fog, cold and dank and full of death." Tolui shuddered. He wiped his face again, as if to rub off the memory of that touch.

Then Skylitzes cried out a name. "Skotos!" he exclaimed, and made the sun-sign again. Goudeles, not normally one to call on his god at every turn, joined him. Gorgidas frowned. He did not follow the Videssian faith, but there was no denying that Tolui's description bore an uncanny resemblance to the attributes the imperials gave Phos' evil opponent.

"What if it is?" said Arghun, to whom Skotos and Phos

were mere names. "What business does a spirit you Videssians worship have on the steppe? Let him look out for himself here. This is not his home."

"We do not worship Skotos," Skylitzes said stiffly, and
began explaining the idea of a universal deity.

Gorgidas cut him off. "Avshar is no god, nor spirit, either,"
he said. "When Scaurus fought him in Videssos, he cut him
and made him bleed. And beat him, too, in the end."

"That's so," Arigh said. "I was there—that was when I
met you, remember, V'rid'rish? Two big men, both good with
their swords."

"I didna stay for the shindy, bad cess for me," the Gaul
said. "I went off wi' a wench instead, and not one to waste
such a braw fight over, either, the clumsy quean." The memory still rankled.

Irnek scratched his head. "I do not like going ahead blind."

"Finding meaning in foretellings that have to do with battles is always chancy," Tolui said, "though it is worth trying.
Men's passions cloud even the spirits' vision, and dark spells
surround this struggle and veil it more thickly in shadows.
Soon we will not need to wonder. We will know."

Arghun's far-flung scouts picked up the approaching army
while it was still more than a day's ride northeast of the Arshaum. Against most foes they would have gained an advantage from such advanced warning, but with Avshar's sorcery
they were themselves not hidden.

The Arshaum turned to meet Varatesh's horsemen, shaking out into battle order as they rode. They were, Viridovix
saw, more orderly in their warfare than the Khamorth. The
latter fought by clan and by band or family grouping within
the clan, with each family patriarch or band leader a general
in small. Though the Arshaum also mustered under their
khagans, each clan was divided into squads of ten, companies of a hundred, and, in the large clans, regiments of a
thousand. Every unit had its appropriate officer, so that
commands passed quickly through the ranks and were executed with a precision that astonished the Gaul.

"They might as well be legionaries," he said to Gorgidas,
half complaining, as a company of Arghun's plainsmen thundered by, broke into squads, and then re-formed. They carried
out the evolution in perfect silence, taking their cues from
black and white signal flags their captain carried.

The Greek grunted something in reply. He had been in more battles than he cared to remember, but always as a physician, fighting only in self-defense, relying on the legionaries for protection. The Arshaum, however well organized they were by nomad standards, had no place for such noncombatants. Even Tolui and his fellow shamans would take up bows and fight like any of their poeple once their magicking was done.

Thorough as usual, Gorgidas checked his equipment with great care, making sure his *gladius* was sharp, that his boiled-leather cuirass and small round shield had no weak spots, that all the straps on his horse's tackle were sound and tight. "You'll make a warrior yet," Viridovix said approvingly. He was careless in many ways, but went over his gear as exactingly as the Greek had.

"The gods forbid," Gorgidas said. "But there's no one to blame but me, should anything fail." He felt a curious tightness in his belly, half apprehension, half eagerness to have it over, one way or another—a very different feeling from the one he had known as a legionary physician. Then his chief reaction to battle had been disgust at the carnage. This twinge of anticipation made him ashamed.

When he tried to exorcise it by speaking of it aloud, Viridovix nodded knowingly. "Och, indeed and I've felt it, the blood lust, many's the time. Hotter than fever, stronger than wine, sweeter than the cleft between a woman's thighs—" He broke off, his smile going grim as he remembered Seirem and how she died. After a few seconds he went on, "And if your healing could find a cure for it, now, that'd be a finer thing nor any other I could name."

"Would it?" Gorgidas tossed his head. "Then how would those cured ever resist the outrages of wicked men?"

The Celt tugged at his mustaches. "To the crows with you, you carper! Here we've gone and chased ourselves right round the tree, so you're after saying there's need for warring, and it's me who'd fain see the end of it. Gaius Philippus, the sour auld kern, would laugh himself sick to hear us."

"You're probably right, but he'd think the argument was over the shadow of an ass. He's not much for rights or wrongs; he takes what he finds and does what he can with it. Romans are like that. I've often wondered if it's their greatest wisdom or greatest curse."

A couple of companies of Arshaum trotted ahead of the

main body, to skirmish with the Khamorth and test their quality. Some of the plainsmen bet that the sight of them alone would be enough to scatter Varatesh's followers. Batbaian glowered, unsure whether to hope they were right or be angry at hearing his people maligned.

The skirmishers returned a little before nightfall; a few led horses with empty saddles, while several more men were wounded. Their comrades shot questions at them as the Arshaum set up camp. "It was strange," one said not far from Gorgidas. "We ran into two bands of Hairies, outriders like us, I suppose. The first bunch fired a few shots and then turned tail. The others, though, fought like crazy men." He scratched his head. "So who knows what to expect?"

"And a fat lot o' good all that did," Viridovix grumbled. "The omadhaun might as well be Tolui—or Gavras back in Videssos, come to that—for all the news we get from him."

In the light of the campfires, the dozen naked men were spread-eagled on the ground, as if staked out; though no ropes held them, they could not move. Some fearfully, others smiling like so many wolves, the Khamorth watched them as they lay. "See the rewards cowardice wins," Avshar said, his voice filling Varatesh's camp. He made a swift two-handed pass; his robes flapped like vulture's wings.

There was a rending sound. One of the helpless men shrieked as first one shoulder dislocated, then another; a louder cry came from another man as a thighbone ripped free from its hip-socket. Varatesh bit his lip as the screams went on. He was no stranger to using cruelty as a weapon, but not with the self-satisfied relish Avshar put into it.

The cries bubbled down to moans, but then, one by one, screams rang out again when limbs began to tear away from bodies. Blood spouted. The shrieks faded, this time for good.

"Bury this carrion," Avshar said into vast silence. "The lesson is over."

Varatesh gathered his courage to protest to the wizard-prince. "That was too much. You will only bring down hatred on us both."

Perhaps sated by the torment, Avshar chuckled, a sound that made Varatesh want to hide. "It will encourage them," he said carelessly. "What do I care if they hate me, so long as they fear me?" He chuckled again, in gloating anticipation.

"Come tomorrow, the Arshaum will envy those wretches. The sorcery is cumbersome, but very sure."

The scout was bleeding from a cut over his eye, but did not seem to notice. He rode his lathered pony up to Arghun and sketched a salute. "If they hold their pace, the main body of them should hit us in an hour or so."

The khagan nodded. "My thanks." The scout saluted again and hurried off to rejoin his company. Arghun turned to his sons and councilors. "It's of a piece with the rest of the reports we've had."

"So it is," Irnek said. "About time for me to get back to my clan. Good hunting, all." Several lesser khagans also rode away from the gathering under the standard of Bogoraz's coat.

"And you, Tolui," Arghun said. "Are you ready?"

"As ready as I was when you asked me before." The shaman smiled. He still carried his devil-mask under one arm; the day was warm and sunny, and he would have sweltered, putting it on too soon. "I can cast the spell, that I know. Whether it will do as we hope . . ." He shrugged.

Dizabul said, "I hope it fails." He mimed shooting a bow and made cut-and-thrust motions. "The slaughter will be greater if we overcome them hand-to-hand." His eyes glowed at the prospect.

"The slaughter among us, too, witling!" Arigh snapped. "Think of your own men first."

Dizabul bridled, but before the quarrel between the two brothers could flare again Arghun turned to the Videssian party and said quickly, "Well, my allies, does it suit you to fight this day?"

Skylitzes' nod was stolid, Pikridios Goudeles' glum: the chubby bureaucrat was no soldier and made no secret of it. Agathias Psoes reached over his shoulder, drew an arrow from his quiver, and set it in his bow.

Batbaian already carried a shaft nocked. "Here I hold with Dizabul," he said. His one-eyed grin was a hunting beast's snarl.

"And I as well, begging your pardon, Arigh dear," Viridovix said. Shading his eyes with his hand, he stared out over the plain, grimly eager for the first sight of a Khamorth. "Plenty of vengeance to be taken today—aye, and heads, too."

"A victory will do, whatever the means," Gorgidas said. "If we are to assail Yezd, I'd sooner see an easy one, to keep our army strong." He had to work to hold his voice steady. He could feel his pulse hammering; the lump in his throat was like some horrid tumor. He had heard many soldiers say there was no time for such pangs when the fighting started. He waited, hoping they were right.

Trumpets blared on the left; signal flags wigwagged. "They've spotted them!" Arigh exclaimed. He peered at the flags and what they showed of troop movements. "Irnek's falling back. They must have him flanked."

"Then their wing is exposed for us to nip off," his father replied. The khagan gestured to his standard-bearer, who flourished Bogoraz's caftan high overhead on its long lance. Signalmen displayed banners to swing the army west. The *naccara*, the deep-toned Arshaum war drum, thuttered out its commands. The drummer, in his constantly exposed position at the van, was one of the few nomads who protected himself with chain mail.

"Forward!" Arghun called, exhilarated by the prospect of action at last. Gorgidas flicked his horse's reins. It trotted ahead with the rest. Only Tolui and his fellow shamans held their place, making last preparations and awaiting the order to begin.

Viridovix pulled close to the Greek. "Fair useless you'll feel for a longish while," he warned. "There's a deal of shooting to be done or ever it comes to sword work." Gorgidas dipped his head impatiently. He had seen the nomads practicing with their composite bows and thought he knew what they could do.

Those moving dots—friends or foes? The Arshaum had no doubts. In one smooth motion they drew their bows to their ears, let fly, and were slammed back into their saddles, whose high cantles absorbed the force of the recoil. Riders and horses ahead crashed to the ground, dead at the hands of men whose faces they never saw.

Gorgidas' eyes went wide. Shooting at a mark was one thing, hitting moving targets from horseback at such a range something else again.

Not all the Khamorth went down; far from it. An arrow zipped past the Greek with a malignant whine, then several more. One of Psoes' troopers yelped and clutched his leg. An Arshaum tumbled from his horse. A nomad to his rear trampled him, but with a shaft through his throat he did not know it. Gorgidas abruptly understood what Viridovix had meant. He brandished his sword and shouted curses at Varatesh's men, those being his only weapons that could reach them.

The missile duel went on, both sides emptying their quivers as fast as they could. Now and again a band would gallop close to the enemy line, fire a quick volley of heavy, broad-headed arrows at their foes, and then dart away. For longer-range work they used lighter shafts with smaller, needle-sharp points, but those lacked the penetrating power of the stouter arrows.

Steppe war was fluid, nothing like the set-piece infantry battles the Romans fought. Retreat held no disgrace, but was often a ploy to lure foes to destruction. With their tighter command structure, the Arshaum had the better of the game of trap and countertrap. Time and again they would pretend to flee, only to signal flying columns to dash in behind the overbold Khamorth and cut them off.

Then the fighting turned savage, with the surrounded nomads making charge after desperate charge, trying to hack their way back to their comrades. Though it was on horseback, that was the sort of warfare Viridovix understood. He spurred toward the thickest action, and found himself facing a Khamorth bleeding from cuts on cheek and shoulder and with an arrow sunk to the fletching in his thigh.

The plainsman might have been wounded, but nothing was wrong with his sword arm. His face a snarling mask of pain, he cut at the Celt backhanded, then came back with a roundhouse slash Viridovix barely managed to beat aside.

They traded sword strokes. Viridovix' reach and long straight blade gave him an edge, but the nomad's superior horsemanship canceled it. He needed no conscious thought to twist his mount now this way, now that, by pressure of his knees, or to urge it in close when one of Viridovix' cuts left him off balance. Only the Gaul's strong arm let him recover in time to parry. The Khamorth's saber cut his trousers; he felt the flat kiss his leg.

But the plainsman's horse betrayed him in the end. An arrow sprouted in its hock with a meaty *thunk*. It screamed and reared, and for a moment its rider had to give all his attention to holding his seat. Before he could recover, Viridovix' sword tore out his throat. He toppled, horrified surprise the last expression his face would wear.

The Gaul felt none of the fierce elation he had expected, only a sense of doing a good job at something he no longer relished. "Och, well, it needs the doing, for a' that," he said. Then he stopped in dismay at his own words. "The gods beshrew me, I'm fair turned into a Roman!"

Not far away, Goudeles was fighting a Khamorth even fatter than he was. The nomad, though, knew what he was about and had the pen-pusher in trouble. He easily turned the Videssian's tentative cuts and had pinked Goudeles half a dozen times; luck was all that had kept him from dealing a disabling wound.

"Don't kiss him, Pikridios, for Phos' sake!" Lankinos Skylitzes roared. "Hack at him!" But the dour Videssian officer was hotly engaged himself, with no chance to come to Goudeles' rescue. The bureaucrat gritted his teeth as another slash got home.

Gorgidas raked his pony's flanks with his spurs and galloped past cursing horsemen toward Goudeles and his foe. He shouted to draw the Khamorth's attention from Goudeles. The plainsman glanced his way, but only for a moment; seeing a bearded face, he took the Greek for one of Varatesh's followers, come to help finish off his enemy.

He realized his mistake barely in time to counter Gorgidas' thrust. "Who are you, you flyblown sheepturd?" he bellowed in outrage, cutting at the physician's head. He was a powerful man, but Gorgidas was used to fencing with Viridovix and knocked the blow aside. Then it was easy to thrust again, arm at full extension, all the weight of his body behind it. The Khamorth fought with the edge, not the point; battle reflex had saved him the first time. His eyes went wide as Gorgidas' *gladius* punched through his boiled-leather jerkin and slid between ribs.

A rugged warrior, he cut at the Greek again, but his stroke had no strength behind it. Bright blood bubbled from his nose. A stream of it poured out of his mouth as he tried to gulp air. His curved shamshir dropped from his hand. His eyes rolled up in his head; he slumped over his horse's neck.

"Bravely done, oh, bravely!" Goudeles was shouting, all but cutting off Gorgidas' ear as he waved his saber about. The physician stared at the scarlet smear on his own sword point. The legionaries were right, it seemed: there was no time for fear, or even thought. The body simply reacted—and a man was dead.

He leaned to one side and vomited onto the blood-spattered grass.

The sour stuff was still stinging his nose when another plainsman, grimly intent on battling out of the Arshaum trap, stormed at him, scimitar smashing down in an arc of death. Though the nausea had filled his eyes with tears, the Greek brought up his shield to ward off the blow. He felt the light wood framework splinter and hurled the ruined target away. The second Khamorth had no more idea how to defend himself against the stabbing stroke than had the other, but Gorgidas' thrust was not as true. The nomad reeled away, clutching a shoulder wound.

The second time, the Greek discovered, he felt only anger that his opponent had escaped. That disturbed him worse than his earlier revulsion.

Close combat ran all along the battle line as arrows were exhausted. The fight, which had begun with the two sides facing north and south, wheeled to east and west as the right wing of each overlapped the other's left and made it give ground. If the Arshaum had gained any advantage, it was tenuous. Varatesh's outlaws, though they were rulers now, still fought with the renegade fury of men who had nothing to lose. The clans forced into alliance with them were less ferocious, but the sight of the white-robed figure on his charger behind them reminded them that retreat held more terrors than standing fast.

Viridovix cut another swordsman from the saddle, then found himself facing a Khamorth who carried a light lance in place of shamshir or bow. It was his turn to be outreached; he did not care for it. Luckily the press was heavy; the lancer had no chance to charge and build momentum. He jabbed at Viridovix' face. The Gaul ducked, seized the shaft below the head, and dragged the Khamorth toward him.

His first stroke with his potent Gallic sword hewed through the lance. Its owner, who was tugging against him with all his strength, almost flew over his horse's tail when the shaft broke and the opposing pressure disappeared. His arms flailed wildly for balance. Viridovix slashed again. The Khamorth screamed briefly, half his face sheared away.

Batbaian was wreaking a revenge to dwarf the Celt's.

He had slewed his fur cap around so one earflap hid his empty socket and he looked no different from any other Khamorth. He would strike, snakelike, and be gone before a victim knew to whom he had fallen. When three Arshaum assailed him, not recognizing him either, he lifted the cap for a moment. They drew back, knowing what that dreadful scar meant.

Arigh's chest was splashed with blood—not his own. "Ha, we begin to drive them!" he shouted excitedly. Varatesh's left was falling back, a retreat that was no feint. Here and there Khamorth pulled out of line and rode north for their lives. Others stubbornly battled on, but could not hold against the greater flexibility of their foes and the fury of the band that fought beneath the standard of Bogoraz' coat.

Then an Arshaum pitched forward with a black-feathered shaft driven clean through him. Another fell, and another; a horse crashed to the ground, an arrow in its right leg. Two more animals tumbled over it, spilling their riders. One nomad rolled free; the other was crushed beneath his pony's barrel.

Far behind the Khamorth line, Avshar plied his bow with deadly virtuosity. He had kept his quiver filled against the chance of disaster, and when it threatened he turned it back. He outranged even the nomads; his accuracy was fearsome. As its leaders died, the Arshaum advance staggered and began to ebb, like a wave running down a beach.

"That is the wizard?" Arghun said. The khagan's legs were weak, but there was nothing wrong with his arm; more than one Khamorth had fallen to his sword. As he spoke, another Arshaum lurched in the saddle, clutching at an arrow in his belly. His scrabbling hands went limp; he slid to the ground.

"That is Avshar," Gorgidas said. With a mixture of dread, hate, and an awe he loathed himself for feeling; he looked across the lines at the wizard-prince who had chosen himself as Videssos' nemesis. The tall, white-robed figure did not deign to notice him. One by one his deadly shafts went out, as if fired by some murderous machine.

"Whatever sort of sorcerer he is, he is no mean man of his hands," Arghun said with a face like iron, watching another of his men cough blood and die. "He will break us if he holds to it much longer; we cannot stand up under such archery."

For Viridovix and Batbaian, no awe mingled with their hate at the sight of Avshar; it burned hot and clean. With one accord, they spurred their ponies forward, ready to cut their way through all the Khamorth who stood between them and the sorcerer. But the Arshaum did not press the charge with them, and Varatesh's men took fresh courage from the mighty power at their back. Gaul and plainsman killed and killed again, but could not force a breakthrough by themselves.

Them Avshar seemed to recognize, for he bowed contemptuously in the saddle and gave a mocking wave as he slung his bow over an armored shoulder and rode from that part of the field.

Far away on his army's right wing, Varatesh shook his head for the hundredth time, trying to keep the blood welling from the cut on his forehead from running into his eyes. He was exhausted, snatching panting breaths on his pony, which was wounded, too. His hand trembled from his weariness; the shamshir he grasped felt heavy as lead.

And this Irnek in front of him was a very devil. Beaten at the outset when his men were outflanked, he had somehow regrouped, steadied his line, and fought back with a savagery that chilled even the longtime outlaw. One lesson Varatesh had learned: never to trust an Arshaum retreat, no matter how panic-stricken it seemed. That mistake had cost him the slash over his eye and nearly his life with it.

But it was past noon, and Irnek was not retreating any more. His riders pressed foward, probing for weaknesses and making the most of whatever they found. Lacking their enemies' discipline, the Khamorth in retreat only opened themselves to greater danger. They wavered; a few more pushes would crack them.

Varatesh bawled for a messenger, despising himself as he did so. He had thought to win this battle without help from Avshar, to free himself once and for all from the wizard's domination. Now he was on the point of losing. Having had a taste of life as Royal Khagan, he would not go back to outlawry, the best fate he could expect from failure.

The words gagged him, but he brought them out: "Ride to Avshar and tell him to let it begin."

* * *

Arghun shouted for a courier. A young Arshaum appeared at his side, face gray-brown with dust save for streaks washed clean by sweat. The khagan said, "We stand at the balance. Ride back to Tolui and tell him to let it begin."

The nomad hurried away.

"Get yourself gone, you lumpish clot," Avshar snarled. "If I waited for Varatesh's leave for my sorceries, his cause would have foundered long before this. Go on, begone, I say." The quailing Khamorth wheeled his pony and fled.

The wizard-prince forgot him before he was out of sight. The conjuration over which he labored sucked up his attention like a sponge. If the barbarian had broken into his spell-casting half an hour from now, his life would not have been enough to answer for the interruption.

Avshar drew a fat viper from a saddlebag. The snake thrashed wildly, trying to strike, but his grip behind its head was sure and inescapable. His mailed fingers tightened; bone crunched dully. He threw the broken-backed serpent, still alive, onto the small fire that smoked in front of him. The flames leaped up to engulf it.

He began a preliminary incantation, chanting in an archaic tongue and moving his hands through precise passes. Even so early in the spell, a mistake could mean disaster. He intended no mistakes.

Clouds passed across the sun. With the edges of his perception, he felt another power—a tiny one, next to his— making magic. When his chant was done, he allowed himself the luxury of laughter. A rain summons, was it? If his foes thought him so lacking in imagination as to repeat the walls of fire he had loosed against Targitaus' riders, all the better. He had nothing so trivial in mind.

As a temple went up brick by brick, so with one spell upon another was his sorcery built. He laughed again, liking the comparison. But despite his grim amusement, he did not let himself be tempted out of methodical precision for the sake of speed. Even for a wizard of his might, summoning demons was not undertaken lightly. Calling and then controlling them taxed him to the utmost; if his will slipped once, they would turn and rend him in an eyeblink of time.

He could count on the fingers of both hands the invocations he had performed in all the centuries since he first recognized the dominance of Skotos in the world. There had been the dagger-imprisoned spirit which should have drunk the accursed Scaurus' soul, but somehow failed; and a few decades before that a conjuring which did not fail at all—the fiend that slew Varahran, the last King of Kings of Makuran, in his bed and opened his land to the Yezda. Before that, it had been more than a hundred years.

His reverie vanished as the gathered power of the demon swarm he was raising heaved against his control. He restrained them harshly, sent them torment for daring to set themselves against him. Their howls of anguish rang in his mind. When he had punished them enough, he resumed the slow, careful business of preparing them for release—on his terms.

This time his laughter was full of expectant waiting. As demons went, each member of the swarm was small and weak. So is a single bee or wasp. Several hundred, all enraged together, are something else again. The Arshaum would go down as if scythed.

Avshar would have rubbed his hands together at the prospect, had they not been full of a certain powder. He cast it into the fire. The flames flared in blue, malignant violence. Fell voices cried out from the heart of the blaze, roaring, demanding. He quieted them, soothed them. "Soon," he said. "Soon."

A faint, halfhearted squib of thunder rumbled overhead—like a windy man with too many beans in him, the wizard-prince thought scornfully. Rain pattered down, a few drops here and there. The pulsing fire ignored them. It was no longer consuming wood and brush, but the force of the wizard's spirit. He felt strength drain from him, but what he had left would suffice.

He raised his hands above his head in a sinuous pass and began the hypnotically rhythmic canticle that would guide the first of the swarm to do his bidding. A shape began to flicker, deep within the leaping blue flames. It turned this way and that, blindly, until it chanced to face him. It bowed low then, recognizing its master.

Avshar dipped his head in acknowledgment, but warned in a voice like rime-covered stone, "See to it thou remembrest, aye, and thy brethren with thee."

The demon cringed.

* * *

Varatesh hardly heard the mutter of thunder in the distance; he was beating down an Arshaum's stubborn guard and finally cutting the man from the saddle. Nor had he thought much about the dark scudding clouds suddenly filling the sky—doubtless some side-effect of Avshar's wizardry. He had not made any deep inquiries into that. He did not want to know.

A raindrop splashed on his cheek, another on the palm of his left hand. The thunder came again, louder. He felt a light touch on the back of his neck and brushed at it automatically. His hand closed around something small and soft. It wriggled against his fingers.

He opened his hand. A tiny tree frog, green mottled with brown, sat frozen on his palm, its golden eyes wide with fear, the sac under its throat swelling and deflating at each quick breath.

Varatesh shouted in horrified disgust and threw the little creature as far as he could, then wiped his hands frantically on his buckskin trousers. With their cold slimy skins and thin, peeping voices, frogs housed the spirits of the dead, according to Khamorth legend. Even hearing them was bad luck; to touch one was infinitely worse, a sign he would soon die himself.

Shaken, he tried to put the evil omen out of his thoughts and concentrate on the fighting again. Then another froglet dropped from the sky, to tangle itself in the long hair of his pony's mane. Its pale legs thrashed and kicked. Yet another landed on Varatesh's knee. It hopped away before he could bring down his fist and smash it. There was another phantom touch at the side of his neck; a little frog with clinging toepads skittered wildly across his face, too fast for him to kill it. He spat and blinked, over and over. His stomach churned.

Varatesh was almost thrown from his horse when the rider on his right, who was swatting at himself like a madman, lost control of his mount and sideswiped him. "Careful, you slubberer!" he cried. The other did not seem to hear him. Still smashing away at frogs, he rode ahead with no thought for his own safety and quickly fell, easy meat for a grinning Arshaum's saber.

Too late, Varatesh understood the clouds above the field

were no part of Avshar's sorcery. Frogs fell from them in streams, in torrents, in a deluge, and as they fell, chaos spread through the Khamorth ranks. Some men fled, screaming in terror. Others, like the luckless fellow who had collided with the outlaw chief, were too unstrung by the frogs' dreadful prophecy to think of their own safety—and thus helped fulfill it. And the hard cases who put aside panic and omens alike were too few to hold back the Arshaum, who stormed forward as they saw their foes in confusion.

Fury banished fright from Varatesh. He roared foul oaths, trying to rally his unmanned followers. "Stand!" he shouted. "Stand, you stoneless spunkless sheep-hearted cravens!" But they would not stand. Neither his words nor his savage sword work stemmed the growing rout. By ones and twos, by groups, by whole bands, his army streamed away north, back toward their familiar pastures, and he with them.

Viridovix howled his glee as the frogs rained down and the nomads began to waver. "Look at the little puddocks, will you now, falling from the skies!" he chortled. Several fell on him. He felt very kindly toward them and let them stay; they were safer than they would be under the horses' pounding hooves.

He rode close to Gorgidas and slapped the Greek on the back so hard that he whirled round, sword in hand, thinking himself attacked. "Sure and you're a genius, you and your puddocks!" the Gaul cried. "D'you see the whoresons flapping about like hens wi' the heads off 'em, not knowing whether to shit or go blind? They're addled for fair!"

"So it would seem," Gorgidas agreed, watching two Khamorth gallop full tilt into each other. He picked a frog off his cheek. It sprang away as he was trying to set it on top of his fur cap. "Tolui and the rest of the shamans are doing splendidly, aren't they?"

Viridovix clapped a hand to his forehead. "Is that all you'll say?" he said disgustedly. "You might as well be a dead corp, for all the relish you take from life. Where's the brag? Where's the boast? Where would Tolui and the whole lot o' he-witches be, outen your scheme to play with?"

"Oh, go howl!" Gorgidas said, but a grin stretched itself across his spare features as he watched the Khamorth lines dissolve under the froggy cloudburst like men of salt caught in the rain. *"Brekekekex!"* he shouted in delight. *"Brekekekex! Koax! Koax!"*

Viridovix looked at him strangely. "Is that what a frog's after saying in your Greek? Gi' me a good Celtic puddock any day, who'll croak his croak and ha' done."

The physician had no chance to come up with a sharp answer. Three Khamorth were riding at him and the Gaul, stout-spirited warriors sacrificing themselves to buy time for their comrades' escape. He recognized Rodak son of Papak. The onetime envoy spurred toward him, still shouting, "Varatesh!" Gorgidas had no chance to use his thrusting attack. It was all he could do to save himself from Rodak's whirlwind assault. He yelped as the Khamorth's saber scored a bleeding line down his arm.

Then Rodak's head leaped from his shoulders. As every muscle in the spouting corpse convulsed, Batbaian pushed on to the next outlaw and hewed away half his hand. With a shriek, the Khamorth jammed it under his other arm to try to stem the bleeding. He spun his horse round and rode for his life. Batbaian galloped to Viridovix' aid against the third. After his mutilation and the slaughter of his clan, mere frogs held no terror for him.

Viridovix killed his man before Batbaian reached him. The young Khamorth stared at the standards in Varatesh's army. They were in disarray, some moving in one direction, some in another, others shaking as if their bearers were taken by an ague.

"I know those clans," he said. "They cannot all be corrupt —the Lynxes, the Four Rivers clan, the Spotted Goats, the Kestrels. . . ." He spurred forward toward the Khamorth, crying, "To me! To me! Rise now against Varatesh and his filthy bandits! The Wolves!" he shouted, and followed it with the howling war cry of his clan.

A chill ran up Viridovix' spine. Only Batbaian could raise that shout now. No, there was another—had not Targitaus and he shared blood in brotherhood? He threw back his own head and howled, took up the cry himself. "The Wolves! Are you hearing me, you dung-eating mudsouls? The Wolves!" He pounded after Batbaian. Even in their confusion, heads whipped round among the Khamorth to listen.

A flood of fleeing Khamorth came up from the south, Arshaum riding in pursuit. "Irnek's turned them!" Arigh said. "He's rolling them up!"

"Aye!" said his father. "If we strike now, we can bag the lot of them." Arghun seized the lance that carried Bogoraz' coat from the standard bearer. He leveled it at the milling Khamorth, who were losing any semblance of order as the new wave of fugitives crashed through bands still fighting. "At them!" he cried. Hard on the heels of Batbaian and Viridovix, the Gray Horse Arshaum charged.

When the first frog dropped from the sky, Avshar thought it a freak of nature and crushed it under his boot. Then another one fell, and then a handful of them. A few hundred yards ahead, the sound of battle changed. The wizard-prince lifted his head, wary as an old wolf at a shift of wind.

Sensing his distraction, the demon cowering in the sorcerous fire lashed out with all its might, trying to break free from his control. Avshar staggered. "Test me, wilt thou?" he roared, gathering all his powers to hurl against the rebellious fiend. It resisted, but could not draw on the full power of its swarm; its mates were not yet entirely on the plane where it battled. He beat it back and lashed it with agony it had never imagined. With a final gesture of sublime hatred, the wizard-prince severed the connection between the swarm leader and its comrades.

Aghast, solitary in a way it had never known, the demon wailed and yammered. "Less than thou deservest, traitorous maggot!" Avshar hissed.

He readied the cantrip that would reunite the swarm with its leader and bring them through to do his bidding, but had no time to cast it. While he and the demon had fought, the battle ahead was collapsing. Khamorth galloped by, too unstrung by frogs and Arshaum to fear the wizard any more. And the Arshaum themselves could only be seconds behind, hot for revenge against his archery.

His fists balled in fury. It all but choked him—outdone by a two-copper bit of conjuring! But he had survived too long to yield to rage's sweet temptation. He bounded atop his great black charger—no time for a spell of apportation, even if he were not spent by his earlier magics. His long-sword rasped out. Cold iron, then, and nothing else.

No, not quite. As the wizard touched spurs to the stallion's flanks, he swung his sword arm in a quick, intricate pattern.

The blue flames of his balefire died; the demon within sprang free.

Avshar pointed east. "Slay me the leader of that accursed rabble, and then I give thee leave to get hence and join thy fellows once more."

The demon's claws clutched hungrily. Its slanted eyes were still filled with horror at aloneness. It mounted to the air on black, leathery batwings and circled above the field to seek its commanded quarry.

The wizard-prince did not watch it go. He was already galloping south, away from the fleeing Khamorth. They were a broken tool, but he had others.

Viridovix paid no attention when the druids' stamps on his sword flared to golden life. They had been gleaming gently for some time from Tolui's sorcery, and he was deep in the press, laying about him for all he was worth. He kept shouting the Wolves' war cry, though his throat was raw and his voice hoarse. Several times he had heard answering shouts that did not come from Batbaian and once saw a pair of Khamorth chopping at each other with axes. Varatesh's jerry-built power was cracking at the first defeat.

As if the name was enough to conjure the man, he spied the outlaw chief not fifty feet away, using the strength of his fine horse to force his way through the crush. Varatesh's eyes locked with his. Viridovix raised his sword in challenge. Varatesh nodded, once, and turned his mount's head. He struck one of his own men across the shoulders with the flat of his shamshir. "Make way, there! This is between the pair of us!"

They moved cautiously toward one another, each aware of his opponent's strengths. At swords afoot Viridovix would have been confident; he was a better man with the blade than Varatesh ever would be. But the nomad's lifelong rapport with his horse canceled the Gaul's advantage.

Confident in his horsemanship, Varatesh struck first, a cut at the Celt's head that Viridovix easily beat aside. The outlaw chief swung up his blade in salute. "A pity it must end this way. Had the spirits made the world but a little different, we might have been friends, you and I."

"Friends, is it?" Viridovix wheeled his horse, slashed; with liquid grace, Varatesh ducked under the stroke. Memories swam behind the Gaul's eyes until a red mist all but robbed him of vision: Varatesh kicking him in the point of the elbow to warn against escape when he was the renegade's captive; a butchered camp—oh, and one body in particular—the remembrance of Seirem smote him like a blow; a thousand blinded men stumbling along with weeping red empty sockets, tied to half a hundred left one-eyed to guide them. "Friends wi' the likes o' you, you murthering sod? The Empire's Skotos'd spit on you." He cut again, anger lending his arm fresh force. Varatesh grunted as he turned the slash. The next one got home.

Pain twisted the Khamorth's mouth, but from Viridovix' words, not the wound. "I know what you think," he said, and the Celt could not help but believe him. "Those outrages I was forced to, and the ones before as well. I loathe myself for every one. It was do as I did or die, after I was wrongly outlawed." His voice was full of desperate pleading, as though he was trying to convince himself and Viridovix both that he spoke truly.

For a moment the Gaul felt sympathy, but then his eyes grew hard and his hand tightened once more on his sword hilt. "A man flung into a dungheap can climb out and wash himself, or he can wade deeper. Think on the choice you made."

The explosive rage that made Varatesh dangerous to friend and foe alike turned his handsome features into a mask more frightening than the one Tolui wore. He showered blows on Viridovix, using his lighter, quicker blade to strike and then strike again, never giving the Celt a chance to reply. Viridovix dodged in the saddle, parrying as best he could. He felt steel cut him, but battle fever ran too high to let him know the hurt yet.

Not so his horse; it squealed and bucked when Varatesh laid open its shoulder. Viridovix flew over its head. He landed heavily on his side. As Varatesh wheeled his own beast to come round and finish the job, the Gaul scrambled to his feet. He grabbed at his pony's reins, hoping he could mount before the Khamorth was upon him. He missed. The pony, wild with pain, ran off still leaping and kicking.

Varatesh's gore-smeared grin was a ghastly thing to see. Viridovix hefted his sword and planted his feet firmly, though facing a horseman afoot was a fight with only one likely ending.

Just as Varatesh urged his horse at the Gaul, another rider hurtled toward him out of the crowd of fighters watching the single combat. The outlaw chief whirled to face the unexpected attack, but too late. Batbaian's scimitar rose and fell. "For my father!" he cried. Blood spurted. He slashed again. "My mother!" Varatesh reeled. "Seirem!" Two cuts, forehand and back, delivered with savage force. "And for me!" Varatesh gave a bubbling scream as the sword hacked across his face, giving Batbaian exact retribution for his own disfigurement.

The renegade toppled to the ground, lay still. "Take his horse," Batbaian called to Viridovix. He hurried forward. Varatesh groaned and rolled over onto his back. Viridovix swung up his sword to finish him, but the outlaw's one-eyed dying stare transfixed him.

Varatesh's mouth worked. "Outlawed wrongly . . . not . . . my fault," he choked out. "Swear . . . Kodoman drew knife . . . first." He coughed blood and died, the dreadful insistence still set on his face.

The pony did a nervous dance step as Viridovix' unfamiliar weight swung into the saddle, but it bore him. The Celt glanced at Varatesh's corpse. "D'you suppose he was telling the truth, there at the end?"

Batbaian frowned. "I don't care. He earned what he got." He hesitated, looked for a moment as young as his years. "I'm sorry I broke into the duel."

"I'm not, lad," Viridovix said sincerely. He was starting to feel his wounds. "For all he was a cullion, the kern was as bonny a fighter as ever I faced; belike he had me there. And," he added quietly, "you gave him your reasons for it." Satisfied, Batbaian nodded.

Their chief's fall spurred on the rout of the Khamorth. They fled north, pressed hard by Arghun's forces. The khagan waved the standard over his head, urging his riders on. Flanked by his two sons, he caught up with Viridovix and Batbaian at the spearhead of the attack. "You know him, the one you brought down?" he said.

"Aye," said Batbaian; Viridovix, almost as brief, amplified: "Varatesh, it was."

Arghun's face lit with the smile of a general who sees victory assured, the smile of a man for whom war still holds joy. "No wonder they break, then! Well fought, both of you."

Viridovix grunted; Batbaian said nothing. Dizabul and even Arigh scowled at their churlishness, but the Gaul did not care. Some triumphs were too dearly won for rejoicing.

Someone was plucking at his sleeve. He turned to find Gorgidas by his side; it was like meeting someone from another world. "Still alive, are you?" he said vaguely.

The Greek's answering grin was haggard. "Through no fault of my own, I think. Wherever I get the chance hereafter, I'll stick to writing up battles instead of fighting in them—safer and less confusing, both." He grew businesslike, drawing a long strip of wool from his saddlebag. "Let me tie up your arm. That slash that got through your cuirass will have to wait until we have time to get it off you."

For the first time, Viridovix realized that the dull ache in his chest was not just exhaustion; he felt warm wetness trickling down his ribs and saw the rent in his boiled-leather armor. A flesh wound, he decided, since he had none of the shortness of breath that went with a punctured lung.

He held out his arm to Gorgidas for bandaging, then jerked it away. The druids' marks were yellow fire down the length of his sword. But the rain of frogs, having served its purpose, was slackening. "Avshar!" the Gaul shouted, looking wildly in every direction for the wizard-prince.

But when the danger came, it dropped from the skies like Tolui's frogs, hurtling down like a stooping hawk. Arghun suddenly groaned. The standard went flying from his hands and fell to the ground as he pitched forward on his horse, clawing at the crow-sized horror that clung to the back of his neck.

It was clawing too, its talons ripping through sinew and softer flesh. Its razor-sharp beak tore deeply into him; everyone close by heard bone break. Batwings overlay the khagan's shoulders like the shadow of death. His struggles lessened.

Arigh and Dizabul cried out together; no one could have said which of their swords first descended on the demon's back. But its armored integument turned their blades. It glared hatred at them through slit-pupiled eyes red as the westering sun and did not loose its hold.

Then Viridovix slashed at the creature. The druids' stamps flashed like lightning as his sword cleaved the unearthly flesh; he blinked and shook his head, half dazzled by the explosion of light. The demon shrieked, a high, thin squall of anguish. Foul-smelling ichor sprayed from it, spattering the Gaul's sword hand. He jerked it away; the stuff burned like vitriol.

Still screaming, the demon dropped off Arghun and thrashed in its death throes. In a rage born of disgust and dread, Virdovix hacked it clean in two. The wailing stopped, but each half quivered on with unnatural vitality. Then, when it was truly dead, its flesh crumbled to fine gray ash and blew away on the breeze.

"Out of my way, curse you!" Gorgidas said, pushing past the Celt and Arigh to reach Arghun's side. The khagan was slumped over his horse's back; Gorgidas sucked in a sharp, dismayed breath when he saw the gaping wound Arghun had taken. The khagan's face was gray, his eyes rolled back in his head. Gorgidas stanched the flow of blood as well as he could and groped for a pulse. He felt none.

Near panic, the physician reached into himself for the healer's trance. He felt his awareness of his surroundings, of everything but Arghun's dreadful injuries, slip away. Laying his hands on them, he sent out the healing power with all the force at his command. But there was nothing to receive it, no spark of life for it to jump to. He had felt that awful emptiness before, trying to save Quintus Glabrio when his lover was far past saving.

Slowly Gorgidas returned to himself. He looked from Arigh to Dizabul and spread his hands, wet with their father's blood. "He is gone," he told them. His voice broke and he could not go on; Arghun had treated him like a son these last few months, in gratitude for his life. This time it was a gift Gorgidas could not give him.

Dizabul and Arigh shed no tears; that was not the Arshaum way. Instead they drew their daggers and gashed their own cheeks, mourning with blood rather than water. Then, knives still in their hands, they stared at each other with sudden hard suspicion. One of them would be khagan, and Arghun had named no successor.

When Arghun's standard fell, the pursuit of the fleeing Khamorth broke down in confusion as the Arshaum reined in to find out what had happened. As they did, they followed his sons in marking his passage with their own blood. Lankinos Skylitzes unhesitatingly imitated the nomads; the rest of the Videssian embassy party mourned in their own way.

"Where did the wizard run?" Arigh called to the growing crowd of men around him. He jerked his chin northwards at the cloud of dust that marked the flight of the broken Khamorth. "If he's with that rabble, I'll chase them till I fall off the edge of the world."

Several of Irnek's men spoke to their own chieftain, who rode forward and bowed in the saddle to Arigh and Dizabul both, with nicely calculated impartiality. They eyed each other again. Irnek smiled, quickly erased it. *He's setting them against each other while they're groggy with grief,* Gorgidas realized, *to weaken the Gray Horses and advance his own Black Sheep clan.* He had thought that tall, cool Arshaum had a ready wit—the fellow maneuvered like a Videssian.

Irnek's words, though, could not have been rehearsed, not when he had just learned of Arghun's death. He said, "A giant in white mantlings on a great horse cut his way through my riders and headed south." His warriors shouted confirmation; one had been disarmed by a stroke of Avshar's broad-sword, and counted himself lucky not to have lost his head as well.

"Anthrax take the Hairies, then! Let them run," Arigh said. His wave encompassed a score of his clansmen. "Get fresh horses from camp and be after the wizard. I don't care how fast that big black stallion is—aye, I've seen it. He has no remounts, and we'll run him down, soon or late." He grinned wolfishly at the prospect.

As the riders hurried away, Dizabul rounded on his brother, angrily demanding, "Who are you, to give orders so?" One of Irnek's eyebrows might have twitched, but his features were too well schooled to give away much of what he was thinking.

"And who are you, to say I may not?" Arigh's voice was silky with danger. The Gray Horse Arshaum surreptitiously jockeyed for position, some lining up behind one brother, some behind the other. Gorgidas was dismayed to see how much support Dizabul enjoyed. He had largely recovered from the ignominy of backing Bogoraz, and many of his clanmates were more comfortable with him than with Arigh after Arghun's elder son had spent so much time in Videssos, away from the steppe.

Irnek sat quiet on his horse, weighing the balance of forces.

"A moment, gentlemen!" Pikridios Goudeles forced his way through the crowd to Arigh and Dizabul. The dapper envoy was sadly draggled, covered with blood, dust, and sweat. His voice had nothing wrong with it, though, rolling out rich and deep in the trained phrasing of the rhetorician. "The command is sensible, no matter who gives it."

He could not be as grandiloquent in the Arshaum tongue as in his own Videssian, but by now he spoke it fairly well. Agrhun's sons turned their heads to listen. He continued, "Consider who gains from your disunity at the moment of victory—only Avshar. Suppressing him is your chiefest goal; all else comes afterward. Is it not so?"

"Truth," Arigh said soberly. Dizabul still glowered, but nodded in reluctant agreement. The Gray Horse clansmen visibly relaxed. Irnek's mouth was a little tight, but he bobbed his head Goudeles' way, respecting the diplomat for his skill.

But then Batbaian spoke out: "It is *not* so!" Heads swung his way in surprise. He said, "With Varatesh dead—may the ghosts of hungry wolves gnaw his spirit's privates forever—and Avshar routed, what needs doing is setting Pardraya right once more, so their wickedness can never flourish here again." He trotted his pony a few paces north, toward the vanished Khamorth. "Are you with me, V'rid'rish?"

The Gaul started; he had not expected the question. The naked appeal on Batbaian's face tore at him, and life with Targitaus' clan, though very different from the one he had known in Gaul, had had some of the same easygoing freedom to it. Two summers before, he had been ready to desert Videssos for Namdalen, but now when he probed his feelings he found only a small temptation and a regret that it was not greater.

He shook his head sadly. "I canna, lad. Avshar's the pit o' the peach, I'm thinking, and my foeman or ever I came to the plains. I willna turn away from him the now."

Batbaian slumped like a man taking a wound. "I'll go alone, then. I have my duty, just as you think you have yours." Viridovix flinched at his choice of words. The Khamorth said, very low, "There will always be a place for you in my tents." He wheeled his horse and started to ride away.

"Wait!" Irnek called. Batbaian reined in. The Arshaum chieftain said, "Would you ride with my men at your back? With your Hai—" He choked the word off. "—ah, people in disarray, we can make you master as far east as the plains run."

Here, thought Gorgidas, was truly one with an eye toward the main chance. Batbaian might have been reading his mind, for he barked out two syllables of a laugh. "If I said yes to that, Arshaum, your men would be riding on my back, not at it. I'll not be your bellwether for you, with my ballocks cut off and a chime round my neck to lead my folk to your herding. We remember how you drove the last of us east over the Shaum a lifetime ago. You hunger for Pardraya, too, now, do you? Thank you all the same, but I'll win or fall on my own."

"Will you?" Irnek said. He was still smiling, but with his mouth only; his eyes had gone flinty. His men stirred, looking to him for orders. Batbaian hesitated, then reached for his shamshir.

But Arigh rapped out, "By the wind spirits, he does as he pleases. He's paid the price for the right." This once, Dizabul backed his brother. A mutter of agreement rose from the riders of the Gray Horse Arshaum, who knew and admired Batbaian's quality. They stared in challenge at Irnek's Black Sheep.

Irnek refused to be drawn. His laugh came, easy and natural-sounding. "A dismal state of affairs, when Arshaum are reduced to arguing over the fate of a Hairy." He no longer wasted politeness on Batbaian, but waved him away. "Go, then, if it suits you." Batbaian gave Arigh a sketched salute, Viridovix another. He trotted north. The twilight gloom swallowed him.

"'Tis Royal Khagan he'll be one day, I'm thinking," Viridovix whispered to Gorgidas.

"I'd say you're right, if he lives," the Greek replied. He was remembering the wand Tolui had used to symbolize the Khamorth, and how its pieces had begun to burn. With Varatesh dead and his power shattered, civil war would run through the clans of Pardraya, one-time collaborators against their vengeful foes. Batbaian, he was sure, knew the danger he was riding into.

As darkness fell, the Arshaum ranged over the field, stripping corpses and slitting the throats of those Khamorth who still moved—and those of Arshaum who knew themselves mortally wounded and sought release from pain. The shamans, Gorgidas with them, did what they could for those less seriously hurt. The physician used the healing art on two badly injured warriors with good results, then tottered and almost fell; combined with the day's exertions, the fatigue the healer's trance brought with it left him shambling about in a weary daze.

Most corpses remained above ground, to await the services of carrion birds and the scavengers of the plains. Only Arghun and a couple of fallen subchiefs from other clans received burial. The Gray Horse Arshaum worked by firelight to dig a grave large and deep enough to hold him and his pony. Tolui cut the beast's throat at the edge of the pit, in accordance with the nomads' custom. Either Arigh or Dizabul might have done so, but neither would yield the other the privilege.

Gorgidas got back to camp as that quarrel was winding down. He collapsed by a fire with the rest of the embassy party and gnawed mechanically at a chunk of smoked meat. It must have been past midnight; the crescent moon was long set.

Arghun's sons flared at each other again, shouting furiously. "You spoiled, stupid puppy, why should you deserve the rule?"

"A fine one to talk you are, coming back after years to try and rob me—"

"Not long will they be going on like that," Viridovix said with glum certainty; he had been in faction fights of his own. "A word too many and it's out swords and at 'em!"

The Greek feared he was right. The insults were getting louder and more personal. "You'd futter a mangy sheep!" Dizabul hissed.

"No. I wouldn't risk taking your pox from it."

"And here's more trouble," Viridovix said as Irnek came striding briskly between campfires. "What's he after?"

"His own advantage," Gorgidas said.

Arghun's sons fell silent under Irnek's sardonic eye. He was older and more experienced than either of them; his simple presence was a weapon. "I trust I'm not interrupting," he said, earning a glare from Dizabul and a hard frown from Arigh.

"What is it?" Arigh snapped, with hauteur enough to make the leader of the Black Sheep pause.

Irnek, as was his way, recovered well. "I have something to tell the Gray Horse khagan," he said, "whichever of you that may be." He did not stop to savor their sputters, but went on, "As your—friend? client?—Batbaian made it clear my clan was not welcome east of the Shaum, I have decided the only proper thing for us to do is return to our lands and herds in Shaumkhiil. We've been too long away, anyhow. We leave tomorrow."

Both brothers exclaimed in dismay. Dizabul burst out, "What of your fancy promises of help?" He had reason to be disconcerted; Irnek led a good quarter of the Arshaum forces.

"What do you call this past day's work?" Irnek retorted, with some justice. "I lost nearly a hundred men killed, and twice as many wounded—help enough, I'd say, for a fight that wasn't my own in the first place." He turned on his heel and stalked away, leaving Dizabul still expostulating behind him.

"You must be a farmer, to find your land so dear," the young prince jeered. Irnek's back stiffened, but he kept walking.

"Good shot!" Arigh said, slapping his brother on the shoulder. His anger at the Black Sheep leader put the damper on the quarrel with Dizabul, at least for the moment. He shouted to Irnek, "We'll go on without you, then!" Irnek shrugged without breaking stride.

Gorgidas' head and Goudeles' came up at the same instant; their eyes met in consternation. "They don't see their danger. How do we fix it?" Gorgidas demanded.

"Do we?" Goudeles said. "Better for the Empire if we leave it alone."

Viridovix and Lankinos Skylitzes looked at them as if they had started speaking an unknown tongue. But Gorgidas said angrily, "We do! There's no justice in loading all the risk on them and having them ruined on their pastures as well. Besides, I like them."

"Amateurs," Goudeles sighed. "What do likes matter, or justice?" Even so, he gave a few sentences of pithy advice, very much what Gorgidas had also been thinking. Their friends' eyebrows rose in sudden understanding. The pen-pusher finished, "Do you want to put it to them, or shall I?"

"I will," Gorgidas said, his knees creaking as he rose. He started to walk over to the Arshaum, then turned back to Goudeles. "Tell me, Pikridios, if justice does not matter, how are you different from Avshar?" He did not wait for an answer.

Arghun's sons were running up their light felt tents when the Greek approached. Arigh nodded in a friendly enough way, Dizabul curtly. The physician still wondered whether he had been glad or sorry to see his father saved from Bogoraz' hemlock. He would probably never know.

In time-honored Hellenic tradition, he put his business in the form of a question. "What do the two of you think Irnek will do in Shaumkhiil while we chase after Avshar?"

"Why, go back to his herds," Dizabul said before he realized the question was out of the ordinary. Arigh saw it quicker. He had been using the heavy pommel on the hilt of his dagger to hammer tent pegs; he threw the weapon down with an oath.

"The answer is, anything he pleases," he ground out. "Who'd be there to stop him?"

"We can't let him get away with that," Dizabul said fiercely. Where the fortunes of the Gray Horses were touched, they stood in perfect accord; what use to be khagan of a ruined clan?

"Would you forget why we're here, then, and what we owe Yezd? All the more, now." Arigh eyed his younger brother with comtempt. Not far away, nomads were still filling in Arghun's grave.

"N-no, but what can we do?" Dizabul said, troubled. Arigh chewed his lip.

"May I suggest something?" Gorgidas asked. Again, Arigh nodded first, Dizabul following warily. When he saw he had their consent, he went on: "This could be one time when having both of you as leaders will work for you, not against. One could go ahead and move on Yezd, while the other took part of your force back across the Shaum to your stretch of the steppe. It need not be nearly as big as Irnek's band, only enough to make him think twice about starting trouble."

The Greek watched them calculate. Whichever one held to the pursuit of Avshar would keep the greater part of the army, but the other would have the chance to solidify his position on his native ground with the rest of the clan. If they bought the scheme, he thought he knew who would pick which role— Goudeles had set it up to make each half attractive to one of them.

They came out of their study at the same time. "I'll go back," Dizabul said, while Arigh was declaring, "Come what may, I push on." They looked at each other in surprise; Gorgidas kept his face straight. The imperials knew tricks Irnek had never thought of.

After that, the haggle was over how many riders would go on, how many back to Shaumkhiil. Not all the nomads accompanying Dizabul would be Gray Horse clansmen; some of the clans that had sent out smaller contingents were also nervous about Irnek's intentions.

"I mislike giving away so many men," Arigh said to Gorgidas when agreement was finally reached, "but what choice have I?"

The physician was so tired he hardly cared what he said; it was almost like being drunk. "None, but I don't think numbers matter much. By himself Avshar outnumbers all of us." Arigh rubbed his slashed cheek, nodded somberly.

Swords clashed. Pressed hard, Nevrat Sviodo gave ground. Her foe slashed at her legs. She barely turned the blow with her saber and had to retreat again. The next cut came high. Again her parry was just in time. Sweat ran into her eyes. It burned. She did not have even an instant to blink it away, for her opponent was sidling forward, a nasty grin on his face.

A quick flurry of steel—an opening! Nevrat ducked a cut, stepped in close. Her wrist knew what to do then. Her foe reeled away.

He was still grinning. She scowled at him, her eyes dark and dangerous. "Curse you, Vazken, did you let me get home there? Don't try that again when you practice with me, or you'll end up bleeding for real."

Vazken placatingly spread his hands. "It's hard to make myself go all out against a woman."

"Do you think the Yezda match your courtesy?" Nevrat snapped. She suspected she had seen more combat than her partner on the drill field—scouting was a chancier business than fighting in line. She did not say so. Vazken would only have stomped off in a huff.

She also did not want to practice with him any more. If not fully tested, how could she get better?

Seeing her cousin Artavasdos riding up was something of a relief. She had the excuse she needed to escape from Vazken without telling him to go to the ice. She greeted Artavasdos with a dazzling smile.

He had to work to return it. She realized with surprise that

114

he was frightened. "What is it" she asked, steering him away from Vazken. One thing the sometimes stolid Vaspurakaners learned in Videssos was the joy of gossip.

Artavasdos understood that, too. He waited until Vazken was well out of earshot before he dismounted and offered her a stirrup, saying, "Climb up behind me. I've been sent to fetch you. We'll ride double into the city."

"Fetch me?" She made no move to mount. "By whom?"

"Alypia Gavra," her cousin said, adding, "If I don't get you to her fast, we're both for it." The answer sent her scrambling onto Artavasdos' horse. He hardly waited for her to slide behind his saddle before he sprang up, seized the reins, and sent the horse back toward the city walls at a fast trot.

"Phos!" Nevrat exclaimed. "I can't meet the princess like this. Look at me—in these leathers I look like a Yezda. I stink like one, too. Let me stop at the barracks to change and at least sponge myself off a little."

"No," Artavasdos said flatly. "Speed counts for everything now."

"You'd better be right."

He hurried west along Middle Street. When he turned north off it, Nevrat said, "Do you know where you're going?"

"Where I was told to," he said. She felt like reaching forward and wrenching a better answer out of him, but with difficulty forbore. If this was a joke, she thought grimly, Thorisin's palace would get itself a new eunuch, cousin or no.

A few minutes later, Nevrat burst out, "By Vaspur Phos' firstborn, are you taking us to the High Temple?" The great shrine had been growing against the sky since Artavasdos left Middle Street, but Nevrat had not thought much about it— following their own version of Phos' faith, the Vaspurakaners did not worship along with imperials. Now, though, the High Temple was too close to ignore.

Artavasdos turned in the saddle to give Nevrat a respectful look. "You're very close. How did you guess?"

"Never mind." She would rather have been wrong. She slid off the horse with a sigh of relief as Artavasdos tethered it outside the stucco building at the edge of the High Temple courtyard. Together, cautiously, they went to the door of the patriarchal residence. Nevrat grasped the knocker and rapped twice.

Even she had not expected Balsamon to answer himself.

"Come in, my friends, come in," he said, beaming. Nevrat felt his smile like warm sunshine; no wonder, she thought, the Videssians loved him so well.

"Where are your retainers, sir?" she asked as he led her and her cousin down a corridor.

"I have but the one," Balsamon said, "and Saborios is off on a bootless errand. Well, not quite, but more than he thinks." He laughed. Though Nevrat did not see the joke, she found herself grinning, too.

The patriarch led the two Vaspurakaners into his disreputable study. He and the young woman waiting there cleared space for them to sit. She was quite plainly dressed, but for a necklace of emeralds and mother-of-pearl; Nevrat took a moment to realize who she was.

"Your Highness," she said, and began a curtsey, but Alypia help up a hand to stop her.

"We have no time for that," she said, "and in any case, the favor I am going to ask of you I ask as a friend, not as a princess."

"Don't worry, my dear, Saborios will be bootless a while longer," Balsamon told her.

"Not even Nepos knows how long his spell will hold," Alypia retorted. Quickly, as if begrudging every word, she explained to Nevrat, "Saborios—he's my uncle's watchdog here—is off taking a pair of Balsamon's blue patriarchal boots to be redyed. So long as Nepos' magic works, he won't notice the *very* long wait he's having for them. Nor —Nepos hopes—will anyone detect that I am not back in the palace complex. But he cannot juggle the two magics forever, so we must hurry with our business here."

"Then let me ask at once what you want of me, your Highness," Nevrat said, carefully not abandoning Alypia's formal title, "and ask you why you choose to call me friend when we have never met."

Artavasdos gasped at her boldness, but Alypia nodded approvingly. "A fair question. We are, though, both friends of Marcus Aemilius Scaurus."

Her quiet statement hung in the air a moment. "So we are," Nevrat said. She studied the princess and added, "You are a good deal more than that, it seems."

Despite his role as go-between, Artavasdos looked about ready to flee. Nevrat paid no attention to him; she wanted to see how Alypia would react. Balsamon, though, spoke first:

"It also seems Scaurus somehow infects everyone who knows him with his own blunt speech." Had his words been angry, Nevrat would have been as frightened as her cousin, but he sounded amused.

"Hush," Alypia told him. She turned back to Nevrat. "Yes, he and I are a good deal more than friends, as you put it. And because of that, he has been sent to what will almost surely be his death." She explained what Thorisin required for Marcus to redeem himself.

"Zemarkhos!" Nevrat exclaimed. Having traveled so long with Gagik Bagratouni's men, she knew more than she ever wanted to of the fanatic priest's pogrom against all Vaspurakaners. Anything to hurt him sent hot eagerness surging through her. But she agreed with Alypia—she did not think Scaurus had a chance against him.

When she said so, the princess sagged against the back of her couch in dismay. Nevrat abandoned her half-formed thought of telling Alypia that Marcus had wanted her, too. That might have cured an infatuation, but she was convinced Alypia felt more—and so did Scaurus, if he was willing to beard Zemarkhos for her sake.

"Tell me what to do," she said simply.

Alypia's eyes glowed, but she wasted no time on thank-yous. "To destroy Zemarkhos, I think Marcus will have to have an army at his back. His Romans and those who have joined them are in Garsavra. If you rode to tell them what has happened to him, what do you think they would do?"

Nevrat never hesitated. Give Bagratouni another chance for revenge? Give Gaius Philippus—no, it would be Minucius; Gaius Philippus was with Scaurus—the chance to save his beloved commander? "Charge for Amorion, and Phos spare anything in their way."

"Exactly what I thought," Alypia said, eager now for the first time.

Nevrat looked at her in wonder. "You would do this, in spite of your uncle's command?"

"Command? What command?" Alypia was the picture of innocence. "Balsamon, you as patriarch must be well informed of what goes on in the palaces. Has his Imperial Majesty ever ordered me not to send word to Garsavra of Marcus' dismissal?"

"Indeed not," Balsamon said blandly, though he could not keep the corners of his mouth from twitching upward.

Only because Thorisin never dreamed you would, Nevrat thought. She did not say that. What she did say was, "I think Marcus is a very lucky man, Princess, to have you care for him."

"Is he?" Alypia's voice was bitter and full of self-reproach. "His luck has an odd way of showing itself, then."

"So far," Nevrat said firmly.

"You'll go, then?"

"Of course I will. Senpat will be furious with me—"

"Oh, I hope not!" Alypia exclaimed. "I would have gone through him—"

"—because he'll be stuck here in the city," Nevrat said.

At the same time the princess was concluding, "—but with his duties here, I thought he would have trouble getting away inconspicuously."

They stared at each other and started to laugh. Nevrat flashed the thumbs-up gesture the Romans used. She was unsurprised to find Alypia knew what it meant. The princess said, "How will I ever repay you for this?"

"How else?" Nevrat said. At Alypia's puzzled look, she explained: "Invite me to the wedding, of course."

They laughed again. "By Phos, I will!" Alypia said.

"Most touching, my children," Balsamon put in. "But I suggest we bring our pleasant gathering to an end, before this poor lad jitters himself to death." He made a courteous nod toward Artavasdos, who did seem on the point of expiring. "And, even more to the point, before my *dear* colleague Saborios at last returns with my boots."

After embracing Nevrat, Alypia left first, by a back way. Then Balsamon led Nevrat and her cousin out to Artavasdos' horse. "It matters less if Saborios should happen to see you," he said. "He'll merely think me daft for consorting with heretics." One of his shaggy eyebrows rose. "Surely I've given him better reason than that." He patted Nevrat's arm and went back inside.

The two Vaspsurakaners were still close to the High Temple when a priest came by carrying a pair of blue boots. He had an upright bearing and rugged features, but his face was vaguely confused.

"Don't gape at him like that," Nevrat hissed in Artavasdos' ear. Her cousin ostentatiously looked in the other direction. He was not cut out for intrigue, Nevrat thought. But it did not matter. Past a glance any man might have sent an attractive woman, Saborios paid no attention to either of them.

Nevrat began thinking about what she had agreed to try, and also began worrying. From Garsavra to Amorion was no small journey, and many Yezda roamed between the two towns. Could the legionaries force their way through? More to the point, could they do it in time?

"The only thing to do is find out," she muttered to herself. She grinned. What better omen to start with than sounding like Scaurus?

Riding west through the lush farming country of the coastal plain, Nevrat became certain she was being followed. She could see a long way in the flatlands, and the horseman on her trail was noticeably closer than he had been when she first spotted him early that morning.

She checked her bowstring to make sure it was not frayed. If Thorisin was fool enough to send a single rider after her, he would regret it. So, even more pointedly, would the rider. Not many imperials, she thought proudly, could match her at the game of trap and ambush.

She did spare concern for Balsamon, Alypia Gavra, and her cousin Artavasdos. She wondered what had gone wrong, back in the city. Maybe Saborios had noticed something amiss in spite of the sorcerous befuddlement Nepos cast on him, or maybe Nepos had just tried keeping too many magics in the air at once, like a juggler with too many cups.

On the other hand, maybe pincers and knives had torn the truth from Artavasdos, who could not hide behind rank.

In the end, none of that mattered. What did matter was the fellow coming after her. She glanced back over her shoulder. Yes, he was closer. He had a good horse—not, Nevrat thought, that having it would help him.

A couple of mule-drawn cars, piled high with clay jugs full of berries, were coming toward her. She swerved behind them. They hid her from view as she rode off the road into the almond orchard along the verge.

One of the farmers with the carts called, "Old Krates don't like trespassers on his land."

"To the ice with him, if he begrudges me a quiet spot to squat a minute," Nevrat said. The farmers laughed and trudged on.

Nevrat walked into the orchard and tethered her horse to a

tree out of sight from the roadway. She gave the beast a feed-bag so it would not betray her with a neigh. Then she took her bow and quiver and settled down to wait, well hidden by bushes, for her pursuer.

Something with too many legs crawled up under her trousers and bit her several times, just below her knee, before she managed to kill it. The bites itched. Scratching at them gave her something to do.

Here came the fellow at last. Nevrat peered through the leaves. Like her, he was riding one of the nondescript but capable horses the Videssians favored. She set an arrow in her bow, then paused, frowning. She wished she could see better from her cover. Surely no Videssian would wear a cap like that one, with three peaks and a profusion of brightly dyed ribbons hanging down in back. . . .

She rose, laughing, her hands on her hips, the bow forgotten. "Senpat, what *are* you doing here?"

"At the moment, being glad I found you," her husband replied, trotting his horse up to her. "I was afraid you'd gone off the road to give me the slip."

"I had." Nevrat's smile faded. "I thought you were one of Thorisin's men—the more so," she added, "as you told me you were staying in the city the other night when I left."

Senpat grinned at her. "The thought of sleeping alone for who knows how long grew too disheartening to bear."

Her hands went to her hips again, this time in anger. Her eyes flashed dangerously. "For that you would risk us both? Have you all of a sudden gone half-witted? The very reason I got this task was that your leaving the capital might be noticed. You were trailing me—how many imperials are after you?"

"None. My captain felt very bad when I got a letter from home bidding me return at once because my older brother had just died of snakebite. The same thing had happened to him three years ago, which is why I had Artavasdos write the letter that way. For good measure, he wrote it in Vaspurakaner, which Captain Petzeas doesn't read."

"You have no older brother," Nevrat pointed out.

"Certainly not now, poor fellow, and Petzeas has the letter to prove it." Senpat arched an elegant eyebrow. "Even if anyone who knows differently hears of it, it'll be too late to matter."

"Oh, very well," Nevrat grumbled. She could never stay

annoyed at her husband for long, not when he was working so hard to charm her. And he was right—the imperials were unlikely to see through his precautions. Still: "It was a risky thing to do."

Senpat clapped a hand to his forehead. "This, from the woman who rode out alone from Khliat after Maragha? This, from the woman who, if I know her as the years have given me a right to, is itching to tangle with the Yezda or Zemarkhos or both at once?" Nevrat hoped he did not see her guilty start, but he did, and grinned. He went on, "I don't expect to keep you out of mischief, but at least I can share it with you. And besides, Scaurus is a friend of mine too."

Again Nevrat wondered whether he would say that if he knew the Roman had made a move in her direction. Probably, she thought—Marcus was at low ebb the past fall, but took a no when he heard one even so. Senpat would likely chuckle and say he could not fault the tribune's taste.

Nevrat did not intend to find out.

She said, "Come with me while I get my horse. I tied him up in the nut orchard so I could do a proper job of ambushing you."

"Hmmp. I suppose I should be honored." As they scuffed through last year's dry leaves, Senpat remarked, "Nice quiet place."

"A couple of locals told me old Krates, who I take it owns the orchard, doesn't care for intruders."

"He doesn't seem to have troubled you any while you were setting up your precious ambush." Senpat put a hand on Nevrat's shoulder. "Do you suppose he might stay away a while longer?"

She moved toward him. "Shall we find out?"

"I still say you shouldn't have shot Krates' dog," Nevrat told her husband a few days later.

By then they were almost to Garsavra, but Senpat still sounded grumpy. "You're right. I should have shot Krates, for showing up when he did."

"We've made up for it since."

"Well, so we have." Senpat peered toward the town ahead. "Why does it look different?"

"The Romans have been busy," Nevrat said. A man-high earthwork wall, faced with turf so it would not melt in the rain, surrounded Garsavra. It has been unfortified for hundreds of years, but times were changing in Videssos' westlands, and not for the better. From the direction in which she was coming, Nevrat could see two openings in the wall, one facing due north, the other east. She was dead certain a matching pair looked west and south. "They've turned the place into a big legionary camp."

"Sounds like what Gaius Philippus would do—there's nothing he likes better." Senpat chuckled. "I wonder if he had the Romans knock down half the buildings in town so he could make the streets run straight between his gates."

Nevrat shook her head. "He's not wasteful. Look at the way they made the Namdalener motte-and-bailey part of their works." She found the senior centurion too single-mindedly a soldier to be easy to like, but she was always glad they were on the same side.

The sentries at the north gate were Vaspurakaners, men from Gagik Bagratouni's band. They brightened at the approach of two of their countrymen. Still, their questions were brisk and businesslike—Roman drill working, Nevrat thought as the foot soldiers stood aside to let her and Senpat into Garsavra.

Sextus Minucius made his headquarters where Scaurus and Gaius Philippus had before him, in what had been the city governor's residence. He was a handsome young man, taller than most of the legionaries, with blue-black stubble that darkened his cheeks and chin no matter how often he shaved.

He greeted Senpat and Nevrat warmly, but with a trace of awkwardness. He had been only a simple trooper when they first attached themselves to the legion; now he outranked them. At their news, though, he abruptly became all business. His face went hard as stone.

"Gaius Philippus, too, eh?" he murmured, half to himself. He followed it with something in Latin that Nevrat could not follow. Seeing her incomprehension brought him back to the here-and-now, and to Videssian. "Sorry. It sounds like him, I said. The two of you had best wait here while I send for Bagratouni and Pakhymer. They ought to hear your story firsthand, to give me the best advice."

That last sentence killed any doubts Nevrat had about who was in charge at Garsavra. In his firm, unhesitating acceptance of duty, Minucius sounded much like Scaurus.

The orderly outside his office was a Roman. His hobnailed *caligae* clattered on marble flooring as he dashed off to fetch the officers his commander wanted.

Laon Pakhymer showed up first. Somehow that surprised Nevrat not at all. Nothing took Pakhymer by surprise—the light cavalry officer from Khatrish had a nose for trouble and a gift for exploiting it.

Minucius was pacing impatiently by the time Gagik Bagratouni arrived, though the Vaspurakaner was prompt enough. He embraced Senpat and Nevrat in turn. He had known them since he and they still held estates in Vaspurakan, before the Yezda invasions forced so many nobles from their native land.

"So," he said at last, turning to Minucius. "I am glad to see them, yes, but is this occasion enough to drag me from my quarters?" His voice was deep and deliberate, a fit match for his solid frame and strong, heavy features, the latter framed by an untrimmed beard as dark and thick as Minucius' would have been.

"Yes," the Roman said flatly. Nevrat exchanged glances with her husband; not many men could withstand Bagratouni's presence when he chose to exert it. Minucius nodded their way. "Seeing them is one thing, hearing them something else again."

Nevrat told most of the story, Senpat filling in details and adding how he had managed to get out of the city to join her. That earned him an admiring grin from Pakhymer. Nevrat saw how her husband drew himself up with pride; praise from the Khatrisher was praise from a master schemer.

When they were through, Bagratouni did what Nevrat had known he would—he slammed his fist down on the table in front of him and roared, "My men march now! Give me Zemarkhos, Phos, and I will ask for nothing more in this life!"

Minucius was the one who surprised her. He waited until Bagratouni's thundering subsided a little, then told the Vaspurakaner, "Your men march nowhere without my leave, Gagik."

Bagratouni's beard swallowed most of his dark flush of anger, but not all. "Who are you to tell me what to do? I am a *nakharar*, a lord of Vaspurakan, and I act with my retainers as I will."

"You are not in Vaspurakan," Minucius said, "and you

have taken Roman service as commander of a maniple. Do you remember that, or not?"

Nevrat leaned forward, afraid Bagratouni would throw himself at the Roman. "With Zemarkhos in front of me, I remember nothing," the *nakharar* ground out. "How do you propose to stop me from slaying him, as is less than he deserves?"

"With my men, if I have to," Minucius said evenly. "There are more Romans than Vaspurakaner legionaries in Garsavra. Look at me, Gagik. Do you doubt I would use them if you disobey my orders? I value your counsel; you know that. But I will have your obedience and I will do what I must to get it."

Bagratouni studied the younger man. The silence stretched. "You would," the Vaspurakaner said wonderingly. "Very well, then, what are your orders?" He spat the last word at Minucius.

"Why, to go after Scaurus, of course," the Roman said at once. He was not as calm as he wished to seem; sweat beaded on his forehead.

"Why this game, if we want the same thing?" Bagratouni exclaimed.

"I know how you feel about the Yezda, and about Zemarkhos. I don't blame you, Gagik, but I need you to remember you go as part of my forces, not have you haring off on your own."

Laon Pakhymer spoke up. "How will the Emperor feel when *you* go haring off on your own? No different from you about Gagik, I expect."

Suddenly and disarmingly, Minucius grinned. It made him look very young indeed. "Probably not. But there are more Romans than Videssian troops in Garsavra, too, so what is he going to do about it?"

"Not bloody much, except pitch a fit." Pakhymer grinned, too, his teeth white in a scraggly beard that rode high on his cheeks to cover pockmarks. He looked delighted at the prospect.

"If you take back Amorion for him, Thorisin won't care about the wherefores," Nevrat said to Minucius.

"She's right." Pakhymer turned his impudent smile her way. She suspected he approved of her person more than of her idea, but having men look at her did not bother her. Rather the reverse, unless they went further than looking, and Pakhymer knew better than that.

"If the Yezda kill all of us along the way, of course, we won't care what Thorisin thinks," Minucius said. "I'm glad we gave Yavlak something to think about when he raided last winter—his clans won't want any part of us."

"You leave Yavlak to me," Pakhymer said. "I bought an attack on the Namdaleni from him when we needed it; I expect a little gold will get him not to mind us marching through his land."

"Videssos' land," Minucius said, frowning.

"Yavlak's there, the Emperor's not. Do you really want to risk having to fight your way through and wasting Phos knows how much time?"

Minucius bit his lip. Nevrat saw Pakhymer had found the magic word to tempt him, despite his abhorrence for dealing with the Yezda in any way but at sword's point. He drummed his fingers, muttered again in Latin. Nevrat heard a familiar word, but could not follow the phrase.

But in the end, the Roman said, "No. If we move fast, Yavlak won't dare try troubling us."

Unlike Bagratouni, Pakhymer knew determination when he heard it. "You're the boss," he said with the casual wave he used for a salute. "Not much point to more talk, then, is there? Let's get ready to go." He got up and left. Bagratouni followed a moment later.

Minucius rose, too. "The Khatrisher is right. Time to get moving."

"May I ask you something first?" Nevrat said. Minucius paused. She went on, "I thought I heard you say Marcus' name, but I didn't know what the rest of that meant."

The Roman looked, of all things, embarrassed. "That'll teach me to talk to myself. Do you really want to know?" He waited till she nodded, then said sheepishly, "I was just asking myself what Scaurus would do in this spot. Now I'm off. One thing he wouldn't do is waste time."

Senpat Sviodo strummed the strings of his pandoura as he rode; he guided his horse with his knees. His song and the plashing of the Arandos River were the only music to accompany the column marching west. The Roman army, unlike its Videssian equivalent, mostly traveled in silence.

Nevrat, along with everyone else, was glad for the Arandos. The westlands' central plateau was nothing like the lush coastal lowlands. Away from running water, the sun baked the land to dust.

Her husband's song jangled to a stop. Two Khatrishers from Pakhymer's cavalry screen were riding back toward the main body of foot soldiers with a third man between them. "Yezda," Senpat said unnecessarily. The fellow was dressed in nomad leathers and carried a small round shield daubed here and there with whitewash—a truce sign.

At Minucius' signal, the buccinators trumpeted the legionaries to a halt; when they needed it, the Romans did not despise music. The Yezda rode up to him and said in loud, bad Videssian, "What you doing on land belong to mighty Yavlak?"

"Marching on it, not that it is Yavlak's," the Roman commander said. He ignored the Yezda's effort to stare him down; having outfaced Gagik Bagratouni, he was more than equal to this smaller challenge. "And if Yavlak doesn't care for it, let him recall what happened when he tried visiting Garsavra."

"He stack up your corpses like firewood," the Yezda herald blustered.

"Let him try. But tell him this—for now I have no quarrel with him. If I have to turn aside to deal with him, the only land he will claim is enough to bury him in. Now get out. I've wasted enough time on you."

Minucius nodded to the buccinators. They blew advance. The army tramped forward. The Yezda had to swing his horse into a sidestep to keep from being ground into the dirt. Scowling, he wheeled and trotted away.

"Trouble," Nevrat said, watching his angry back.

Senpat answered, "Mm, maybe not. Yavlak's no fool and he is still smarting from last winter. Besides, it will take some time for him to gather enough men to fight, even if he wants to. By the time he does, we may be past the stretch of country he holds." But as he spoke, he stowed his precious pandoura in its soft leather cover and began checking the fletching on the arrows in his quiver. Nevrat did the same.

Despite such forebodings, no trouble came that day. One reason, Nevrat was sure, was the speed with which the legionaries moved. As they were traveling along a river, they needed to carry only iron rations; no cumbersome wagons impeded their march. Dash might have been a better word—they fairly flung themselves up the Arandos.

At the end of the first grueling day, when the legionaries were building their familiar fortified camp, Nevrat asked Minucius, "How do you go so fast? I've seen cavalry armies that would have trouble matching your pace."

"We Romans train for it from the minute we join the legions," he answered. No doubt he was tired; his face was red and wet, his voice hoarse. But he was ready for more, managing a worn grin as he went on, "We call ourselves 'mules,' you know, for all the marching we do in full kit. And by now, all these Vaspurakaners and imperials have been with us long enough to keep up."

"If I had to bet, I'd say Yavlak will lead his horsemen to where we were early this afternoon."

"I hope he stays away. But if not, let's hope you're right." Minucius looked around, as he did every minute or so. "No, you idiot!" he bellowed at a Khatrisher. "Water your damned horses downstream from camp, not up! The fornicating Arandos is muddy enough already, without them stirring up more muck for us to drink."

Despite being the only woman in camp, Nevrat shared a tent with her husband unconcerned and would have worried no more had she been among the legionaries without him. It was not just that she was as handy with weapons as most men. After all the dangers she had shared with the Romans, none of them would have annoyed her, any more than he would a sister.

The next day, she saw a few Yezda. The nomads fled at the sight of the legionaries and looked back over their shoulders in disbelief at seeing troops loyal to Videssos pushing through country they had come to think of as theirs. Never were they in numbers enough to offer combat.

Later that afternoon, a Khatrisher rear guard came galloping up to warn that a real force of nomads was approaching from behind the Romans. Minucius gave Nevrat a Roman salute, holding his clenched fist out at arm's length in front of him. She waved her hat in reply.

Horns brayed. "Form lines to the rear!" Minucius shouted. With the smoothness of endless drill, the legionaries performed the maneuver.

"Where do you want us?" Laon Pakhymer asked.

"Out front, to foul up their archery." Minucius studied the ground. "And put a few squads over there, in that little copse. The gods willing, the Yezda will be too busy with us to study it much. If your men pop out at the right time, they'll count for a lot more than their numbers." Pakhymer nodded and bawled orders in the lisping Khatrisher dialect.

As soon as he was finished, Senpat called, "Shall we ride with you?"

"I'd sooner your lady asked that," Pakhymer said, and waited for Nevrat's snort before continuing, "but aye, come ahead. Another couple of good bows won't do us any harm."

"You have a care, mistress," one of the horsemen said as Nevrat passed him. "Get in trouble, and we'll all try and save you—and we might mess ourselves up to do it." He spoke with the half-joking tone Khatrishers often used, but Nevrat knew he meant what he said.

She was warmed and irritated at the same time. "I thank you," she said "I expect I'll manage." The Khatrisher nodded and waved.

The Yezda were not far behind the scout who brought news of them. Already Nevrat saw them emerging from the dust their ponies kicked up and heard the thunder of the horses' hooves.

"You've done this before, lads," Pakhymer told his men, calm as if he were discussing carting home a sack of beans. "Pick your targets while you're shooting and help your mates when the sabers come out."

A horse's skull on a pole—Yavlak's emblem-advanced. Closer, closer . . . Nevrat drew her bow back to her ear, let fly. The string lashed across the leather bracer on her wrist. She did not wait to see if her arrow hit; she was reaching for another while the first was still descending.

Here a horse stumbled, there another shrieked like a woman in labor when it was struck. Men were shouting, too, both from wounds and to terrify their foes. Icy fear shot through Nevrat when she saw blood on her husband's face. "A graze," Senpat reassured her when she cried out. "I'll let my beard get a little fuller to hide the scar, if it bothers you."

"Don't be an idiot." In itself, that kind of minor wound was nothing. But it reminded Nevrat how easy it was to find worse, and how little anyone could do to evade the death flying through the air.

The arrow duel, though, did not last as long as in the usual nomad engagement. Yavlak seemed intent on forcing the issue. His riders bulled through the Khatrishers, who, outnumbered, were forced aside. Nevrat understood why when she yeard Yavlak yelling toward the Roman standards: "With muds and snows you us once beat! Not we gets revenge!"

Senpat's face wore a grim smile. "Does he really think so? He hasn't brought near enough men, looks like to me."

Nevrat never heard him. She was hotly embroiled with a Yezda whose arms seemed as long as an ape's. She could parry his sword strokes, but her counters did not reach him.

Then the fellow suddenly grinned and moved in to fight at closer quarters. Nevrat recognized the new light in his eyes. It was not battle fury, but simple lust; he had realized he was facing a woman. His tongue flicked over his lips in slow, deliberate obscenity.

But he was no great swordsman, not when Nevrat could get at him at last. Her saber bit between his neck and shoulder. He howled a curse as he reeled away. Nevrat never knew whether her blow finished him—battle was often like that. She had to throw up her sword just in time to turn another nomad's slash and lost track of the first.

The heat of combat lessened, at least for the Khatrishers. Yavlak flung his horsemen at the legionaries. Senpat clapped a hand to his forehead in disbelief. "He's an idiot," he shouted. "He thinks they'll break and run."

"Probably the only foot soldiers he's faced since Maragha are herders with bows and axes trying to keep his men from running off their sheep." Nevrat's hand clamped down hard on her sword hilt in delighted anticipation of the shock the nomad chief was about to get.

Watching from the flank, she saw at once that Senpat had been right; Yavlak did not have enough men to take on the legionaries. He tried, regardless. Shouting and brandishing their swords, the Yezda spurred toward the waiting lines of shields. If they could force a breach, numbers would not matter.

The horns cried out, echoing Minucius' dropped arm. With a single great cry that cut cleanly through the random yells of their foes, the Romans cast their heavy javelins at the Yezda. An instant later, another wave of spears flew. The legionaries drew their stubby thrusting swords and surged forward, peering over the tops of their semicylindrical *scuta*.

The first ranks of the Yezda were in hideous confusion.

The volleys of *pila* had blunted the momentum of their charge, emptying saddles and felling horses. Yet they could not turn tail and flee, the usual nomad tactic when pressed, because their comrades behind them were still trying to push up and get in the fight. The result was a few minutes of slaughter.

Watching the legionaries swarm over the Yezda, Nevrat thought of ants. Usually the Romans operated at a disadvantage in numbers and gave better than they got. With an edge, they were terrifying. A hamstrung horse screamed. Even before it fell, two soldiers beset its rider, one from either side. He did not last long. Another Roman turned a nomad's slash with the edge of his big, heavy shield, then used its weight to push the Yezda off balance. Another legionary stabbed him in the back; boiled leather could not keep out steel.

The Yezda could not even seek to outflank their opponents. The Arandos anchored the Romans' right wing, while Pakhymer's Khatrishers covered the left. And at close quarters, even mounted the nomads were no match for the disciplined, armored veterans Minucius led. Remembering ravaged fields and burned keeps in Vaspurakan, Nevrat found only fierce delight in their predicament.

But an army of infantry cannot wreck horsemen unless they stay to fight. The Yezda the legionary advance had not caught began pulling away, first by ones and twos, then in larger groups. Then the concealed Khatrisher squadron came galloping out of ambush, emptying their quivers as fast as they could into the Yezda flank. Retreat turned to rout.

"Ride over to Minucius," Pakhymer bawled in Nevrat's ear. She started; she had not noticed him come up. "Find out how far he wants us to chase the buggers."

The Roman's answer came promptly: "Only far enough to be sure they're in no shape to re-form. I want to get moving again. This mess has cost us close to half a day."

"Not much else, though." Hardly any of the men on the ground were legionaries.

The young man inside Minucius peeped out for a moment from behind the stern commander's mask. "It did work well, didn't it? Yavlak got what anyone too eager gets." His eyes flicked to Bagratouni's men, who were grimly making certain all the downed Yezda were corpses.

"On my way back to Pakhymer, shall I stop and thank

Gagik for you, for not breaking ranks in his own eagerness to get at the nomads?"

"Thank him for obeying orders?" Minucius' astonishment was perfectly real. "By the gods, no! He does what he does because I command it, not as a favor to me."

"He's right," Senpat said in their tent that night when Nevrat told him of the exchange. They were lying side by side on the bedroll, too tired after the fight for anything more, but too keyed up to sleep.

"Of course he's right." Nevrat brushed back a wet lock of hair from her cheek—washing the grime and sweat from it was the only pleasure for which she'd had the energy after the legionaries made camp. She went on, "But how did he make Bagratouni see that, after all he's suffered from the Yezda? What happened back in Garsavra means nothing now—the Romans would never turn on Gagik's men here, not in the middle of enemy-held country."

"I suppose not," Senpat half agreed, "though I wonder what would happen if Minucius gave the order. I'm glad we don't have to find out. Still, you're right; that's not what held Gagik back."

"What, then?"

"Do you really want to know what I think? I think over the last couple of years, without ever quite knowing it, Bagratouni has gone from being a *nakharar* to a—what do they call it?—a centurion, that's right. This Roman discipline digs deep into a man. I'm just glad it hasn't set its hooks too deep in us."

Nevrat thought about that. Imagining Gagik Bagratouni as a clean-shaven Roman made her smile, but she decided her husband had a point. The *nakharar* had snarled at Minucius, but in the end he obeyed. The Bagratouni she had known of old, affronted so, might well have made the legionary commander carry out his threat.

After a while, she said, "If the Romans have no hold on us, why are we here by the Arandos instead of back in the capital following the Avtokrator's orders?"

Only a snore answered her. She rolled over. A few minutes later she was asleep herself.

Yavlak had fought the Romans once before they began their drive to the west, but had learned little from his earlier defeat. The nomad chieftains further into the interior of the central plateau knew nothing of the newcomers and were foolish enough to believe they could run them off with whatever forces they scraped together on the spur of the moment.

A couple of stinging defeats taught them otherwise. Word spread quickly from one clan to the next. After that, the Yezda left them alone. In fact, the nomads fled before them, flocks and all.

"I found another abandoned camp ahead of us," Nevrat reported to Minucius at an evening council after her return from a scouting run. "The tracks leading out of it look two or three days old."

"Senseless," the Roman said. Stubble rasped as he rubbed his chin. "If they left us alone, we wouldn't go after them. You'd think they'd have noticed that by now."

"Do you miss them?" Nevrat teased.

"Not even slightly." Again she saw the amused youngster through Minucius' grave shell, but only for a moment. He went on, "I mistrust what I don't understand, though."

"It is the nomads' way," Bagratouni said. "When a strong clan comes, the weak ones move aside. They will be fighting among themselves now, over grazing land, and shifting all about in more country than we could hope to march to in a year." Somber satisfaction at the prospect filled his voice.

Laon Pakhymer's eyes lit with mock indignation. "Ha! Are you saying my noble ancestors were forced off the steppe into Khatrish, instead of being the great heroes our minstrels sing of?"

Bagratouni took him literally. "It could be so, but with the original push hundreds of miles away."

"Are we going to push the Yezda into Amorion ahead of us, then?" Minucius said slowly.

Nevrat and Senpat exchanged glances of consternation; neither had worried about that. Gagik Bagratouni's big hands curled into fists. "Better, maybe, if we do. Zemarkhos and the Yezda deserve each other. The more they fight, the easier time we have coming after."

"Normally I would agree and be grateful," Minucius said, his face troubled. "But, the gods willing, Scaurus and Gaius Philippus are also in Amorion, or getting close. We came to rescue them, after all, not to throw more calamities down on them."

With his gift for pointing out what was so obvious as to be easily overlooked, Pakhymer broke the worried silence that followed. "Well, it's a bit late to turn back, isn't it?"

Nevrat thought about the Khatrisher's wry comment the next day, when she and her husband spotted the horseman coming up along the Arandos after the legionaries. The two Vaspurakaners had rotated back to rear guard, with some of Pakhymer's men riding in front of the army.

Senpat gave a puzzled grunt as he looked back over his shoulder. "Fellow doesn't sit his horse like a nomad."

"So he doesn't," Nevrat agreed after a moment's study. The Yezda, like the Khatrishers and other folk ultimately of Khamorth stock, used very short stirrup leathers and rode with their knees drawn up. The unknown kept his legs down at his horse's side.

"There just seems to be the one of him." Senpat whistled three notes from a Vaspurakaner hunting song, then set an arrow in his bow. "Cover me—I saw him first."

Her chance to argue forestalled by that last, offhand remark, Nevrat trailed her husband at easy bowshot range as he approached the stranger. The two men talked briefly before Senpat waved an all-clear. Her bow still across her lap ready to grab, she came up.

"He's not a Yezda, Nevrat." Senpat's face bore a faintly bemused expression. "His name is Arsakes Akrounos—he's an imperial courier."

Looking at Akrounos, Nevrat Sviodo was not surprised. He had the air of unimpressive competence the job required. If he was nonplused at finding a woman on patrol, he never let on. All he said was, "I have a dispatch for your leader."

"We'll get you to him," Nevrat said.

Like most Videssians, Akrounos liked to hear himself talk. He gossiped on about this and that as he rode west between Nevrat and Senpat. Unlike many of his countrymen, he gave nothing away with his chatter, and Nevrat was sure no detail escaped his eyes as he trotted past the marching lines of legionaries.

Minucius tramped along at the front of the column. "Is he now?" he said when Senpat explained who and what Akrounos was. He stepped to one side to let the Romans pass him as he eyed the courier with scant liking. "All right, I suppose he can speak his piece."

For the first time, Akrounos looked annoyed; he was used to warmer welcomes. He rummaged in a saddlebag and produced a parchment that prominently displayed the imperial sunburst seal. With a flourish, he handed it down to Minucius.

The Roman handed it back, discomfiting him again. "Suppose you just tell me the gist. Sorry and all that, but I don't read Videssian very fast."

"Surely you can guess—" Akrounos began.

Minucius cut him off. "Why should I guess, with you here? Say what you have to say or go home."

"*What?*" Now the courier was openly scandalized; no one spoke so to imperial representatives. Mastering himself with a visible effort, he broke the seal on the document he carried. "'His Imperial Majesty Thorisin Gavras, Avtokrator of the Videssians, to Sextus Minucius, commanding my Majesty's forces at Garsavra: greetings. I regret to learn that you have forgotten your obedience to me and—'"

"The gist," Minucius said. "I haven't the time to waste on this."

Akrounos took a moment to put his thoughts in order; saying things short and clear did not come easy to Videssians. At last he said, "Return your force to Garsavra and in his mercy the Emperor will overlook your brief defection."

"I thought as much." Minucius folded his arms. "No."

Again Akrounos hesitated, expecting some further answer. When he saw he would get none, he cried, "Why such ingratitude? Did the Empire not take you in when you were homeless, feed you when you were hungry?"

The Roman frowned. Nevrat's respect for Thorisin Gavras' wits, already high, went up another notch. The argument he had given his courier to cast in Minucius' face appealed to the legionary's strong sense of duty.

But Minucius said, "We follow Scaurus first, not Gavras. And we've earned our keep with blood. Besides, your master sent my two commanders off to die alone. Where's the charity in that, Akrounos?"

The soldiers marching by growled in agreement with Minucius' words. A couple of them hefted *pila* and glowered at Akrounos. Minucius quelled them with a gesture.

Bagratouni's contingent replaced a maniple still almost wholly Roman. Akrounos called to the Vaspurakaner, "Do you, too, prefer some outland mercenary as your lord, rather than the Emperor?"

"Why not?" Bagratouni had been listening to the exchange all the while. "Did not Scaurus take us in when we were homeless, feed us when we were hungry?" His deep-set eyes gleamed as he placed the barb. Akrounos' face froze. Bagratouni nodded gravely to Minucius and walked on.

Senpat murmured in Vaspurakaner, "It would take more than Thorisin to keep Gagik from going after Yezda—and after Zemarkhos."

"But he doesn't say that," Nevrat replied in the same tongue. "He answers as a Roman centurion would—another sign you were right."

"I will take your answer back to his Imperial Majesty," Akrounos was saying to Minucius.

"Stay with us," the Roman urged. "You were lucky to come this far once by yourself. Think how slim the odds are of getting back whole."

The courier shrugged. "As may be. I have my loyalty, too, and the Emperor will need to hear the news I bring."

"Go, then," Minucius said, waving a hand in recognition of Akrounos' courage. "I am not your enemy, or Thorisin's either."

"Ha!" Akrounos turned his horse sharply and trotted east. Minucius marched double time in the opposite direction to catch up to the head of his column. He did not look back.

The legionaries marched northwest along the Ithome River after it joined the Arandos. Amorion was only about three days away. Anticipation grew among the troopers, in the Romans for the chance to rescue their tribune and in the Vaspurakaners for that reason and at the prospect of striking a blow at the hated persecutor of their people.

Just when Nevrat began to hope Zemarkhos was too busy with his theological rantings to bother about such mundane details as frontier guards, a Khatrisher scout rode back to the army bearing a helmet, saber, and bow as trophies.

"A pair of the buggers tried to jump me," he reported to Minucius. "I shot the one this junk used to belong to, but the other whoreson got away. They were imperials, not Yezda."

The Roman commander sighed. "I wish you'd picked off both of them, but you did well to get the one." The scout grinned at the praise.

"So much for surprise," Laon Pakhymer observed. "If I were you, Sextus, I'd expect attack later today."

"Even Yavlak waited to gather some of his forces," Minucius protested.

"Yavlak seeks only loot and blood," Bagratouni said. "Myself, I think Pakhymer is right. The foul, lying cur of a Zemarkhos has his men deluded into thinking Phos will lift them straight to heaven if they die doing the madman's will."

Minucius shook his head in wonder. "What idiocy." Again he reminded Nevrat of Scaurus, to whom the sectarian quarrels among Phos' worshipers meant nothing. As for herself, she had grown up with the Vaspurakaner version of the faith and never thought of changing. Some Vaspurakaners in the Empire did, to rise more quickly. Their countrymen had a word for them—traitor.

"I can't believe any soldier would be so stupid," Minucius insisted. Pakhymer and Bagratouni argued, but could not change his mind. The louder they shouted, the more he set his strong chin and looked stubborn.

Nevrat thought they were right. She wondered what would have made Marcus see reason. She caught Minucius' eye and said, "Don't let your not sharing a belief blind you into thinking it isn't real. Remember how Bagratouni and his men joined yours."

The Roman pursed his lips. Pakhymer was sharp enough to stay quiet and let him think, and to kick Bagratouni in the ankle when he would have kept on wrangling. Finally Minucius said, "We'll march with maniples abreast. That way we can shift quickly into line if we have to."

He shouted orders, at the same time swearing under his breath at the delay they would cause. Pakhymer winked at Nevrat, then startled her by saying in fair Vaspurakaner, "You have more than logic behind your words."

Minucius looked up sharply. Nevrat had not thought he knew any of her language either.

"Can't trust anyone any more," Senpat chuckled when he rode up from patrol a few minutes later. But the amusement rode lightly on his voice, and on his face. He and Nevrat had not had to flee Zemarkhos' pogrom, but they had seen the fanatic priest's venom at Bagratouni's vanished home in Amorion before the battle of Maragha.

This time the outriders gave only brief warning. "Curse you, how many?" Minucius shouted when a Khatrisher came galloping in to cry that horsemen were chasing him.

"Didn't stop to count 'em," the scout retorted. He ignored Minucius' glare. Nevrat giggled. The freewheeling Khatrishers had a talent for getting under the Romans' skins.

"Form line!" Minucius commanded. He nodded to Laon Pakhymer. "You were right, it seems. Can your men buy us some time to deploy?"

"Hurry," Pakhymer said, waving to the rapidly approaching cloud of dust to the west. Smooth as on a parade ground, the legionaries were already moving into position. That seemed to annoy Pakhymer as much as his own soldiers' cheerful rowdiness irritated Minucius.

"Come on, come on!" Pakhymer bawled to his men. "Don't you know what a rare privilege it is to die for an officer who'll admit he was wrong?" He sent Senpat and Nevrat a languid wave better suited to some great lord. "Would you care to join the ball? The dancing will begin shortly."

Bowstrings had begun to thrum. The cavalry troop trading arrows with the Khatrishers seemed hardly more orderly than so many Yezda; they knew nothing of the intricate maneuvers Videssian military manuals taught. But they knew nothing of retreat either, though Nevrat saw how few they were compared to their foes.

"Zemarkhos!" they shouted. "Phos bless Zemarkhos!"

That war cry infuriated Gagik Bagratouni's men. They sent it back with obscene embellishments. The leader of Zemarkhos' men whipped his head around. Even fighting Roman-fashion, Bagratouni's followers were recognizable for what they were by their stocky builds and thick black beards.

"Vaspurs!" the leader howled. He swung his sword toward them.

Laon Pakhymer was a cool professional. He had his horsemen sidling out to flank Zemarkhos' irregulars, threatening them with encirclement if they did not withdraw. Neither he nor anyone else who thought only in military terms would have expected them to hurl themselves straight for the legionary line.

Because the charge was such a surprise, it succeeded better than it should have. Nevrat shot at an onrushing Videssian at point-blank range and, to her mortified disgust, missed. She ducked low, grinding her face into the coarse hair of her horse's mane. She heard his blade hiss bare inches above her head. Then he was past, still yelling Zemarkhos' name.

Once through the cavalry screen, the Videssians spurred straight for Bagratouni's men. The rest of the army did not seem to exist to them, save as an obstacle between them and their chosen prey. The volly of *pila* they took slowed them, but they came on regardless. A dying horse bowled over three Vaspurakaners and gave Zemarkhos' men a breach to pour into. They stabbed and slashed at the targets of their hatred. The Vaspurakaners fought back as savagely.

But the battle did not stay private long. The Roman maniples by Bagratouni's moved up and swung in on the sides of Zemarkhos' troop. And behind them, the Khatrisher cavalry swiftly re-formed to close off escape.

"The cork's in the bottle now!" Senpat shouted. He yelled a challenge to one of the harried band in front of him: "Here, scum, what about me? I am a prince of Vaspurakan, too!" All the Vaspurakaners styled themselves princes, for they claimed descent from the first man Phos created.

Senpat's foe fought with desperation and fanaticism. That helped even the fight, since Senpat was a better swordsman. But the Videssian never saw Nevrat, a few paces away, draw her bow. This time her aim was true. The man crumpled.

"Did you doubt me?" Senpat demanded.

"I've learned from the Romans, too. I take no chances."

"Good enough. I won't complain over unspilled blood, especially when it's mine." Senpat urged his horse ahead. Nevrat followed. She had saved arrows and she used them now to wicked effect.

At last even fanaticism could not maintain Zemarkhos' men. A remnant of them disengaged and tried to fight their way clear. A few did; more died in the attempt. The whole sharp little fight had lasted only minutes.

Minucius came up to Gagik Bagratouni. The Roman commander's walk was wobbly; a fresh dent in his helmet showed why. His wits still worked, though. "Well fought, Gagik. Let's talk to some of the prisoners, to see what's ahead for us."

The Vaspurakaner spread large hands. "Prisoners? What a pity—there don't seem to be any." His eyes dared Minucius to make something of it.

"Ah, well, we'll find out soon enough," Minucius said. He looked round for Pakhymer, who, predictably, was not far away. "Can you send your scouts out a bit further, Laon? It wouldn't do to get hit by a big band of those madmen without warning."

"I'll see to it." The cavalry leader sounded more serious than usual as he gave his orders. The rough handling Zemarkhos' irregulars gave his men in that first charge did not sit well with him, even if the Khatrishers had gained a measure of revenge.

The trumpets blared advance. The army moved ahead. Senpat finished bandaging a small cut on the side of his horse's neck. "We've done all this," he said, "and we don't even know if Scaurus ever made it to Amorion."

"I know," Nevrat said. "I keep wondering how he'd fare if he ran into some of Zemarkhos' zealots."

"He's not a Vaspurakaner," her husband pointed out.

"So he isn't. I hadn't thought of that. But even if he's got to the city, what can he hope to do?" Nevrat dug her heels into her horse's ribs. "As Minucius said, we'll find out soon enough."

VI

A CATAPULT THUMPED. A STONE BALL BIGGER THAN A MAN'S head hissed through the air, almost too fast for the eye to follow. It buried itself in the soft ground at the edge of the steppe. The wind blew away the puff of dust it raised.

Viridovix shook his fist at the fortress, which lay like a beast of tawny stone in the mouth of the pass that led south into Erzerum. Like fleas on the back of the beast, men scurried along the battlements. "Come out and fight, you caitiff kerns!" the Gaul shouted.

"That was a warning shot," Lankinos Skylitzes said. "At this range they could hit us if they cared to."

Pikridios Goudeles sighed. "We built too well, it seems, we and the Makuraners, the one time we managed to work together."

Gorgidas touched his saddlebag. He had written that tale down a few days before, when Goudeles told it at camp. Centuries ago the two great empires saw it was in their joint interest to keep the steppe nomads from penetrating Erzerum and erupting into their own lands. The northern passes were beyond the permanent power of either of them, but Makuran had provided the original construction money to fortify them, with Videssos contributing skilled architects and an annual subsidy to the local princelings to keep the strong points garrisoned. Now Makuran was no more and the Videssian subsidy had ceased when the Empire fell on hard times these past fifty years, but the Erzrumi still manned the forts; they warded Erzerum as well as the lands farther south.

"Show parley," Arigh ordered, and a white-painted shield

went up on a lance. Trying to force one of the narrow passes would have been suicidal, and the great mountains of Erzerum, some in the distance still snow-covered though it was nearly summer, offered no other entranceways.

A postern gate opened; a horseman carrying a like truce sign and riding a big, rawboned mountain beast came toward the Arshaum. Arigh quickly chose a party to meet him: himself, Goudeles and Skylitzes—the one for his diplomatic talent, the other for his command of the Khamorth tongue, which anyone at the edge of Pardraya should know —and Tolui. At Goudeles' suggestion, he added one of Agathias Psoes' troopers who knew some Vaspurakaner; the "princes" had dealt with their northwestern neighbors before Videssos' influence reached so far, and affected some of them greatly.

"May I come, too?" Gorgidas asked.

"Always looking to find things out," Arigh said, half amused, half scornful. "Well, why not?" Viridovix asked no one's leave, but rode forward with the rest, cheerfully pretending not to see Arigh's frown.

The Erzrumi waved them to a halt at a safe distance. He looked much like a Vaspurakaner—stocky, swarthy, square-faced, and hook-nosed—but he trained his curly beard into two points. His gilded cuirass, plumed bronze helmet, and clinging trousers of fine silk proclaimed him an officer. He was within five years either way of forty.

He waved again, this time in peremptory dismissal. "Go back," he said in the plains speech; he had a queer, hissing accent. "Go back. We will crush you if you come further. I, Vakhtang, second chief of the castle of Gunib, tell you this. Are we simpletons, to open our country to murderous barbarians? No, I say. Go back, and be thankful we do not slay you all."

Arigh bridled. Goudeles said hastily, "He means less than he says. He has a Videssian style to him, though a debased one."

"Videssian, eh? There's a thought." The Arshaum's years at the imperial capital had given him a good grasp of the language. He used it now: "Why the high horse, fellow? We have no quarrel with you or yours. It's Avshar we're after, curse him."

Vakhtang's eyebrows rose to his hairline. "I know what that speech is, though I do not use it." He seemed to take a first good look at the group in front of him. In their furs and leathers, Gorgidas, Goudeles, Skylitzes, and Psoes' soldier—his name was Narbas Kios—might have been Khamorth, if odd ones. But Arigh and Tolui were something else again. And Viridovix, with his drooping mustaches, red hair spilling from under his fur cap, and pale freckled skin, was unlike any man the Erzrumi captain had seen. His careful composure deserted him. "Who *are* you people, anyway?" he blurted.

Goudeles nudged Narbas the trooper, who rode forward a couple of paces. "Make sure he understands you," the penpusher said. Vakhtang showed fresh surprise when Narbas spoke hesitantly in the Vaspurakaner tongue, but stifled it. He gave a regal nod.

"Good," Goudeles said. He paused; Gorgidas could see him discarding the florid phrases of Videssian rhetoric to stick with ideas Kios could put across. "Tell him Skylitzes and I are envoys of the Avtokrator of the Videssians. Tell him where the Arshaum are from, and tell him they've come all this way as our allies against Yezd. We only ask a safe-conduct through Erzerum so we can attack the Yezda in their own land. Here, give him our bona-fides, if he'll take them."

He produced the letter of authority Thorisin had given him, a bit travel-worn but still gorgeous with ink of gold and red and the sky-blue sunburst seal of the Videssian Emperors. Skylitzes found his letter as well. Holding one in each hand so he could draw no weapon, Narbas offered them to Vakhtang. The officer made a show of studying them. If he spoke no Videssian, Gorgidas was sure he could not read it, but he recognized the seals. Few men in this world would not have.

The Erzrumi gravely handed the letters back. He spoke again, this time in the throaty Vaspurakaner language. Narbas Kios translated: "Even this far north, he says, they know of Yezd, and know nothing good. They have never yet let a nomad army past their forts, but he will take what you said to the lord of Gunib."

"Tell him we thank him for his courtesy," Arigh said, and bowed from the waist in the saddle. Viridovix watched his friend with surprised respect; a roisterer in Videssos, the Arshaum was learning to be a prince.

Vakhtang returned Arigh's compliment and turned to go

back to the fortress. Before he got far, Tolui rode out of the parley group and caught him up. Vakhtang spun in alarm and started to reach for his sword, but stopped after a glance at the shaman; though not in his regalia, Tolui still had a formidable presence. He put his hand on the captain's arm and spoke to him in the few words of Khamorth he had learned from Batbaian: "Not—fight you. Not—hurt you. Go through, is all. Oath."

His broken speech seemed to have as much effect on Vakhtang as Goudeles' arguments and letters both. Gorgidas saw the self-important bureaucrat redden as the officer gave Tolui what was plainly a salute, putting both clenched fists to his forehead. Then he clasped the shaman's hand before releasing it and urging his horse into a trot. The postern gate swung open to readmit him.

"Now what?" Gorgidas asked.

"We wait," Arigh said. Gorgidas and the Videssian fidgeted, but with nomad's patience Arigh sat his horse quietly, ready to wait there all day if need be. After a while the main gate of the fortress of Gunib opened a little. "They trust us—some, at least," Arigh said. "Now we do business."

Flanked by a small bodyguard of lancers in scaled mail came Vakhtang and another, older man whose gear was even richer than his. Age spots freckled the backs of his hands, Gorgidas saw as he drew close, but there was strength in him. He had the eyes of a warrior, permanently drawn tight at the corners and tracked with red. He inspected the newcomers with a thoroughness Gauis Philippus might have used.

At last he said, "I am Gashvili, Gunib's lord. Convince me, if you can, that I should give you leave to pass." His voice was dry, his heavy features unreadable.

He heard the tale they had given Vakhtang, but in more detail. He kept interrupting with questions, always searching ones. His knowledge of Pardrayan affairs was deep, but not perfect; he knew of Varatesh's rise to power and the magical aid Avshar had given him, but thought the latter a Khamorth sorcerer. When Arigh told how the wizard-prince had fled southward, Gashvili rammed fist into open palm and growled something sulfurous in his own language.

"Day before yesterday we let one through who answered to your account of him," he said when he had control of a speech the men from the plains could follow. "He claimed he was a

merchant beset by bandits on the steppe. As there was just the
one of him and he was no Khamorth, we had no reason to
disbelieve him."

Suddenly all of Arigh's party was shouting at once. For all
their hopes, for all their anticipation, they had not run Avshar
to earth. He must have had some magic to make his stallion
run night and day, far past the normal endurance of any horse.
The beast had gained steadily on the Arshaum, tireless in the
saddle though they were. Then a rainstorm covered its tracks,
and they lost the trail.

"Well, whatever is your honor waiting for?" Viridovix
cried. "Why are you not after calling yourself's men out to be
riding with us to take the spalpeen, the which'd be worth a
million years o' this sitting on the doorstoop o' nowhere." The
Gaul wanted to leap down from his pony and shake sense into
Gashvili.

The noble's mouth twitched in amusement. "Perhaps I
shall." He turned to Arigh. "You ask me to take a heavy
burden on myself. What guarantees would I have from you
that it shall be as you say, and that your army will not
plunder our fair valleys once you get past me here? Will
you give hostages on it, to be held in Gunib as pledge
against bad faith?"

"As for pledges," Arigh said at once, "I will swear my own
people's oath, and any that suit you. Are you a Phos-worshiper like the Videssians? He seems not a bad god, for
farmer-folk."

The Arshaum meant it as a compliment, though Skylitzes'
face was scandalized. Gashvili shook his head, setting silver
curls bouncing under his gilded helm. "For all the blue-robes'
prating, I and most of mine hold to the old gods of sky and
earth, rock and river. I am a stubborn old man, and they
humor me." His tone belied the self-mockery; he was proud
his people followed his lead.

"No trouble there, then," Arigh said. His manner
abruptly harshened. "But what is this talk of hostages? Will
you give me hostages in turn, so no man of mine will be
risked without knowing that, if he dies from treachery, some
Erzrumi's spirit will go with him to serve him in the next
world?"

"By Tahund of the thunders, I will, and more!" Gashvili
spoke with sudden hard decision. "I and all but a skeleton
garrison will ride with you. With the Khamorth in disorder,

the pass will be safe this year. And," he added, looking shrewdly at Arigh, "having watch-hounds along will no doubt encourage you to keep your fine promises."

"No doubt," Arigh said, so blandly that Gorgidas stared at him. This one, he thought, has nothing to fear from haughty Dizabul, however handsome Arghun's younger son might be. Still mild, Arigh went on, "You'll have to keep up with us, you know."

The fortmaster chuckled. "You may know the steppe, but credit me with some idea of my business here. We'll stick tight as burrs under your horses' tails." He rode to brush cheeks with Arigh. "We agree, then?"

"Aye. Bring on your oath."

"It is better done by night." Gashvili turned his head. "Vakhtang, go tell the men to get ready to—" But Vakhtang was already trotting back toward Gunib, waving to show all was well. Gashvili laughed out loud. "My daughter knew what she was about when she chose that one."

The Arshaum and the Gunib garrison spent the afternoon warily fraternizing. No plainsman was invited into the fortress, and Gashvili made it clear his vigilance had not relaxed. Arigh was offended at that until Goudeles reminded him, "He is going against generations of habit in treating with you at all."

Through Sklylitzes—who looked acutely uncomfortable as he translated—an Erzrumi priest, a wizened elder whose thick white beard reached his thighs, explained his people's way of binding pledges to Tolui. The shaman nodded thoughtfully when he was done, saying, "That is a strong ritual."

In a way, the Erzrumi oath-taking ceremony reminded Gorgidas of the one the Arshaum had used to pledge the Vi- dessian party and Bogoraz of Yezd against threat to Arghun. At twilight the priest, whose name was Tzathmak, lit two rows of fires about thirty feet long and three or four feet apart. "Will he be walking through them, now?" asked Viridovix, who had heard about but not seen the Arshaum rite.

"No; the ways here are different," Goudeles said.

In striped ceremonial robe, Tzathmak led one of the fort's scavenger dogs out to the fires. Tolui joined him in his fringed shaman's regalia and mask. Together they prayed over the dog, each in his own language. Tolui called to his watching countrymen, "The beast serves as a sign of our agreement."

Normally nothing could have made the dog walk between the two crackling rows of flame, but at Tzathmak's urging it padded docilely down them. "As the dog braves the fire, so may the peace and friendship between us overcome all obstacles," Tolui said. Tzathmak spoke in his own tongue, presumably giving Gashvili's men the same message.

At the far end of the fires stood a muscular Erzrumi, naked to the waist and leaning on a tall axe not much different from the sort the Halogai used. When the dog emerged, he swung the axe up in a glittering arc, brought it whistling down. The beast died without a sound, cut cleanly in two. All the Erzrumi cried out at the good omen.

"May the same befall any man who breaks this pact!" Tolui shouted, and the Arshaum, understanding, yelled their approval, too.

Gashvili could roar when it suited him. "Tomorrow we ride!" he cried in the Khamorth tongue. Both groups yelled together then—the Arshaum raggedly, for not all of them had even a smattering of Khamorth, but with high spirits all the same.

"Effective symbolism, that, if a bit grisly," Goudeles remarked, pointing toward the sacrificed dog.

"Is that all you take it for?" Gorgidas said. "As for me, I'd sooner not chance finding out—I remember what happened to Bogoraz too well."

"Gak!" the bureaucrat said in horror. He tenderly patted his middle, as if to reassure himself no axeblade, real or sorcerous, was anywhere near.

Viridovix squinted with suspicion at the new valley shimmering in the sultry heat-haze ahead. "Sure and I wonder what'll be waiting for us here."

"Something different," Gorgidas said confidently. At the first sight of the Arshaum army's outriders, herders were rushing their flocks up into the hills and peasants dashing for the safety of their nobles' fortresses. Other men, armored cavalry, were moving together in purposeful haste.

Viridovix snorted at the Greek. "Will you harken to the Grand Druid, now? That's no foretelling at all, at all, not in this Erzerum place. Were you after saying 'twould be the same, the prophecy'd be worth the having."

"With your contrariness, you should feel right at home," the physician snapped. He clung to his patience and to the subject. "It makes perfectly good sense for every little valley here to be nothing like any of its neighbors."

"Not to me, it doesn't," Viridovix and Arigh said in the same breath.

The Arshaum continued, "My folk range over a land a thousand times the size of this misbegotten jumble of rocks, but all our clans make up one people." He looked haggard. Seven separate bands of Erzrumi were with the nomads, and as overall leader he had the thankless job of keeping them from one another's throats. They used five different languages, were of four religions—to say nothing of sects—and were all passionately convinced of their own superiority.

"You have the right of it, Arigh dear," Viridovix backed him. "In my Gaul, now, I'll not deny the Eburovices, the tribe southwest o' my own Lexovii, are a mangy breed o' Celt, but forbye they're Celts. Why, hereabouts a wight canna bespeak the fellow over the hills a day's walk away, and doesna care to, either. He'd sooner slit the puir spalpeen's weasand for him."

Lankinos Skylitzes said, "We Videssians hold that Skotos confounded men's tongues in Erzerum when the natives fell away from Phos' grace by refusing to accept the orthodox faith."

"No need to haul in superstition for something with a natural cause," Gorgidas said, rolling his eyes. Seeing Skylitzes bristle, he demanded, "Well, how does your story account for the men of Mzeh riding with us? They're as orthodox as you are, but the only Videssian they have is learned off by rote for their liturgy. Otherwise not even Gashvili can follow their dialect."

The officer tugged at his beard in confusion, not used to the notion of testing ideas against facts. Finally he said, "What is this famous 'natural cause' of yours, then?"

"Two, actually." The Greek ticked them off on his fingers. "First, the land. Size means nothing. Shaumkhiil and Gaul are open countries. People and ideas move freely, so it is no wonder they aren't much different from one end to the other. But Erzerum? It's all broken up with mountains and rivers. Each valley makes a bastion, and since none of the peoples here could hope to rule the whole land, they've been able to keep their own ways and tongues without much interference."

He paused for a gulp of wine. Erzerum's vintages were rough, but better than kavass. Down in the valley, behind a covering stream, the band of cavalry was moving two by two into position at the edge of the stream. Bright banners snapped above them.

Gorgidas put the wineskin away; he would rather argue. "Where was I? Oh, yes, the second reason for Erzerum's diversity. Simple—it's the rubbish-heap of history. Every folk beaten by Makuran, or Videssos, or even by Vaspurakan or the peoples of Pardraya, has tried to take refuge here, and a good many pulled it off. Thus the Shnorhali, who fled the Khamorth when they entered Pardraya who knows how long ago—their remnant survives here."

"Isn't he the cleverest little fellow, now?" Viridovix said, beaming at the Greek. "Clear as air he's made the muddle, the which had me stymied altogether."

"Clear as fog, you mean," Skylitzes said. He challenged Gorgidas: "Does your fine theory explain why the Mzeshi *are* orthodox? You brought them up, now account for them. By your rules they should have taken their doctrine from the heretic Vaspurakaners, who were the first people close to them to follow Phos, even if wrongly."

"An interesting question," the physician admitted. After thinking a bit, he said slowly, "I would say they are orthodox for the same reason the Vaspurakaners aren't."

"There you go, speaking in paradoxes again," Skylitzes growled.

"These Greeks are made for talking circles round a body," Viridovix put in.

"To the crows with both of you. There is no paradox. Look, Vaspurakan liked Videssos' religion, but was afraid the influence of the Empire would come with its priests. So the 'princes' worked out their own form of the faith, which satisfied them and kept the Empire at arm's length. But Vaspurakan was to the Mzeshi what Videssos was to Vaspurakan: a land with attractive ideas to borrow, but maybe risky to their freedom, too. So they decided for orthodoxy. Videssos is too far away to be dangerous to them."

Skylitzes wore a grimace of concentration as he worked that through, but Goudeles, who had been quiet till now, said,

"I like it. It makes sense. And not only does it show why the Mzeshi are orthodox and the 'princes' not, it also makes clear why Khatrish, Thatagush, and Namdalen keep clinging to their own pet heresies."

"Why, so it does," Gorgidas said. "I hadn't thought of that. Well, a good theory should be able to cover a wide range of cases." He paused and waved back toward the varied groups of new allies. "Erzerum is a wide range of cases by itself."

Arigh said, "To me this history of yours only makes so much fancy talk. I'm just glad the one thing all these hillmen can get together on is hating Yezd."

"Right you are," Skylitzes said, and the others nodded. Though most of the Yezda had roared east against Vaspurakan and Videssos, enough raiders had pushed north to rape and loot and kill among the Erzrumi valleys that the locals, whatever tiny nation they might claim, welcomed Yezd's foes. That was the only reason Arigh could control them at all. Hitting back was too sweet a prospect to jeopardize with their own petty quarrels.

The Arshaum waved for a messenger. "Fetch me, hmm, let's see, Hamrentz of the Khakuli. Let's see what he can tell us about these horsemen ahead." The riders were still deploying along their stream; through the dust their mounts kicked up, the sun glinted off spearpoints.

Hamrentz, whose holding lay a couple of days' ride north, was a thin, gloomy man with enormous hands. He wore a mail coif, but the rest of his armor was a knee-length shirt of leather covered with bone scales. Though he spoke some Videssian, he followed the Four Prophets of Makuran and had lines from their writings tattooed on his forehead.

When Arigh put the question to him, his doleful features grew even longer; one of his verses almost disappeared in a deep fold of skin. "This is—how would you say?—the Vale of the Fellowship. So they call it here, let me say. They are no cowards. I give them so much. I have seen them fight. But to their neighbors they are the—" He used a guttural obscenity in his own language, adding an equally filthy gesture.

Arigh repeated the scurrility with a grin. It was one to fill the mouth and soothe the angry spirit. "I know that's foul," he said. "What exactly does it mean?"

"What it says, of course," Hamrentz said. "In this language, I do not know the words." He seemed offended. The rest of his answers were hardly more than grunts. "You will find out, and then you will understand," he finished cryptically, and rode off.

Arigh looked at his advisors, who shrugged one by one. Goudeles said, "You might summon one of the others."

"Why waste my time when I can see for myself? Come along, if you care to." The Arshaum raised his voice. "Narbas, to us! The further south we get, the more of these people speak Vaspurakaner."

They hoisted the truce sign and trotted down toward the stream. Behind them, several Erzrumi contingents erupted in hisses, catcalls, and the whistles some of the hillmen used for jeers. Viridovix scratched his head. "You'd think these Fellowship laddies the greatest villains left unkilled, sure and you would, the way the carry on. To see 'em, though, why, they're better-seeming soldiers than half we have wi' us."

The troops drawn up on the far side of the little river were indeed disciplined-looking, well-horsed, and well-armored in crested helms, mail shirts under surcoats, and bronze greaves. They numbered archers as well as lancers. The Arshaum scouts, not wanting to start a war by accident, were keeping a respectful distance from the border stream.

A few of the locals nocked arrows or let their horses move a couple of paces forward as Arigh's party drew close, but in the center of their line a black-bearded giant in an orange coat nodded to his companion, a younger man whose surcoat matched his. The latter blew three bright notes from a coiled horn. At once the horsemen settled back into watchful waiting.

Perhaps drawn by the action of the leaders, Viridovix ran an eye down the line. "Will you mark that, now? Pair by pair they are, matched by their coats." The others saw he was right. One pair wore light green, the next scarlet, then ocher, then the deep blue of woad; remembering a tunic of that exact shade he had once owned, the Celt ached for his lost forests.

"How quaint," Goudeles said, with the disdain he showed any non-Videssian custom. "I wonder what it might signify."

Gorgidas felt himself go hot, then cold. He was suddenly sure he understood Hamrentz's obscenity. In a way he hoped he did, in a way not; if not altogether satisfying, his life had been simple for some time now. Were he right, it might not long stay so.

He had only a moment to reflect; with a sudden toss of his head, the big man in orange spurred forward into the stream, which proved only belly-deep on his mount. Without a second thought, his comrade with the horn followed. Cries of alarm rang along the line. The big man shouted them down.

With his size and his horse's—it was one of the big-boned mountain breed—he towered over Arigh. But the Arshaum, backed by a much bigger army, met his stare with a king's haughtiness; he had learned a great deal, treating with the Erzrumi. The local gave a rumbling grunt of approval. He said something in his own language. Arigh shook his head. "Videssian?" he asked.

"No," the black-bearded chief said; it seemed the only word he knew. He tried again, this time in throaty Vaspura-kaner. Narbas Kios translated: "The usual—he wants to know who we are and what in the name of Wickedness we're doing here."

"They follow the Four Prophets, then," Skylitzes said, recognizing the oath.

"In the name of Wickedness it is, with Avshar and all," Viridovix said.

"Aye." Arigh began to explain their goal. When he said "Yezd," both the locals growled; the younger one reached for the spiked mace on his hip. Thanks to Gunib and the other forts in the passes, the only nomads they had seen were Yezda raiders from the south, and thought Arigh was identifying himself as one. They laughed when Kios made them understand their mistake. "All we ask is passage and fodder," Arigh said. "You can see from the bands with my men that we did not plunder their countryside. We'll all loot to glut ourselves in Yezd."

Black-Beard jerked his chin toward the Erzrumi with the Arshaum. "I care not a turd for them. But," he admitted, "they are a sign you tell some of the truth." He could not keep a glow from his eyes, the glow that comes to any hillman's face when he thinks of the booty to be taken in the flatlands below.

He shook himself, as if awaking to business from a sweet dream. "You have given your names; let it be a trade. Know me to be Khilleu, prince of the Sworn Fellowship of the Yrmido. This is Atroklo, my—" He dropped back into his own tongue. Atroklo, who by the fuzziness of his beard could not have been far past twenty, smiled at the prince when his name was mentioned.

Gorgidas knew that smile, had felt it on his own face years —a lifetime!—ago, before he left provincial Elis for Rome and whatever it might offer. No, he thought, his life would not be the same.

Khilleu was laughing in his beard; his face was heavy-featured but open, a good face for a leader. "So you'd poke the Yezda, eh? I like that, truly I do."

Atroklo broke in in their language, his voice, surprisingly, not much lighter than his chieftain's bass. Khilleu pursed his lips judiciously and gave an indulgent wave, as if to say, "You tell it." Atroklo did, in halting Vaspurakaner: "That wizard you speak—spoke—of, I think he pass through here."

From the way all eyes swung toward him, he might have been a lodestone. He reddened with the almost invisible flush of a swarthy man, but plowed ahead with his story. "Four days ago we find in field a black stallion, dead, that none of us knows." He had given up on the past tense of his verbs. "It is a fine horse once, I think, but used to death. Used past death, I mean—never I see an animal so worn. A skeleton, lather long caked on sides, one hoof with no shoe and down to bloody nub. Cruel, I think then. Now I think maybe magic or desperate, or both. No tackle is with this dead horse, and next day our noble Aubolo finds two of his best beasts missing. Who thief is, he does not know then and does not know now."

"Avshar!" Arigh's companions exclaimed together; it was, Gorgidas thought, becoming a melancholy chorus. "Four days!" the Arshaum chief said bitterly. "See, we've lost another two to him. These Erzrumi can't stay with us; they only slow us down."

Khilleu had watched them closely; attitudes spoke for much, even if he could not follow their talk. He and Atroklo dropped into a low-voiced colloquy in the Yrmido tongue. The prince returned to Vaspurakaner. "I begin to believe you," he said, looking straight at Arigh. "We too have suffered from the southern jackals, more than once. I ask you two questions: Would you have the Sworn Fellowship at your side? And will our charming neighbors," he continued, irony lurking in that resonant bass, "bear with our coming?"

"As for the first, why not? One Erzrumi slows us as much as a thousand, and you look to have good men. As for the other, Hamrentz of the Khakuli said you were no cowards."

"Among other things," Atroklo guessed. His laugh and Khilleu's did not sound amused.

"Here's another argument for you, then," Sklyitzes put in. "These Arshaum here outnumber all the hillmen with us three to one."

"A point," Khilleu said. He spread his hands. "In the end, what choice have I? You have not three, but ten times my numbers. Oh, we could hold out in our keeps if we would, but stop your passage? No." Again, his chuckle was grim. "So I will leap on the snow leopard's back, hold onto its ears, and pray to the Four to petition the kindly gods not to let it turn aside for my sheep."

Atroklo blew a different call on his horn; Gorgidas watched a vein pulse at his temple. He must have played the signal for truce. The Sworn Fellowship abandoned their defensive stand at the edge of the stream and formed up into a long column.

"You will answer to me if you betray us," Khilleu warned Arigh. "Tell that to Hamrentz and the rest, too; for all your numbers, I vow it."

"No," Arigh said. "I will tell them they will answer to me."

"Spoken like a king!" Khilleu cried when Narbas translated. "I would have bid you to a feast at my keep this night for my own honor's sake, but now I see I may enjoy the evening. Bring all these here. Invite my neighbor chiefs, too; some may come." Wry mirth edged his voice. "There will be pleasures for every taste, not merely our own."

"I will eat with you outside your castle, but not in it," Arigh answered. He did not need Goudeles' hisses or Sky-litzes' surreptitious wave to make him wary of the squat, square pile of masonry toward which the Yrmido chief was pointing.

Atroklo started an angry exclamation, but Khilleu cut him off. "Can't say I blame you," he told the Arshaum. "My Lio is a strong keep; if I intended mischief, I could hole up there for ten years. Outside it will be—at sunset? Good. Best your men camp here—not only, I admit, because there is good water, but also to keep as much distance between you and my people as we can."

He waited, watching Arigh narrowly, ready to judge his sincerity by how he reacted. "Till sunset," was all the nomad said. He wheeled his horse, leaving Khilleu to make the best of the economical plains style.

Hamrentz, whose respect for the Yrmido was grudging but real, agreed to banquet with them, as did Gashvili, who owned frankly that he knew nothing about them for good or ill. The other Erzrumi leaders said no, with varying degrees of horror. One, Zromi of the Redzh, took up his hundred horsemen and rode from home at the thought of the Yrmido joining the expedition. "Good riddance," Skylitzes said. "We gain more here than we lose, seeing the last of his band of thieves."

Though troopers stayed on the walls of Lio, its drawbridge came down. Retainers kept scurrying in and out of the castle, running up trestle tables and benches outside the moat. Cookfires smoked in the castle forecourt. Along with the reek of the midden, the breeze brought the savory smell of roasting mutton. Viridovix' nostrils twitched of their own accord; he patted his belly in anticipation.

But appetite did not keep him from carefully inspecting the arrangements as Arigh's party rode up through ripening fields of wheat and barley. He found himself satisfied. "If they were after mischief, now," he said, tethering his horse, "they'd put us all together in a body instead of amongst their own. Then archers on the wall could hardly be missing us, e'en in sic torchlight as this. As is, they'd be apt to shoot holes in their chiefs, the which'd win 'em no thanks, I'm thinking."

"Hardly," Gorgidas answered. He brushed a bit of lint from his embroidered tunic, wishing the grease spot on his trousers had come cleaner. He was in Videssian dress; the last thing he wanted tonight was for the Yrmido to take him for a steppe nomad.

There was courtesy, if no more, in the greeting Khilleu and Atroklo gave their guests. The two of them seemed inseparable friends. They rose together to bow the newcomers to their places. Viridovix found himself between a chunky Yrmido a few years older than he was and a lean one a few years younger. The one knew a couple of words of Khamorth, the other none. Both were politely curious about his strange looks, but went back to their wine when they found they could not understand him.

He raised his pewter mug and a serving girl filled it. He watched her hips work as she moved away. After Seirem he had vowed he would stay womanless for life, a promise easy enough to keep in the Arshaum army as it traveled across the plains. But time wore away at grief, and his body had its own demands. When a wench among the Mzeshi made her interest plain, he had not backed away. Half a night behind a haystack was a small thing; it could not erase what he had known before.

No women of quality sat with the men. Most of the Erzrumi held to that custom, perhaps borrowed from Makuran. Used to the freer ways of the nomads, Viridovix missed them. Just by being there, they livened a gathering.

Gorgidas also noted their absence and drew his own conclusions from it. There was a pair of Yrmido to either side of him, one set somber in black slashed with silver, the other gaudy in scarlet and yellow. None of them shared a language with him. He sighed, resigning himself to a long evening. The maid who served him wine smiled invitingly. His answering look was so stony that she tossed her head in disdain.

Unexpectedly, one of the men across the table spoke in accented Videssian: "May I this tongue on you practice? When I a lad was, I served two years as hired soldier in the Empire before my brother died and I his holding inherited. I Rakio am called."

"Glad to know you," Gorgidas said heartily, and gave his own name. Rakio, he judged, was in his late twenties. Neither handsome nor the reverse, his face had character to it, with a beard trimmed closer than the usual Yrmido style, a chipped tooth his smile showed, and a nose whose imperious thrust was offset by an eyebrow that kept quirking whimsically upward. Pleasant fellow, the Greek thought.

Then the food appeared, and he forgot Rakio for some time. His year on the steppe had made him all too used to lamb and goat, though it was enjoyable to have them broiled with cloves of garlic rather than hastily roasted over a dung fire. But peas, spinach, and steamed asparagus were luxuries he had almost forgotten, and after months of flat, chewy wheatcakes, real bread, still soft and steaming from the ovens, brought him close to ecstasy.

He let his belt out a notch. "That was splendid."

Rakio was grinning at him. "I once had to eat with a squad of Khamorth," the Yrmido said. "I how you feel know."

The Greek poured a small libation on the ground and raised his mug high. "To good food!" he cried, and drank. Laughing, Rakio emptied his own cup. So did Goudeles, a couple of tables away. The plump bureaucrat's ears were as sharp as his pleasure in eating.

A minstrel wandered among the feasters, accompanying his songs with the plangent notes of a pandora. A juggler kept half a dozen daggers in the air, his hands a blur of speed. Someone tossed him a coin. He caught it without dropping a knife. Two dancers carrying torches leaped back and forth over upturned swords.

When the girl with the wine came past again, Viridovix slid an arm around her waist. She did not pull away, but smiled down at him. She put out a forefinger to stroke his fiery mustache, not the first time his coloring had drawn a woman's eye in these dark-haired lands. He nibbled at her fingertip. She snuggled closer.

Khilleu boomed something in Vaspurakaner. The men who spoke that tongue shouted agreement. Narbas Kios said to the Gaul, "He asks you not to take her away for tumbling until she's emptied her jug."

"Only fair, that." Viridovix patted the girl's rump. "Soon, my pretty," he murmured. Without a word in common, she understood him. Arigh had already contrived to disappear into the night with the buxom wench who had fetched meat to his table. Gashvili and Vakhtang were gone, too. Khilleu looked on benignly, glad his guests were contented. No Yrmido had left.

Gorgidas let his own serving wench pass by again. Rakio's eyebrows rose. "She does not you please? You would prefer another? Fatter? Thinner? Younger, perhaps? We would not you have lonely." His concern sounded real.

"My thanks, but no," the physician said. "I do not care for a woman tonight."

Rakio gave a comic shrug, as if to say the foreigner was mad, but perhaps harmlessly so. Gorgidas stared down at his hands. He knew what he wanted to say, but had no notion of how to say it without risking grave offense. Yet he was so sure. . . .

He gave up on the dilemma for the moment when another

servitor brought a tray of candied fruit. But that was soon done. The thing could be avoided no longer, unless he had not the nerve to broach it at all.

He felt his heart pound as though he were a nervous youth. Through a dry mouth he said, as casually as he could, "There are many fine pairs of your men here tonight."

Rakio caught the faint emphasis on "pairs." This time the eyebrow went up like a warning flag. "Most foreigners would say that we foul vices practice." The Yrmido regarded Gorgidas with the suspicion years of outsiders' despisal had ingained in his people.

"Why should that be?" Remembering Platon's golden words, Gorgidas gave them back as well as he was able: "If the man who loves is caught doing something ugly, he would sooner be caught by anyone, even his father, than by his lover. And because lovers, feeling this way, would do anything rather than show cowardice before each other, and would do their best to spur each other on in battle, an army of them, however small it was, might conquer the world."

It was said. With bleak courage, the Greek waited to be wrong, waited for Rakio to scorn him. The Yrmido's jaw dropped. He shut it with a snap and broke into excited speech in his own tongue. Then the men in black and silver on Gorgidas' left and the bright peacocks on his right were clasping his hand, pounding his back, pressing food and wine on him and shouting noisy toasts.

Relief washed over him like sweet rain. He disentangled himself from a bear hug, then jumped as someone he had not heard coming up behind him tapped him on the shoulder. Viridovix grinned down at him. "Friendlier they are to you than they were for me, and you such a sobersides and all."

Gorgidas nodded at the girl on the Gaul's arm, who was plainly impatient at the delay. "To each his own."

"Och, aye, and this one's mine. Are you not, my sweet colleen?" She shrugged at his words, but giggled when he nuzzled her neck. He led her away from the feast, then let her find a quiet spot for the two of them. There was a stand of apple trees just out of bowshot from the castle of Lio and in the middle of it, the Gaul discovered, a small grassy patch. He spread his cloak with a flourish; the grass was soft as any bed, and sweeter-smelling.

The girl—he thought her name was Thamar—was eager

as he. They helped each other off with their clothes; she was smooth and soft and warm in his arms. They sank together to the cloak, but when he rose on knees and elbows to mount her she shook her head vehemently and let loose a torrent of incomprehensible complaint.

Finally, with gestures, she made him understand the Yrmido did not favor that style of lovemaking. "Well, whatever suits you, then," he exclaimed, spreading his hands in acquiescence. "I'm ever game for summat new."

She rode him reversed, her hands at either side of his calves. A drop of sweat fell on his thigh. It was, the Gaul thought, a different view of things. "Though indeed," he muttered to himself, "one a pederast might be finding more gladsome than I."

Then suddenly everything the Gaul had seen in the Yrmido country came together. He shouted laughter, so that Thamar looked back at him in mixed surprise and indignation. "Nay, lass, it's nought to do with you," he said, stroking her ankle.

But he was still chuckling. "Sure and I see why you're after doing it this way, is all," he said, as if she could understand his speech. "Och, that Gorgidas, the puir spalpeen! Puir like the cat that fell in the cream jar, I'm thinking. Where were we, now?" He applied himself with a will.

Gorgidas had got his hosts to grasp that he was no Videssian and told them something of how he had come to the Empire and of the customs of his lost homeland. Naturally, most of their questions centered on one area. With the contempt their neighbors had heaped on them for centuries, they found it astonishing past belief that an outsider could see them with sympathy.

The Greek spoke of the military companionships of Sparta, of Athens' more genteel ways, and at last of the Sacred Band of Thebes, whose hundred-fifty pairs of lovers had fallen to the last man against Philip of Macedon and his son, Alexander the Great.

That account brought his listeners, whose number had grown as the night wore on, close to tears. "How then?" asked Rakio, who had been interpreting. "Did they show outrage to their bodies?"

"In no way," Gorgidas answered. "When Philip saw that all of them had taken their death wounds in front, he said, 'Woe to those who think evil of such men.'"

"Ahh," said all the Yrmido when Rakio was done translating. They bent their heads in a moment of silent respect for the men almost three hundred years dead. Moved past speech himself, Gorgidas shared it with them.

After a time his unquenchable curiosity reasserted itself. He said, "You've listened to me. May I ask you in return how your own Sworn Fellowship came to be?"

Rakio scratched his head. "Came to be? Always it was. Since before the time of Fraortish, first of the blessed Four, it was."

That, Gorgidas knew, was another way of saying forever. He sighed, but not too deeply; there were more vital things than history. He said to Rakio, "Is your Sworn Fellowship all pairs, as the Theban Scared Band was? So it would seem, but for you, from the feasters here."

"More closely look. See over there—Pidauro and Rystheu and Ypeiro. They are a three-bond—and their wives with them, it is said. Another such there is, though tonight they are on patrol in the south. And there are a fair number such as myself. 'Orphans' we are named. I no life-partner yet have, but because I am my father's eldest son, I still when I reached manhood became a member of the Fellowship."

"Ah," the Greek said, annoyed at himself—seeing Rakio alone should have answered that for him. To hide his pique, he took a long drink of wine. It sent recklessness coursing through him. He said, "Will you not take offense at a personal question from an ignorant foreigner?" Rakio smiled for him to go on. He asked, "Are you an 'orphan' because you, ah, do not care to follow all the ways of the Fellowship?"

Rakio frowned in thought, then realized what Gorgidas, as an outsider, had to be trying to say. "Do I only like women, mean you?" He translated the question into his own language. All the Yrmido hooted with glee; someone threw a crust of bread at him. "I only am slow settling down," he said unnecessarily.

"So I gather," Gorgidas said, dry as usual.

That eyebrow of Rakio's was twitching again. This time, a look of frank speculation was on the Yrmido's face. Gorgidas dipped his head, then remembered how little that gesture meant to non-Greeks. He nodded slightly. When the torches round the feasting table guttered low, he and Rakio left hand in hand.

From the top of the pass the Erzrumi called the Funnel, the Arshaum and their allies could spy in the southwestern distance the river Moush. It sparkled like a silver wire, reflecting the afternoon sun. Beyond the green fertile strip along the bank of the stream lay the dun-colored flatlands where the Yezda ruled.

The plainsmen raised a cheer to see their goal at last, but Viridovix was not sorry when they started down the southern slope of the Funnel and that bare brown terrain disappeared once more. "A worse desolation it looks than the Videssian plateau," he said, "the which I hadna thought possible."

"It's desert away from water," Goudeles admitted, "but where the land is irrigated it can be fantastically rich. You'll see that, I'd say, in the valleys of the Tutub and the Tib—they raise three crops a year there."

"I dinna believe it," the Gaul said at once. Thinking of his own land's cool lush fruitfulness, he could not imagine this bake-oven of a country outdoing it, water or no.

But Skylitzes backed his countryman, saying, "Believe as you will; it's true regardless. They call the land between the Tutub and the Tib the Hundred Cities because it can support so many people. Or could, rather; it's fallen on evil times since the Yezda came."

"Honh!" Viridovix said through his nose. He changed the subject, asking "Where might Mashiz be, once we're after sacking these Hundred Cities o' yours?"

"It might be on the far side of the moon," Goudeles said, adding mournfully, "but it's not, worse luck. The cursed town is nestled in the foothills of the mountains of Dilbat, just west of the Tutub's headwaters."

When the army camped that night, the Celt drew lines in the dirt to help him remember what he had learned. He explained his scratchings to Gorgidas, who copied them on wax with quick strokes of his stylus. "Interesting." The Greek snapped his tablet closed. He said, "I'm off to the Yrmido camp. Their customs promise to make a worthwhile digression for my history."

"Do they now?" Viridovix tried not to laugh at how transparent his friend could be. The physician had used the same excuse three nights running. Twice he had not come back till past midnight; the other time he spent the whole night with the Sworn Fellowship.

"Well, yes," Gorgidas answered seriously. "Their account of the first Yezda incursion into Erzerum, for example—confound it, what are you smirking about?"

"Me?" The Celt aimed for a look of wide-eyed innocence, an expression which did not suit his face. He gave up and chortled out loud. "Sure and it's nae history alone you're finding with the Yrmido, else you'd not be sleeping like a dead corp and wearing that fool grin the times you're awake."

"What fool grin?" Viridovix' parody made the Greek wince. He threw his hands in the air. "If you already know the answer, why ask the question?"

"Begging your pardon I am," Viridovix said quickly, seeing the alarm that always came to Gorgidas when his preference for men was mentioned by someone who did not share it. "All I meant by it was that it's strange for fair, seeing a sour omadhaun like your honor so cheery and all."

"Go howl!" From long habit, the physician searched Viridovix for the sort of killing scorn the Yrmido met from all their neighbors. He did not find it, so he relaxed; it was not as though the Gaul had just discovered the way his habits ran.

Viridovix slapped him on the back, staggering him a little. On his face was honest curiosity. "Might you be telling me now, how do you find it after a year with women?"

"After a year my way, how would you find a wench?"

The Gaul whistled. "I hadna thought of it so. I'd marry her on the spot, beshrew me if I didn't."

"I'm in no danger of *that*," Gorgidas said, and they both laughed. There was more than one kind of truth in his words, though, the physician thought. Rakio would never come close to filling the place Quintus Glabrio had in his heart.

True, the Yrmido, like most of his countrymen, was brave to a fault, and he had the gift of laughter. But he was hopelessly provincial. Despite his travels in Videssos, he cared for nothing beyond his own valley, while for Gorgidas the whole world seemed none too big. And where Glabrio and Gorgidas had shared a common heritage, Rakio's strange syntax was the least reminder of how different his background was from the Greek's. Finally, the Yrmido

openly scoffed at fidelity. "Faithfulness for women is," he
had said to Gorgidas. "Men should enjoy themselves."

Enjoying himself the physician was. Let it last as long as it
would; for now it was good enough.

With their speed, the Arshaum expected to swarm over
the river Moush and into Yezd before its defenders were
ready to receive them. There again, they reckoned without
Avshar. The wizard-prince, still ahead of his enemies, had
given his followers warning. The boat-bridges leading north
into Erzerum had been withdrawn. Squadrons of nomad
horse patrolled the Moush's southern bank. Better-drilled
troops, men of Makuraner blood, guarded the river's ford
with catapults.

Against the advice of all the Erzrumi commanders, Arigh
tried to force one of the river-crossings in the face of the
Yezda artillery and was repulsed. The stonethrowers reached
across the Moush, which even his nomads' bows could not.
And the catapults shot more than stones. Jugs of incendiary
mix crashed among he Arshaum, splashing fire all about.
Horses and men screamed; there was nearly a panic before the
plainsmen drew back out of range.

Arigh shouldered the blame manfully, saying, "I should
have listened. They know more of this fighting with engines
than I do." He scratched at the pink, shiny scars on his cheek.
"From now on I will stay with what we do best. Let the Yezda
have to figure out how to meet me."

"That is a wise general speaking," said Lankinos Skylitzes,
and the Arshaum's eyes lit.

He proved as good as his word, taking advantage of the
plainsmen's mobility and skill at making do. Under cover of
night he sent a hundred Arshaum over the widest part of the
Moush, swimming with their horses and carrying arms and
armor in leather sacks tied to the beasts' tails. As soon as they
were across and starting to remount, the rest of their countrymen followed.

By sheer bad luck, a single Yezda spied the forerunners
just as they were coming out of the river. He raised the
alarm and managed to escape in the darkness. The Yezda
were steppemen themselves; they reacted quickly. The fight
that blew up was no less fierce for being fought half-blind.
The Arshaum struggled to expand their perimeter, while
their opponents battled to crush them and regain control of

the riverbank before the bulk of the army could cross.

Viridovix stripped naked and splashed into the Moush just after the advance force. Some of the Arshaum hooted at him. "What good will a sword do, when you can't see what to hit?" someone called.

"As much good as a bow," he retorted, "or are your darts after having eyes of their own?"

When his pony clambered up onto the southern bank of the Moush, he let go of its neck and armed himself with frantic haste. Not long ago he would have gone to a fight sooner than to a woman, most times, but that was gone forever. Yet the Yezda ahead were obstacles between him and Avshar. For that he would kill them if he could.

He could hear them shouting ahead as he mounted his pony and spurred toward the fighting. He understood their cries, or most of them; the dialect they spoke was not that far removed from the Khamorth tongue of Pardraya.

A rider appeared ahead of him, indistinct in the starlight. "Can you bespeak me, now?" he called in the speech he had learned in Targitaus' tent.

"Aye," the other horseman said, reining in. "Who are you?"

"No friend," Viridovix said, and slashed out. The Yezda fell with a groan.

An arrow snarled past the Gaul's ear. He cursed; it had come from behind him. "Have a care there, ye muck-brained slubberers!" he roared, this time in the Arshaum language. The cry in the alien tongue drew another Yezda to him. They fenced half by guess. Viridovix took a cut on his left arm and another above his knee before a double handful of Arshaum came galloping up and the Yezda fled.

His mates were beginning to give ground all along the line. The company that had happened to be close by was big enough to face Arigh's first wave, but more and more Arshaum were emerging, dripping, from the Moush and going into action. It was not the nomad way to fight a stand-up battle against superior numbers. The Yezda scattered, saving themselves but yielding the position.

It was too dark for signal flags. The *naccara* drum boomed. Arigh's messengers rode orders up and down the line: "Hurry west for the ford!" Picking their way over unfamiliar ground, the Arshaum obeyed. Their Erzrumi allies paced them on the far side of the Moush. The heavily armored mountaineers could not cross the river as easily as the plainsmen; it was up to the Arshaum to win them safe passage.

Viridovix hoped they would take the guards at the ford by surprise, but they did not. A ring of bonfires made the space round the enemy camp bright as day. Catapult crews stood to their weapons; darts, stones, and jars of incendiary were piled high by the engines. Cavalry in ordered rows waited for the Arshaum. The firelight gleamed from their corselets and lances. No irregulars these, but seasoned troops of the same sort Videssos produced, Makuraner contingents fighting for their land's new masters.

Arigh's white grin was all there was to see of him. "This will be easy—only a couple hundred of them. We can flatten them before they get reinforced." He confidently began deploying his men.

As he was sending messengers here and there, a single figure from the enemy lines rode out past the bonfires toward the Arshaum. He loomed against the flames, tremendous and proud. Viridovix' heart gave a painful leap; he was sure that huge silhouette had to belong to Avshar. Then the horseman turned his head and the Gaul saw his strong profile. A mere man, he thought, disappointed; the wizard-prince's mantlings would have hidden his face.

The rider came closer, brandishing his spear. He shouted something, first in a language Viridovix did not understand but took to be Makuraner, then in the tongue of Vaspurakan, finally in the Yezda dialect. The Celt could follow him there: "Ho, you dogs! Does any among you dare match himself against me? I am Gusnaph, called with good reason the Feeder of Ravens, and fourteen men I have struck down in the duel. Who among you will join them?"

He rode back and forth, arrogant in his might, crying his challenge again and again. The Arshaum murmured among themselves as those who understood translated for the rest. No one seemed eager to answer Gusnaph. Aboard his great horse, armored head to foot, he might as well have been a tower of iron. He laughed scornfully and made as if to return to his own lines.

Viridovix whooped and dug his heels into his pony's flanks. "Come back, you idiot!" he heard Skylitzes yell. "He has a lance to your sword!" The Gaul did not stop. Even with a won battle, he had leaped to fight Scaurus; had he not, the

fleeting thought went by, he would still be in Gaul. But he had
not hesitated then and did not now. An enemy leader slain was
worth a hundred lesser men.

Gusnaph turned, swung up his lance in salute, then lowered it and thundered at the Celt. He grew bigger with terrifying quickness. The spear was fixed unerringly on Viridovix'
chest, no matter which way he swerved.

At the last instant the Gaul feinted again, and again Gusnaph met the move—too well. The lancepoint darted past the
Celt's shoulder as their horses slammed together in collision.

Both men were thrown. They landed heavily. Viridovix
scrambled to his feet. He was faster than Gusnaph, whose
armor weighed him down. His lance lay under his thrashing
horse. He reached for a weapon at his belt—a shortsword, a
mace, a dagger; Viridovix never knew which. The Gaul
sprang forward. Gusnaph was still on one knee when his
sword crashed down. The Makuraner champion fell in the
dirt.

Following the custom of his own nation, Viridovix bent,
chopped, and raised Gusnaph's dripping head for the rest of
the enemy to see. He let out a banshee wail of triumph.
There was an awful stillness on the other side of the fires.

With the resilience of the nomad breed, Viridovix' pony
was on its feet and seemed unhurt, though Gusnaph's charger
was screaming enough to make the Celt think it had broken a
leg. The steppe animal shied from the smell of blood when he
approached it with his trophy.

He set the head down. "I've no gate to nail it to, any road,"
he said to himself. The pony side-stepped nervously, but let
him mount. He waved his sword to the Arshaum, who were
erupting in a cloudburst of cheers. "Is it summat else you're
waiting for, then?" he shouted.

The plainsmen advanced at the trot. Their foes hardly
waited for the first arrows to come arcing out of the night, but
fled, abandoning their tents, the catapults, and the ford. The
first hint of morning twilight was turning the sky pale when
Arigh stood on the bank of the Moush and waved to the
Erzrumi to cross.

They came over band by band, the water at the ford
lapping at their horses' flanks. Gorgidas crossed with the
Sworn Fellowship, just behind Rakio. In his boiled leather,
armed only with a *gladius*, he felt badly out of place among
the armored Yrmido, but he had discovered Platon was

right. He would do anything before he let his lover think him afraid.

The Yezda managed a counterattack at dawn, nomad archers fighting in the familiar style of the plains. But as they had only faced the Arshaum during the night, the Erzrumi took them by surprise. They shouted in dismay as the plainsmen's line opened out and the big mountain horses crashed down on them.

With the Yrmido, Gorgidas was at the point of the wedge. There were a few seconds of desperate confusion as the Sworn Fellowship and the rest of the Erzrumi speared Yezda out of the saddle and overbore their light mounts. Some fell on their side, too; an Yrmido just in front of the physician flew from his horse, his face bloodily pulped by a morningstar. His partner, tears steaming down his cheeks, killed the nomad who had slain him.

The Greek slashed at a Yezda. He thought he missed. It did not much matter. The advance rolled ahead.

Gashvili shouted something in Vaspurakaner to Khilleu. The lord of Gunib had a dent in his gilded helmet, but was undismayed. Khilleu, grinning, gave back an obscene gesture. "What was that?" Gorgidas asked Rakio, who was tying up a cut on the back of his hand.

"Says Gashvili, 'You damned fairies can fight.'"

"He's right," the Greek said with a burst of pride.

"Why not?" To Rakio, war came as naturally as breathing. He touched spurs to his horse, driving against the Yezda. Gorgidas' steppe pony snorted in affront when he spurred it, but followed.

Then, quite suddenly, the enemy was reeling away, each man fleeing to save himself, with no thought of holding together as a fighting force. The Arshaum and Erzrumi cheered each other till they were hoarse. The way clear before them, they pushed into Yezd.

VII

GAIUS PHILIPPUS SLAPPED AT A HORSEFLY BUZZING ROUND the head of the bony gray nag he was riding. It droned away. He growled, "I'm amazed this arse-busting chunk of buzzards' bait has enough life in it to draw flies. *Get* up, you mangy old crock! Make it to Amorion by sundown and you can rest."

He jerked on the reins. The gray gave him a reproachful look and came out of its amble for a few paces' worth of shambling trot. It blew until its skinny sides heaved, as if the exertion were too much for it. As soon as it thought it had satisfied him, it fell back into a walk. "Miserable gluepot," he said, chuckling in spite of himself.

"It's an old soldier, sure enough," Marcus said. "Be thankful it's not better—it didn't tempt the Yezda into trying to steal it."

"I should hope not!" Gaius Philippus said, taking perverse pride in his decrepit mount. "Remember that one whoreson who looked us over a couple of days ago? He fell off his pony laughing."

"As well for us," the tribune answered. "He was probably a scout for a whole band of them."

At that thought he slipped out of the bantering mood. The journey inland from Nakoleia was much worse that he had expected. The port was still in Videssian hands, but its hinterland swarmed with Yezda, who swooped down on farmers whenever they tried to work their fields. If the Empire had not kept the city supplied by sea, it could not have survived.

Most of the villages on the dirt track that led south were deserted, or nearly so. Even a couple of towns that had kept their ancient walls through the centuries of imperial peace now stood empty. The Yezda made growing or harvesting crops impossible, and so the towns, though safe from nomad siege, withered. He wondered how many had died when they were forced to open their gates, and how many managed to get away.

It occurred to him that the devastation the nomads were inflicting on the westlands had happened on a vastly greater scale long before, when the Khamorth swarmed off the edge of the steppe into Videssos' eastern provinces. He shook his head. No wonder those lands had fallen into the heresy of reckoning Skotos' power equal to that of Phos; evil incarnate must have seemed loose in the world.

A squad of horsemen came round a bend in the road, trotting briskly north. Their leader swung up an arm in warning when he caught sight of the Romans, then brought it down halfway as he recognized they were not Yezda. He rode up to inspect them. Scaurus saw that he had helmet, shortsword, and bow, but no body armor. His men were similarly equipped and mounted on a motley set of animals. The tribune had met their like on the road the day before— Zemarkhos' men.

The squad leader drew the sun-sign over his heart. Marcus and Gaius Philippus quickly imitated him; it would have been dangerous not to. "Phos with you," the Videssian said. He was in his late twenties, tall, stringy, scarred like a veteran, with disconcertingly sharp eyes.

"And with you," the tribune returned.

A tiny test had been passed; the Videssian's head moved a couple of inches up and down. He asked, "Well, strangers, what are you doing in the dominions of the Defender of the Faithful?" Having heard Zemarkhos' self-chosen title from the riders he had come across yesterday, Marcus did not blink at it.

"We're for the holy Moikheios' *panegyris* at Amorion," he said, giving the cover story he and Gaius Philippus had worked out aboard the *Seafoam*. "Maybe we can sign on as caravan guards with one of the merchants there."

The squad leader said, "That could be." He studied the tribune. "By your tongue and hair, you are no Videssian, but you do not look like a Vaspurakaner. Are you one of the Namdalener heretics?"

For once Marcus was glad of his blondness; though it marked him as a foreigner, it also showed he was not of the sort Zemarkhos' men killed on sight. He recited Phos' creed in the version the Empire used; the Namdaleni appended "On this we stake our very souls" to it, an addition which raised the hackles of Videssian theologians. Gaius Philippus followed his lead. He went through the creed haltingly, but got it right.

The horsemen relaxed and took their hands away from their weapons. "Orthodox enough," their chief said, "and no one will take it ill if you hold to that usage. Still, you'll find that many, out of respect for our lord Zemarkhos, add 'We also bless the Defender of thy true faith,' after 'decided in our favor.' As I say, it is optional, but it may make them think the better of you in Amorion."

"'We also bless the Defender of thy true faith,'" Scaurus and Gaius Philippus repeated, as if memorizing the clause. Zemarkhos, it seemed, had a perfectly secular love of self-aggrandizement, no matter how he phrased it. The tribune kept his face blank. "Thanks for the tip," he said.

"It's nothing," the Videssian answered. "Outlanders who come to the true belief of their own accord deserve to be honored. Good luck in town—we're off to watch for Yezda thieves and raiders."

"And filthy Vaspurakaners, too," one of his men added. "Some of the stinking bastards are still skulking around, for all we can do to root 'em out."

"That's not so bad," said another. "They make better sport than bustards, or even foxes. I caught three last winter." He spoke matter-of-factly, as he might of any other game. Scaurus' twinge of regret at his hyprocrisy over the creed disappeared.

The squad leader touched a forefinger to the rim of his helmet, nodded to the Romans, and started to lead his troops away. Gaius Philippus, who had been mostly silent till then, called after him. He paused. The senior centurion said, "I was through these parts a few years ago and made some good friends at a town called Aptos. Have the Yezda got it, or Zemarkhos?"

"It's ours," the Videssian said.

"Glad to hear it." Marcus suspected Gaius Philippus was

mostly worried about Nerse Phorkaina, the widow of the local noble; Phorkos had died at Maragha. She was the only woman the tribune had heard Gaius Philippus praise, but when the legionaires had wintered at Aptos the veteran did nothing at all to let her know his admiration. Fear of one sort or another, Marcus thought, found a place to root in everyone.

Amorion was no great city, even next to Garsavra, only a dusty town in the middle of the westlands' central plateau. Without the Ithome River, the place would have had no reason for being. But the only two times Marcus had seen it, it was jammed past overflowing, first by Mavrikios Gavras' army marching west toward disaster and now with the *panegyris*.

Twilight was descending when the Romans rode between the parallel rows of commercial tents outside the city. Thorisin had been right; in the crush they were just another pair of strangers. A merchant with the long rectangular face and liquid eyes of the Makuraners laughed in staged amazement at the price a Videssian offered him for his pistachioes. Half a dozen turbaned nomads from the desert south of the Sea of Salt—slender, big-nosed men with a family likeness— were packing up their incenses and quills of spice till morning. They had camels tethered back of their tent; Marcus' horse shied at the unfamiliar stink of them.

A priest dickered with a fat farmer over a mule. The rustic's respect for the blue robe was not making him drop his price any. Somehow a Namdalener merchant had found his way to Amorion with a packhorse-load of clay lamps. He was doing a brisk business. The priest bought one after the mule seller laughed in his face.

"I don't see *him* making it hot for heretics," Gaius Philippus remarked.

"Seems to me 'heretics' and 'Vaspurakaners' mean the same thing to Zemarkhos," Scaurus answered. "He's got himself and his people worked into such a froth about them that he has no time to stew over anybody else's mischief."

The senior centurion grunted thoughtfully. Caravan masters, lesser merchants, swaggering guardsmen, and bargain hunters represented a great sweep of nations, some heterodox, others outside Phos' cult altogether, yet every one of them carried on undisturbed by the clergy. But not a single Vaspurakaner was to be seen, although the land of the "princes"—as they called themselves—was not far north-west of Amorion, and although many of them had settled round the city after Yezda assaults made them flee Vaspura-kan. Zemarkhos' pogroms had done their work well.

The Romans rode past a caravan leader—a tall, wide, swag-bellied man with a shaved head, great jutting prow of a nose, and drooping black mustachioes almost as splendid as Viridovix'—cursing at a muleteer for letting one of his beasts go lame. He swore magnificently, in several lan-guages mixed to blistering effect; his voice was the bass crash of rocks thundering down a mountainside. By unspo-ken joint consent, Scaurus and Gaius Philippus pulled up to listen and admire.

The caravaneer spotted them out of the corner of his eye. He broke off with a shouted, "And don't let it happen again, you motherless wide-arsed pot of goat puke!" Then he put meaty hands on hips in a theatrical gesture that matched his clothes—he wore a maroon silk tunic open to the waist, baggy wool trousers dyed a brilliant blue tucked into gleaming black knee-high boots, a gold ring in his right ear, and one of silver in his left. Three of his teeth were gold, too; they spar-kled when he grinned at the Romans. "You boys have a prob-lem?"

"Only trying to remember what all you called him," Gaius Philippus said, grinning back.

"Ha! Not half what he deserves." A chuckle rumbled deep in the trader's chest. He gave the Romans a second, longer look. "You're fighters." It was not a question. With a broad-bladed dagger and stout, unsheathed cutlass on his belt, the caravaneer recognized his own breed. "I'm short a couple of outriders—are you interested? I'll take the both of you in spite of that horrible screw you're riding there, gray-hair."

"Why did you think I wanted your curses?" Gaius Phi-lippus retorted.

"Don't blame you a bit. Well, what say? It's a goldpiece a month, all you can eat, and a guardsman's share of the profits at the end of the haul. Are you game?"

"We may be back in a day or two," Marcus said; it would not do to refuse outright, for their story's sake. "We have business to attend to in town before we can make plans."

"Well, you can paint me with piss before I tell you I'll hold the spots, but if I haven't filled 'em by then, I'll still think about you. I'll be here—between the damn Yezda and all this hooplah over the Vaspurs, things are slow. Ask for me if you don't see me; I'm Tahmasp." The Makuraner name explained his slight guttural accent and his indifference to Zemarkhos' persecution, except where it interfered with trade.

Someone bawled Tahmasp's name. "I'm coming!" he yelled back. To the Romans he said, "If I see you, I'll see you," and lumbered away.

Gaius Philippus booted his horse in the ribs. "Come on, you overgrown snail." He said to Marcus, "You know, I wouldn't half mind serving under that big-nosed bastard."

"Never a dull moment," Scaurus agreed. The centurion laughed and nodded.

At any other time of the year Amorion would have shut down with nightfall, leaving its winding, smelly streets to footpads and those few rich enough to hire link-bearers and bodyguards to hold them at bay. But during the *panegyris* of the holy Moikheios, the town's main thoroughfare blazed with torches to accomodate the night vigils, competing choirs, and processions with which the clergy celebrated their saint's festival.

"Buy some honied figs?" called a vendor with a tray slung over his shoulder. When Marcus did, the man said, "Phos and Moikheios and the Defender bless you, sir. Here, squeeze in beside me and grab yourselves a place—the big parade'll be starting before long." The Defender again, was it? The tribune frowned at the hold Zemarkhos had on Amorion. But he had an idea how to break it.

Practical as always, Gaius Philippus said, "We'd best find somewhere to stay."

"Try Souanites' inn," the fig seller said eagerly. He gave rapid directions, adding, "I'm called Leikhoudes. Mention my name for a good rate."

To make sure I get my cut, Marcus translated silently. Having no better plan, he made Leikhoudes repeat the directions, then followed them. To his surprise, they worked. "Yes, I have something, my masters," Souanites said. It proved to be piles of heaped straw in the stable with their horses at the price of a fine room, but Scaurus took it without argument. Each stall had a locking door; Souanites might see his place near empty the rest of the year, but he made the most of the *panegyris* when it came.

After they stowed their gear and saw to their animals, Gaius Philippus asked, "Do you care anything about this fool parade?"

"It might be a chance to find out what we're up against."

"Or get nailed before we're started," Gaius Philippus said gloomily, but with a sigh he followed the tribune into the street.

They took a wrong turn backtracking and were lost for a few minutes, but the noise and lights of the main street made it easy to orient themselves again. They emerged a couple of blocks down from where they had turned aside to go to Souanites' and promptly bumped into the fig seller, who had been working his way through the gathering crowd. His tray was nearly empty. he spread his hands apologetically. "I'm sorry I no longer have such a fine view to offer you."

"We owe you a favor," Marcus said. With Leikhoudes between them, he and Gaius Philippus elbowed their way to the front of the crowd. They won some black looks, but Scaurus was half a head taller than most of the men and Gaius Philippus, though of average size, did not have the aspect of one with whom it would be wise to quarrel. Leikhoudes exclaimed in delight.

They were just in time, though the first part of the procession left the Romans fiercely bored. The company of Zemarkhos' militia drew cheers from their neighbors, but looked ragged, ill-armed, and poorly drilled to Marcus. They held the Yezda off with holy zeal, not the spit and polish that made troops impressive on parade. Nor was the tribune much impressed by the marching choruses that followed. For one thing, even his insensitive ear recognized them as rank amateurs. For another, most of their hymns were in the archaic language of the liturgy, which he barely understood.

"Are they not splendid?" Leikhoudes said. "There! See, in the third row—my cousin Stasios the shoemaker!" He pointed proudly. "Ho, Stasios!"

"I've never heard any singers to match them," Scaurus said.

"Aye, but plenty to better them," Gaius Philippus added, but in Latin.

Another chorus went by, this one accompanied by pipes, horns, and drums. The din was terrific. Then came a group of Amorion's rich young men on prancing horses with manes decorated by ribbons and trappings bright with gold and silver.

The noise of the crowd turned ugly as a double handful of half-naked men in chains stumbled past, prodded along by more of Zemarkhos' irregulars with spears. The prisoners were stocky, swarthy, heavily bearded men. "Phos-cursed Vaspurakaners!" Leikhoudes screeched. "It was your sins, your beastly treacherous heresy that set the Yezda on us all!" The crowd pelted them with clods of earth, rotten fruit, and horse-dung. In a transport of fury, Leikhoudes hurled the last of his figs at them.

Marcus set his jaw; beside him Gaius Philippus shifted his feet and swore under his breath. They had no hope of making a rescue; to try would get them ripped to pieces by the mob.

The growls around them turned to cheers. "Zemarkhos! His Sanctity! The Defender!" With neighbors watching, no one dared sound halfhearted.

Before the fanatic priest marched the parasol bearers who symbolized power to the Videssians, as the lictors with their rods and axes did in Rome. Marcus whistled when he counted the flowers of blue silk. Fourteen—even Thorisin Gavras was only entitled to twelve.

As if oblivious to the adulation he was getting, Zemarkhos limped down the street, looking neither right nor left. His gaunt features were horribly scarred, as were his hands and arms. Limp and scars both came from the big prick-eared hound that paced at his side.

The hound was called Vaspur, after the legendary founder of the Vaspurakaner people. Zemarkhos had named it long before Maragha, to taunt the Vaspurakaner refugees who fled to his city. Finally Gagik Bagratouni had his fill of such vilification. He caught priest and dog together in a great sack, then kicked the sack. Striking out in pain and terror, Vaspur's jaws had done the rest.

Marcus, who had been at Bagratouni's villa, had persuaded the *nakharar* to let Zemarkhos out, fearing his death as a martyr would touch off the persecution the priest had been fomenting. Maybe it would have, but looking back, the tribune did not see how things could have gone worse for the "princes." He wished he had let Vaspur finish tearing Zemarkhos' life away.

The hound paused, growling, as it padded past the

Romans. The hair stood up along its back. It had been close to three years, and the beast had only taken their scent for a few minutes; could it remember? For that matter, would Zemarkhos know them again if he saw them? Scaurus suddenly wished he were a short brunet, to be less conspicuous in the crowd.

But the dog walked on, and Zemarkhos with it. The tribune let out a soft sigh of relief. The priest had been dangerous before, but now he carried an aura of brooding power that made Marcus wish he could raise his hackles like Vaspur. He did not think mere temporal authority had put that look on Zemarkhos' ruined features; something stranger and darker dwelt there. By luck, it was directed inward now, growing, feeding on the priest's fierce hate.

Still shouting, "Phos watch over the Defender," the crowd fell in behind Zemarkhos as he made his way into Amorion's central forum. They swept Scaurus and Gaius Philippus with them. More Videssians filled the edges of the square; the newcomers pushed and shoved to find places.

The spear-carrying guards forced their Vaspurakaner captives into the middle of the forum. They released the ends of the chains they held. One took a short-handled sledge from his belt and secured each prisoner by staking those free ends to the ground. A couple of the Vaspurakaners tugged at their bonds, but most simply stood, apathetic or apprehensive.

The guards moved away from them in some haste.

Zemarkhos limped toward the prisoners. Beside him, Vaspur barked and snarled, showing gleaming fangs. "Is he going to set the hound on them?" Gaius Philippus muttered in disgust. "What did they do to him?"

Marcus expected the dog to go for the prisoners in vengeance for Bagratouni's treatment of Zemarkhos. That made a twisted kind of sense. But at the priest's command it sat next to him. Zemarkhos' profile was predatory as a hunting hawk's as he focused his will on the Vaspurakaners.

He extended a long, clawlike finger in their direction. The crowd quieted. The priest quivered; Scaurus could fairly see him channeling the force that boiled within him. In a way, he thought, it was an obscene parody of the ritual healer-priests used to gather their concentration before they set to work.

But Zemarkhos did not intend to heal. "Accursed, damned,

and lost be the Vaspurakaner race!" he cried, his shrill voice searing as red-hot iron. "Deceitful, evil, mad, capricious, with wickedness twice compounded! Malignant, treacherous, beastly, and obstinate in their foul heresy! Accursed, accursed, accursed!"

At every repetition, he stabbed his finger toward the captives. And at every repetition, the crowd bayed in bloodthirsty excitement, for the Vaspurakaners writhed in torment, as if lashed by barbed whips. Two or three of them screamed, but the noise was drowned in the roar of the crowd.

"Accursed be the debased creatures of Skotos!" Zemarkhos screeched, and the prisoners fell to their knees, biting their lips against anguish. "Accursed be their every rite, their every mystery, abominable and hateful to Phos! Accursed be their vile mouths, which speak in blasphemies!" And blood dripped down into the Vaspurakaners' beards.

"Accursed be these wild dogs, these serpents, these scorpions! I curse them all, to death and uttermost destruction!" With as much force as if he cast a spear, he shot his finger forward again. Their faces contorted in terror and agony, their eyes starting from their heads, the Vaspurakaners flopped about on the ground like boated fish, then subsided to twitching and finally stillness.

Only then did Zemarkhos, unwholesome triumph blazing in his eyes, stalk up to them and spurn their bodies with his foot. The crowd, fired to the religious enthusiasm that came all too readily to Videssians, shouted its approval. "Phos guard the Defender of the Faithful!" "Thus to all heretics!" "The true faith conquers!" One loud-voiced woman even cried out the imperial salutation: "Thou conquerest, Zemarkhos!"

The priest gave no sign the acclaim moved him. Urging Vaspur to his feet, he limped off toward his residence. He fixed his unblinking stare on the crowd and said harshly, "See to it you fall not into error, nor suffer your neighbor to do so."

His people, though, were used to his unbending sternness and cheered him as though he had granted them a benediction. They streamed out of the plaza, well pleased with the night's spectacle.

As they were making their way back to their meager lodgings, Gaius Philippus turned to Marcus and asked, "Are you sure you want to go through with what you planned?"

"Frankly, no." The strength of Zemarkhos' wizardry, fueled with a fanatic's zeal and a tyrant's rage, daunted the tribune. He walked some paces in silence. At last he said, "What other choice do I have, though? Would you sooner be an assassin, sneaking through the night?"

"I would," Gaius Philippus answered at once, "if I didn't think they'd catch us afterward. Or, more likely, before. But I'm glad I'm no big part of your scheme."

Marcus shrugged. "The Videssians are a subtle folk. What better to confound them with than the obvious?"

"Especially when it isn't," the veteran said.

Dawn the next day gave promise of the ferocious heat of the Videssian central plateau, the kind of heat that would quickly kill a man away from water. The horse trough in which Scaurus washed his head and arms was blood-warm.

He had no appetite for the loaf he bought from the innkeeper. Gaius Philippus finished what was left after polishing off his own. It was not, Marcus knew, that the other felt easier because he was sure of his safety. Had their roles been reversed, the unshakable centurion would not have eaten a bite less.

They stayed in the shade of the stable until early afternoon, drawing curious glances from the horseboys and the guests who came in to take their beasts.

When the shadows started to grow longer again, Marcus unpacked his full Roman military kit and donned it all—greaves, iron-studded kilt, mail shirt, helmet with high horsehair crest, scarlet cape of rank. Even in the shadows, he began to sweat at once.

Gaius Philippus, still in cloth, clambered aboard his spavined gray. He led the tribune's saddled horse after him as he emerged from the stable and leaned down to clasp hands with Scaurus. "I'll be ready at my end, not that it'll make any difference if things go wrong. The gods with you, you great bloody fool."

A good enough epitaph, Marcus thought as the senior centurion clopped away. His own progress was as leisurely as he could make it; in armor under that blazing sun he understood, not for the first time, how a lobster must feel boiled in its shell.

He collected a crowd of small boys before he got to Amorion's chief street. The youngsters had grown used to soldiers, but not ones so resplendent as he. He gave out coppers with a free hand; he wanted to attract all the notice he could. He asked, "Is Zemarkhos preaching today?"

Some of the lads perked up at mention of the priest, while others watched the tribune with blank faces; not through love alone did Zemarkhos rule Amorion. One of the boys who had smiled said, "Aye, so he is, sir. He talks in the plaza every day, he do."

"Thanks." Scaurus gave him another coin.

"Thank *you*, sir. Are you going to go listen to him? I can see, sir, you've come from far away, maybe even just to hear him? Isn't he a marvel? Have you ever run across his like?"

"That I haven't, son," the Roman said truthfully. "Yes, I'm going to listen to him. I may," he went on, "even speak with him."

The corpses of the Vaspurakaners still lay in their agonized postures in the center of the square. They did nothing to slow the furious buying and selling of the *panegyris*, which went on all around them. Two rug sellers had set up stalls across from each other, and loudly sneered at one another's merchandise. A swordsmith worked a creaking grindstone with a foot pedal as he sharpened customers' knives. A plump matron examined herself in a merchant's bronze mirror, looking for flaws in the speculum and in her makeup. She put it down with a reluctant nod; the haggling began in earnest.

Sellers of wine, nuts, roasted fowls, ale, fruit juice, figs, little spiced cakes, and a hundred other delicacies wandered through the eager crowd, crying their wares. So did strongmen sweating under the great stones they had heaved over their heads, strolling musicians, acrobats—including one who walked on his hands and had a beggar's tin cup tied to his leg—trainers with their performing dogs or talking ravens, puppeteers, and a host of other mountebanks.

And so, for all Zemarkhos' ascetic prudery, did prostitutes, drawn with the other merchants to the *panegyris*' concentration of wealth. Marcus spied Gaius Philippus, well posted at the edge of the square, talking with a tall, dark-haired woman, attractive in a stern-faced way. Perhaps she reminded him of Nerse Phorkaina, the tribune thought. She slid her dress off one shoulder for a moment to show the centurion her breasts. Startled, Marcus laughed—perhaps she didn't, too.

As the street lad promised, Zemarkhos was exhorting a good-sized gathering. Flanked by several spear-carrying guardsmen, he stood, Vaspur at his side, behind a portable rostrum. He emphasized his points by pounding it with his fists. Scaurus did not need to have heard the first part of the harangue to know what it was about.

"They are Skotos' spawn," Zemarkhos was shouting, "seeking to corrupt Phos' untarnished faith through the vile mockery of it they practice in their heretical rites. Only by their destruction may right doctrine be preserved without blemish. Aye, and by the destruction of those deluded heresy-lovers in the capital, whose mercy on the disbelievers' bodies will be justly requited with torment to their souls!"

The audience cheered him on, crying, "Death to the heretics! Zemarkhos' curse take the hypocrites! Praise the wisdom of Zemarkhos the Defender, scourge of the wicked Vaspurakaners!"

Flicking his crimson cape round him, Marcus worked his way toward Zemarkhos' podium. He cut an impressive figure; people who turned to grumble as he pushed past them muttered apologies and stepped back to let him by. Soon he stood in the second or third row, close enough to see the veins bulging at Zemarkhos' throat and on his forehead as he ranted against his chosen victims.

"Anathema to those who spring from Vaspurakan, the root-stock of every impurity!" he screamed. "May they be cast into Skotos' outer darkness for their wicked inspirer to devour! They are the worst of all mankind, howling like wild dogs against our correct faith—hardhearted, stiff-necked, vain, and insane!"

Marcus pushed his way to the very front of the audience. "Rubbish!" he shouted, as loud as he could.

He heard gasps all around him. Zemarkhos' mouth was open for his next pronouncement. It hung foolishly for a moment as the priest gaped; it had been years since anyone opposed him. Then he waved to his guards. "Kill me this blasphemous oaf." Grinning, they stepped forward to obey.

"Yes, send your dogs to do your work," the Roman jeered. "Too stupid to learn, are you? Look what happened to you when you tried that with your precious Vaspur. You're a scrawny, murderous fraud and you deserve every scar you have."

Several people near Scaurus scrambled away, afraid they might somehow be tainted by his sacrilege. Vaspur snarled.

The guards, no longer grinning, hefted their spears in anger. The tribune set his hand to the hilt of his sword, but kept his eyes riveted on Zemarkhos. Confident in his own power, the priest gestured to his men again. They growled, but gave way.

"Very well, madman, let it be as you wish; you are as fit a subject as my other for the proof of Phos' power within me." Zemarkhos' eyes glittered with consuming hunger. As he measured Scaurus, his stare reminded the tribune of that of an old eagle, ready to stoop.

Then the zealot priest's eyebrows twitched, surprise returning humanity to his expression. "I know you," he rasped. "You are one of the barbarians who preferred the company of Vaspurakaners to my exposition of the truth. Your repentance will come late, but none the less certain for that."

"Of course I'd sooner have guested with them than with you. They're whole men, not twisted, venomous fanatics, 'hardhearted, stiff-necked, vain, and insane!'" Marcus quoted with insulting relish. The crowd gasped again; Zemarkhos jerked as if stung.

"'Whole men,' is it?" he returned. His stabbing finger darted at the Vaspurakaners he had slain. "There they lie, a mort of them, given over to death by Phos' just judgment."

"Horseshit. Any evil wizard could work the same, without taking Phos' mantle for himself in the bargain." The tribune sneered. "Phos' power! What nonsense! If you weren't so damned cruel, Zemarkhos, you'd be a joke, and a lame one at that. Go on, show everyone here Phos' power—if it comes through you, strike *me* dead with it."

"No need to beg," Zemarkhos said, his voice an eager whisper. "I will give you what you want." He did not move, but seemed nonetheless to grow taller behind the podium. Marcus could all but see the power he was summoning to himself. His eyes were two leaping back flames; his whole body quivered as he aimed his dart of malice.

His arm shot toward the tribune. Scaurus stumbled under the immaterial blow and wished for his *scutum* to hold up against it. His ears roared; his sight grew dark; agony filled his mind like the kiss of molten lead. He bit his lip till he tasted blood. Dimly he heard Zemarkhos' cackle of cruel, vaunting laughter.

But he held on to his sword, though he kept it in its

sheath. Zemarkhos' fanatic zeal powered his magic to a strength to match any Marcus had seen since he came to Videssos, but the druids' charms were equal to it. "You'll have to do better than that," he called to Zemarkhos, and stood straight once more.

The hatred on the priest's face was frightening, making him into something hardly human. He gathered all his might within him and loosed it in a single blast of will. This time, though, the Gallic blade's ward spells were already alive and easily turned aside the thrust. Scaurus barely flinched.

The tribune stretched his mouth into a grin. "I don't think Phos is paying much attention to you," he said. "Try again— maybe he's doing something important instead."

The crowd muttered at his effrontery, but also at Zemarkhos' failure. The priest readied another curse, but Marcus saw in his eyes the beginning of doubt, sorcery's fatal foe. The third attack was the weakest; the tribune felt vague discomfort, but did not show it.

"There—do you see?" he shouted to the folk around him. "This old vulture tells lies with every breath he takes!" He forbore to mention that he would have been lying dead in the dirt without his sword's unseen protection.

"You have sold your soul to Skotos and stand under his shield!" Zemarkhos shrieked, his voice cracking. His harsh features were greasy with sweat; he panted like a soldier after an all-day battle.

That was a cry to get Scaurus mobbed, but he was ready for it. "Hear the desperate liar, grabbing at straws! Do you not teach, Zemarkhos, that Phos will beat Skotos in the end? Or are you a Balancer all of a sudden, one of those Khatrisher heretics who do not profess that good is stronger than evil?"

At another time, the expression the priest wore might have been funny. He had thrown charges of heresy past counting, but never expected to catch one, or to see his very piety discredited. "Kill him!" he started to scream to his guardsmen, but a cabbage flew out of the crowd and caught him in the side of the head, sending him sprawling off the podium. Not all of Amorion had enjoyed living under his religious tyranny.

Nor had all hated it, either; the cabbage-flinger went down with a shriek as the man in front of him whirled and stabbed him in the side. He kicked savagely at the man he had knifed, then fell himself as the woman beside him smashed a clay water jug over his head.

"Dig up Zemarkhos' bones!" she screamed—the Videssian cry for riot. A hundred voices took up the call. A hundred more rose in horror, shouting, "Blasphemers! Heretic lovers!"

Zemarkhos scrambled to his feet. Two men rushed him, one swinging a chunk of firewood, the other barehanded. Growling horribly, Vaspur leaped for the first man's throat. He threw up his arms to protect himself. Vaspur tore them to the bone; the man dropped his club and fled, dripping blood. One of the priest's guards speared the unarmed man. He stared in amazement at the point in his belly, crumpled, and fell.

"Murderer! See the murderer!" that same woman cried. Her voice was loud and coarse as a donkey's bray and rang through the square. Before the guard could pull his pike free, she led the charge at him. He went down and did not get up. "Dig up Zemar—" Her cry was abruptly cut off as another guard reversed his spear and clubbed her with it. A moment later an uprooted paving stone dashed out his brains.

"Death to those who mock the Defender!" a wild-eyed youth shouted, and was fool enough to punch Marcus in his ironclad ribs. The tribune heard knuckles break. The young man howled. The tribune kicked him in the stomach before he could think of something worse to do; the youth folded up like a fan.

Armed, armored, and well-trained in the midst of rioting civilians, Scaurus enjoyed a tremendous edge. He swung his sword in great arcs, not so much to strike as to keep a little space around him. The sight of a yard of edged steel in the hands of someone who knew how to use it made even the most fiery zealot think twice. The tribune began slipping through the mob toward Gaius Philippus.

His worst worry was Zemarkhos' guardsmen, but the three or four of them still standing had all they could do holding the rioters back from their master. His curses now rained on the crowd that had followed him so long. But in civil strife as in battle, uproused passion went far to protect against magic. And as one intended victim after another did not drop, the priest's assurance failed him. He turned and fled, robe flapping about his shanks as he forced them into a hobbling run.

A fusillade of stones and rubbish followed him. Several missiles landed; he staggered and went to one knee. More struck the dog Vaspur. It howled and leaped as far as the chain Zemarkhos still held would let it. When the chain went taut the dog fell heavily, half-throttled.

Its snarl sent everyone close by scrambling back. The closest target for its fury was its master. Zemarkhos screamed "No!" as Vaspur sprang for him. The dog's teeth tore at his throat. The scream rose higher and shriller for a moment, then bubbled away to silence.

Zemarkhos' backers cried out in horror, but his foes raised a great hurrah. His death did nothing to end the riot. By then, everyone in the square had been hit from behind at least once and struck back blindly, keeping fights going and starting new ones. Some went through the crowd with more purpose, looking for old enemies to pay back.

The mob also began to realize no one would keep them from plundering whatever traders whose goods took their fancy. The first merchant's stall went over with a crash. Friends and foes of Zemarkhos forgot their quarrel and looted it together.

"Phos and no quarter!" bellowed a squat, brawny man in a butcher's leather apron. He rampaged through the crowd, heavy fists churning. Marcus wondered whose side he was on, and wondered if he knew himself.

Someone bludgeoned the tribune. His helmet took the worst of the blow, but he still staggered. He whirled by reflex and felt his sword bite. His attacker groaned, fell, and was trampled. He never did see the fellow.

Across the plaza, a disappointed looter cursed because all of a ring seller's best opals had already been stolen before he got a chance at them. "It's not fair!" he yelled, paying no attention to the jeweler who lay unconscious on the ground a few feet away, a thin stream of blood trickling down the side of his face.

"Cheer up," another man said. "There's bound to be better stuff in the merchants' tent city outside of town."

"You're right!" the first rioter exclaimed. "And most of those buggers are heretics or out-and-out heathens, so they must be fair game." He had been howling against Zemarkhos, but only because his brother-in-law had fallen victim to the priest. Now he filled his lungs and shouted, "Let's clean out those rich whoresons who come here just to cheat us every year!"

The cheers were like the baying of wolves. Brandishing torches and makeshift weapons, the mob streamed north through Amorion's streets, hot for loot. Most houses were slammed tight against the riot, but the tide of excitement swept more than a few men from them.

Marcus fought his way across the current toward Gaius Philippus. The veteran's *gladius* was in his scarred fist; his feet dangled outside the stirrups. Just before the tribune made it to him, a rioter tried to steal the roan he was leading. Disdaining the sword, the centurion raked out with his left foot. The nailed soles of his *caligae* shredded the Videssian's back. The man howled like a whipped dog; when he turned to run, Gaius Philippus sped him along with a well-aimed toe to the fundament.

As Scaurus mounted, the senior centurion scowled at him. He grumbled, "You could have waited a bit before you started the brawl. I might have had time for a quick one against the wall with that tart, but as soon as the ruction got going she ran off to lift whatever wasn't nailed down. Easier than friking, I suppose."

"Go howl." Marcus booted his horse forward. He took off his crested helmet and threw away his cape, trying to look as little like the man who had set Amorion aboil as he could.

It helped, but not as much as he wanted. "Pawn of Skotos!" an old bald man yelled, rushing at him with looted dagger in hand. But the tribune's horse was a trained warbeast from the imperial stables. It reared and struck out with iron-shod hooves. The man toppled, his knife flying through the air.

"This wretched slug I'm on would kill itself if it tried that," Gaius Philippus said envyingly. The gray was not at risk; one display was enough to make the rioters keep their distance. Undisturbed for the moment, the Romans rode the mob's current north.

"What now?" the senior centurion asked, shouting to be heard. "Back to Nakoleia?"

"I suppose so," Marcus said, but he still hesitated. "I do wish, though, I had a token to prove Zemarkhos dead."

"What are you going to do, go back and take his head so you can toss it at Thorisin's feet the way Avshar gave you

Mavrikios'?" When Scaurus did not answer at once, Gaius Philippus turned astonished eyes on him. "By the gods, you're thinking of it!"

"Yes, I'm thinking of it," the tribune said heavily. "After all this, I'm damned if I'll leave Gavras any excuse for cheating me. I have to be sure he can't."

"He can if he wants to, anyway—that's what being Emperor is all about. All going back'll do is get you killed to no purpose." Gaius Philippus paused a moment. "Now you listen to me and see if I don't argue like some fool Greek sophist—shame Gorgidas isn't here to give me the horse-laugh."

"Go on."

"All right, then. Without Zemarkhos, do you think this town can hold off the Yezda long? What'll *they* be doing? Sitting back with their thumbs up their arses? Not bloody likely. And even Thorisin can't help noticing them being here instead of that maniac in a blue robe."

"You're not wrong," Marcus had to admit. "Gavras won't thank us for giving them Amorion, though."

"Then why didn't he give *you* an army, to keep them out of it? You know the answer to that as well as I do." Gaius Philippus drew the edge of his hand across his throat. "You've done what he told you to; he can't complain over what happens next."

"Of course he can; you just showed me that yourself." But Marcus realized Gaius Philippus was right. Zemarkhos was done, and without troops the tribune could not help Amorion. "Very well, you have me. Let's get out while we can."

"Now you're talking." Gaius Philppus bullied a resentful lope out of his horse and slapped its bony flank when it tried to slack off. "Not this time, you don't." Soon he and Marcus were near the front of the mob. The centurion grinned maliciously at the rioters around them. "They'd best enjoy their loot while they can. The Yezda'll swarm down on 'em like flies on rotten meat."

"So they will." Marcus swore in sudden consternation. "And one of the ways they'll come swarming is out of the north, straight down the path we need to use."

"A pox! I hadn't thought of that. We were lucky when we got here, not seeing more than a few scattered bands." Gaius Philippus rubbed his scarred cheek. "And they'll be hot for plunder, too, when they come across us. Bad."

"Yes." Buildings were beginning to thin out as they got near the edge of town; like most cities in the once-secure Videssian westlands, Amorion had no wall. Ahead, Marcus could see the tents of wool, linen, and silk, the merchants' assembly that rose like mushrooms after a rain, only to disappear once the *panegyris* was over. "I have it!" he exclaimed, wits jogged by them. "Let's take that Tahmasp up on turning guardsman. There's booty in his caravan, aye, but only the biggest band of raiders would dare have a go at him. He'd bloody any smaller bunch."

"You've thrown a triple six!" Gaius Philippus said. "The very thing!" He bunched the thick muscles in his upper arms. "We may get to have another whack at these jackals around us, too. I wouldn't mind that one bit." Like most veteran soldiers, he loathed mobs, as much for their disorder as for their looting habits.

The tent city was already in an uproar when the Romans reached it. The first wave of rioters had come just ahead of them; they were running from one vendor to the next, snatching what they could. The buyers already there were catching the fever, too, and joining the mob. Several bodies, most of them locals, lay bleeding in the dirt.

But the mob's onset was not the only thing sowing confusion. Merchants were frantically shutting up displays, taking down tents, and loading everything onto their horses, donkeys, and camels. Some were nearly done; they must have started at first light, long before Scaurus touched off the scramble at Amorion.

"Now where was Tahmasp lurking?" Gaius Philippus growled. The Romans had counted on finding him by his main tent, which was an eye-searing saffron that had glowed even in the twilight of the night before. But it was already down.

"There, that way, I think," Marcus said pointing. "I remember that blue-and-white striped one wasn't far from him."

They rode forward. "Right you are," Gaius Philippus said, spotting the yellow canvas baled up on horseback. There was no sign of the caravan master, though traders who traveled with him were still dashing about finishing their packing.

Despite the chaos, the mob left Tahmasp's caravan alone. A good forty armored guardsmen, most of them mounted, formed a perimeter to daunt the most foolhardy rioters. Some had drawn bows, others carried spears or held sabers at the ready. They had the mongrel look of any such company, with no matching gear and men who ranged from a blond Haloga through Videssians and Makuraners to robed desert nomads and even a couple of Yezda. They were all scarred, several missing fingers or an ear, and probably four-fifths of them outlaws, but they looked like they could fight.

They bristled as the Romans approached. "Where's Tahmasp?" Marcus shouted to the man he figured for their leader, a short, dark, hatchet-faced Videssian who wore his wealth—his hands glittered with gold rings, his arms with heavy bracelets. His sword belt and scabbard were crusted with jewels, and the torque round his neck would have raised the envy of Viridovix or any Gallic chieftain. Baubles aside, he looked quick and dangerous.

"He's bloody well busy," he snapped. "What's it to you?"

Gaius Philippus spoke up, in piping falsetto: "Oh, the wicked fellow! He's got me in trouble, and my daddy's coming after him with an axe!" The guard chief's jaw dropped; several of his men doubled over in laughter. In normal tones, the centurion rasped, "Who are you, dung-heel, to keep people from him?"

The other purpled. Marcus said hastily, "He said for us to come see him if we were looking for spots in your troop. We are."

That got them a different kind of appraisal from Tahmasp's rough crew. Suddenly the gaudy little troop leader was all business. His darting black eyes inspected the puckered scar on the tribune's right forearm, his sleeveless mail shirt. "Funny gear," he muttered. He gave Gaius Philippus a hard once-over. "Well, maybe," he said. He called to the Haloga, "Go on, Njal, fetch the boss."

"What idiocy is this?" Tahmasp boomed as he came up at a heavy run. He glared at his guard chief. "This had better be good, Kamytzes. These boneheads with me this trip couldn't figure out how to put a prick where it goes, let alone—" He broke off, recognizing the Romans. "Ha! Done with your precious 'business,' are you?"

Somewhere behind Marcus, a rioter yelled as a merchant slammed a box closed on his hand. "You might say so," the tribune said.

Tahmasp's eyes glinted, but he rolled his shoulders in a massive shrug. "The fewer questions I ask, the fewer lies I get back. So you two want to join me, eh?" Receiving nods, he went on, "You've soldiered before—no, don't tell me about it; I'd sooner not know. That makes things easier. You know what orders are. Pay and all I told you about already. Steal, and we'll stomp you the first time; stomp you again, harder, and kick you out naked the next. Try and run out on us, and we'll kill you if we can. We don't like bandits planting spies."

"Fair enough," Marcus said. Gaius Philippus echoed him.

"Good." The caravaneer's bushy eyebrows went down as he frowned. "I forgot to ask—what do I call you?"

They gave their praenomens. "Never heard those before," Tahmasp said. "No matter. You, Markhos, from now on you are in Kamytzes' band. Once we are on the move, that is right flank guard. And you, Gheyus—" His Makuraner accent made the veteran's name a grunt. "—you belong to Muzaffar and left flank patrol." He pointed to a countryman of his, a tall, thin man with coal-black hair going gray at the temples and an aristocratic cast of features marred by a broken nose.

Tahmasp saw the Romans look at each other. He laughed until his big belly shook—not like so much jelly, as Balsamon's did, but like a boulder bouncing up and down. "I don't know you bastards," he pointed out. "Think I'll let you stay together and maybe plot who knows what? Not frigging likely."

He might not be a Videssian, Marcus thought, but his mind worked the same way. No help for it; taking precautions kept Tahmasp alive.

Gaius Philippus asked the caravaneer, "What's all your hurly-burly about? Seems you were going to get out even before the riot started—and 'most everybody else up here with you." As if to punctuate his words, another merchant company pulled away, the traders lashing their animals ahead. The lash fell on looters, too, driving them away with curses and yelps.

"I'd have to have my head stuffed up my backside to stay. A rider came in this morning with news of a thundering big army pushing east up the Ithome toward us. That says Yezda to me, and I'm not blockhead enough to sit still and wait for 'em."

"You called it," Scaurus said to Gaius Philippus. The approaching force had to be the nomads, he thought. Thorisin had hardly begun mobilizing when Marcus was expelled from the city; he doubted whether an imperial force could even have reached Garsavra.

"Enough of this jibber-jabber," Tahmasp declared. "We've got to get out of here fast, and standing around chinning don't help. Some of the stupid sods with me would hang around to sell a Yezda the sword he'd take their heads with the next second. Kamytzes, Muzaffar, these two are your headache now. If they give trouble, scrag 'em; we got on without 'em before, and I'll bet we can again." He turned and clumped away, shouting, "Isn't that bleeding tent down yet? Move it, you daft buggers!"

Kamytzes ordered Marcus forward with a brusque gesture. Muzaffar smiled at Gaius Philippus, his teeth white against swarthy skin. When he spoke, his voice was soft and musical: "Tell me, what do you call that steed of yours?"

"This maundering old wreck? The worst I can think of."

"A man of discernment, I see. That would seem none too good." He beckoned to the veteran to join him. "If you are one of us, you are facing the wrong way."

Tahmasp's caravan pulled out less than an hour after the Romans took service with him. Forty guards seemed an impressive force when the caravan was gathered together, but, even eked out by merchants, grooms, and servants, they were pitifully few once it stretched itself along the road. Divided into three-man squads, Kamytzes' troop patrolled its side of the long row of wagons, carts, and beasts of burden, while Muzaffar's took the other.

Marcus looked for Gaius Philippus, but could not see him.

What might have been a bad moment came just outside Amorion, when the rioters were still thick as fleas on a dog. A double handful of them attacked Scaurus and the squadmates he had been assigned, Njal the Haloga and a lean, sun-baked desert nomad who spoke no Videssian at all. The tribune heard his name was Wathiq.

Some of the looters tried to keep the guards in play while the rest went for the donkeys behind them. Against their own kind, the simple plan would have worked. But

Njal, wielding his axe with a surgeon's precision, sliced off one rioter's ear and sent him running away shrieking and spurting blood. Marcus cut down another before the fellow could jump in to hamstring his horse. Wathiq turned in the saddle and shot one of the men who had run past them in the back. The rioters gave it up as a bad job and fled, while the three professionals grinned at each other.

Njal and Wathiq could talk to each other after a fashion in broken Makuraner. Through the Haloga, the tribune learned Wathiq had backed the wrong prince in a tribal feud and had to flee. Njal himself was exiled for being too poor to pay blood-price over a man he had killed. Scaurus gave out that he was a wandering mercenary down on his luck, a story the other two accepted without comment. He had no idea whether they believed him.

The Roman thought nothing of it when Tahmasp led his charges west; with enemies coming from the opposite direction, he would have gone the same way to get maneuvering room.

They camped by the Ithome. With summer's heat drawing near, the river was already low in its bed, but it would flow the year around. On the parched central plateau, that made it more precious than rubies.

Each squad of guards shared a tent; Marcus gave up the idea of any private planning with Gaius Philippus. Still, he thought, with Latin between them, their talk would be safe enough from prying ears. But when he went looking for the centurion at the cookfires, he discovered his comrade's squad had picket duty the first watch of the night. Kamytzes had given him, Wathiq, and Njal the mid-watch. From what he had seen of Tahmasp's methods, he suspected that was no accident.

The blocky caravaneer hired the best, though. His cook somehow managed a savory stew out of travelers' fare of smoked meats, shelled grain, chick-peas, and onions. The very smell of it had more substance than the thin, sorry stuff Thorisin Gavras' jailers had dished out.

The tribune settled down by a fire to enjoy the stew, but before he got the spoon to his lips, one of the other guardsmen stumbled over him. Marcus' bowl went flying. The trooper was a Videssian, thicker through the shoulders than most imperials, with a gold hoop dangling piratically from his left ear. "Sorry," he said, but his mocking grin made him out a liar.

"You clumsy—" Marcus began, but then he saw the rest of the guards watching him expectantly and understood. Any new recruit could look forward to a hazing before veterans would accept him.

His tormentor loomed over him, fists bunched in anticipation. Without standing up, the tribune hooked his foot back of the other's ankle. The Videssian went down with a roar of rage; Scaurus sprang on top of him.

"No knives!" Kamytzes shouted. "Draw one, and it's the last thing you'll do!"

The two fighters rolled in the dirt, pummeling each other. The Videssian rammed a knee at Marcus' groin. He twisted aside just enough to take it on the point of the hip. He grabbed his opponent's beard and pulled his face down into the dust. When the other tried for a like hold on him, his hand slipped off the tribune's bare chin.

"Ha!" someone exclaimed. "Some point to this shaving business after all."

The Roman saw sparks when the guard's fist smashed into his nose. Blood streamed down his face; he gulped air through his mouth. He punched the Videssian in the belly. The fellow was so muscular it was like hitting a slab of wood, but one of the tribune's blows caught him in that vulnerable spot at the pit of the stomach. The guard folded up, the fight forgotten as he struggled to breathe.

Marcus climbed to his feet, gingerly feeling his nose. There was no grate of bone, he noted with relief, but it was already swelling. His voice sounded strange as he asked Kamytzes, "Have I passed, or is there more?"

"You'll do," the little captain said. He nodded at the tribune's foe, who was finally starting to do more than gasp. "Byzos there is no lightweight."

"Too true," Scaurus agreed, touching his nose again. He helped Byzos up and was not sorry to see he had scraped a good piece of hide off the Videssian's cheek. But the guard took his hand when he offered it. The fight had been fair and was no tougher an initiation rite, the tribune decided, than the branding that sealed a man to a Roman legion.

"Pay up, chief," one of the guards said. Kamytzes, looking sour, pulled off a ring and gave it to him.

Marcus frowned, not caring to have his new commander

resentful at having lost money on account of him. "If you want to get your own back," he said, "bet on my friend Gaius when his turn comes after he gets off watch."

"With his head full of gray?" Kamytzes stared. "He's an old man."

"Don't let him hear you say that," the tribune said. "Tell you what; make your bets. If you lose, I'll make them good for you—and here are your witnesses to see I said so."

"The bigger fool you, but I'm glad to take you up on it. Never turn down free money or a free woman, my father always told me, and money won't give you the clap."

When the squad rode out on picket duty, Njal said, "You'd best be richer t'an you look, outlander. T'at Kamytzes, he might almost be a Namdalener for gambling." He said something to Wathiq, who nodded vigorously and pantomimed a man rolling dice.

"I'm not worried," Marcus said, and hoped he meant it.

The watch passed without incident; only the buzz of insects and a nightjar's chuckling call broke the stillness. Videssos' constellations, still alien to the tribune after nearly four years, rolled slowly across the heavens. Making idle talk with Njal, he learned the Halogai recognized constellations altogether different from the patterns the imperials saw in the sky. Wathiq, it turned out, had another set still.

It seemed a very long time before the late-watch squad came to relieve them. They shook their heads when Scaurus asked whether they knew how Gaius Philippus had done. "We sacked out soon as our tent was up," one said for all. "Take more than a brawl to wake us, too—hate this bloody last watch of the night."

As Marcus was yawning himself, he could hardly argue. Back at the camp, the fires had died into embers; even gossipers and men who had stayed up for a last cup or two of wine were long since abed. "Come morning you'll know," Njal consoled Scaurus as they slid into their bedrolls. The tribune fell asleep in the middle of a grumble.

Tahmasp announced the dawn not with trumpets, but with a nomad-style drum whose deep, bone-jarring beat tumbled men out of bed like an earthquake. Bleary-eyed, Marcus splashed water on his face and groped for his tunic. He was still mouth-breathing; his nose felt twice its proper size.

After the sweaty closeness of the tent, the smell of wheatcakes sizzling was doubly inviting. Marcus stole one from the griddle with his dagger, then tossed it up and down till it was cool enough to hold. He devoured it, ignoring the cook's curses. It was delicious.

A nudge in the ribs made him whirl. There stood Kamytzes, looking like a fox who had just cleaned out a henhouse. The troop leader handed him a couple of pieces of silver. "I made plenty more," he said, "but this for the tip."

"Thanks." Marcus pocketed the coins. He looked round for Gaius Philippus, but Muzaffar's half of the guard troop was billeted at the far end of the camp. Turning back to Kamytzes, he asked, "How did he do it?"

"They picked a big hulking bruiser to go at him, all muscles and no sense. From the way he came swaggering over, a blind idiot would have known what he had in mind. Your friend hadn't had time to sit down to his supper yet. He made as if he didn't notice what was going on until the lout was almost on top of him. Then he spun on his heel, cold-cocked the bugger, dragged him over to the latrine trench, and dropped him in—feet first; he didn't want to drown him. After that he got his stew and ate."

Scaurus nodded; the encounter had the earmarks of the senior centurion's efficiency. "Did he say anything?" he asked Kamytzes.

"I was coming to that." The cocky officer's eyes gleamed with amusement. "After a couple of bites he looked up and said to nobody in particular, 'If anything like that happens again, I may have to get annoyed.'"

"Sounds like him. I doubt he need worry much."

"So do I." Filching a wheatcake the same way Marcus had, Kamytzes bustled away to help Tahmasp get the caravan moving.

They were on the road by an hour and a half after sunrise—not up to the standard of the legions, but good time, the tribune thought, for a private band of adventurers. Tahmasp went up and down the line of merchants who traveled with him, blasphemously urging them to keep up. "What do you think you are, a eunuch in a sedan chair?" he roared at one who was too slow to suit him. "You move like that, we'll fornicating well go on without you. See how fast you'll run with Yezda on your tail!" The trader mended his pace; the caravaneer had no more potent threat than leaving him behind.

As they had the day before, they traveled west. Marcus waved to Tahmasp as he came by on his unceasing round of inspections. "What is it?" the flamboyant caravaneer asked genially. "Kamytzes tells me you carved yourself a place," he said, chuckling, "though you'll not gain favor by making your nose as big as mine."

"As I wasn't born with it that way, I'll be as glad when it's not," the tribune retorted. Happy to find Tahmasp in a good mood, he asked when the caravan would swing north toward the Empire's ports on the coast of the Videssian Sea.

Tahmasp dug a finger in his ear to make sure he had heard correctly. Then he threw back his head and laughed till tears streamed down his leathery cheeks. "North? Who's ever said a word about north? You poor, stupid, sorry son of a whore, it's Mashiz I'm bound for, not your piss-pot ports. Mashiz!" He almost choked with glee. "I hope you enjoy the trip."

VIII

"SURRENDER!" LANKINOS SKYLITZES BAWLED UP TO THE Yezda officer atop the mud-brick wall.

The Yezda put his hands on his hips and laughed. "I'd like to see you make me," he said. He spat at the Videssian, who was interpreting for Arigh.

"Och, will you hear the filthy man, now?" Viridovix said. He shook his fist at the Yezda. "Come down here and be doing that, you blackhearted omadhaun!"

"Make me," the officer repeated, still laughing. He gestured to the squad of archers beside him. They drew their double-curved bows back to their ears. The sun glinted off iron chisel-points; to Gorgidas every shaft seemed aimed straight at him. The Yezda said, "This parley is over. Pull back, or I will fire on you. Fight or not, just as you please."

To give the warning teeth, one of the nomads put an arrow in the dirt a couple of feet in front of Arigh's pony. He sat motionless, staring up at the Yezda, daring them to shoot. After a full minute, he nodded to his party and made a deliberate turn to show the town garrison his back. He and his comrades slowly rode off.

The moment they left the shade of the wall, the blasting heat of the river-plain summer hit them once more with its full power. Viridovix wore an ugly hat of woven straw to protect his fair skin from the sun, but he was red and peeling even so. The sweat that streamed down his face stung like vinegar. Armor was a chafing torment no amount of bathing could ease.

Arigh cursed in a low monotone until they were well away

195

from the city, not wanting to give the Yezda officer the satisfaction of knowing his anger. The drawn-up lines of his army, banners moving sluggishly in the sweltering air, made a brave show. But without the siege train they did not have, assaulting a walled town with ready defenders would cost more than they could afford to lose.

"May the wind spirits blow that dog's ghost so far it never finds its way home to be reborn," Arigh burst out at last, bringing his fist down on his thigh in frustration. "It galls me past words not to watch him drown in his own blood for his insolence, crying defiance at me with his stinking couple of hundred men."

"The trouble is, he knows what he's about," Pikridios Goudeles said. "We haven't the ladders to go at the walls of this miserable, overgrown village, whatever its name is—"

"Erekh," Skylitzes put in.

"A fitting noise for a nauseating town. In any case, we don't have the ladders and we can't do much of a job making them because the only trees in this bake-oven of a country are date palms, with worthless wood. To say nothing of the fact that if we sit down in front of a city instead of staying on the move, all the Yezda garrisons hereabouts will converge on us instead of each one being pinned down to protect its own base."

"Are you a general now?" Arigh snarled, but he could not argue against the pen-pusher's logic. "This will cost us," he said darkly. When he drew closer to his assembled soldiers, he waved to the southwest and yelled, "We ride on!"

He gave the order first in the Arshaum speech for his own men, then in Videssian so Narbas Kios could translate it into Vaspurakaner for the Erzrumi. The mountaineers' ranks stirred; it would have taken a deaf man to miss their resentful mutters. Some of the Erzrumi were not muttering. Part of the Mzeshi contingent shouted their fury at the Arshaum chief and at those of their own leaders content to remain with the plainsmen.

One of their officers advanced on Arigh. Dark face suffused with rage, he roared something at the Arshaum in his own strange language, then brought himself under enough control to remember his Vaspurakaner. His accent was atrocious; Narbas Kios frowned, trying to be sure he understood. At last he said, "He calls you a man of little spirit." From the savage scowl on the Mzeshi's face, Gorgidas was sure Narbas was shading the translation. The trooper went on, "He says he came to fight, and you run away. He came for loot, and has won a few brass trinkets his own smiths would be ashamed of. He says he was tricked, and he is going home."

"Wait," Arigh said through the Videssian soldier. He went through Goudeles' arguments all but unchanged, and added, "We are still unbeaten, and Mashiz still lies ahead. That has been our goal all along; stay and help us win it."

The Mzeshi frowned in concentration. Gorgidas thought he was considering what Arigh had said, but then he loudly broke wind. His face cleared.

"Not the most eloquent reply, but one of unmistakable meaning," Goudeles remarked with diplomatic aplomb.

Smirking triumphantly, the officer trotted back to his followers and harangued them for a few minutes. They shouted their agreement, brandishing lances and swords. Their harness and chain mail jingled as they pulled away from their countrymen and started back to their mountain home. Several individual horsemen peeled away from the remaining men of Mzeh to join them.

Arigh had his impassivity back as they began to grow small against the sky. "I wonder who the next ones to give up will be," he said. Already a good third of the Erzrumi had abandoned the campaign and turned back.

Viridovix blew a long, glum breath through his mustaches. "And it all started out so simple, too," he said. Fanning out as they crossed the Tutub, the Arshaum had fallen on three or four towns before startled defenders realized an enemy was loose among the Hundred Cities. It was as easy as riding through open gates; there was next to no fighting and, in spite of Mzeshi complaints, they came away with their horses festooned with booty.

But it had not stayed easy long. Not only were the cities shut up against attack, Yezda raiders began the hit-and-run warfare they shared with the Arshaum. Two scouts were ambushed here, a forager there. The Yezda lost men, too, but they had the resources of a country to draw on. Arigh did not.

He gave his commands to the *naccara* drummer, who boomed them out for the whole army to hear. It shifted into traveling order, with what was left of the Erzrumi heavy cavalry in a long column in the center, flanked and screened by the Arshaum.

Gorgidas rode with Rakio, near the front of the Erzrumi formation. Most of the Sworn Fellowship was hurrying back to the Yrmido country; Khilleu did not relish giving up the campaign, but he did not dare leave his land unprotected when his unfriendly neighbors were going home. A fair number of "orphans" and a handful of pairs, mostly older men, stayed on.

The physician flattered himself that Rakio was still with the army for his sake. Certainly the Yrmido found no delight in the journey itself. "What strange country this is," he said. He pointed. "What is that little hill, out of the flat plain rising? Several of them I have seen here."

Gorgidas followed his pointing finger. It was truly not much of a hill, perhaps not even as tall as the walls around Videssos, but in the dead-flat river plain it stood out like a mountain, springing up so abruptly he did not think it could be natural.

Having no idea how it came about, he poised tablet and stylus before he called out the question to whoever might hear it. Skylitzes was not far away, talking with Vakhtang of Gunib. He raised his head. "It's the funeral marker for a dead town," he told the Greek. "You've seen how they build with mud brick hereabouts. They have to; it's all there is in this country. No stone here to speak of, Phos knows. The stuff is flimsy, and the people don't care for work any more than they do anywhere else. When a house or a tavern falls down, they rebuild on top of the rubble. Do it enough times, and there's your hillock. That should be plain to anyone, I'd think."

Gorgidas scowled at the officer's patronizing tone. Skylitzes let out one of his rare, short laughs. "See how it feels to get a lecture instead of giving one," he said. Ears burning, Gorgidas quickly stowed his tablet.

Rakio did not notice his lover's discomfiture; he was still complaining about the countryside. "It looks like it leprosy has. What parts are in crop seem rich enough, but there are so many patches of desert, ugly and useless both."

Overhearing him, Skylitzes said, "Those are new; blame the Yezda for them. They made them by—"

"Destroying the local irrigation works," Gorgidas interrupted. He was not about to have his self-esteem tweaked twice running. "Without the Tutub and the Tib, this whole land would be waste. It only grows where their waters reach. But the Yezda are nomads—what do they care about crops?

Their herds can live on thorns and thistles, and if they starve away the farmers here, so much the better for them."

"Just what I would have said," Skylitzes said, adding, "but at twice the length."

"What are you arguing about?" Vakhtang demanded in the plains speech. When Skylitzes had translated, the Erzrumi advised Gorgidas, "Pay no attention to him. I have not known him long, but I see he bites every word to test it before he lets it out."

"Better that way than the flood of drivel Goudeles spouts," the officer said, not missing the chance to score off the man who was a political rival back in Videssos.

Vakhtang, though, favored the bureaucrat's more florid style of oratory. "Meaning can disappear with not enough words as well as from too many."

They hashed it back and forth the rest of the day as they rode through farmland and desert. It made for a good argument; there were points on both sides, but it was not important enough for anyone to take very seriously.

With empty fields all around, Gorgidas forgot he was at war. Rakio, though, knew at a glance what that emptiness meant. "They hide from us," he said. "Peasants always do. In a week come, and the fields will be full of farmers."

"No doubt you're right," the Greek sighed. It saddened him to think that to the locals he was only another invader.

"Yezda!" The peasant was short, stooped, and naked, with great staring eyes. He pointed to an artificial mound on the southern horizon, larger and better-preserved than the one Rakio had noticed a couple of days before. He rapidly opened and closed his hands several times to show that they were numerous.

Arigh frowned. "Our scouts saw nothing there this morning." He glanced at the native, who repeated his gestures. "I wish you spoke a language some one of us could follow." But the farmer had only the guttural tongue of the Hundred Cities, reduced to a patois by centuries of subjection to Makuran and the Yezda.

He smiled ingratiatingly at the Arshaum chief, pantomiming riders going up to tether their horses in the ruins. He pointed to the sun, waved it through the sky backwards. "This was yesterday?" Arigh asked. The local shrugged, not understanding. "Worth another look," Arigh decided. He ordered a halt and sent a squad of riders out to examine the hillock.

It was nearly twilight when they came back. "Nothing around there," their leader told Arigh angrily. "No tracks, no horseturds, no signs of fire, nothing."

The peasant read the scout's voice and fell to his knees in the dirt in front of Arigh. He was shaking with fear, but kept stubbornly pointing south. "What's he sniveling about?" Gorgidas asked, walking up after seeing to his pony.

"He claims there are soldiers up on that hillock there, but he lies," the Arshaum answered. "He's cost us hours with his nonsense; I ought to cut off his ears for him for that." He gestured so the native would understand. The local cringed and went flat on his belly, wailing out something in his own language.

Gorgidas scratched his head. "Why would he put himself in danger to lie to you? He has no reason to love the Yezda; see how well he lives under them." Every rib of the farmer's body was plainly visible beneath his dirty skin. "Maybe he's just trying to do you a favor." The Greek wanted to believe that; he did not like being put on the same level as the Yezda.

"Where are the warriors, then?" Arigh demanded, putting his hands on his hips. "If you tell me my scouts are going blind, you might as well cut your own throat now."

"Blind? Hardly—we'd be dead ten times over if they were. But still . . ." He eyed the peasant, who had given up moaning and was gazing at him in mute appeal. The physician's trained glance caught the faint cloudiness of an early cataract in the man's left eye. His mind made a sudden leap. "Not blind—but blinded? Magic could hide soldiers better than rubble or brush."

"That is a thought," Arigh admitted. "If I'd taken this lout—" He stirred the peasant with his foot; the fellow groaned and covered his face, expecting to die the next instant. "—more seriously, I'd have sent a shaman to smell the place out." He became the brisk commander once more. "All right, you've made your point. Get Tolui and round up a company of men, then go find out what's going on."

"Me?" the Greek said in dismay.

"You. This is your idea. Ride it or fall off. Otherwise I have no choice but to think Manure-foot here a spy, don't I?"

Arigh, Gorgidas thought, was getting uncomfortably good at making people do what he wanted. "A concealment spell?" Tolui said when the doctor found the shaman eating curded mares' milk. "You could well be right. That's not battle magic; whoever cast it could not mind if it fell apart as soon as his men burst from ambush."

He drew his tunic over his head and undid the drawstring of his trousers with a sigh. "In this weather the mask is a torment, and the robe is of thick suede. Ah, well, better by night than by day."

"Round up a company," Arigh had said, but Gorgidas had no authority over the nomads, who did not fancy taking orders from an outsider. Tolui's presence finally helped the Greek persuade a captain of a hundred to lead out his command. "A hunt for a ghost stag, is it?" the officer said sourly. He was a broken-nosed man named Karaton, whose high voice ruined the air of sullen ferocity he tried to assume.

His men grumbled as they wolfed down their food and resaddled their horses. Karaton worked off his annoyance by swearing at Gorgidas when the physician was the last one ready. Still, it was not quite dark when they rode for the mound that had once been a city.

Rakio caught up with them halfway there. He gave Gorgidas a reproachful look as he trotted up beside him. "If you go to fight, why not me tell?"

"Sorry," the physician muttered. In fact he had not thought of it; he always had to remind himself that his comrades did not share his distaste for combat. Rakio was as eager as Viridovix once had been.

The hillock was ghostly by moonlight. Atop it Gorgidas could see stretches of wall still untumbled; his mind's eye summoned up a time when all the brickwork was whole and the streets swarming with perfumed men dressed in long tunics and carrying walking sticks, with veiled women, their figures robed against strangers' glances. The place would have echoed with jangling music and loud, happy talk. It was silent now. Not even night birds sang.

Like a good soldier, Karaton automatically sent his men to surround the base of the hill, but his heart was not in it. He waved sarcastically. "Ten thousand hiding up there, at least."

"Oh, stop squeaking at me," Gorgidas snapped, wishing he had never set eyes on the peasant in the first place. He hated looking the fool. In his self-annoyance he did not notice Karaton stiffen with outrage and half draw his saber.

"Stop, both of you," Tolui said. "I must have harmony around me if the spirits are to answer my summons." There was not a word of truth in that, but it gave both men a decent excuse not to quarrel.

Karaton subsided with a growl. "Why call the spirits, shaman? A child of four could tell you this place is dead as a sheepskin coat."

"Then fetch a child of four next time and leave me in peace," Tolui said. Echoing from behind the devil-mask he wore, his voice carried an otherworldly authority. Karaton touched a finger to his forehead in apology.

Tolui drew from his saddlebag a flat, murkily transparent slab of some waxy stone, which was transfixed by a thick needle of a different stone. "Chalcedony and emery," he explained to Gorgidas. "The hardness of the emery lets a man peering through the clear chalcedony pierce most illusions."

"Give it to me," Karaton said impatiently. He squinted up to the top of the mound. "Nothing," he said—but was there doubt in his voice? Tolui took the seeing-stone back and handed it to Gorgidas. Things at the crown of the hillock seemed to jump when he put it to his eye, but steadied quickly.

"I don't know," he said at last. "There was a flicker, but . . ." He offered the stone to Tolui. "See for yourself. The toy is yours, after all; you should be able to use it best."

The shaman lifted the mask from his head and set it on his knee. He raised the stone and gazed through it for more than a minute. Gorgidas felt the backwash of his concentration as he channeled his vision to penetrate semblance and see truth.

The physician had never thought much about Tolui's power as a sorcerer. If anything, he assumed the shaman was of no great strength, as he had been second to Onogun until Bogoraz poisoned Arghun's old wizard because he favored Videssos. Since then Tolui's magic had always been adequate, but the Greek, not seeing him truly tested, went on reckoning him no more than a hedge-wizard mainly interested in herbs, roots, and petty divinations.

He abruptly realized he had misjudged the shaman. When Tolui cried, "Wind spirits, come to my aid! Blow away the cobwebs of enchantment before me!" the night seemed to hold its breath.

A howling rose above the hillock, as of a storm, but no wind buffeted Gorgidas' face. Then Karaton shouted in amazement while his men drew bows and bared swords. Like a curtain whisked away from in front of a puppet-theater's stage, the illusion of emptiness at the crest of the hill was swept aside. Half a dozen campfires blazed among the ruins, with warriors sprawled around them at their ease.

The first arrows were in the air before Karaton could give the order to shoot. A Yezda pitched forward into one of the fires; another screamed as he was hit. A different scream went up, too, this one of fury, as the pair of wizards with the enemy felt their covering glamour snatched away.

"Up and take them!" Karaton yelled. "Quick, before they get their wits about them and go for weapons and armor!"

Shouting to demoralize the Yezda further, his men drove their ponies up the steep sides of the hill, then dismounted and scrambled toward the top on foot. Gorgidas and Rakio were with them, grabbing at shrubs or chunks of brick for handholds. Looking up toward the crest, the Greek saw the campfires and running figures of the Yezda shimmer and start to fade as their sorcerers tried to bring down the veil once more. But Tolui was still working against them, and the fear and excitement of their own men and the Arshaum ate at their magic as well. The fires brightened again.

A pony thundered downhill past Gorgidas. A daredevil Yezda, seeing his only road to safety, took that mad plunge in the dark and lived to tell of it. His horse reached level ground and streaked away. "That is a rider!" Rakio exclaimed. A crash and a pair of shrieks, one human, the other from a mortally injured pony, told of a horseman who tried the plummet and failed.

Several more mounted Yezda broke out down the path they would have taken to attack the Arshaum army. Most, though, stunned by the unexpected night assault, were still throwing saddles on their beasts or groping for sabers when Karaton's men reached them.

As he gained the top of the mound, Gorgidas stumbled over an upthrust tile. An arrow splintered against masonry not far from his head. Rakio hauled him to his feet. "You crazy are?" he shouted in the Greek's ear. "Get out your sword."

"Huh? Oh, yes, of course," Gorgidas said mildly, as if being reminded of some small blunder in a classroom. Then a Yezda was in front of him, shamshir whistling at his head. He had no room for fine footwork. He parried the stroke, then another that would have gutted him. The Yezda feinted low, slashed high. Gorgidas did not feel the sting of the blade, but warm stickiness ran down the side of his neck, and he realized his ear had been cut.

He thrust at the Yezda, who blocked and fell back awkwardly, confused by the unfamiliar stroke. Gorgidas lunged. At full extension he had a much longer reach than the nomad thought possible. His *gladius* pierced the Yezda's belly. The man groaned and folded up on himself.

Most of the enemy, outnumbered two to one, drew back for a stand at a small courtyard whose ruined walls were still breast high. The Arshaum hacked at them over the bulwark and sent arrows and stones into their crowded ranks. Unable to stand that punishment for long, the Yezda surged out again and with the strength of desperation broke through their foes' lines. Karaton squalled in outrage as Yezda hurled themselves down the hillside with no thought for broken bones or anything but escape.

Only a few got that far; the Arshaum cut down the greater part of them as they fled. One of the Yezda wizards, a shaman in robes hardly less fringed than Tolui's, fell in that mad chase, a sword in his hand in place of the magic that had failed him.

The other sorcerer was made of different, and harsher, stuff. Gorgidas thought he saw motion down a narrow alleyway and called out in the Arshaum tongue, "Friend?" He got no answer. *Gladius* at the ready, he stepped into the rubble-choked lane.

A campfire flared behind him. The sudden brightness showed him that the alley was blind—and that it trapped no ordinary Yezda. For a moment the red robe and jagged tonsure meant nothing to the physician. Then ice walked up his spine as he recognized Skotos' emblems.

The wizard's face, Gorgidas thought, would have revealed his nature even in the absence of other signs. A man who knows both good and evil and with deliberate purpose chooses the latter will bear its mark. The eyes of the dark god's votary gave back the fire like a wolf's. The skin was drawn taut on his cheeks and at the corners of his mouth, pulling his lips back in a snarl of hate. But it was not directed at the Greek; he was sure the wizard wore it awake and asleep.

The physician edged forward. He saw the other had only a short dagger at his belt. "Yield," he called in Videssian and the Khamorth tongue. "I would not slay you out of hand."

As it focused on Gorgidas, the wizard's sneer tightened.

His hands darted out, his lips twisted in soundless invocation. Mortal fear lent his spell force enough to strike despite the chaos of battle. Gorgidas staggered, as if clubbed from behind. His sight swam; his arms and legs would not answer; the sword fell from his hand. The air rasped harshly in his throat as he struggled to breathe. He slipped to one knee, shaking his head over and over to try to clear it.

The spell had been meant to kill; perhaps only the discipline of the healer's art gave the Greek strength of will enough to withstand it even in part. He was groping for his blade as the sorcerer came up to him. The dagger gleamed in the wizard's hand, long enough to reach a man's heart.

The wizard knelt for the killing stab, a vulpine smile stretched over his lean features. Gorgidas heard a dull thud. He thought it was the sound of the knife entering his body. But the Yezda sorcerer reeled away with a muffled grunt of pain. The power of the spell vanished as his concentration snapped.

Gorgidas sprang for the wizard, but someone hurtled by him. A sword bit with a meaty thunk. The Yezda thrashed and lay still; Gorgidas smelled his bowels let go in death.

"You crazy are," Rakio said, wiping his blade on his sleeve. It was statement this time, not question. He seized the Greek by the shoulders. "Are you too stupid not to go wandering away from help and get caught alone?"

"So it would seem. I'm new to this business of war and don't do the right thing without thinking," Gorgidas said. He drew Rakio into a brief embrace and touched his cheek. "I'm glad you were close by, to keep me from paying the price of my mistake."

"I would want you for me to do the same," the Yrmido said, "but would you be able?"

"I hope so," Gorgidas said. But that was no good answer, and he knew it. They heard an Arshaum shout not far away and rushed to his aid together.

Fewer than half the Yezda managed to get away or to hide well enough in the ruins to escape their enemies' search. The rest, but for a couple saved to question later, were cut down; the Arshaum captured a good three dozen horses. The cost was seven dead and twice that many wounded.

"That was a true lead," Karaton said to Gorgidas, the nearest thing to an apology he would give a non-Arshaum. He lay on his belly while the Greek stitched up a gash on the back of his calf. The wound was deep, but luckily ran along the muscle instead of across it; it did not hamstring him. A clean, freely bleeding cut, it did not require the healing art to mend.

Karaton did not flinch as the needle entered his flesh again and again, or even when the physician poured an antiseptic lotion of alum, verdigris, pitch, resin, vinegar, and oil into the wound. "You should have kept that wizard of theirs alive," the commander of a hundred went on, his tone perfectly conversational. "He would have been able to tell us more than these no-account warriors we have." Without liking the man, the Greek had to admire his fortitude.

"I was almost sorry for having lived through the encounter myself," he told Viridovix much later that night. The Celt was yawning, but Gorgidas was still too keyed up to sleep. Having seen the peasant who had warned them loaded with gold and sent home, he kept hashing over the fight.

"The shindy would've been easier for you lads, I'm thinking, were you after having me along," Viridovix interrupted. Most times he would have heard his friend out gladly, but his eyes were heavy as two balls of stone in his head.

"Aye, no doubt you would have stomped the hill flat with one kick and saved us the trouble of fighting," Gorgidas said tartly. "I thought you over your juvenile love for bloodletting."

"That I am," the Gaul said. "But for one who prides himself on the wits of him, you've no call to be twitting me. If it was magic you suspected, now, couldna this glaive o' mine ha' pierced it outen the folderol and all puir Tolui went through?"

"A plague! I should have thought of that." Hardly anything annoyed Gorgidas worse than Viridovix coming up with something he had missed. Sitting back combing his mustaches with his fingers, the Celt looked so smug Gorgidas wanted to punch him.

"Dinna fash yoursel' so," he said, chuckling. "Forbye, you won and got back safe, the which was the point of it all." He laid a large hand on the Greek's shoulder.

Gorgidas started to shrug it away in anger, but had a better idea. He gave a rueful laugh and said, "You're right, of course. I wasn't very clever, was I?" Viridovix' baffled expression made a fair revenge.

* * *

The Yezda band slashed through Arigh's cavalry screen, poured arrows into the Erzrumi still with his army, and fled before the slower-moving mountaineers could come to grips with them. Arshaum chased the marauders through the fields. Wounded men reeled in the saddle; as Gorgidas watched, one lost his seat and crashed headlong into the trampled barley. The locals, he thought, would find the corpse small compensation for the hunger those swathes of destruction would bring come winter.

As the last of the Yezda were ridden down or got away, their pursuers returned. A couple led new horses, while more showed off swords, boots, and other bits of plunder. Even so, Viridovix clucked his tongue in distress over the skirmish. "Och, the more o' the Hundred Cities we're after passing, the bolder these Yezda cullions get. 'Tis nobbut a running fight the last two days, and always the Erzrumi they're for hitting."

"It works, too." Gloom made Pikridios Goudeles unusually forthright. Of the hillmen, all had seen enough of the lowlands, but for a couple of hundred adventurers from various clans and Gashvili's sturdy band, who still reckoned themselves bound by oath. Casualties and desertions reduced their count by a few every day.

"Tomorrow will be worse," Skylitzes said. Hard times loosened his tongue as they checked Goudeles'. "The Yezda have our measure now. They know which towns we can reach and which are safe from us. The garrisons are coming out to reinforce the bushwhackers who've dogged us all along."

Viridovix did not like the conclusion he reached. "We'll be fair nibbled to death, then, before too long. We havena the men to spare."

"We should have," Goudeles said. "But for the mischance of battle on the steppe and for the squabbles among the Arshaum themselves, we would be twice our present numbers."

Skylitzes said, "I served under Nephon Khoumnos once, and he was always saying, 'If ifs and buts were candied nuts, then everyone would be fat.'" His eyes traveled to Goudeles' belly. "Maybe he was thinking of you."

Reminding the bureaucrat of their political rivalry back in Videssos proved unwise. "Maybe," Goudeles said shortly. "I'm sure the good general's philosophy is a great consolation to him now."

Appalled silence fell. Avshar's wizardry had killed Khoumnos at Maragha. Goudeles reddened, knowing he had gone too far. He hurriedly changed the subject. "We'd also be better off if the Erzrumi had not proved summer soldiers, going home when things turned rough."

Some truth lay in that, but after his gaffe his companions were not ready to let him off so easily. "That is unjust," Gorgidas said, doubly irritated because of the implied slur on Rakio's countrymen. "They came to fight for themselves, not for us, and we've seen how the Yezda keep singling them out for special attention."

"Aye; to make them give up." Goudeles was not about to abandon his point. "But when they do, they get off easy while we pay the price of their running out. Deny it if you can." No one did.

Gorgidas' side of the argument, though, received unpleasant confirmation later that afternoon. The bodies of several Erzrumi who had been captured in a raid the week before were hung on spears in Arigh's line of march. With the time to work on them, the Yezda had used their ingenuity. Among other indignities, they had soaked their prisoners' beards in oil before setting them alight.

Arigh buried the mistreated corpses without a word. If they were meant to intimidate, they had the opposite effect. In cold anger, the Arshaum hunted down a squad of Yezda scouts and drove them straight into the lances of the mountaineers still with them. The enemy horsemen did not last long. The evening's camp held a grim satisfaction.

But the Yezda returned to the attack the next day. The iron-studded gates of one of the larger of the Hundred Cities, Dur-Sharrukin, swung open to let out a sally party, while two troops who had been shadowing the Arshaum nipped in from either flank.

They were still outnumbered and could have been badly mauled, but Arigh threw the bulk of his forces at Dur-Sharrukin's gate. If he could force an entrance, the city was his. The Yezda gate-captain saw that, too. He was, unfortunately, a man of quick action. He put a shoulder to the gate himself and screamed for his troops to help. The bar slammed into place seconds before the Arshaum got there. Much of the garrison was trapped outside, but the town was secure.

The plainsmen milled about in confusion just outside Dur-Sharrukin. In their dash for the gate they had pulled away from the Erzrumi, and the Yezda flanking attack fell on the hillmen.

Gashivili's company stopped one assault in its tracks. Used to clashing with the Khamorth at the edge of the steppe, the lord of Gunib's veterans waited till the Yezda drew close enough to be hurt by a charge and then, with nice timing, delivered a blow that brought a dozen lightly armed archers down from their horses at the first shock and sent the rest galloping away for their lives.

On the other wing the combat went less well. The free spirits who had clung with the Arshaum acknowledged no single commander. They grouped together by nation or by friendship, and each little band did as it pleased. Lacking the discipline for a united charge, they tried to fight nomad-style, and the nomads had much the better of it.

"Stay close to me," Rakio called to Gorgidas as the first arrows whipped past them. The Yrmido swung his lance down and roweled his big gelding. He thundered toward a Yezda who was restringing his bow. On a more agile mount, the other had no trouble eluding him, but his grin turned to a snarl as he saw Gorgidas bearing down on him behind Rakio.

The Greek rode a steppe pony himself and was thrusting at the Yezda as the latter snatched out his saber. A backward lean saved him from Gorgidas' sword, but another "orphan" from the Sworn Fellowship speared him out of the saddle. All the remaining Yrmido, about fifteen of them, stuck close together; even now, few of the other Erzrumi would have anything to do with them.

They cut down a couple of Yezda more and took injuries in return. One was shot in the shoulder, another wounded in the leg by a sword stroke. His foe's saber cut his horse as well. Crazed with pain, it leaped into the air and galloped wildly away, by good fortune toward Gashvili's troops. One of their rear guard rode out to the hurt warrior, helped bring his beast under control, and hurried him into the safety of their ranks.

"That is well done," Rakio said. "These men of Gunib decent fellows have themselves shown to be. Some here would let the Yezda take him."

Back at Dur-Sharrukin, the Arshaum were reversing themselves and riding to help their allies. The Yezda, seeing that their advantage would soon be gone, battled with redoubled vigor, to do all the damage they could before they had to retreat.

The Yrmido took the brunt of that whirlwind assault, and, because they were who they were, the rest of the Erzrumi did not hurry to help them. Gorgidas parried blow after blow and dealt a few of his own. "Eleleleu!" he shouted—the Greek war cry.

He wished he could use a bow; arrows flew by him, buzzing like angry wasps. He noticed his left trouser leg was torn and wet with blood and wondered foolishly if it was his.

Through the tumult he heard Viridovix' yowling battle paean. "Eleleu!" he yelled, and waved his hat to show the Celt where he was. The wild Gallic howl came again, closer this time. He thought he could hear Skylitzes' cry as well; Goudeles was apt to be noisier before a fight than during.

Rakio shouted and flung both hands up in front of his face. A little kestrel stabbed claws into the back of one wrist, then screeched and streaked away to its Yezda master. Another Yezda landed a mace just above Rakio's ear. The Yrmido slid bonelessly to the ground.

Gorgidas spurred his pony forward, as did the two or three men of the Sworn Fellowship who were not fighting for their own lives at that instant. But Rakio had got separated from them by fifty yards or so. Though Gorgidas burst between two Yezda before either could strike at him, more were between him and his lover, too many for him to overcome even had he had a demigod's strength and Viridovix' spell-wrapped blade.

He tried nonetheless, slashing wildly, all fencing art forgotten, and watched with anguish as a Yezda leaped down from his horse to strip off Rakio's mail shirt. The Yrmido stirred, tried groggily to rise. The Yezda grabbed for his sword, then saw how weak and uncertain Rakio was. He shouted for a comrade. Together they quickly lashed Rakio's hands behind him, then heaved him across the first warrior's saddlebow. Both men remounted and trotted off toward the west.

The Yezda were breaking contact wherever they could as the Arshaum drew near. Gorgidas' chase stopped as soon as it began. An arrow tore through his pony's neck. The horse foundered with a choked scream. As he had been taught, the Greek kicked free of the stirrups. The wind flew from him as he landed in the middle of yet another trampled grain field, but he was not really hurt.

Viridovix was almost thrown himself as he stormed toward Gorgidas. He was spurring his horse so hard that blood ran down its barrel. At last it could stand no more and tried to shake him off. He clung to his seat with the unthinking skill a year's waking time in the saddle had given him.

"Get on, ye auld weed!" he roared, slapping the beast's rump. He saw its ears go back and slapped it again, harder, before it could balk. Defeated, it ran. "Faster now, or it's forever a disgrace to sweet Epona you'll be," he said as he heard Gorgidas' war cry ring out again. As if the Gallic horse goddess held power in this new world, the pony leaped forward.

The Celt shouted himself, then cursed when he got no answer. "Sure and I'll kill that fancy-boy my ain self, if he's after letting the Greek come to harm, him such a fool on the battlefield and all," he panted, though he would sooner have been flayed than have Gorgidas hear him.

He hardly noticed the Yezda horseman in his path, save as an obstacle. One sword stroke sent the other's shamshir flying, a second laid open his arm. Not pausing to finish him, Viridovix galloped on.

Though the physician was in nomad leathers, the Celt recognized him from behind by the straight sword in his hand and by the set of his shoulders, a slump the self-confident Arshaum rarely assumed. "'Twill be the other way round, then," the Gaul said to himself, "and bad cess to me for thinking ill o' the spalpeen when he's nobbut a dead corp."

But when he dismounted to offer such sympathy as he could, Gorgidas blazed at him: "He's not dead, you bloody witless muttonhead. It's worse; the Yezda have him."

Having seen the grisly warning in the army's path, Viridovix knew what he meant. "No help for it but that we get him back, is there now?"

"How?" Gorgidas demanded, waving his hand toward the retreating Yezda. As was their habit, they were breaking up and fleeing every which way. "He could be anywhere." Clenching his fists in despair, the physician turned on Viridovix. "And what is this talk of 'we'? Why should you care what happens to my catamite?" He flung the word out defiantly, as if he would sooner hear it in his own mouth than the Gaul's.

Viridovix stood silent for a moment. "Why me? For one thing, I wouldna gi' over a dead dog to the Yezda for prisoner. If your twisty Greek mind must have its reasons, there's one. For another, your *friend*," he emphasized, turning his back on the hateful word, and on his own thoughts of a few minutes before, "is a braw chap, and after deserving a better fate. And for a third," he finished quietly, "didn't I no hear you tried to chase north over Pardraya all alone, the time Varatesh took me?"

"You shame me," Gorgidas said, hanging his head. Memory of Rakio's remarks when the Yrmido had saved him came scalding back.

"Och, I didna aim to," Viridovix said. "If kicking the fool arse o' you would ha' worked the trick, it's that I'd have done, and enjoyed it the more, too."

"Go howl!" The physician could not help laughing. "You fox of a barbarian, no doubt you have the rescue planned already."

"That I don't. Your honor has made the name for being the canny one. Me, I'd sooner brawl nor think—easier and less wearing, both."

"Liar," Gorgidas said. But his wits, once the Gaul had dragged him unwilling from despondency, were working again. He said briskly, "We'll need to see Arigh for soldiers, then, and Tolui, too, I think. What better than magic for tracking someone?"

To their surprise and anger, Arigh turned them down flat when they asked him for a squad. None of their arguments would change his mind. "You've chosen a madman's errand," he declared, "and one I do not expect you to come back from. Kill yourselves if you must, but I will not order any man to follow you."

"Is that the way a friend acts?" Viridovix cried.

"It is how a chief acts," the Arshaum returned steadily. "What sort of herdsman would I be if I sought a lost sheep by sending twenty more to meet the wolves? I have all my force to think of, and that is more important than any one person. Besides, if the Erzrumi is lucky he is dead by now." He turned away to discuss the evening's campsite with two of his commanders of a hundred.

That what he said had a great deal of truth in it did not help. Gorgidas was coldly furious as he went looking for Tolui. He found the shaman and learned that Arigh had preceded him. When he put his request to Tolui, the nomad shook his head, saying, "I am ordered not to accompany you."

"Och, and what's a wee order, now?" Viridovix said airily. "They're all very well when you'd be doing what they tell you with or without, but a bit of a bother otherwise."

Tolui raised an eyebrow. "My head answers for this one." Seeing Gorgidas about to explode, he stopped him with an upraised hand. "Softly, softly. I may be able to help you yet. Do you have anything of your comrade's with you?"

From his left wrist the physician drew off a silver bracelet stamped with the images of the Four Prophets. "Handsome work," Tolui remarked. He reached behind him, took the staring devil-mask of his office from his saddlebag, and lowered it over his head. "Aid me, spirits!" he called softly, his voice remote and disembodied. "Travel the path between the possession and the man and show the way so the journey may be made in this world as well as in your country."

He cocked his head as if listening. With an annoyed toss of his head, he got out his fringed oval summoning drum. "Aid me, aid me!" he called again, more sharply, and tapped the drumhead in an intricate rhythm. Gorgidas and Viridovix started when an angry voice spoke from nowhere. Tolui laid his command on the spirit, or tried to, for it roared in protest. With drum and voice he brought it to obedience and flung out his hands to send it forth.

"They have your view of orders," he said to Viridovix.

"Honh!" The Celt waited with Gorgidas for the spirit's return. Watching the Greek's set features, all the more revealing in their effort to conceal, he knew what pictures his friend was imagining. He had his own set, and it was not hard to substitute Rakio's face for Seirem's.

Tolui repeated that odd, listening pose, then grunted in satisfaction and handed the bracelet back to Gorgidas. Accepting it, the physician was puzzled until he noticed the faint bluish glow crowning the head of the leftmost prophet. Answering the unspoken question, the shaman said, "There is your guide. As the direction of your search changes, the light will shift from figure to figure, from west to north to east to south; it will grow brighter as you near your goal."

He waved aside thanks. Gorgidas and Viridovix hurried away; the sun was low in the west, and the army slowing as it prepared to camp. Somewhere the Yezda would be doing the same, Gorgidas thought—if they had not made a special stop already.

As they rode away, someone shouted behind them. Viridovix swore—was Arigh going to stop them after all? He lay his sword across his knees. "If himself wants to make a shindy of it, I'll oblige him, indeed and I will."

Their pursuer, however, was no Arshaum, but one of the Yrmido, a quiet, solid man named Mynto. "I with come," he said in broken Vaspurakaner, of which the Greek and Celt had picked up a handful of words. He was leading a fully saddled spare horse. "For Rakio."

Viridovix smacked his forehead with the heel of his hand. "What a pair o' cullions the two of us make! We'd have had the poor wight riding pillion, and belike wrecking our horses for fair."

Gorgidas was marshaling what Vaspurakaner he knew. "Big danger," he said to Mynto. "Why you come?"

The Yrmido looked at him. "Same reason you do."

The answer was one the physician might have been as glad not to have, but there could be no arguing Mynto's right to join them. "Come, then," the physician said. Viridovix managed to swallow a grin before the Greek turned his way.

The peaks of Dilbat hid the sun. The day's vicious heat subsided a little. Night in the land of the Hundred Cities had a beauty missing from the flat, monotonous river plain by day. The sky was a great swatch of blue-black velvet, with the stars' diamonds tossed carelessly across it.

The horsemen, though, had little chance to enjoy the loveliness. Swarms of mosquitoes rose, humming venomously, from the fields and the edges of the irrigation channels to make the journey a misery. The riders slapped and cursed, slapped and cursed. Their mounts' tails switched back and forth as they did their best to whisk the bugs away. Gorgidas was reminded of the fight between Herakles and the Hydra; for every insect he mashed, two more took its place.

The mosquitoes particularly tormented Viridovix, whose face in the starlight was puffed and blotchy. "Dogmeat I'll be before long," he said sadly, waving his arms in a futile effort to frighten the biters away.

Thanks to a swollen bite over one eye, Gorgidas had to squint to see the bracelet that was steering them. "North," he said after a bit, as the blue radiance began to shift, and then, a little later, "More west again." He had no doubt the glow was stronger than it had been when they set out.

As well as they could, the three of them tried to decide what they would do when they found Rakio. More than language hindered them; much depended on how many enemies held the Yrmido and what they would be doing to him when the rescuers arrived. Viridovix made the key point: "We maun be quick. Any long fight and we're for it, and no mistake."

They skirted one Yezda camp without being spotted; the bracelet was still guiding them northwest. Soon after, a squadron of Yezda rode past them only a couple of hundred yards away. No challenges rang out; the squad leader must have taken them for countrymen. "No moon—good," Mynto whispered.

"Bloody good," Gorgidas said explosively once the Yezda were out of earshot.

He was hiding the bracelet in his sleeve to conceal its brightness when he and his companions passed the mound that marked yet another abandoned city. As they came round it they saw several fires ahead and men moving in front of them. When the physician checked the bracelet, its glow almost dazzled him. "That must be it."

"Yes." Mynto pointed. He was farsighted; they had to draw closer before the unmoving figure by one of the fires meant anything to the Greek. He caught his breath sharply. No wonder the man did not move—he was tied to a stake.

"Ready for sport, are they, the omadhauns?" Viridovix said. "We'll give them summat o' sport."

They made plans in low mutters, then almost had to scrap them at once when a sentry called a challenge from out of the darkness. "Not so much noise, there," Viridovix hissed at the Yezda in the Khamorth speech they shared, doing his best to imitate the fellow's accent. "We've a message for your captain from the khagan himself. Come fetch it, an you would; there's more stops for us after the one here."

The sentry rode forward, not especially suspicious. He was only a few feet away when he exclaimed, "You're no—" His voice cut off abruptly as Mynto hurled half a brick at his face. He went over his horse's tail.

They waited tensely to see whether the noise would disturb the Yezda in the camp. When it was clear the enemy had not noticed, Viridovix said, "Here's how we'll try it, then," and shifted into his lame Vaspurakaner, eked out with gestures, so Mynto could follow.

"That place is mine," Gorgidas protested when the Gaul came to his own role.

"No," Viridovix said firmly. "Mynto has his chain-mail coat, and I this whopping great blade and all the practice using it. Each to the task he's suited for, or the lot of us perish, and Rakio, too. Is it aye or nay?"

"Yes, damn you." Having lived his life by logic and reason, the physician wished he could forget them.

"You'll get in a lick or two, that you will," Viridovix promised as they moved in. They kept their horses to a walk, advancing as quietly as they could. The Yezda around the fires went about their business. One walked up to Rakio and slapped him across the face with the casual cruelty so common among them. Several others laughed and applauded.

Gorgidas could hear them plainly. With his comrades, he was less than fifty yards from the campfires before one of the Yezda turned his head their way—close enough for them to see his eyes go big and round and his mouth drop open in astonishment.

"Now!" Viridovix bellowed, snatching the reins of the spare horse from Mynto. Spurring their beasts, they stormed forward.

They were at a full gallop when they crashed down on the startled Yezda, shouting at the top of their lungs. In the first panic-filled moments, they must have seemed an army. The Yezda scattered before them. Men screamed as lance pierced or pounding hooves trampled. One soldier dove into a fire to escape a swing of Viridovix' sword and dashed out the other side with his coat ablaze.

Gorgidas swerved sharply toward the ponies tethered beside the camp. Viridovix had been right; already a couple of Yezda were there, clambering onto their horses. He cut them down, then rode through the rearing snorting animals, cutting lines and slashing at the horses themselves. He screeched and flapped his arms, doing everything he could to madden the beasts and make them useless to their masters.

Cries of fright turned to rage as the Yezda realized how few their attackers were. But Mynto in their midst was working a fearful slaughter, alone or not. His charger's iron-shod feet cracked ribs and split skulls; his spear killed until the clutch of a dying warrior wrenched it from his grasp. Then he pulled his saber free and, bending low in the saddle, slashed savagely at a pair of Yezda rushing toward him. One spun and fell, the other reeled away with a hand clapped to his slit nose.

In the chaos Viridovix made straight for Rakio. He sprang down from his horse beside the Yrmido. The Yezda had not really begun to enjoy themselves with their prisoner. He was bruised and battered, one eye swollen shut, a trickle of blood starting from the corner of his mouth where the last slap had landed. His mail shirt, of course, had gone for booty. His undertunic, ripped open to the waist, showed that his captors had tested their daggers' edges on his flesh.

But he was conscious, alert, and not begging to die. "Sorry your evening to disrupt," he said, moving his wrists so Viridovix could get at his bonds more easily. The Celt sliced through them and stooped to free his ankles. As he did so, a sword bit into Rakio's post just above his head. He half rose, bringing his dagger up in the underhanded killing stroke of a man who knows steel. A Yezda shrieked, briefly.

Rakio staggered once the thongs that bound his feet were cut. When Viridovix steadied him, he turned his head and kissed the Gaul square on the mouth. "I am in your debt," he said.

Sure his face was redder than his hair, Viridovix managed to grunt, "Can ye ride?"

"It is ride or die," the Yrmido said.

Viridovix helped him onto the horse Mynto had brought and set his feet in the stirrups. Hands still too numb to hold the reins, Rakio clasped them round the horse's neck.

Viridovix seized the lead line and vaulted aboard his own pony. With a wild howl of triumph, he dug his spurs into its flanks and slapped its muzzle when it turned to bite. Neighing shrilly, it bolted forward. A Yezda leaped at Rakio to tear him from the saddle, but spied Mynto bearing down at him and thought better of it. A crackle of excited talk ran between the two Sworn Fellows.

The Gaul's screech cut through the turmoil as easily as his knife tore flesh. With a skill he had not had till he went to the steppe, Gorgidas used the reins, the pressure of his knees, and a firm voice to steer his pony through the loosed animals that plunged and kicked all around him. He pounded after his comrades.

By the time he caught up with them, Rakio was in control of his own horse and Viridovix had let the lead line go. He rode close to the Yrmido and reached out to clasp his hand. "As I said I would be, I am here," he said.

Eyes shining, Rakio nodded, but winced at the Greek's touch; his hand was still puffy from trapped blood. "Sorry," Gorgidas said, the physician's tone and the lover's inseparable in his voice. "Are you much hurt?"

"Not so much as in another hour I would have been," Rakio said lightly. "All this looks worse than it is." He reached out himself, carefully, and ruffled the Greek's hair. "You were brave to come looking for me; I know that you are no warrior born." Before Gorgidas could say anything to that, he went on, "How did you find me?"

"Your gift." Gorgidas lifted his arm to show Rakio the bracelet, its light now vanished. He explained Tolui's magic.

"You have a greater one me given," the Yrmido said. With equestrian ability Gorgidas still could not have matched, he leaned over to embrace the physician.

"Och, enough o' your spooning, the twa o' ye," Viridivox said, the memory of Rakio's kiss making him speak more gruffly than he had intended. He was far too set on women for it to have stirred him, but it had not revolted him, either, as he would have expected. He pointed back to the Yezda camp. "Pay attention behind. They're coming round, I'm thinking. Bad cess for us they're so quick about it."

The confused cries and groans of the wounded were fading in the distance, but Gorgidas could also hear purposeful orders. When he turned his head, he saw the first pursuing riders silhouetted against the campfires. He cursed himself for not doing a better job of scattering their horses.

Viridovix brought him up short. "Where was the time for it? Nought to be gained worrying now, any road."

More familiar with the ground than their quarry, the Yezda closed the gap. An arrow clattered against a stone somewhere behind them. It was a wild, wasted shot, but others would come closer before long. Viridovix bit his lips. "The sons o' pigs'll be overhauling us, the gods send 'em a bloody flux."

"Up the mound, then?" Gorgidas said unhappily. They had agreed the dead city would make a refuge at need, but had hoped they would not have to use it. "We'll be trapping ourselves there."

"I ken, I ken," the Gaul replied. "But there's no help for it, unless your honor has a better notion. Sure as sure they're running us down on the flat. In the ruins we'll make 'em work to winkle us out, at least, and maybe find a way to get off. It's a puir chance, I'm thinking, but better than none."

Having seen the Yezda caught in a similar position, Gorgidas knew just how slim the chance was, but some of them had indeed escaped. And without cover, he and his comrades could not shake off their pursuers; Viridovix was right about that, too. The physician jerked on the reins, changing his pony's direction. The others were already making for the artificial mound.

Shouts from behind said their swerve had been marked. By then they were reining in sharply, slowing their beasts to a walk as they picked their way up the steep, cluttered sides of the mound. Mynto, heaviest in his armor, dismounted and climbed on foot, leading his horse. His companions soon had to follow his example.

Rakio came up side by side with Viridovix. Fighting through brush and shattered masonry that shifted under his feet at every step, the Celt paid little attention until Rakio nudged him. He turned. Even by starlight, the puzzlement was plain on Rakio's face. "Why are you here?" he asked, softly so Gorgidas and Mynto could not overhear. "I thought you my enemy were."

Once he had untangled that, Viridovix stared at the Yrmido. "And would you be telling me whatever gave ye sic a daft notion, now?"

"You had been sleeping with Gorgidas for a year." Rakio set out what seemed to him too obvious to need explaining. "It only natural is for you to be jealous, with me taking him away from you. Why you aren't?"

All that kept the Gaul from laughing out loud was that it would draw the Yezda. "Och, what a grand ninny y'are. 'Twas nobbut sleeping in the tent of us, that and some powerful talk. A finer friend nor the Greek there couldna be, for all his griping, but the next man's arse I covet'll be the first."

"Really?" It was Rakio's turn for amusement. No matter what he knew intellectually of other peoples' ways, emotionally the Sworn Fellowship's customs were the only right and proper ones to him. "I am sorry for you."

"Why are you sorry for him?" Gorgidas asked; Rakio had forgotten to keep his voice down.

"Never you mind," Viridovix told him. "Just shut up and climb. The losels ahint us'll be here all too quick."

But when the Greek looked back to see how close the Yezda were, he watched, dumfounded, as they trotted east past the mound. From their shouts to one another, they still thought they were in hot pursuit of Rakio and his rescuers. Mynto said something in the Yrmido tongue. Rakio translated: "A good time for them to lose their wits, but why?"

The question was rhetorical, but answered nonetheless. From the top of the hillock a thin voice called, "Come join me, my friends, if you would." At first Gorgidas thought he was hearing Greek, then Videssian. From the muffled exclamations of the others, he was sure they felt the same confusion; Viridovix gave a startled answer in his musical Celtic speech. In whatever language they heard the summons, none of them thought of disobeying, any more than they might a much-loved grandfather.

Before long they had to tether their horses and help each other with the last rugged climb to the hill's crest. The same jumble of eroded mud-brick walls and buildings Gorgidas had seen at the would-be Yezda ambush presented itself here, made worse because no fires lit it. The voice came again: "This way." They stumbled through the ruins of what might once have been the town marketplace and came at last to work that was not ancient—a lean-to of brush and sticks, propped against a half-fallen fence.

There was motion as they approached. A naked man emerged, at first on hands and knees before painfully getting to his feet. He raised his left hand in a gesture of blessing that was new to Gorgidas and Viridovix, but which Rakio and Mynto returned. "In the names of a greater Four, I welcome the four of you."

Gorgidas wondered how the hermit knew their number; his eyes were white and blind. But that wonder was small next to the physician's amazement that he could stand at all. He was the most emaciated human being the Greek had ever seen. His thighs were thinner than his knees; the skin fell in between his sharply etched ribs, or what could be seen of them behind a matted white beard. But for his blindness, his face might once have been princely; now he resembled nothing so much as a starved hawk.

While Gorgidas was taking the measure of the physical man, Viridovix penetrated at once to his essence. "A holy druid he is," the Gaul said, "or more like one nor any priest I've yet found here." Bowing to the hermit, he asked respectfully, "Was it your honor kept the Yezda from chasing us here?"

"A mere sending of phantoms," the other said. Or so the Celt understood him; watching, he did not see the holy man's lips move.

He was surprised when the hermit bowed to him in turn, then looked him full in the face with that disconcerting, empty gaze. He heard, "I have broken my rule of nonintervention in the affairs of the world for your sake; you carry too much destiny to be snuffed out in some tiny, meaningless scuffle."

They were all looking at Viridovix now, the two Yrmido in bewilderment, Gorgidas appraisingly. He could feel the truth emanating from the man. So could Viridovix, who protested, "Me? It's nobbut a puir lone Celt I am, trying to stay alive— for the which I maun thank you, now. But wish no geases on me."

Gorgidas cut in, "What destiny do you speak of?" This was no time, he thought, for Viridovix to have an uncharacteristic fit of modesty.

For the first time the hermit showed uncertainty. "That I may not—and cannot—tell you. I do not see it clearly myself, nor is the outcome certain. Other powers than mine cloud my view, and the end, for good or ill, is balanced to within a feather's weight. But without this stranger, only disaster lies ahead. Thus I chose to meddle in the ways of man once more, though this is but one of the two required pieces."

"Och, a druid indeed," Viridovix said, "saying more than he means. Is it so with your oracles, too, Greek?"

"Yes," Gorgidas said, but he caught the nervousness in the Gaul's chuckle.

Rakio spoke in the Yrmido language; with his gift of tongues, the holy man understood. Gorgidas caught only a couple of words; one was "Master," the title priests of the Four Prophets bore. The physician waited impatiently for the hermit's reply.

"I have made this hill my fortress against temptation since before the Yezda came," he said, "seeking in negation the path the sweet Four opened to a better life ahead. But I failed; my faith tottered when the murderers swept out of the west and laid waste my land and my fellow believers with no sign of vengeance being readied against them. Often I wondered why I chose to remain alive in the face of such misery; how much easier it would have been to let go my fleshly husk and enjoy bliss forever. Now at last I know why I did not."

He tottered forward to embrace Viridovix. The Celt had all he could do to keep from shying; not only was it like being hugged by a skeleton, but he did not think the holy man had washed himself since he took up his station a lifetime ago. Still worse, that confident touch told again of the holy man's certainty about his fate. He was worse afraid than in any battle, for it tore his freedom from him as death never could.

He pulled away so quickly the hermit staggered. Mynto righted the old man, glaring at the Celt. "Begging your honor's pardon," Viridovix said grudgingly. He looked to his comrades. "Should we not be off with us the now, with the Yezda so befooled and all?"

They started to agree, but the holy man quivered so hard Viridovix thought he would shake himself to pieces. He grasped the Celt's arm with unexpected strength. "You must not go! The fiends yet prowl all about, and will surely destroy you if you venture away. You must stay and wait before you try to return to your friends."

Mynto and Rakio were convinced at once. Gorgidas shrugged at Viridovix' unvoiced appeal. "Whatever else the man may be," the physician pointed out, "we've found him wizard enough to outfox the Yezda. Dare we assume he doesn't know what he's talking about?"

"Put that way, nay," the Gaul sighed, "but och, I wish we did."

Had he known the wait would stretch through four days, Gorgidas would have taken his chances on the Yezda. With Mynto there, he did not feel easy with Rakio, the more so because Rakio seemed to enjoy teasing him by playing up to his onetime lover. Nor was Viridovix, kicking against what the holy man insisted was to be his destiny, any better company. The Gaul, by turns somber and angry, either moped about in moody silence or snarled defiance at the world.

That left the hermit. Gorgidas did his best to draw the man out, but he was as faith-struck as the most fanatical Videssian priest. The Greek learned more than he really wanted to know about the cult of the Four Prophets, as much by what the hermit did not say as by what he did. Like Rakio and Mynto, he never mentioned his god or gods, reckoning the divinity too sacred to pollute with words, but he would drone on endlessly about the Prophets' attributes and aspects. Caught for once without writing materials, Gorgidas tried to remember as much as he could.

The first morning they were there, he asked the holy man his name, to have something to call him by. The hermit blinked, in that moment looking like an ordinary, perplexed mortal. "Do you know," he answered, "I've forgotten." He did not seem to mind when Gorgidas followed Rakio's usage and called him "Master."

He refused in horror to share the field rations the Greek and his comrades had with them. With ascetic zeal, he ate only the roots and berries he grubbed from the ground himself. His water came from the one well that had not fallen in since the dead city he lived in was abandoned. It was warm, muddy, and gave all four of his guests a savage diarrhea.

"No wonder the wight's so scrawny," Viridovix said, staggering up the hill after a call of nature. "On sic meat and drink I'd be dead in a week, beshrew me if I wouldn't."

Despite everything, though, the Celt did not urge his fellows to leave before the hermit said it was safe. For the first two days, Yezda constantly trotted past the mound. One band had a red-robed sorcerer with it. Gorgidas' heart was in his mouth lest the wizard penetrate the defenses of the place, but he rode on.

When the holy man finally gave them leave to go, the physician felt he was being released from gaol. And, like a warden cautioning freed prisoners against new crimes, the hermit warned: "Ride straight for the main body of your companions and all will be well with you. Turn aside for any reason and you will meet only disaster."

"We scarcely would do anything else," Rakio remarked as the hillock grew smaller behind them. "In this flat, ugly land there precious few distractions are." Perhaps seeking one, he winked at Mynto. Gorgidas ground his teeth and pretended not to see.

Following the Arshaum army did not rate the name of tracking. War's flotsam was guide enough: unburied men and horses swelling and stinking under the merciless sun, trampled canal banks where scores of beasts had drunk, a burnt-out barn that had served as a latrine for a regiment, discarded boots, a broken bow, a stolen carpet tossed aside as too heavy to be worth carrying.

The four riders drove their horses as hard as they dared; the Arshaum, unburdened now by many allies, would be picking up the pace. They saw no Yezda, save as distant specks. "You had the right of it," Viridovix admitted to Gorgidas. "Himself knew whereof he spoke. But for the draff and all, we might be cantering in the country."

The next morning rocked their confidence in the hermit's powers. Dust warned of the approaching column before it appeared out of the south, but they were in a stretch of land gone back to desert after the Yezda wrecked the local irrigation works, and the baked brown earth offered no cover. The column swerved their way.

"Out sword!" Viridovix cried, tugging his own free. "Naught for it but to sell oursel's dear as we may."

Mynto drew his saber, a handsome weapon with gold inlays on the hilt. He patted the empty boss on the right side of his saddle and said something to Rakio. "He wishes he had his spear," Rakio translated. Irrepressible, he added an aside to Gorgidas: "It was a long one."

"Oh, a pest take Mynto and his spear, and you with them," the physician snapped. He could feel his sweat soaking into the leather grip of his *gladius*. The shortsword fit his hand as well as any surgical knife, and he was beginning to gain some skill with it. But the size of the oncoming troop only brought despair at the prospect of a hopeless fight.

He could see men in armor through the swirling dust, their lances couched and ready. What that meant escaped him until Viridovix let out a wordless yowl of glee and slammed his blade into its sheath. "Use the eyes of you, man," he called to the Greek. "Are those Yezda?"

"No, by the dog!" Along with his comrades, Gorgidas booted his horse toward the Erzrumi.

Rakio identified them. "It is Gashvili's band from Gunib."

Though he kept shouting and waving to show the mountain men he was no enemy, trepidation stirred in Viridovix. Frightful oaths had bound Gashvili to ride with the Arshaum. If he was forsaking them, would he leave witnesses to tell of it? The Gaul did not draw his sword again, but he made sure it was loose in the scabbard.

His alarm spiked when the men of Gunib almost rode him and his companions down in spite of their cries of friendship. Only as the Erzrumi finally pulled up could he see them as more than menacing figures behind their lanceheads. They were reeling in the saddle, red-eyed with fatigue; every one was filthy with the caked dust of hard travel. Scraps of grimy cloth covered fresh wounds. Clouds of flies descended to gorge on oozing serum or new blood. Most of the troopers did not bother slapping them away.

"They're beaten men," the Celt said softly, in wonder. He looked in vain for Gashvili's gilded scale-mail. "Where might your laird be?" he asked the nearest Erzrumi.

"Dead," the fellow replied after a moment, as if he had to

force himself to understand the Khamorth tongue Viridovix had used.

"The gods smile on him when he meets them, then. Who leads you the now?"

Vakhtang made his way through his men toward the newcomers. He surveyed them dully. "I command," he said, but his voice held no authority. He was a million miles from the coxcomb who had come out to confront Arigh's men in front of Gunib. His two-pointed beard made an unkempt tangle down the front of his corselet, whose gilding was marred by sword stroke and smoke and blood. The jaunty feather was long gone from his helm. Out of a face haggard and sick with defeat his eyes stared, not quite focused, somewhere past Viridovix' right ear.

He was worse than beaten, the Gaul realized; he was stunned, as if clubbed. "What of your oath to Arigh?" he growled, thinking to sting the ruined man in front of him back to life. "Gone and left him in the lurch, have you now, mauger all the cantrips and fine words outside your precious castle?"

As lifelessly as before, Vakhtang said, "No. We are not forsworn." But in spite of himself, his head lifted; he met Viridovix' eyes for the first time. His voice firmed as he went on. "Arigh himself and his priest Tolui absolved us of our vow when the army began to break up."

"Tell me," Viridovix said, overriding cries of dismay from Gorgidas and then in turn from Rakio and Mynto as Vakhtang's words were rendered into Videssian and the Yrmido speech.

The story had an appalling simplicity. Yezda in numbers never before seen had come rushing up out of the south to repeat on a vastly larger scale the pincer tactics they had tried in front of Dur-Sharrukin. They were better soldiers than the Arshaum had seen before, too; a prisoner boasted that Wulghash the khagan had picked them himself.

All the same, Arigh held his own, even smashing the Yezda left wing to bits against a tributary of the Tib. "No mean general, that one," Vakhtang said, growing steadily more animated as he talked. But his face fell once more as newer memories crowded back. "Then the flames came."

Viridovix went rigid in the saddle. "What's that?" he barked. He jerked at a sudden pain in his hands. Looking down, he willed his fists open and felt his nails ease out of his flesh.

He did not need the Erzrumi's description to picture the lines of fire licking out to split apart and trap their makers' foes; Avshar had shown him the reality in Pardraya. As Vakhtang continued, though, he saw that Arigh had not had to face the full might of the spell. The noble said, "It was battle magic; our priests and shamans fought it to a standstill, in time. But it was too late to save the battle; by then our position was wrecked past repair. That was when your Arshaum gave us leave to go. The gods be thanked, we mauled the Yezda enough to make them think twice about giving chase."

"Begging your pardon, I'm thinking you saw nobbut the second team," Viridovix said. "Had himself been working the fires and not his mages—a murrain take them—only them as he wanted would ever ha' got clear."

"As may be," Vakhtang said. A few of his men bristled at the suggestion that less than Yezd's best had beaten them, but he was too worn to care. "All I hope now is to see Gunib again. I am glad we came across you; every sword will help on our way home."

Gorgidas and then Rakio finished translating; silence fell. The two of them, the Gaul, and Mynto looked at each other. Wisdom surely lay with retreat in this well-armed company, but they could not forget the hermit's warning that changing course would bring misfortune. In the end, though, that was not what shaped Viridovix' decision. He said simply, "I've come too far to turn back the now."

"And I," Gorgidas said. "For better or worse, this is my conflict, and I will know how it ends."

As nothing else had, their choice tore the lethargy from Vakhtang. "Madmen!" he cried. "It will end with an arrow through your belly and your bones baking under this cursed sun." He turned to the two Yrmido, his hands spread in entreaty, and spoke to them in the Vaspurakaner tongue.

Mynto gave a sudden, sharp nod. He and Rakio got into a low-voiced dispute; from what little Gorgidas could follow, he was echoing Vakhtang's arguments. Rakio mostly listened, indecision etched on his features. When at last he answered, Mynto's lips thinned in distress. Rakio shifted to Videssian: "I will travel south. To disregard the words of the holy hermit after he his gifts from the Four has shown strikes me as the greater madness."

When Mynto saw he could not sway his countryman, he embraced him with the tenderness any lover would give his

beloved. Then he rode forward to join the men of Gunib.
Vakhtang brought both fists to his forehead in grateful salute.

"I wish you the luck I do not expect you to have," he told
the other three. He waved to his battered company. They
started north on their lathered, blowing horses, the jingle of
their harness incongruously gay.

Soon dust and distance made Mynto impossible to pick out
from the men of Gunib around him. Rakio let out a small sigh.
"He is a fine, bold fellow, and I him will miss," he said. His
eyes danced at Gorgidas' expression.

Viridovix caught the byplay. He rounded on the Ymrido.
"Is it a puss-cat y'are, to make sic sport? Finish the puir wight
off or let him be."

"Will you shut up?" Gorgidas shouted, scarlet and furious.

Laughing, Rakio looked sidelong at the Gaul. "You are
sure it is not jealousy?" He went on more seriously: "Should I
tell Mynto all my reasons for going with you two? That only
would hurt him to no purpose."

Having reduced both his companions to silence, he set out
south along the trail Vakhtang's men had left. They followed.
Neither met the other's eye.

IX

Money clinked in Marcus' palm. "Four and a half," Tahmasp said. "One for your month with us, the rest your fair share of the pot." Two of the goldpieces were Yezda, stamped with Yezd's leaping panther and a legend in a script the tribune could not read. The rest came from Videssos. Even in Mashiz, imperial gold was good.

Gaius Philippus stepped up to take his pay. "We'd have earned more in time served if you'd not taken the southern route," he said.

Tahmasp made a sour face. "More in profit, too." The lands between the Tutub and the Tib would have given him twice the trade his desert-skirting track yielded, but a barbarian invasion had thrown the Hundred Cities into confusion.

The caravaneer folded each Roman in turn into a beefy embrace. "You bastards sure you won't stick around till I set out again?"

"A couple of months from now?" Marcus shook his head. "Not likely."

"Not that I care a flying fart what happens to you," Tahmasp said, a frown giving his gruff words the lie, "but two men riding through the Yezda by themselves stand the same chance of coming out whole as two eggs about to be scrambled."

"Actually, I think we may do better alone," the tribune answered. "At least we won't draw nomads the way your traveling madhouse does." The Yezda had swarmed thick as flies the first two weeks out of Amorion. To ride away then would have been death, even without Tahmasp's vow of destruction to deserters.

Later they might have escaped with ease, but by then the shared dangers of three desperate fights and endless hours of picket duty and talk around campfires had welded them indissolubly to the company. It was easy to abandon strangers; not so, friends. And so, Scaurus thought, here we are in the heart of Yezd, all for loyalty's sake.

It seemed strange and not very fair.

Tahmasp pumped Gaius Philippus' hand, slapped Marcus on the back. As always, he set himself; as always, he staggered. "You have the wits of a couple of sun-addled jackasses, but good luck to you. If you live—which I doubt—maybe we'll meet again." The caravaneer turned away. To him they were finished business.

They led their horses out of the fortified warehouse into the shadows of Mashiz' afternoon. Marcus could look east and see the sun still shining brightly, but the peaks of Dilbat brought an early twilight to the city. In a way it was a blessing, for it cut the Yezda summer's heat. Yezd made Videssos' central plateau temperate by comparison.

"What now?" Gaius Philippus asked, his mind firmly on the problem of the moment. "Me, I'm for shagging out of here right away. Tahmasp is welcome to this place."

Marcus nodded slowly. More shadows than the ones cast by the mountains of Dilbat hung over Mashiz. He looked around, trying to pinpoint the source of his unease. It was not the buildings; he was sure of that much. The eye grew used to thin towers topped by onion domes, to spiral ramps instead of stairways, to pointed arches wider than the doors beneath them, and to square columns covered with geometric mosaics. Mashiz seemed fantastically strange, but Makuraner architecture was only different, not sinister.

The Yezda, but two generations off the steppe, were not builders. They had put their mark on Mashiz all the same. The tribune wondered what the sack had been like when the city fell. Every other block, it seemed, had a wrecked building, and every other structure needed repair. That air of decay, of a slow falling into ruin, was part of the problem, Scaurus thought.

But only part. A disproportionate number of ravaged buildings had been shrines of the Four Prophets; the Yezda had been as savage toward Makuran's national cult as they were to

the worship of Phos. As the Romans headed for the city's
market, they passed only a couple of surviving shrines. Both
were small buildings that had probably once been private
homes, and mean ones at that.

Further west, toward the edge of Mashiz, stood another
temple once dedicated to the Four: a marvelous red granite
pyramid, no doubt the Makuraner counterpart to Phos' High
Temple in Videssos. The Yezda, though, had claimed it for
their own. Scored into every side, brutally obliterating the
reliefs that told the story of the Four Prophets, were Skotos'
twin lightningbolts. A cloud of thick brown smoke rose above
the building. When the breeze shifted and sent a tag end of it
their way, Marcus and Gaius Philippus both coughed at the
stench.

"I know what meat that is," the senior centurion said
darkly.

The people of Mashiz, Scaurus reflected, lived with that
cloud every day of their lives. No wonder they were furtive,
sticking to the deeper shadows of buildings as they walked
along the street, looking at strangers out of the corners of their
eyes, and rarely talking above a whisper. No wonder a born
swaggerer like Tahmasp spent most of his time on the road.

In Mashiz, the Yezda swaggered. Afoot or on horse, they
came down the middle of the road with the arrogance of con-
querors and expected everyone else to stay out of their way.

The Romans saw priests of Skotos for the first time; they
seemed a ghastly parody of the clergy who served Phos. Their
robes were the color of drying blood—to keep the gore of
their sacrifices from showing, Marcus thought grimly. Their
dark god's sigil was blazoned in black on their chests; their
hair was shorn into the double thunderbolt. The locals ducked
aside whenever a pair of them came by; even the Yezda appeared nervous around them.

They did not speak to Scaurus, which suited him.

To his relief, something like normality reigned in the marketplace. The sights and sounds of commerce were the same
wherever men gathered. He needed no knowledge of the guttural Makuraner tongue to understand that this customer
thought a butcher was cheating him, or that that one was
going to outhaggle a wool merchant if it took all night.

Marcus was afraid he would have to bargain by dumb
show, but most of the venders knew a few words of Videssian:
numbers, yes, no, and enough invective to add flavor to no.

He bought hard cheese, coarse-ground flour, and a little griddle on which to cook wheatcakes. As a happy afterthought, he added a sackful of Vaspurakaner-style pastries, a rich mixture of flour, minced almonds, and ground dates, dusted with sugar.

"'Princes' balls,'" the baker said, chuckling, as he tied the neck of the sack. Marcus had heard the joke before, but his answering laugh got a couple of coppers knocked off the price.

"Anything else we need?" he asked Gaius Philippus.

"A new canteen," the centurion said. "The solder's come loose from the seam on this one, and it leaks. Maybe a patch'll do, but something, anyway. The kind of country this is, losing water could kill you in a hurry."

"Let's find a tinker, then, or a coppersmith." To Marcus' surprise, there did not seem to be any tinkers wandering through the square, nor did the baker understand the Videssian word. "Not something they have here, I gather. Oh, well, a smith it is."

The coppersmiths' district was not far from the marketplace. The baker pointed the way. "Three blocks up, two over."

The Romans heard a scuffle down a sidestreet. So did several locals, who paid no attention; if it was not happening to them, they did not want to know about it. But when Scaurus and Gaius Philippus came to the alleyway, they saw a single man, his back to a mud-brick wall, desperately wielding a cudgel against four attackers.

They looked at each other. "Shall we even up the odds?" Marcus asked. Without waiting for an answer, he sprang onto his horse. Gaius Philippus was already mounting. He had a better beast than the gray these days, a sturdy brown gelding with a white blaze between the eyes.

The robbers whirled as the drumroll of hoofbeats filled the narrow street. One fled. Another threw a dagger at the tribune, a hurried cast that went wild. Scaurus' horse ran him down. The third bravo swung a mace at Gaius Philippus, who turned the stroke with his *gladius* and then thrust it through the fellow's throat. The last of the robbers grappled with him and tried to pull him from the saddle, but their would-be victim sprang out to aid his unexpected rescuers. His club caved in the back of the bandit's skull.

Marcus rode after the footpad who had run, but the fellow

escaped, vanishing in a maze of twisting alleys the tribune did not know. When he got back, the man he had saved was bending over the trampled robber, who groaned and thrashed on the ground. Pulling out a penknife, he jerked the bandit's head back and cut his throat.

Scaurus frowned at such rough-and-ready justice, but decided the robber was probably lucky not to fall into the hands of whatever passed for a constabulary among the Yezda.

The man rose, bowing low to one Roman and then to the other. He was about Marcus' age and nearly as tall as the tribune, but with a much leaner frame. His face was long and gaunt, with hollows below the cheekbones. His eyes, somber and dark, also looked out from hollows.

He bowed again, saying something in the Makuraner language. Marcus had picked up just enough of it to be able to answer that he did not understand. Without much hope, he asked, "Do you speak Videssian?"

"Yes, indeed I do." The fellow's accent was thicker than Tahmasp's, but also more cultured. "May I ask my rescuers' names?"

The Romans looked at each other, shrugged, and gave them.

"I am in your debt, sirs. I am Tabari." He said that as if they ought to know who Tabari was. Marcus tried to seem suitably impressed. Gaius Philippus grunted.

Just then, a squad of archers came dashing round the corner. Someone finally must have let the watch know a fight was going on. The leader of the Yezda saw the robber's body lying on the ground in a pool of blood and growled something to his men. They turned their bows on the Romans and Tabari.

Scaurus and Gaius Philippus froze, careful not to do anything threatening with the swords they still held. Tabari strode forward confidently. He spoke a couple of sentences in the Yezda tongue. The city guards lowered their weapons so fast that one dropped an arrow. Their commander bowed low.

"As I said, I am Tabari," said the man the Romans had rescued, turning back to them, "minister of justice to my lord the great khagan Wulghash." Suddenly his eyes no longer looked somber to Marcus. They looked dangerous. Justice, these days, meant prison to the tribune, and he had seen more of prison than he ever wanted to.

Tabari went on, "As a small token of my gratitude, let me present you at the court banquet this evening. Surely my lord

Wulghash will take notice of your courage and generosity and reward you as you deserve. My own resources, I fear, are too small for that, but know you have my undying gratitude."

"Wulghash? Oh, bloody wonderful!" Gaius Philippus said in Latin.

"Surely you do us too much honor," Marcus said to Tabari, doing his best to frame a polite refusal. "We know nothing of courts or fancy manners—"

"My lord Wulghash does not insist on them, and I tell you he will be delighted to show favor to the men who saved his minister of justice, even if," Tabari's voice held irony, "they were unaware of his rank." He spoke to the Yezda underofficer, who bowed again. "Rhadzat here will take you to the palace. I would escort you myself, but I fear I have pressing business this dead dog of a robber and his confederates interrupted. I shall see you there this evening. Until then, my friends."

"Until then." Marcus and Gaius Philippus echoed him with a singular lack of enthusiasm.

Unlike the rambling Videssian palace complex, the court at Mashiz was housed in a single building. The great stone blocks from which it was built looked as if they had been ripped from the mountains' heart. Studying the smoothly weathered outwalls, Marcus guessed the palace had been a citadel before Mashiz was a city.

Once inside the outwalls, a couple of Yezda from Rhadzat's squad peeled off to lead the Romans' horses to the stables. Knowing the care the Yezda lavished on their own beasts, Scaurus was sure his would get fine treatment from them. It did nothing to ease his mind. Being away from their mounts would only make flight harder for the Romans.

Rhadzat conducted the tribune and senior centurion to the palace entrance, where a steward eyed him and them with distaste. The servitor was of Makuraner blood, slim, dark, and elegant, wearing a brocaded caftan and sandals with golden clasps. His haughty air vanished when the Yezda officer explained why they had come. Graceful as a cat, he bowed to the Romans.

He called into the palace for another servant. When the man arrived, the steward spoke to the Romans in his own tongue. Marcus shrugged and spread his hands. A ghost of the doorman's sneer returned. "You please to follow him," he said, his Videssian slow and rusty but clear enough.

Their guide knew only Makuraner and the Yezda speech. He chattered on, not caring whether they understood, as he led them up a ramp of green marble polished till it reflected the light of the torches that hung in gilded sconces every few feet along the wall. His soft-soled slippers did better on the smooth surface than the Romans' *caligae*; he giggled out loud when Gaius Philippus skidded and almost fell.

The couches in the waiting room were stuffed with down and upholstered in soft suede. The sweetmeats that the palace servitors brought came on silver trays and filled the mouth with delicate perfume. Watching shadows move across the ornate wall hangings, Marcus felt like a fly gently but irresistibly trapped in spider silk.

The room was in twilight by the time the court official returned to take the Romans away. At the entrance to the throne room he surrendered his charges to another chamberlain, an elderly Makuraner eunuch whose caftan was of almost transparent silk.

He had some Videssian. "No need for proskynesis when you present yourself before Khagan Wulghash," he said, sniffing in disapproval at his master's barbarous informality. "A bow will do. He keeps his grandfather's ways—as if a lizard-eating nomad's customs were valid." Another sniff. "He even allows his primary wife a seat beside him." A third sniff, louder than the other two.

Marcus did not pay much attention. The throne room was long and narrow; the tribune felt his shoes sinking into the thick wool of the carpet as he walked toward the distant pair of high ivory seats ahead. Without turning his head too much, he tried to spot Tabari. In the flickering torchlight, one man looked like the next.

With its moving shadows, the light of the torches did a better job showing up the reliefs on the walls behind the nobility of Yezd. Like the defaced ones on the temple that now belonged to Skotos, they were carved in a florid style that owed nothing to Videssian severity. One was a hunting scene, with some long-forgotten Makuraner king slaying a lion with a sword. The other—Marcus' eyes went wide as he recognized the regalia of the man shown kneeling before another king on horseback. Only an Avtokrator wore such garb.

Beside him, Gaius Philippus gave a tiny chuckle. "I

wonder what the imperials have to say about *that* in their histories," he whispered.

A herald was coming forward from the thrones as the Romans approached them. He raised their hands above their heads—no easy feat; he was several inches shorter than Gaius Philippus—and cried out in the Makuraner and Yezda tongues. Scaurus caught his own name and the centurion's.

Applause washed over the Romans. A couple of Makuraner lords, seeing they were foreigners, cried out "Well done!" in Videssian. The tribune finally spotted Tabari, sitting close to the front. He and the other Makuraners cheered louder and longer than their Yezda counterparts. It was a heady moment, though Marcus wondered how many of the clapping men had led armies into the Empire.

The herald led them toward the thrones. The khagan sat on the right-hand one, which was higher than the other. Wulghash wore a headdress like those of the Makuraner kings remembered on the throne room walls, a high, conical crown of stiff white felt, with earflaps reaching nearly to his shoulders. A vertical row of gems ran up from edge to peak; a double band of horsehair made a diadem across the khagan's forehead.

Marcus sized Wulghash up—he had never wanted to meet the ruler of Yezd, but would not waste what chance had set before him. The khagan was swarthy, about fifty. His thick beard, cut square at the bottom, was salt-and-pepper, with salt gaining. His square features had a hard cast partly offset by tired, intelligent eyes. He was wide shouldered and well made, his middle only beginning to thicken.

"Careful," Gaius Philippus said. "He's not one to mess with." Scaurus gave a small nod; that fit his view exactly.

The herald stopped the Romans just past the end of the carpet, at a stone smoothed by thousands of feet over the centuries. They made their bows, to fresh applause. It grew even louder when Wulghash came down to clasp their hands —his own was hard, dry, and callused, more like a soldier's than a bureaucrat's—and embrace them.

"You have saved a valued member of my court, and have my friendship for it," Wulghash said. His Videssian was polished as any courtier of Thorisin's. "Allow me to present you to my senior queen, Atossa." He nodded to the woman on the lower throne.

Studying Wulghash so, the tribune had hardly noticed her.

She was about the khagan's age and handsome still. She smiled and spoke in the Makuraner tongue. "She apologizes for being unable to thank you in a language you know," Wulghash translated.

Marcus returned the first compliment that popped into his mind: "Tell her she is as kind as she is beautiful." Atossa regally inclined her head. He nodded back, thoughts whirling. Here with a friendly hand on his shoulder stood Videssos' sworn enemy, the man Avshar named master. If he jerked his dagger from his belt, thrust—

He did not move. To violate Wulghash's generosity so was not in him. What point in fighting Avshar if he fell to his methods? That thought brought him closer to understanding Videssos' dualism than he had ever come.

A pipe's clear whistle cut through the court chatter. Everyone brightened. "The feast is ready," Wulghash explained, "and about time, too." He handed Atossa down from her throne; she took his arm. The Romans fell in line behind the royal couple.

The banquet hall, though merely a palace chamber, was nearly as large as the Hall of the Nineteen Couches in Videssos. Torchlight sparkled off the blue crystal and gold and silver foil of the abstract mosaic patterns on the walls. As guests of honor, Scaurus sat at Wulghash's right while Gaius Philippus was on Atossa's left.

The khagan rose to toast them. He drank wine, as did the nobles Marcus had picked as Makurani. Most of the Yezda chieftains preferred their traditional kavass. When a skin of the fermented mares' milk reached the tribune, he slurped for politeness' sake and passed it to Wulghash. The khagan wrinkled his fleshy nose and sent it on without drinking.

"There is also date wine, if you care for it," he told the Roman. Marcus declined with a shudder. He had sampled the stuff on the journey with Tahmasp. It was so sweet and syrupy as to make the cloying Videssian wine seem pleasantly dry.

Some of the food was simple nomad fare: wheatcakes, yogurt, and plain roast meat. Again, though, Wulghash liked Makuraner ways better than those of his ancestors. Enjoying grape leaves stuffed with goat and olives, an assortment of roasted songbirds, steamed and sauteed vegetables, and mutton baked in a sauce of mustard, raisins, and wine, Scaurus decided he could not fault the khagan's taste. And at sizzling rice soup he positively beamed; he had met it in a Makuraner cafe in Videssos that first magic winter night with Alypia Gavra.

The thought of her made the celebration strange and somehow unreal. After fighting the Yezda for years, what was he doing here making polite small talk with a prince whose people were destroying the land he had taken for his own? And what was Wulghash doing as that prince? He seemed anything but the monster Scaurus had pictured, and no ravening barbarian either. Plainly a capable ruler, he was as much influenced by Makuran's civilization as the great count Drax was under Videssos' spell. His presiding over the devastation the Yezda worked posed a riddle the tribune could not solve.

He got his first clue when a dispatch rider, still sweaty from his travels, brought the khagan a sheaf of messages. Wulghash read rapidly through them, growing angrier with each sheet. He growled out a stream of commands.

When the messenger interrupted with some objection or question, the khagan clapped an exasperated hand to his forehead. He wrote on the back of one of the dispatches with quick, furious strokes. Then he wet the signet ring he wore on the middle finger of his right hand in mustard sauce and stamped a smeary, yellow-brown seal on his orders. Goggling, the messenger saluted, took the parchment, and hurried away.

Wulghash, still fuming, drained his ivory rhyton at a gulp. He turned to Marcus. "I have days I think all my captains idiots, the way they panic at shadows. They've been raiding Erzerum since my grandfather's time—is it any wonder the hillmen strike back? I know the cure for that, though. Hit them three ways at once so their army breaks into all its little separate groups and they're nothing much. We've already started that; all we have to do is keep on with it. And the heads have started going up into their valleys. They'll think a long time before they stir out again."

"Heads?" the tribune echoed.

"Killed in battle, prisoners, what does it matter?" Wulghash said with ruthless unconcern. "So long as the Erzrumi recognize most of them, they serve their purpose."

The khagan slammed his fist down on the table; Atossa touched his left arm, trying to soothe him. He shook her off. "This is *my* land," he proudly declared to Scaurus, "and I intend to pass it on to my son greater than it was when I received it from my father. I have beaten Videssos; shall I let a pack of fourth-rate mountain rats get the better of me?"

"No," Marcus said, but he felt a chill of fear. Wulghash's wish was irreproachable, but the khagan did not care what steps he took to reach it. The man on that path, the tribune thought, walks at the edge of the abyss. To cover his unease, he asked, "Your son?"

As any father might, Wulghash swelled with pride. "Kho-bin is a fine lad—no, I cannot call him that now. He has a man's years on him, and a little son of his own. Where does the time go? He watches the northwest for me, making sure the stinking Arshaum stay on their side of the Degird. There will be trouble with them; the embassy I sent last year won no success."

Scaurus concealed the excitement that coursed through him. If the Yezda embassy had failed, perhaps the Videssian mission to the steppe tribes was faring well. He wondered how Viridovix and Gorgidas were and even spared a moment's thought for Pikridios Goudeles. The pen-pusher was a rogue, but a slick one.

Only a few drops of wine came from the silver ewer when Wulghash lifted it to refill his drinking-horn. "I need more, Harshad," he called, absentmindedly still using Videssian. A Yezda at the foot of the table looked up when he heard his name. Seeing him scratch his head, the khagan realized his mistake and repeated the request in his own language.

Grinning now, Harshad muttered a few words into his beard and moved his fingers in a quick, intricate pattern over the wine jar in front of him. It rose smoothly until it was a couple of feet above the table, then drifted toward Wulghash. Gaius Philippus had been cutting the meat from a pork rib; he looked up just as the jar floated past him. He dropped his knife.

None of the Yezda or Makuraner nobles took any special notice of the magic. A small smile on his lips, Wulghash said, "A little sorcery, that one." He pointed at Gaius Philippus' cup and spoke in a language Marcus almost thought he knew. The cup lifted, glided over to the floating ewer. The wine jar tipped and poured, then straightened as the cup was full. Wulghash gestured again. The cup returned to Gaius Philippus; the wine jar settled to the table. The khagan filled his rhyton the ordinary way.

Gaius Philippus was staring at his cup as if he expected it to get up and shoot dice with him. "Merely wine," Wulghash assured him, tasting his own. "Better than what we had, in fact. You are not very familiar with wizardry, are you?"

"More than I want to be," the veteran answered. He picked up the cup in both hands and emptied it at a gulp. "That *is* good. Could you pass me the jar for more?" He managed to laugh when Wulghash lifted the ewer with the same exaggerated care he had given the cup.

The khagan turned back to Marcus who had done his best not to show surprise at the magic. That best, apparently, was not good enough, for Wulghash said, "How is it sorcery seems so strange to you? You must have seen magecraft enough among the Videssians." His gaze was suddenly sharp; the tribune remembered he had thought the khagan's eyes intelligent the moment he saw him. Now they probed at the Roman. "But then, you have an accent I do not know and you talk with your comrade in a tongue I do not recognize—and I know a good many."

He saw the Roman's face turn wary, and said, "I do not mean to frighten you. You are my friends, I have promised you that. By all the gods and prophets, were you the Avtokrator of the Videssians you could leave my table in safety if you had that pledge." He sounded angry at himself and Scaurus both; more than anything, that made the tribune believe him.

The khagan went on, "As a friend, though, you make me wonder at you, all the more when magic startles you despite the blade you carry." This time Marcus could not help jumping. Wulghash's chuckle was dry as boots scuffing through dead leaves. "Am I a blind man, to miss the moon in the sky? Tell me of yourself, if you will, as one friend does for another."

Marcus hesitated, wondering what Wulghash might have heard of Romans from Avshar or from the spies the khagan had to have in Videssos. The story he decided on was a drastically edited version of the truth. Saying nothing of the rest of the legionaries, he gave out that he and Gaius Philippus were from a land beyond the eastern ocean, forced to flee to these strange shores by a quarrel with a chieftain. After serving as mercenaries for Videssos, they had to flee again when Scaurus fell foul of the Emperor—he did not say how. Tahmasp's caravan, he finished truthfully, had brought them to Mashiz.

"That scoundrel," Wulghash said without rancor. "Who knows how much trade tax and customs revenue he cheats me out of every year?" He studied the tribune. "So Gavras outlawed you, did he? With his temper, you should be thankful you're still breathing."

"I know," Scaurus said, so feelingly the khagan gave that dry chuckle again.

"You have poor luck with nobles, it appears," Wulghash remarked. "Why is that?"

The tribune sensed danger in the question. As he cast about for a safe answer, Gaius Philippus came to his rescue. "Because we have a bad habit—we speak our minds. If one high-born sod's greedy as a pig at the swill trough or the next is a liverish son of a whore, we say so. Aye, it gets us in trouble, but it beats licking spit."

"Liverish, eh? Not bad," Wulghash said. As Gaius Philippus had intended, he took it to refer to Thorisin. He seemed reassured—the centurion's raspy voice and blunt features were made for candor.

The khagan looked musingly from one Roman to the other. "I know nothing of the countries beyond the eastern sea," he said. "Past Namdalen and the barbarous lands on the southern shore of the Sailors' Sea, our maps are blank. You could teach me a great deal." He went on, as his smile exposed strong yellow teeth, "And you were officers with Videssos. No doubt you will be able to tell me quite a lot about your sojourn there as well. Shall I have an apartment prepared for you here in the palace? That would be most convenient; I think we will be spending a good deal of time together over the next couple of weeks."

"We would be honored," Marcus said, and knew he had told Wulghash another lie.

To the Romans' dismay, the khagan was good as his word. He was full of questions, yet did not really subject them to a serious interrogation, asking almost as much about their homeland as about Videssos and its armies. Those questions Scaurus answered honestly, after the initial deception about the eastern ocean. Sometimes he and Gaius Philippus disagreed sharply; he came from the urban upper class, while the centurion was a product of farm and legion.

Wulghash was that rarity, a good listener. His queries always moved arguments along and convinced Scaurus afresh of his brain. His secretary Pushram, who wrote down the Romans' replies, asked no questions. He made a point of seeming bored about everything outside the khagan's court. It was a mischievous sort of boredom, for he was a skinny little brown man with outsized ears and amazingly flexible features.

Well into the second week of the Romans' presence at court, a servant came by with a tray of eggplant slices cooked in cheese and oregano. Wulghash took one. "That's excellent," he exclaimed. "Much better than usual. Here, fellow, give my friends some, too."

"Very nice," Marcus said politely, though in fact he found the eggplant bland and its sauce too sharp. Gaius Philippus, no timeserver, left his slice half-eaten.

Pushram, however, screwed up his face into a blissful expression. "Most glorious eggplant! Handsome to look upon, delicate on the tongue, full of flavor and of pleasing texture, a comestible to be esteemed for all the multifarious ways it may be prepared, each more delicious than the next. Truly a prince —no, let me say more: a khagan—among vegetables!"

Scaurus had heard fulsome flattery at the Videssian court, but nothing close to this sycophancy. "Who would want to be a king and have to put up with such tripe?" Gaius Philippus said in Latin.

After a while Wulghash rolled his eyes and went back to questioning the Romans. Pushram's paean of praise never slowed, even while he was recording Marcus' answers. Trying to find some way to shut him up, the khagan took another piece of eggplant, wrinkled his lip, and said, "I have changed my mind. This is vile."

Pushram assumed a look of loathing with a speed that amazed Scaurus. He plucked the eggplant slice from Wulghash's hand and threw it to the floor. "What a foul, noxious weed eggplant is!" he cried. "Not only is it of a bilious color, it brings no more nourishment to mankind than so much grass. Moreover, it makes me burp."

And he was off again, as ready to continue in that vein as to shower the vegetable with compliments. Marcus listened, open-mouthed. Wulghash gave Pushram a look that should have chilled any man's marrow, but the secretary's stream of abuse never faltered. "Enough!" Wulghash finally growled. "Were you not praising eggplant to the skies not two minutes ago, instead of cursing it?"

"Certainly."

"Well?" The word hung in the air like doom.

But Pushram was unruffled. "Well, what?" he said cheerfully. "I am your courtier, not the eggplant's. I have to say what pleases you, not what pleases the eggplant."

"Get out!" Wulghash roared, but he was laughing.

Pushram scurried away anyhow. The khagan shook his head. "Makurani," he said, more to himself than to the Romans. "Sometimes they make me wish my grandfather had stayed on the steppe."

Marcus pointed to the plate of eggplant. "Yet you have taken on many Makuraner ways. If your grandfather was a nomad, he never would have cared for such a dish."

"My grandfather ate beetles, when he could catch them," the khagan said, and then sighed. "Too many of my chiefs think any change from the old customs wrong simply because it is change. Some of the plains ways have their point. What sense does it make to lock away women? Are they not people, too? But on the whole we were barbarians then, and for all their oiliness and foolishness the Makurani have worked out many better ways of living—and of ruling—than we ever knew. Try and tell that to an old nomad who has no thoughts past his flocks, though. Try and make him listen, or obey."

For a moment Scaurus understood him perfectly; he had lived with that feeling of being trapped between two cultures ever since the legionaries came to Videssos.

There was some sort of commotion outside the throne room. Marcus heard shouts of anger, then of fear. Nobles' heads turned as they looked to see what was wrong. A couple of eunuchs trotted toward the door. Wulghash's guards still stood impassive, but the tribune saw arm muscles bunch as hands tightened on sabers.

"Let me by, or regret it evermore!" At the sound of that voice, Marcus and Gaius Philippus were both on their feet and reaching for their swords. Crying out in alarm, the nearest guardsmen broke freeze and sprang at them.

"Stand!" Wulghash shouted, halting the Romans and his own soldiers alike. "What idiocy are you playing at?"

Scaurus was saved the trouble of finding an answer. Back at the entrance to the throne room, the last palace servitors were retreating in dread. Avshar strode down the carpet toward the twin thrones. Despite the thick, soft wool, every bootfall echoed. The muffled thuds were the only sounds in the hall, growing ever louder as he drew close.

No longer were the wizard-prince's robes an immaculate white. They swirled in filthy, dusty tatters round him. As protocol demanded, he stopped just past the edge of the carpet; his head turned from one Roman to the other. "Well, well," he said with horrible good humor, "what have we here?"

He ignored Wulghash, who said sharply, "We have a servant who does not know his master, it seems. Did you forget the respect you owe me, or is this merely more of your natural rudeness?"

Marcus looked at the khagan in surprised admiration. Wulghash showed none of the fear that paralyzed Avshar's friend and foe alike, the fear whose full weight the tribune was feeling now.

The wizard-prince stiffened angrily and gave Wulghash a long measure of his chilling stare, all the worse because his eyes were unseen. The khagan met it, something few men could have done. Fairly bursting with rage, Avshar bent in a bow whose very depth was an insult. "I pray your pardon, your Majesty," he said, but his voice held no apology. He went on, "My surprise betrayed me—seeing these two rogues here, I thought me for a moment I was back in cursed Videssos again, at the damned Avtokrator's court. Tell me, did you capture them in battle or were they taken spying?"

"Neither," Wulghash said, but his eyes slid to the Romans. He asked Avshar, "How is it you claim to have met a couple of no-account mercenaries at the Videssian court? What were they doing there, guard duty?" He still did not sound as if he believed the wizard-prince.

"No-account mercenaries? Guard duty?" Avshar threw back his head and laughed, a horrid sound that sent the nobles closest to him scrambling back in dismay. Its echoes came back cold and spectral from the high-arched roof; a nightjar perched near the top of the throne room wall woke to terror and flapped away. "Is that what they told you?" Avshar laughed again, then gave a colored but largely accurate account of Scaurus' career in Videssos, finishing, "And this other one, the short one, is his chief henchman."

"Bugger yourself," Gaius Philippus said. He stood balanced on the balls of his feet, ready to throw himself at Avshar.

Wulghash ignored the senior centurion. "Is this true?" he asked Marcus in a voice like iron.

Avshar hissed, a serpent on the point of striking. "Have a care what thou dost, Wulghash. Thou couldst yet try me too far, seeking the word of this miscreant espier to weigh it against mine own."

"Be thou still. I act as I list, with or without thy let." The khagan was as fluent as Avshar in the archaic Videssian dialect the wizard-prince often used. Maybe, Marcus thought, Avshar had taught it to him.

Wulghash asked the tribune again, "Is what he says true?"

"Most of it," Scaurus sighed. With Avshar standing there to give him away, what use in lying?

Avshar laughed once more, this time in triumph. "From his own mouth he stands convicted. Give them over to me, Wulghash. The debt I owe them is larger and older than yours. I pledge you, the insult they offered with their base falsehoods shall be requited—oh, yes, a thousand times over." He was all but purring in anticipation. At his gesture, the palace guards edged forward, expecting the khagan's order to seize the Romans.

Wulghash stopped them. "I have told you once, wizard—aye, and times enough before this—that I command here, yet always you seem to forget. Whatever story these men told, before they said a word to me they saved my minister's life. I have made them my friends."

"And so?" Avshar's whisper crawled with menace.

"A favor for a favor. I give them back their lives in exchange for Tabari's." Wulghash turned to Scaurus and Gaius Philippus. "Get your horses. You may leave. No one will pursue you, I vow. I have called you my friends and I do not go back on my word—but you should have trusted me in full. I am no longer happy with you, friends or not. Go on; get out."

Hardly daring believe his ears, Marcus searched the khagan's face. It was stormy with disappointed anger, but he read no deceit. As Wulghash had said of himself, he was as determined in friendship as he was in enmity. "You are a man of honor," the tribune said softly.

"You do well to remind me, for I am tempted to forget." Wulghash waved brusquely for them to be gone.

"Thou dung-headed fool!" Avshar roared before the Romans could move. They froze again; any exit would take them straight past the wizard-prince.

But Avshar had nearly forgotten them in his rage. He screamed abuse at the khagan: "Thou dolt, thou clodpoll, thou idiot puling mousling with fantasies of manhood! Reeking filthy louse-bearded barbarous bastard son of a camel turd, thinkest thou to gainsay *me*? These sneaking spies are mine; get thee down on thy wormish belly and grovel in thanksgiving that I do not serve thee worse than them for thine insolence!"

White about the lips, Wulghash snapped an order in the Yezda tongue to his guards. They drew their weapons and advanced on the wizard-prince.

"Thou'lt not find it so simple to be shut of me as that," Avshar sneered. "Am I as stupid as thyself, to take no precautions against thy childish thoughts of treachery?" He spoke a single word, in Videssian or some darker speech, the trigger to a spell long prepared against this time. The khagan's guards came to a ragged halt. All at once they were looking at Avshar with the devotion a lap dog gives its mistress. "How now, O clever booby?" he chuckled.

Wulghash, though, was wise in the ways of Makuran for reasons stronger than antiquarianism. He knew why the Makuraner kings of old had ordained that men seeking audience with them should halt at a certain spot. His hand darted to a spring cunningly concealed in the arm of his throne. A six-foot slab of stone fell away beneath Avshar's feet.

But the wizard-prince did not drop into the pit below. An abrupt pass let him bestride the empty air like polished marble. Wulghash's nobles moaned; some covered their faces. The khagan's guards—no, Avshar's now—smiled at the new proof of their master's might. Those smiles made Scaurus shudder. Only the soldiers' lips moved. Their eyes stayed bright and blank.

"This farce wearies me," Avshar said. "Let there be an end to it. Look now, Wulghash, on the power thou hadst thought to oppose." Still standing easily on nothing, the wizard-prince threw back the mantlings that always veiled his face.

Even Gaius Philippus, calloused by more than half a lifetime of hard soldiering, could not hold back a groan. His cry was lost in the chorus of horror that swelled and swelled as Avshar turned toward the nobility of Yezd.

Two thoughts raced across Scaurus' mind. The first was that he had gone mad. He wished it were true. And the second was of the myth of Aurora's lover Tithonus. The goddess had begged immortality for him from Jupiter, but forgot to ask that he not grow old.

In his decrepitude, Tithonus had been turned by Jove into a grasshopper. No god had shown Avshar such kindness. Staring—he could not help but stare—the tribune tried to guess how many years had rolled over the sorcerer. He gave up; as well try to reckon how many goldpieces had gone into Phos' High Temple. Imagining such age would have been enough to make the skin prickle into gooseflesh. Seeing it, and seeing it combined with Avshar's undoubted vigor, was infinitely worse.

"Well?" Avshar said into vast silence. "I own eight and a half centuries. Eight hundred years have passed since I learned in the ruins of Skopentzana where true power lay. Which of you puny mayfly men will stand against me now?" There was no answer; there could be no answer. Smiling a lich's smile, the wizard-prince gestured to the guardsmen he had ensorceled. "I rule here. Kill me that lump of offal fouling my throne."

He spoke Videssian, but they understood. They surged toward Wulghash, sabers clenched in their fists.

The khagan was perhaps the only man in the room not paralyzed by dismay. He did not need Avshar's unmasking to know what had served him. No small wizard himself, he had divined that long ago. In his ambition he thought to use the other to exalt himself, to ride to greatness on Avshar's back. For all that arrogance, though, he always remembered tool and user might one day be reversed. And so he pressed another stud mounted on his throne. A hidden doorway swung open behind it. He darted into the tunnel it had concealed.

Avshar howled in fury; the door was secret even to him. "After him, you bunglers," he screamed to the guards, though the blunder had not been theirs.

Pushram sprang up and grappled with the leading guardsman. He was scrawny and carried nothing more deadly than a stylus, but he bought his master a few seconds with his life.

His sacrifice jerked the Romans from their daze. They both seemed to have the same thought at once—better to die fighting than in Avshar's clutches. They tore their swords free and hurled themselves at the wizard-prince's soldiers.

Avshar understood immediately. "Take them alive!" he shouted. "Their end shall not be as easy as they wish."

Sword in hand, a Makuraner noble dashed toward the thrones, rushing to the Romans' aid and to the defense of the khagan. Avshar cursed and moved his gauntleted hands in savage passes. The nobleman crashed to the floor, writhing in torment. "More?" the wizard asked. There were none.

By weight of numbers, the guards forced Scaurus and Gaius Philippus away from the doorway down which Wulghash had vanished. Several rushed after the khagan. The tribune laid about him desperately, but a cleverly aimed slash caught his sword just above the hilt. It flew from his numbed fingers. Knowing how little good it would do, he snatched out his dagger and stabbed at the nearest guardsman. He felt the blade bite and heard a grunt of pain.

Avshar's order hampered his men, who took losses because of it and passed up several sure killing strokes. The Romans battled ferociously, trying to make their foes finish them. Then a guardsman sent his fist clubbing down on the back of Marcus' neck. The tribune toppled. He did not see the Yezda swarm over Gaius Philippus and finally bring him down.

An echoing shout from the secret tunnel's opening returned Scaurus to blurry consciousness. Someone screamed, then silence fell once more. A couple of minutes later, a broad-shouldered guard, staggering under the weight, came out of the doorway with a corpse on his back. It wore royal robes. Marcus had a glimpse of fleshy nose, square-cut gray beard, eyes gone set and staring—no way now to see if intelligence had been there.

Avshar's terrible grin grew wide. "Well done," he said. "Thou'lt be a captain for this day's work. What end did he make?"

As usual, the sorcerer spoke in Videssian, but the guardsman had no trouble with it. He answered in his own tongue. Avshar grimaced impatiently. "What care I that your stupid comrade fell? Incompetence punishes itself, as always. Here, give the body to these others to fling on the midden; hie yourself off to the officers' chambers, to deck yourself with something finer than those rags you wear."

The soldier said something that sounded like a protest of unworthiness. Avshar made his harsh voice as genial as he could, answering, "Nay, thou hast earned it. Hyazdat, Gandutav, take him along and fit him out." Pounding the trooper on the back, the two guards officers led him away.

More guardsmen carried off the corpse that had won him his promotion. Save for those still grasping the tribune and Gaius Philippus, only a couple were left in the throne room.

Avshar did not need them. By himself he cowed the nobility of Yezd, bold haughty Makurani and fierce Yezda alike. Men stared at their shoes, at each other, at the walls, anything to keep from meeting his eyes. He snarled at them. They went to their knees and then to their bellies in proskynesis before him. Some, mostly Makurani, performed the prostration with grace, others were slow and clumsy. But all knelt.

"And thou," Avshar said to Marcus. "I have heard thou wouldst not bend the knee before the Avtokrators. I am greater than they, for I am at once priest and lord, patriarch and Emperor. They shall know my power, and my god's—as shalt thou."

He gave the tribune no chance to refuse; at his command, the guards cast Scaurus at his feet. His boot, still smelling of lathered horse, ground cruelly into the Roman's shoulder. He suddenly asked, "What didst thou with the head of Mavrikios Gavras, when I gave it thee?"

"Buried it," Marcus answered, too startled not to respond.

"A pity; now when I take Thorisin's, the set will remain broken. Perhaps thine shall serve in its stead. Such decisions should not be frivolously made, but then I now enjoy the leisure to choose among the interesting possibilities."

Avshar strode over to the tribune's sword, which still lay where it had fallen. The wizard-prince stooped to pick up the prize, but paused before his hand closed on the hilt—that blade had shown itself dangerous to his spells too many times for him to be easy about touching it. But he did not stay baffled long. He pointed to a noble. "Tabari, come you forward."

"Aye, my lord," the man the Romans had rescued said eagerly. He prostrated himself before the wizard. His face to the floor, he went on, "I am privileged to see you raised at last to your proper estate. Your followers here have waited long for this day."

"As have I," Avshar said. "As have I." The pain behind Marcus' eyes was not the only thing to sicken him now. Bad enough to have saved a Yezda minister. To have preserved one of Avshar's creatures and fallen into the wizard-prince's hand because of it mortified him past bearing.

He hardly noticed when two of the ensorceled guards hauled him to his feet. Another pair did the same with Gaius Philippus, who had also been cast down. The senior centurion struggled in their grasp, but could not break free.

Avshar was saying, "Carry this piece of rusty iron down to my workroom in the dungeons. As minister of justice, you doubtless know them well enough to find the place without difficulty."

Tabari's laugh was not pleasant, except to Avshar. "Oh, indeed, my lord."

"Excellent," he said. "I thought as much. And while you

are about it, guide the guards holding these wretches—"A thumb jabbed toward the Romans—"to the block of cells adjacent. Perhaps the blade will yield up its secrets to me when housed in their flesh."

"What a pleasant prospect," Tabari said, killing any lingering hope Scaurus had for the permanence of his gratitude. Tabari gestured to the tribune's captors. They dragged him away. He heard Gaius Philippus, still swearing, forced along behind him.

Avshar's voice pursued them: "Enjoy this respite while you may, for you shall have none other, ever again."

Tabari waved the guards down a narrow spiral ramp cut into the living rock just outside the throne room. As they descended into the bowels of the palace, a woman's shriek rang out far above. Atossa, Marcus thought dully, must have come into the court. The scream was abruptly silenced.

Gaius Philippus also recognized the cry. "Wulghash has a son," he said.

"What of it? What chance has he, when Wulghash couldn't stand against Avshar in his own palace?"

"Damn little," the veteran sighed. "For a minute, I thought he'd get away—he was ready for anything. Did you hear Avshar howl when that passage opened up? He hadn't a clue it was there."

The guards gave little doglike grunts of devotion to hear their master's name. Otherwise they did not seem to care if their prisoners talked. Wondering whether Avshar's spell had taken more of their wits than that, Marcus tensed to try to break free. Their grip tightened. Nothing wrong with their physical reactions, he saw ruefully.

They did not mind his turning his head this way and that. Several tunnels had already branched off from the ramp. Some held storerooms; from another came the rhythmic clang of a smith's hammer on hot iron. Down and down they went. More than once, they passed workers replacing burned-out torches. Even far underground, the brands burned steadily and did not fill the passageway with smoke. The Makuraner kings, Marcus thought as a puff of cool air touched his cheek, had worked out a better ventilation system than the Videssians used in their prison. He wondered how many men had compared the two.

Gaius Philippus barked laughter when he muttered that

under his breath. "It's nothing to brag of." Scaurus' nod made fresh pain flare in his head.

The tribune's ears clicked before the guards finally turned down a still, lonely side corridor. "Yes, gentlemen, we are almost there," Tabari said. He had been very quiet on the long trip down, nor had the Romans cared to speak to him.

Now at last, though, Marcus turned his head to plead with Wulghash's—no, Avshar's—minister. He did not beg for his life; he had lost hope for it. Instead he said, "Take my sword and strike us down. You owe us that much, if nothing else."

"I am the judge of my debts; no one else." Tabari hefted the Gallic blade. Without warning, he drove it into the back of one of Gaius Philippus' guards. The Yezda groaned and crumpled.

Gaius Philippus acted as if he had been waiting for the blow. He spun and grappled with his other captor, giving Tabari the moment he needed to wrench out the sword.

Scaurus' guards hesitated a fatal instant. Had they shoved him away at once, they might have quickly overwhelmed Tabari and then wheeled round to retake him. As it was, he managed to thrust out a foot and trip one of them. He sprang on the fellow's back, grabbing for his knife wrist.

The Yezda was strong as a bull. They thrashed on the ground. The tribune felt his grip failing. The guard tore his hand free. His dagger slashed along Scaurus' ribs. Gasping, the tribune tried to seize his arm again, all the while waiting for the thrust that would end it. *I made them kill me*, he thought with something like triumph.

The guard snorted, as if in disdain. The weight pressing on Marcus suddenly grew heavier. He groaned and shoved desperately at the Yezda. The guard slid off, knife clattering to the floor as it slipped from his fingers. Another dagger stood in his back. Gaius Philippus pulled it out. Marcus' nose caught the death stench of suddenly loosed bowels.

The other guards were down, too. The one Gaius Philippus had fought lay unmoving. "Bastard had a hard head, but not as hard as a stone floor," the senior centurion said. And Tabari knelt by the last one, wiping the Gallic sword clean on the fellow's caftan.

"You are hurt," the Yezda minister said, pointing to the spreading red stain on Marcus' chest. He helped the tribune shed his tunic, tore rags to try to dress the long cut that ran down from just outside Scaurus' left nipple. The bleeding slowed but did not stop; the rough bandages began to grow soggy with blood.

"That was all an act, you cheering Avshar on up there?" Gaius Philippus demanded. He did not sound as though he believed it, and held his dagger in a knife-fighter's crouch.

"No, not all of it," Tabari said.

Gaius Philippus was poised to hurl himself at the minister. "Hear him out," Marcus said quickly.

Calmly, Tabari went on, "I've long favored Avshar over Wulghash; he will make Yezd mighty. But I have already said once that I judge my debts." He handed Marcus the Gallic sword. The tribune snatched at it; without it, he felt more than half unmanned.

As Scaurus struggled to his feet, Gaius Philippus snapped at Tabari, "Are you crazy, man? When that walking corpse finds out you've let us go, you'll envy what he had planned for us."

"That thought had occurred to me." One of Tabari's dark eyebrows quirked upward. "I will ask you, then, to lay me out roughly—I hope without permanent damage. If I am stunned and battered when found, everyone will think I put up the best fight I could."

"What do we do then?" Marcus said.

"Can you walk?"

Scaurus tried it. The effort it took dismayed him; he could feel blood trickling down his belly. But he said, "If I have to, I can. I'd try flying to keep out of Avshar's hands."

"Then go into the maze of tunnels down here." Tabari pointed to an opening in the rock wall. "They run farther than any man knows these days, except perhaps Wulghash, and he is dead. Maybe you will find a way free. I have no better hope to offer you."

"I think I'd sooner fly," Gaius Philippus muttered mistrustfully, eyeing the blank black hole. But there was no help for it; he realized that as fast as Marcus did.

Tabari drew himself up to stiff attention. "At your service," he said, and waited.

Gaius Philippus approached him, thumped him on the shoulder. "I've never done this as a favor before," he said. In the middle of the sentence, he slammed his left fist into Tabari's belly. As the minister folded, Gaius Philippus' right hand crashed against his jaw. He slumped to the floor.

Rubbing bruised knuckles, the senior centurion opened the

unconscious man's tunic and used the dagger to make a bloody scratch on his chest. "Now they'll figure we thought he was dead."

"Don't forget to cut the tunic, too," Marcus said. Gaius Philippus swore at himself and attended to it. Marcus took canteens from the dead guards—no telling how long the Romans might wander this labyrinth. He wished the Yezda had food with them. When he was finished, he saw Gaius Philippus pulling torches from the sconces set in the tunnel wall. "Why do that? All these ways should have lights ready for us to take."

"Aye, but if we do, whoever comes after us will be able to track us by it," the veteran said, and it was Scaurus' turn for chagrin. Gaius Philippus went on, "Eventually we'll have to start using the torches we come on, but by then we should be lost enough that it won't matter." The centurion's chuckle held no mirth. He strode toward the lightless tunnel entrance. Marcus reluctantly followed. The two Romans plunged in together.

The circle of light behind them shrank, then abruptly vanished as the tunnel veered to the right. Before and behind the flickering glow of the torch was impenetrable black.

Gaius Philippus led, holding the brand high. Marcus did his best to keep up. The cut along his ribs began to stiffen. He did not think he was bleeding any more, but the wound made him slow and weak. In spite of himself, he would fall behind, into the darkness.

When he did, he saw the druids' marks on his sword glowing faintly—magic somewhere, he thought. As long as the gleam stayed dim, he refused to let it worry him.

The way branched every hundred paces or so. The Romans went now left, now right at random. At every turning they put three pebbles by the way they chose. "They'll keep us from doubling back on ourselves," Scaurus said.

"Unless we miss 'em, of course."

"Cheerful, aren't you?" Marcus thought they were deeper underground; his ears had popped again. There was no sign of pursuit behind them. They would have heard it a long way off; but for their own breathing and the faint sound of their feet on stone, the silence was absolute as the darkness.

After a while they paused to rest. They drank a couple of swallows of water. Then, feeling like ants lost in a strange burrow, they wandered on. Once, far off, they saw a lighted corridor and shied away as if it were Avshar in person.

"What's that?" Gaius Philippus said—something was scratched into the side of the tunnel.

"It's in the Videssian script," Marcus said in surprise. "Bring the light close. No, hold it to one side so shadow fills the letters. There, better." He read: "'I, Hesaios Stenes of Resaina, dug this tunnel and wrote these words. Sharbaraz of Makuran took me in the ninth year of the Avtokrator Genesios. Phos guard the Avtokrator and me.'"

"Poor sod," Gaius Philippus said. "I wonder when this Emperor Genesios lived."

"I couldn't tell you. Alypia would know." Her name sent a wave of loneliness washing over Scaurus.

"I hope you get the chance to ask her, not that it looks likely." Gaius Philippus shook a canteen. The tribune did not need the slosh to remind him they only had so much water. A couple of days after that was gone and it would not matter whether Avshar tracked them down or not.

They pressed on. They no longer needed to mark a path. This deep in the maze, long-undisturbed dust held their footprints.

Hesaios' graffito went back to the night that had enfolded it for centuries.

The Romans' only pastime in the tunnels was talk, and they used it till they grew hoarse. Gaius Philippus' stories reached back to the days when Scaurus was a child. The veteran had first campaigned under Gaius Marius, against the Italians in the Social War and then against Sulla. "Marius was old and half-crazy by then, but even in the wreck of him you could see what a soldier he'd been. Some of his centurions had been with him in every fight since Jugurtha; they worshipped him. Of course he made most of them—till his day, landless men couldn't serve in the legions."

"I wonder if that's better," Marcus said. "With no land of their own, they're always beholden to their general, and a danger to the state."

"So say you, who grew up landed," Gaius Philippus retorted, the gut response of a man born poor. "If he can get 'em land, more power to him. What would they do without the army? Starve in the city like that Apokavkos you rescued in Videssos—and not many as bad at thieving as him."

Only women ranked with war and politics for hashing over. Despite his earlier try at sympathy, Gaius Philippus could not understand Marcus' devotion first to Helvis and then to Alypia. "Why buy a sheep if all you want is wool?"

"What do you know? You married the legions." The tribune intended that for a joke, but saw it was true. It gave him pause; he went on carefully, "A good woman halves sorrows and doubles joys." But he had the feeling he was explaining poetry to a deaf man.

He was right. Gaius Philippus said, "Doubles sorrow and halves joy, you ask me. Leaving Helvis out of the bargain—"

"Good idea," Scaurus said quickly. The abandonment was fresh enough still to ache in him every time he thought of it.

"All right. What has Alypia given you, then, that you couldn't have for silver from some tavern wench? I take it you weren't bedding her for ambition's sake?"

"*Et tu*? You sound like Thorisin." From anyone else, the blunt questions would have angered Marcus, but he knew the centurion's manner. He answered seriously. "What has she given me? Besides honest affection, which silver won't buy, her courage outdoes any man's I know of, to hold herself together through all she's endured. She's clever, and kind, and gives everything she has—wisdom, wit, heart—for those she cares about. I only hope to be able to do as much. When I'm with her, I'm at peace."

"You should write paeans," Gaius Philippus grunted. "At peace, is it? Seems to me she's brought you enough trouble for four men, let alone one."

"She's saved me some, too. If not for her, who knows what Thorisin would have done after—" He hesitated; here came the hurt again—"after the Namdaleni got away."

"Oh, aye. Kept you out of jail a few extra months—and made sure you'd be in hotter water when you did land there."

"That's not the fault of who she is; it's the fault of who she was born."

Marcus had hardly noticed the druids' marks stamped into his blade gleaming brighter, but now they were outshining Gaius Philippus' torch. "Hold up," he told the veteran. "There's magic somewhere close." They peered into the darkness, hands tight on their weapons, sure sorcery could only mean Avshar.

But there was no sign of the wizard-prince. Scratching his head, Scaurus took a few steps back the way he had come. The druids' marks grew fainter. "In front, then. Give me the lead, Gaius. The sword will turn magic from me."

They traded places. The tribune slowly moved forward, sword held before him like a shield. The glow from it grew steadily brighter, until the tunnel that had never known daylight was lit bright as noon.

In that golden light the pit ahead remained a patch of blackness. It was three times the length of a man; only a narrow stone ledge allowed passage on either side. Scaurus held his sword over the edge of the pit and looked down. The bottom was wickedly spiked; two points thrust up through the rib cage of a skeleton sprawled in ungainly death.

Gaius Philippus tapped Marcus on the shoulder. "What are you waiting for?"

"Very funny. One more step and I'll keep that fellow down there company." The tribune pointed to what was left of the victim in the pit.

Or so he thought. The senior centurion gave him a puzzled look. "What fellow? Down where? All I see is a lot of dusty floor."

"No pit? No spears set in the bottom of it? No skeleton? One of us has lost his wits." Scaurus had an inspiration. "Here—take my sword."

They both exclaimed then, Marcus because as the sword left his fingers the pit disappeared, leaving what lay ahead no different to the eye from the rest of the tunnel, Gaius Philippus for exactly the opposite reason as he took the blade. "Is it real?" he asked.

"Do you care to find out? Three steps forward and you'll know."

"Hmm. The ledge'll do fine, thanks. We see that with or without." He held out the blade to Scaurus. "You take it in your left hand, I'll hold it in my right, and we'll sidle by crab-fashion, our backs to the wall. We'll both be able to see what we're doing that way—I hope."

As the tribune touched the sword hilt, the pit jumped into visibility again. The ledge was wide enough for the Romans' feet and not much more. Some of the spikes below still gleamed brightly, reflecting the light of the sword; others had rusty points and dark-stained shafts that told their own story.

The Romans were about two thirds of the way across when Marcus stumbled. His foot slipped off the edge, toes curling on emptiness. Gaius Philippus slammed him back against the tunnel wall with a strong forearm. The jar sent anguish through him. When he could speak again, he wheezed, "Thanks. It's real, all right."

"Thought so. Here, have a swig." Even with his sudden sideways leap to save Scaurus, the veteran had not spilled a drop of precious water. Marcus' stomach twisted at the thought of impalement.

The druids' stamps dimmed once more as the Romans put distance between themselves and the pit. Gaius Philippus returned to the lead, his torch a better light than the tribune's blade.

As the sword faded, though, excitement flared in Scaurus. He said, "The Makurani wouldn't have dug that mantrap if it didn't guard the way to something important—the escape route?"

"Maybe." With ingrained pessimism, Gaius Philippus added, "I wonder what else they used to keep unwelcome guests out."

Hope revived brought fresh anxiety. Every branching of the tunnel became a crisis; the wrong choice might mean throwing freedom away. For a while the Romans agonized over each decision. At last Gaius Philippus said, "A pox on it. The dithering doesn't help. One way or the other, we just go." That helped, some.

Scaurus lifted his head like a hunted animal tasting the wind. "Stand still," he whispered. Gaius Philippus froze. The tribune listened, then grimaced at what he heard. The corridors behind them were silent no more. Echoing strangely in the distance, now strong, now faint, came the cries of soldiers and, like the murmur of surf, the sound of trotting feet. Avshar had awakened to his loss.

The Romans did their best to make haste but, battered as they were, could not match the speed of fresh men. The noise of the pursuit grew louder with terrible speed. The Yezda were not searching haphazardly; they must have come across the fugitives' trail in the dust. Perhaps Avshar's magic had led them to it. Marcus wasted a breath cursing him.

But the wizard-prince was not master of all the secrets of the maze below the palace he now held, nor had he readied his minions for them. A dreadful scream reverberated through the tunnels, followed a moment later by two more. One of them went on and on.

The wizard-prince's minions must have probed round the edges of the pit and found at last the narrow ways by the trap.

That was how Scaurus read the silence behind the Romans, a silence broken by a terrified shriek as another Yezda stepped onto deceitfully empty air and fell to his doom.

The tribune shuddered. "They're no cowards, to dare those ledges without being able to tell them from the pit."

"When they're after me, I'd sooner they *were* cravens. But they've had enough for now, sounds like." The loss of that fourth trooper must have dismayed the Yezda past the breaking point. They came no further; soon the only sounds in the tunnels were the groans of the dying men in the pit.

Neither Marcus nor Gaius Philippus said what they both feared, that their respite would not last long. Either their pursuers would find a route that dodged the mantrap, or Avshar would reveal it with his magic so they could get safely past.

When the druids' marks sparked again, the tribune at first thought that had happened and that his sword was reacting to the backwash of the wizard-prince's spell. But the light from the stamping brightened as he went farther and farther from the pit.

"What now?" Gaius Philippus grunted.

"Who knows? It started when that side tunnel joined this one, I think." Scaurus took back the lead, trying to look every way at once. It might not be a pit this time, but vitriol from a spigot in the ceiling, or a blast of fire, or . . . anything.

The uncertainty ate at him, made him start at the shift of his own shadow as he walked. He paused to rest a moment, letting his sword drag in the dust.

Light fountained from the blade, so brilliant the tribune flung up his arms to shield his eyes. The dazzling burst lasted only an instant. Marcus leaped backward, wondering what snare he had tripped. Then he saw the line of footprints stretching out ahead in the dust.

They were invisible to Gaius Philippus until he touched the hilt of the Gallic longsword. "So someone's covering his tracks by magic, is he?" the veteran said. He made a menacing motion with his dagger. "Can't you just guess who?"

"Who else but Avshar?" Marcus said bitterly. How had the wizard-prince got ahead of them? No matter, the tribune thought grimly; there he was. The Romans could not retreat, not with the Yezda in the corridors behind them. No choice but to go on. "He won't take us unawares."

"Or need to." But Gaius Philippus was already moving forward. "We'll stalk him for a change."

As it did all through the tunnel system, the dust went thick and thin by turns, now rising in choking clouds when the Romans scuffed through it, now only a film. The light of Scaurus' sword, though, picked out the sorcerously concealed trail even at its most indistinct.

"Branching up ahead," Gaius Philippus said. "Which direction did the bastard go?" He spoke in a whisper; in these twisting passages, sound carried further than light.

"Left," Marcus answered confidently. But after continuing for about another fifteen feet, the trail disappeared, Gallic magic or no. "What the—" the tribune said. He heard a sudden rush of steps behind him. Knowing he had been tricked again, he whirled with Gaius Philippus for a last round of hopeless combat.

He would remember the tableau forever—three men with upraised weapons, each motionless in astonishment. "You!" they all cried at once, and, like puppets on the same string, lowered their blades together.

"I saw you dead," Marcus said, almost with anger in his voice.

"It was not me you saw," Wulghash replied. The deposed khagan of Yezd wore an officer's silk surcoat over a boiled-leather cuirass, and trousers of fine suede. Trousers and coat were filthy, as was he, but he still bore himself like a king. He went on, "I put my seeming—and my robes—on one of the traitors I slew and took his image for myself when I carried him out. In his arrogance, Avshar did not look past the surface." The khagan spoke matter-of-factly of his sorcery; Scaurus could only imagine his haste and desperation as he had worked, not knowing whether more of the wizard-prince's guards would fall on him before his spells were done. But Wulghash was looking at the Romans with like amazement. "How is it you walk free? I saw you taken by Avshar in truth, not seeming. You have no magic save your sword, and you had already lost that to him."

Marcus hid the blade behind his body before he answered. Wulghash's eyes were watering; he had known little light in the tunnels. The tribune said, "There was no magic to it." He explained what Tabari had done.

"Gratitude is a stronger magic than most of the ones I know." Wulghash grunted. "You conjured more of it from Tabari than I, it seems, if he obeys Avshar now." Scaurus thought the minister of justice lucky he was nowhere near his khagan at that moment.

With characteristic practicality, Gaius Philippus demanded of Wulghash, "So why didn't you flee, once you were wearing another man's face?"

"I would have, but Avshar, his own Skotos eat him, saw fit to promote me for murdering myself, and to give me these gauds." The khagan patted his draggled finery. "That meant I was in his henchmen's company and could hardly up and go. Besides, the glamour I had cast was a weak one. I had no time for better, but it could have worn off at any moment. That *would* have killed me, did it happen while I was still in the palace for his slaves to spot. So when I was finally alone a moment, the best I could think of was to take to the tunnels."

He waved. "Here I am safe enough. I know these ways better than most. They must be learned on foot; masking spells hide much of them—and many traps—from sorcerous prying. Some go back to the Makuraner kings, others I set myself against an evil day; if you ride the snake, watch his fangs. And if you know where to search, there are cisterns and caches of Makuraner bread baked hard as rock to keep forever. Not fare I relish, but I can live on it."

The Romans looked at each other and at their canteens, which held a couple of swallows apiece now. How many times had they missed chances to fill them? Tone roughened by chagrin, Gaius Philippus said, "All right, you escaped Avshar. But this moles' nest must have its ways out. Why didn't you use one?"

Pride rang in Wulghash's answer: "Because I aim to take back what is mine. Aye, I know Avshar has been pickling in his own malice like a gherkin in vinegar these many hundred years, but I am no mean loremaster either. Let me but catch him unawares, and I can best him."

Marcus and Gaius Philippus glanced at each other again. "You do not believe me," the khagan said. "As may be, but with no hope at all I would still be here." His voice, his entire aspect, softened. "Whom else has Atossa to rely on?"

The Romans could not help starting. Wulghash did not miss it. "What do you know? Tell me." He hefted his saber as if to rip the answer from them.

"I fear she is dead," Scaurus said, and told of the shriek from the court room that had been so suddenly cut off.

Wulghash raised the saber again. Before the tribune could

lift his own blade for self-defense, the khagan slashed his own cheeks in the mourning ritual of the steppe. Blood ran into his beard and dripped in the dust at his feet.

He paid it no attention. Pushing past the Romans, he started down the corridor from which he had come. Now he made no effort to conceal his tracks; he cared nothing for magic any more. The sword in his hand was all that mattered to him. "Avshar!" he roared. "I am coming for you!"

Near mad with grief and rage, he could not have stood against the wizard-prince for an instant. Gaius Philippus realized at once the only course that might stay him. He taunted the khagan: "Aye, go on, throw yourself away, too. Then when you meet your woman in the next world you can tell her how you avenged her by getting yourself killed to no purpose."

The jeer served where Marcus' more reasoned tone would have failed. Wulghash whirled with catlike grace. He was close to Gaius Philippus' age, but hardly less a warrior. "What better time to take the spider unawares in the palace than when everything is topsy-turvy after your escape?" He spat the words at the veteran, but that he argued at all showed reason still held him, if narrowly.

"Who'll take whom unawares?" the senior centurion said with a scornful laugh. "The palace, is it? My guess is the son of a whore's not five tunnels behind us, and his guards with him, magicking their way past the spiked pit back there."

That reached Wulghash, though not for the reason Gaius Philippus had expected. "You came this way past the pit?" he demanded in disbelief. "How, without wizardry? That is the deadliest snare in all the tunnels."

"We have this," Scaurus reminded him, motioning with his sword. "It bared the trap before we fell into it—the same way it showed your footprints," he added.

Wulghash's jaw muscles jumped. "Strong sorcery," he said. "Strong enough to draw Avshar were he blind as a cave-fish." He scowled at Gaius Philippus. "You have reason, damn you. With Avshar close by and his magic primed and ready, I cannot hope to beat him now. Best we flee, though saying so gags me."

Still scowling, he turned back to Marcus. "What point in flying, if you carry a lantern calling the huntsmen after you? Leave the sword here."

"No," the tribune said. "When he took me, Avshar feared

to touch it. I will not abandon the best weapon I have, or let him put it to the test at his leisure."

"Ill was the day I met you," Wulghash said balefully, "and I would I had never named you friend."

"Cut the horseshit," Gaius Philippus snapped. "If you'd never met us, you'd be dead yourself, and Avshar running your stinking country anyway."

"So forward a tongue is ripe for the cropping."

The hue and cry from the Roman's pursuers gave a sudden surge. "The wizard's men are past the pit," Marcus said to Wulghash. "You talk like Avshar; maybe you're thinking like him, too, and hoping to buy your own life from them with ours."

"By whatever gods may be, I will never deal in peace with him or his, so long as breath is in me." The khagan paused to think. He set down his saber. His hands flashed through passes; he muttered in the same archaic Videssian dialect Avshar used.

"Your magic will not touch me or my blade," Scaurus reminded him.

"I know," Wulghash said when he could speak normally. "But I can set a spell round you and it both, to befog one seeking it through sorcery. The magic does not touch you, you see; if it did, it would perish. But because of that it only befogs. It will not blind. So, my friends" he said, his tone making it an accusation to flinch from, "can you run with me, since you have proven running the greater wisdom?"

They ran.

X

"THERE IT SITS, MASHIZ ITS AIN SELF, AND DAMN ALL WE can do about it," Viridovix said glumly. He peered through evening twilight toward the Yezda capital from the jumbled hills at the edge of the mountains of Dilbat.

"Aye, one glorious, sweeping charge, and it's ours," Pikridios Goudeles said in ringing tones that went poorly with his dirty buckskin tunic and bandaged shoulder. Sour laughter floated up from the edge of the Arshaum camp where the survivors of the Videssian embassy party and their few friends congregated.

Gorgidas found he could not blame the plainsmen for their bitterness toward the imperials. Despite Arigh's steadfast friendship, most of the nomads felt they had been drawn into a losing campaign for the Empire's sake. And Mashiz, so close yet utterly unattainable, symbolized their frustration.

The cloud of noxious smoke rising from the granite pyramid in the western part of the city did not hide the throng of yurts and tents and other shelters that daily grew greater as Yezd's strength flowed in to the capital. Campfires glittered like stars. At its freshest the Arshaum army would have lost to such a host. Fragmented as the plainsmen were, a determined assault would have swept them away.

The Greek wondered why it had not come. After the blows that broke the Arshaum apart, their foes seemed to have lost interest in them. Daily patrols made sure the scattered bands stayed away from Mashiz, but past that they were ignored. The Yezda even let them make contact with each other, though the mountain country was too broken and too poor for them to regroup as a single force.

"Who comes?" Prevalis Haravash's son barked nervously when an Arshum approached; things were at the point where the imperial trooper from Prista was as leery of his allies as he would have been of the enemy. Then the young sentry relaxed. "Oh, it's you, sir."

Arigh leaned against a boulder set into the side of the hill and looked from Goudeles to Viridovix to Skylitzes to Gorgidas to Agathias Psoes. He slammed a fist down on his thigh. "I don't propose living out my life as an outlaw skulking through these mountains, thinking I'm a hero because I've stolen five sheep or an ugly wench."

"What do you aim to do instead, then?" Psoes asked. The Videssian underofficer had a Roman air of directness to him.

"I don't know, the wind spirits curse it," Arigh glared at the winking field of campfires in the distance.

Skylitzes followed his gaze. He said, "If we skirt them, we can ride for the Empire."

"No," Arigh said flatly. "Even if I could jolly my men into it, I will not turn away from Mashiz while I can still strike a blow. My father's ghost would spurn me if I gave up a blood-feud so easily."

Familiar with the customs of the plains, the Videssian nodded. He tried a different tack. "You would not be abandoning your vendetta, simply getting new allies for it as you did in Erzerum. Seeking the Empire's aid would bring your soldiers round."

"That may be so, but I still will not. In Erzerum I was master of the situation. With Thorisin I would be a beggar."

Gorgidas said, "Gavras is as much Yezd's enemy as you. It's not as if you would be forgetting your fight by seeking his aid."

"No," Arigh repeated. "Thorisin has his own kingdom to rule; his concerns and mine are different. He might have reason to make peace with Yezd for now—what if the Namdaleni still hang over him, as they did last year? I am too weak to be able to take such chances. They would cost me my last freedom of action. If I had something to offer Gavras, now, something to deal with, it might be different. As is, though . . ."

He sighed. "You mean well, all of you, but mercenary captain has no more appeal to me than robber chief as a lifelong trade. What will become of my clan, with Dizabul as their khagan? I must find a way back to Shaumkhiil with my people."

His clipped Arshaum accent added to the urgency of his words. Viridovix marveled at how his friend had grown from a roistering young blood in Videssos to a farsighted chieftain over the course of a year. "Indeed and he's outgrown me," the Gaul murmured to himself in surprise. "I'd go for my revenge and be damned to what came next. Och, what a braw prince he'll make for his people, for he's ever after thinking on the good o' them all."

To Gorgidas, though, Arigh showed the doomed grandeur of a tragic hero. The physician wondered how many defeated lords had been driven into the uplands of Erzerum, vowing to return with victory. But Erzerum was a distant backwater. In Dilbat the Arshaum could only be hunted down.

"What does your shaman say of the omens?" Psoes asked. Having served so long at the edge of the steppe and on it, he was more ready than the other imperials to find value in the nomads' rites. Skylitzes frowned at him.

"He's taken them several times and got no meaning from them. Too close to *that*—" Arigh pointed at the smoking pyramid. He did not need to elaborate. Gorgidas knew the odor that rode those fumes; once he had helped carry corpses from a charred building. Arigh went on, "The very ground is full of pits beneath our feet, Tolui says."

"Heathen superstition." Skylitzes' frown deepened, but he admitted, "One could, I suppose, take that as metaphor for the reek of evil that hangs over Mashiz." He, too, recognized the stench of burned human flesh; the Videssian army used incendiary mixes fired from catapults.

"Metaphor?" Goudeles raised an eyebrow in mocking surprise. "I'd not thought a bluff soldier type like you would know a metaphor if one strolled up and bit your foot, Lankinos."

"Then whose ignorance is showing, mine or yours?"

Viridovix drew a tally mark in the air. "A hit, that." Irritated, Goudeles scowled at him. It irked the bureaucrat that Skylitzes, in his taciturn way, gave as good as he got.

A low, grating sound came from the boulder against which Arigh was leaning. Pebbles and small stones spattered around his feet. He yelped and leaped away. "What's this? Do the rocks walk in this stinking country?"

"Earthquake!" Rakio said it first, with Gorgidas, Skylitzes, and Goudeles a beat behind. But the ground was not really shaking, and no stones fell anywhere but around the gray granite boulder. Gorgidas bit back a startled exclamation. The boulder itself was quivering, as if alive.

"Meta-whatever, eh?" Arigh said triumphantly to Skylitzes. The Arshaum reached for his sword. "Seems more like an ordinary snare to me. Now to close it on the ones who set it—they aimed too well for their own good this time." His companions also drew their blades.

After that grinding beginning, the boulder moved more smoothly. "There is a path for it to run in," Rakio said, pointing. Sure enough, a shallow trench let the great stone move away from the hillside. Blackness showed behind it. "They try to befool us with a secret doorway, eh?" The Yrmido sidled forward on the balls of his feet.

Viridovix started. He remembered Lipoxais the *enaree* in doomed Targitaus' tent. The Khamorth shaman had seen fifty eyes, a door in the mountains, and two swords. The first part of the prophecy had proven such a calamity that the Gaul wanted no part of the second.

The opening in the side of the hill was almost wide enough to admit a man. "Whoever it is lurking in there, I'll cleave him to his navel," Viridovix cried. He pushed past Rakio, his sword upraised.

As he approached the moving chunk of stone, the marks stamped down the length of his blade came to golden life. "'Ware," he called to his companions. "It's Avshar or one of his wizards."

Behind the stone, someone spoke. "I'm losing it, Scaurus. I thought I just heard that great Gallic chucklehead out there."

At the familiar rasp, Viridovix had to make a quick grab to keep from dropping his sword. He and Gorgidas traded wild stares. Then the Celt was shoving the stone out with all his strength. The physician rushed up to help him. The stone overbalanced and fell on its side. Blinking against the glare of the campfires, the two Romans and their comrade stumbled out of the tunnel.

With a whoop of joy, Viridovix flung open his arms. Gaius Philippus returned his embrace without a qualm. Marcus, though, flinched at his touch. "A wound," he explained, courteous even if both he and the senior centurion were bruised, hollow-cheeked, and filthy.

"Phos save me, it is Scaurus," Pikridios Goudeles whispered. For the first time Gorgidas could remember, he sketched the sun-circle over his heart.

The Greek hardly noticed, nor did he pay attention to Arigh shouting to his men that these were, past all expectation, friends. He needed to be no physician to see the Romans were badly battered. "What are you doing here?" he all but shouted at them as he helped ease them down by a fire.

Neither Scaurus nor Gaius Philippus tried to resist his ministrations. "*Khaire*," the tribune said, his voice slow and tired: "Greetings." Gorgidas had to turn his head to hide tears. No one else in this world could have hailed him in Greek. It was like the tribune to do it, exhausted though he was.

Marcus looked from the physician to Viridovix, still hard pressed to understand he was seeing them. "This is a long way from the steppes," he managed at last, an inane effort but the best he had in him.

"A long way from Videssos, too," Gorgidas pointed out. He was also too taken aback to come up with anything deep.

"Is that really you, quack?" Gaius Philippus said. "You look bloody awful with a beard."

"It's better than that face-mange you're sprouting," the Greek retorted. Gaius Philippus sounded exactly as he always had; it helped Gorgidas believe the Romans were really there in front of him. He also had not lost the knack for getting under the physician's skin.

The man who had emerged from the tunnel with Scaurus and Gaius Philippus knelt by the tribune. He was a Yezd, Gorgidas saw, an officer from his gear, but dirty even by the slack standards the Greek had grown used to, and with his face bloody. He used the Empire's tongue, though, with accentless fluency. "Arshaum and Videssians, by whatever gods there be," he said angrily, looking around. Then, to Marcus: "You know these people?"

Provoked by his rough tone, Viridovix put a hand on his shoulder. "Dinna be havering at him so, you. And who might ye be, anyhow? Is it friend y'are, or gaoler?"

The Yezda knocked the Celt's hand aside and looked up at him, unafraid. "If you touch me again without my leave, you will see who I am." The warning was winter-cold. Viridovix' sword came up a couple of inches.

"He's a friend," Marcus said quickly. "He helped us escape. He's called—" He paused, not sure if Wulghash wanted to make himself known.

"Sharvesh," the khagan broke in, so smooth the hesitation was imperceptible. "I was taken when Avshar overthrew Wulghash, but I got free. I spent a while wandering the tunnels, then met these two doing the same." Scaurus admired his presence of mind; but for the name he gave, nothing he said was quite untrue.

Moreover, the news he casually tossed out made everyone forget about him. "Avshar *what*?" Skylitzes, Goudeles, and Arigh exclaimed, each louder than the next.

Wulghash told the tale, creating the impression that he had been one of his own bodyguards who failed to succumb to the wizard-prince's sorcery.

"And so Avshar has a firm grip on Mashiz," he finished. "You are his enemies, yes?" The growl that rose from his listeners was answer enough. "Good. May I beg a horse from you? I have kin to the northwest who may be endangered because of me and I would warn them while I may."

"Choose any beast we have," Arigh said at once. "I would have asked you to ride with us, but it's plain you know your own needs best."

Wulghash gave a stiff nod of thanks. As he started toward the tethered ponies, Marcus got painfully to his feet, despite Gorgidas' protests. "Ah—Sharvesh!" he called.

The khagan of Yezd was too shrewd to miss his alias. He turned and waited for the Roman to join him.

"A favor," Scaurus said, soft enough that only Wulghash could hear. "Treat Viridovix'—he's the tall man with the red hair and mustaches—treat his sword the same way you did mine, so Avshar cannot follow us by it."

"Why should I? I did not name him friend. I have no obligation to him."

"He is my friend."

"So is Thorisin Gavras, I gather, and I am no friend of *his*," Wulghash said coldly. "That argument has no weight with me. And if Avshar pursues you, he cannot come after me. That is how I would have it. No, I will not do what you ask."

"Then why should you go free now? We could hold you with us."

"Go ahead. If you think you can wring magic out of me, how can I stop you from trying?" Every line of Wulghash's body showed his contempt for anyone who would break the bond of friendship. Marcus felt his ears grow hot. After all the khagan had suffered on account of the Romans, he could not force what Wulghash did not want to give.

"Do as you please," the tribune said, and stepped aside.

A little life came into the khagan's face. "Were we to meet again one day, you and I, I could wish you were my friend as well as my friend." Intonation made his meaning clear. He bobbed his head at Scaurus and went off toward the line of horses.

When the Arshaum whose animal he picked protested, Arigh gave the man one of his own ponies as compensation. Satisfied, the nomad gave Wulghash a leg up. He had no trouble riding bareback. With a wave to Arigh, he kicked the horse into a trot and rode up the valley into the mountains.

The tribune returned to the fire; sitting proved no easier than rising had been. "Lay back," Gorgidas told him. "You've earned it."

Scaurus started to relax, then sat up again, quickly enough to wrench a gasp from him. "By the gods," he exclaimed, pointing at the tunnel-mouth, "Avshar himself may be coming out of that hole any minute."

"Ordure!" That was Gaius Philippus. "With all this, I clean forgot the shriveled he-witch. He may have half of Yezd with him, too."

Arigh weighed the choice, to move or fight. "We move," he decided.

The Arshaum broke camp with a speed that impressed even the Romans. Of course, Scaurus thought, there was a great deal less involved than with a legionary encampment—fold tents, mount horses, and travel.

They did not ride far, three or four miles through a pass, south and a bit west so that Mashiz, now northeast of them, was screened from sight by the Dilbat foothills. Though the journey was short, jouncing along on the backs of a couple of rough-gaited steppe ponies left Marcus and Gaius Philippus white-lipped.

When at last they dismounted, Scaurus' distress was so plain that Gorgidas said in peremptory tones, "Shuck off those rags. Let me see you."

No less than officers, physicians learn the voice of command; Marcus obeyed without thinking. The tribune saw Gorgidas' eyes widen slightly, but the Greek was too well schooled to reveal much. His hands moved down the length of the slash, marking Scaurus' reaction at every inch. He muttered to himself in his own tongue, "Redness and swelling, heat and pain," then spoke to Scaurus: "Your wound has inflammation in it."

"Can you give me a drug to check it? We'll be doing more riding than this, I'm sure, and I have to be able to sit a horse."

He thought Gorgidas had not heard him. The Greek sat staring into the fire. But for his deep, regular breathing, he might have been cast from bronze; his features were calm and still. Marcus had just realized he was not even blinking when he turned and laid his hands on the tribune's chest.

The grip was strong, square on the place that hurt worst. Involuntarily, Scaurus opened his mouth to cry out, but he found to his amazement that the physician's touch brought no pain. Very much the opposite, in fact; he felt anguish flowing away, to be replaced by a feeling of well-being he had not known since Avshar took him.

The Greek's fingers unerringly found the most feverish places in the cut. At each firm touch, the tribune felt pain and inflammation leave. When Gorgidas drew his hands away, Scaurus looked down at himself. The cut was still there; he would carry the mark to his grave. But it was only a pale line on his flesh, as if he had borne it for years. He bent and stretched and found he could move freely.

"You can't do that," he blurted. Gorgidas' failure to learn the Videssian healing art had been one of the things that drove him to the plains.

The physician opened his eyes. His face was drawn with fatigue, but he gave the ghost of a grin. "Obviously," he said. He turned to Gaius Philippus. "I think I can deal with you, too, if you want, though like as not you think it's manly to let all your bruises hurt."

"You must have me mixed up with Viridovix," the veteran retorted. "Come on, do what you can, and I'll be grateful. I will say, though, that healing or no healing, beard or no beard, some ways you haven't changed much."

"Good," the Greek said, spoiling the gibe.

When Gorgidas dropped into the healer's trance again, Marcus whispered to Viridovix, "Do you know how he learned the art?"

"The answer there is aye and nay both. Sure and I was there, and you might even say the cause of it all, being frozen more than a mite, but in no condition to make notes for your honor's edification, if you see what I mean. Puir tomnoddy that I was, I thought you back safe and cozy in Videssos, belike wi' six or eight bairns from that Helvis o' yours—by the looks of her, one to keep a man warm o' nights, I'm thinking."

Gaius Philippus' hiss had nothing to do with the hands that squeezed his upper arm. "Did I say summat wrong?" Viridovix asked, then studied Scaurus' face, which had gone grim. "Och, I did that. Begging your pardon, whatever it was."

"Never mind," the tribune sighed. "We have a busy year's worth of catching up to do, though."

Gorgidas came out of his trance and let Gaius Philippus go. "Tomorrow, I beg you, when I can hear it, too," he said. He was scarcely able to keep his eyes open. "For now, all I crave is rest."

After going through the same set of contortions Marcus had, Gaius Philippus gave the physician a formal legionary salute, clenched fist held straight out in front of him. "You do just as you please," he said sincerely. "By my book, you've earned the right."

The touchy Greek raised an eyebrow. "Is that so? We'll see." He waved to a young man in scale mail of a pattern Marcus did not recognize. The fellow ambled over, smiling, and put a hand on Gorgidas' shoulder. The physician said, "This is Rakio, of the Sworn Fellowship of the Yrmido. My lover." He waited for the sky to fall.

"I am pleased you gentlemen to meet," Rakio said, bowing.

"To the crows with you," Gaius Philippus growled at Gorgidas. "You'll not make me out a liar that easily." He stuck out his hand. So did Scaurus. Rakio clasped them in turn; his grip had a soldier's controlled strength. The Romans gave their own names.

"Then you are men from Gorgidas' world," Rakio exclaimed. "Much he about you has said."

"Have you, now?" Marcus asked the physician, but got no answer. Gorgidas was asleep where he sat.

Leaving Rakio to bundle Gorgidas into his bedroll, the Romans wandered through the Arshaum camp. The healing had stripped away their exhaustion as if it had never been, and moving without pain was a pleasure to be savored for its newness. In sheer animal relief, Marcus stretched till his joints creaked. "Seems Viridovix was right," he said. "A busy year indeed."

He spoke Videssian because he had been using it with Rakio. Pikridios Goudeles snapped him out of his reverie with a sardonic jab: "If you have no further profound philosophical insights to offer, you might consider taking counsel with me over our next course of action—unless, of course, you relish Yezd so much that you are enamored of the prospect of remaining here indefinitely. As for myself, I find any place, including Skotos' hell, would be preferable."

"At your service," the tribune said promptly. "With Avshar in the saddle here, the difference between one and the other isn't worth spitting on." He squatted, again feeling the delight of pain-free motion. "First, though, tell me how you got here and what your situation is."

"You still talk like an officer," Goudeles said. He started the story in his own discursive way. Seeing them with their heads together, Skylitzes joined them and boiled the essentials down to a few sentences. The bureaucrat gave him a resentful stare, but took back the conclusion almost by main force: "Arigh will not go east if alliance with Videssos means sacrificing his independence, or if he thinks the Emperor might make peace with Yezd."

"No danger of that," Scaurus said. "When I left Videssos, Gavras was planning this summer's campaign against the Yezda. And as for the other, he'll take allies on whatever terms he can get—he's not so strong himself that he can afford to sneeze at them."

"We have him, then!" Goudeles said to Skylitzes. He reached up to pound the taller man on the back. Marcus glanced at the two of them curiously. The pen-pusher caught the look. With a self-conscious smile, he said, "Once back in the city a while, I shall undoubtedly oppose the soldier's faction once more with all my heart—"

"Not much there," Skylitzes put in.

"Oh, go to the ice. Here I was about to say that spending time amongst the barbarians had changed—at least for the moment—my view of the world and Videssos' place in it, and what thanks do I get? Insults!" Goudeles rolled his eyes dramatically.

"Save your theatrics for Midwinter's Day," Skylitzes said, unperturbed. "Let's talk to Arigh. Now we have news to change his mind."

* * *

Gaius Philippus inspected the *gladius* with a critical eye. "You've taken care of it," he allowed. "A nick in the edge here, see, and another one close to the point, but nothing a little honing won't fix. Can you use it, though? There's the rub."

"Yes," Gorgidas said shortly. He still had mixed feelings about the sword and everything it stood for.

A few feet away, Viridovix was teasing Marcus. "Aren't you the one, now? Bewailing me up, down, and sideways over a romp with Komitta Rhangavve, and then caught 'twixt the sheets with her yourself. My hat's off to you, that it is." He doffed his fur cap.

The tribune gritted his teeth, resigned to getting some such reaction from the Gaul. He looked for words as his pony splashed through the headwaters of the Gharraf River, one of the Tutub's chief tributaries. Nothing much came, even though he was using Latin to keep the imperials he was traveling with from learning of his connection with Alypia. All he could say was, "It wasn't—it isn't—a romp. There's more to it than that. More than with Helvis, too, I'm finding. Looking back, I should have seen the rocks in that stream early on."

Remembering Viridovix' tomcat ways back in Videssos, he expected the Celt to chaff him harder than ever. But Viridovix sobered instead. "One o' those, is it? May you be lucky in it, then. I wasna when I had it and I dinna ken where I'll find the like again." He went on, mostly to himself, "Och, Seirem, it was no luck I brought you."

They rode east in melancholy companionship. The lay of the land was not new to Scaurus, who had come the other way with Tahmasp on a route a little south of the one Arigh was taking. The country was low, rolling, and hilly, the southern marches of the rich alluvial plain of the Hundred Cities. Towns hereabout were small and hugged tight to streambeds. Away from water, the sun blasted the hills' thin cover of grass and thornbushes to sere yellow. There was barely enough fodder to keep the horses in condition.

A scout trotted back over the rise ahead, shouting in the plains speech. Gorgidas translated for the Roman: "A band of Yezda heading our way." He listened some more. "We outnumber them, he says." Marcus grunted in relief. Arigh hardly led six hundred men. A really large company of Yezda going to join Avshar at Mashiz could have ridden over them without difficulty.

As a competent general should, Arigh made his decision quickly. Signal flags waved beside him. The Arshaum deployed from column to line of battle with an unruffled haste that reminded Scaurus of his legionaries. The riders on either flank trotted ahead to form outsweeping wings. The center lagged. Along with his own horse-archers, Arigh kept the remnant of the Erzrumi and the Videssian party there. When he noticed Scaurus studying his arrangements, he bared his teeth in a mirthless grin. "Not enough heavy-armed horsemen to do much good, but if they count for anything, it'll be here."

A messenger came streaking from the left wing, spoke briefly with the Arshaum leader, and galloped away. More flags fluttered. "They've spotted the spalpeens there," Viridovix said, reading the signal. The whole force swung leftward.

No great horseman, Marcus hoped he would be able to control his pony in a fight. Gaius Philippus must have been wrestling with the same worry, for he looked more nervous than the tribune had ever seen him just before combat. He hefted a borrowed saber uncertainly. Gorgidas had offered him his *gladius* back, but he declined, saying, "Better me than you with an unfamiliar sword." The tribune wondered if he was regretting his generosity.

They topped the rise over which the outrider had come. Partly obscured by their own dust, Scaurus saw Yezda galloping away in good order. Viridovix shouted a warning: "Dinna be fooled! It's a ploy all these horse-nomads use, to cozen their foes into thinking 'em cowards."

The pursuing Arshaum on either wing, wary of the trick, kept at a respectful distance from their opponents' main body. Already, though, the faster ponies among them were coming level with the Yezda on slow horses. They did not try to close, but swept wide, seeking to surround the Yezda.

Seeing they might succeed and bag his entire force, the Yezda leader bawled an order. With marvelous speed and skill, his men wheeled their horses and thundered back the way they had come, straight for Arigh and the center of his line. One by one, they rose high in their short-stirruped saddles to shoot.

Marcus had faced a barrage from nomadic archers at Maragha. Then he had been afoot, with no choice but to stand and take it. It had seemed to go on forever. Now he, too, was mounted, in the midst of plainsmen matching the Yezda shot for shot, and then charging the enemy at a pace that left his eyes teary from wind.

An Arshaum horse went crashing down, rolling over its luckless rider. The pony behind it slewed to avoid it, exposing its barrel to the Yezda. An instant later the second beast screamed and foundered a few feet past the first. The plainsman on it kicked free and tumbled over the rough ground, arms up to protect his head.

An arrow bit Scaurus' calf. He yelped. When he looked down, he saw a freely bleeding cut, perhaps two inches long; the head of the shaft had scored the outside of his leg as it darted past. The wound was just below the bottom of his trouser leg. The breeches, borrowed from an Arshaum, fit him well through the waist but were much too short.

Then it was sword on sword, the Yezda trying to hack their way through their foes before the latter could bring all their numbers to bear, Arigh's men battling to keep them in check. Marcus did his best to put himself in a Yezda's way, though to his moritfication the first rider he came near avoided him as easily as if he and his mount had suddenly frozen solid.

Another horseman approached. The fighting was at closer quarters now, and the going slower. The Yezda feinted, slashed. Marcus was lucky to turn the blow; he had to think about everything he did, a weakness easily fatal in combat. His answering stroke almost cut off his horse's ear. The Yezda, seeing he was up against a tyro, let a smile peek through his thick black beard.

His own swordplay, though, had more ferocity than science, and Scaurus, after beating aside a series of roundhouse slashes, felt his confidence begin to return. He could fight this way, even if only on the defensive. The Yezda's grin faded. A fresh surge of combat swept them apart.

The tribune noted with a twinge of envy how well Viridovix and Gorgidas handled themselves on horseback. The Celt's long arm and long, straight blade made him a deadly foe; Gorgidas was less flamboyant but held his own. And there was Gaius Philippus, laying about with his saber as though born to it. Marcus wished he had more of that adaptability.

He was hotly engaged with a Yezda who was a better warrior than the first when the man suddenly wheeled to protect himself from a new threat. Too late; an Erzrumi lance pierced his small leather shield as if it were of tissue, drove deep into his midriff, and plucked him from the saddle. Not since the Namdaleni had Scaurus seen heavy horse in action; he wished Arigh had more mountaineers along.

Those Yezda who could broke out and fled westward. The Arshaum did not pursue—their road was in the opposite direction. The skirmish had cost them a double handful of men. Three times that many Yezda lay dead on the parched ground; several more howled and writhed with wounds that would kill them more slowly but no less surely.

Arigh stood over a Yezda whose guts spilled out into the dry grass. The man whimpered at every breath; he was far past saving. Arigh called Skylitzes to him. "Tell him I will give him release if he answers me truthfully." The Arshaum chief drew his dagger; the Yezda's eyes fixed on it eagerly. He nodded, his face contorted with pain. "Ask him where Avshar intends to take the army he's forming."

Skylitzes put the question into the Khamorth tongue. "Videssos," the Yezda wheezed, tears, oozing down his cheeks. He added a couple of words. "Your promise," Skylitzes translated absently. His face had gone grim, the news was what he had expected, but bad all the same.

Arigh drove his dagger through the Yezda's throat.

"Best be sure," he said, and started to put the question to another fallen enemy, but the soldier died while Skylitzes was translating it. A third try, though, confirmed the first. "Good," Arigh said. "I feel easier now—I'm not leaving Avshar behind."

The Arshaum left their foes where they had fallen. They took up the corpses of their own men and dug hasty graves for them when they came to soft ground by the side of a stream. Tolui spoke briefly as the plainsmen covered over their comrades' bodies. "What is he saying?" Marcus asked Gorgidas.

"Hmm? Just listen—no, I'm an idiot; you don't know the Arshaum tongue." The physician knuckled his eyes. "So tired," he muttered; he had helped heal three men after the skirmish. With an effort, he gathered himself. "He prays that the ghosts of their slain enemies will serve these warriors in the next world."

A thought struck Scaurus. "How strong a wizard is he?"

"Stronger than I first guessed, surely. Why?"

Without naming Wulghash, the tribune explained how his

sword had been partly masked. Gorgidas dipped his head to show he understood. "Aye; Viridovix was tracked across the steppe by his blade. If Tolui can match the magic done for you, it would be no small gain to cover our trail from Avshar." His gaze sharpened. "That sounds like a potent sorcery for a chance-met guardsman to have ready to hand."

Marcus felt himself flush; he should have known better than to try to hide anything from the Greek. "I don't suppose it matters now," he said, and told Gorgidas who the sorcerer was.

The physician had a coughing fit. When he could talk again, he said, "As well you didn't name him in Arigh's hearing. He would have seen Wulghash only as the overlord of Yezd, and an enemy; he would not have spared him for rescuing you. He likes you, mind, but not enough to turn aside from his own plans for your sake."

"He's like his opposite number, then," Scaurus said. "Thorisin, too, come to think of it." He grinned lopsidedly. "Sometimes I was unhappy with Rome's republic, but having seen kings in action, I hope it lasts forever."

That evening Tolui examined the tribune's sword with minute care, then did the same for Viridovix'. "I see what has been done," he said at last, "but not how. Still, I will try to match it in my own way." He quickly donned his fringed regalia, tapped on the oval spirit-drum to summon aid to him.

Scaurus jumped when a voice spoke from nowhere; he had not seen wizardry of this sort before. More and louder drumwork enforced the shaman's command on the spirit.

But the magic in the Gaul's blade must have taken its approach as inimical, for the druids' marks suddenly blazed hot and golden. The spirit wailed. Tolui staggered and cried out urgently, but only fading, derisive laughter answered him.

With trembling hands, he lifted off his leering mask. His wide, high-cheekboned face was pale beneath its swarthiness. In a chagrined voice, he spoke briefly to Gorgidas. The Greek translated: "He says he praises the wizard who disguised your sword, Scaurus. He gave the best he had, but his magic is not subtle enough for the task."

The tribune hid his disappointment. After making sure by gestures that Tolui was all right, he said to Gorgidas, "Worth the try—we're no worse off than we were before."

"Except for the puir singed ghostie, that is," Viridovix

amended wryly, sheathing his blade. "Yowled like a scalded cat, it did."

Later, Gorgidas remarked to Scaurus, "I didn't think Tolui would fail you. He's beaten two magicians at once; Wulghash must be far out of the ordinary, to succeed in putting a spell on your blade."

"Not on, exactly—*around* is closer, I think," the tribune answered. "Even Avshar didn't dare to try making a spell cling to the sword itself."

"As it should be, that," Viridovix said. "The holy druids ha' more power to 'em nor any maggoty wizard, for it's after walking with the true gods that they are." He had utter confidence in the supremacy of his Celtic wise men.

Gaius Philippus snorted. "If your mighty druids are as marvelous as all that, how did Marcus here win his Gallic blade from one of them in battle? And how is it the magic in his sword and yours fetched all of us here, you included, instead of leaving you back in your own country as a properly crafted piece of wizardry would?"

Viridovix looked down his long, straight nose at the senior centurion. "Sure, and I'd managed to forget what a poisonous beetle y'are." He leaned forward to stir up the embers of the fire they were sitting around. That done, he resumed, "For all you ken, 'twas purposed we come here."

The Gaul spoke in reflex defense of the druids, but Gorgidas broke through Gaius Philippus' derisive grunt to say, soberly, "Maybe it was. The hermit in the ruins thought so."

"What tale is this?" Marcus asked; with so much having happened on both sides, neither was caught up on all the other's doings.

The physician and Viridovix took turns telling it. While he listened, Scaurus scratched his chin. Stubble rasped his fingers. One of the first things he had done after regaining his freedom was to borrow Viridovix' razor and scrape off his beard. He kept at it, though shaving with stale grease left a lot to be desired.

When they were through, Gaius Philippus, who was also beardless again, commented: "Sounds like just another priest to me, maybe stewed in his own juice too long. He didn't say what this whacking big purpose was, did he now?"

"To my way of thinking, men make purposes, not the other way round," Gorgidas said. He challenged the veteran: "What would you aim for, given the choice?"

"Ask me a hard one." The laugh Gaius Philippus gave had nothing to do with mirth. "I want Avshar."

"Aye." Viridovix crooned the word, in his eagerness once more looking and sounding the barbarian he had almost ceased to be. "The head of him over my door."

Marcus thought the question hardly worth asking. Beyond what the wizard-prince had done to any of them, he put Videssos in mortal peril. Leaving his own scars—even leaving Alypia—out of the bargain, that alone would have turned the Roman against him forever. For all its faults, Scaurus admired his adopted homeland's tradition of benign rule; he knew how rare it was.

He was rubbing his chin again when his hand stopped cold, forgotten. Very slowly, he turned to Viridovix and asked, "How much would you give to bring him down?"

"Himself?" The Celt did not hesitate. "No price'd be too much."

"I hope you mean that. Listen . . ."

The Arshaum halted at a branching in the road. Neither path east seemed promising. The northern track ran through more of the barren scrub country with which they had already become too familiar, while the other swerved south into what was frankly desert.

Marcus and Gaius Philippus urged Arigh toward the southern route. "You'll enter Videssos sooner, for its border swings further east in the south," the tribune said. "And the Yezda will be fewer. They leave the waste to the desert nomads; there's not enough water to keep their herds alive."

"Then how will we find enough for ourselves?" Arigh asked pointedly.

"It's there, if you know where to look," Gaius Philippus said, "and Scaurus and I do. This is the way we went west with Tahmasp's caravan. Aside from the towns, that pirate knows the name of every little well, and its grandmother's, too. We're no rookies, Arigh; we kept our eyes open."

"A strange route for a caravan master," the Arshaum chief mused. "The Hundred Cities surely offered richer trade."

"Normally, yes, but the fox had wind of invaders turning them upside down." Marcus grinned. "That would have been you, I suppose."

"So it would." Arigh pondered the coincidence. "Maybe the spirits are granting us an omen. Be it so, then." Seldom indecisive long, he waved his followers down the road the Romans suggested.

The air had the smell of hot dust. The sun glared off stretches of sand. Rakio stared through slitted eyes at the baked flatlands he and his comrades were traversing. "Oh, for valleys and streams and cool green meadows!" he said plaintively. "This would be a sorrowful place to die."

"As if the where of it mattered," Viridovix said. "I'll be dead soon enough, here or someplace else." As he had since hearing Scaurus' plan, he sounded more resigned than gloomy. Fey, Gorgidas thought; the Celtic word fit.

For his part, the tribune did his best not to think about the likely fruits of his ingenuity. His role as guide helped. He quickly found the promises he and Gaius Philippus had given Arigh were easier to make than keep. Landmarks looked different from the way he remembered them. The blowing sand was part of the reason. Sometimes hundreds of yards of road disappeared under it.

Worse, he had only made the journey coming west. Seen from the opposite side, guideposts went unrecognized. Only after he had passed them and looked back was he sure of them. "A virtue of hindsight I hadn't realized," he remarked to the senior centurion after they managed to backtrack the Arshaum to the first important water hole.

At the Romans' urging, the plainsmen kept their horses in good order as they let them drink. "If you foul an oasis, the desert men will hunt you down and kill you," Scaurus warned Arigh.

The Arshaum chief was doubtful until Skylitzes said, "Think of the care your clans take with fire on the plains."

"Ahh. Yes, I see," Arigh said, making the connection. "Here fire is no risk; where will it go? But wasting or polluting water must be worth a war."

Sentries' alarms tumbled the Arshaum from their bedrolls at earliest dawn. A band of desert tribesmen was shaking itself out into loose array as it approached from the south. Most of the nomads rode light, graceful horses; a few were on camels. Some of the Arshaum ponies snorted and reared, taking the camels' unfamiliar scent.

"Will they attack without parleying?" Arigh demanded.

"I wouldn't think so, with three of us for their one," Scaurus said. Behind them, the plainsmen were scrambling to horse.

"Never trust 'em, though," Gaius Philippus added. "They turn traitor against each other for the sport of it; outsiders are prey the second they look weak. And have another care, too. Those bows don't carry far, but sometimes they poison their arrows."

Arigh nodded. "I remember that the envoys from their tribes were always at feud with each other in Videssos." He was so thoroughly a chieftain these days that Marcus had almost forgotten his years as ambassador at the imperial city.

The Arshaum gave his attention back to the newcomers. "What's this?"

The desert men had sent a party forward. They came slowly, their hands ostentatiously visible. "You know more about them than anyone else here," Arigh said to the Romans. "Come on." Accompanied by Arshaum archers, they rode out with him toward the approaching nomads.

The desert tribesmen and men from the steppe studied each other curiously. Instead of trousers and tunics, the horsemen nearing the oasis wore flowing robes of white or brown wool. Some wrapped strips of cloth round their heads, while others protected themselves from the sun with scarves of linen or silk. They were most of them lean, with long, deeply tanned faces, features of surprising delicacy, and deep-set eyes as chilly as their land was hot. A couple had waxed mustaches; most preferred a thin fringe of beard outlining the jaw.

They waited for Arigh to speak first and lose face. But the startlement they showed when he asked, "Do you know Videssian?" regained it for him.

"Aye," one of them said at last. His beard was grizzled, his face dark as old leather. The leader, Marcus guessed, as much from the way the rest of the tribesmen eyed him as from the heavy silver bracelets he wore on each wrist. "I am Shenuta of the Nufud." He waved at his men. "Who are you, to use the waters of Qatif without our leave? Your strangeness is no excuse."

Arigh named himself, then said loudly, "I am at war with Yezd. Is that excuse enough?"

It was a keen guess; Shenuta could not keep surprise off his face. He spoke rapidly in his own guttural tongue. Several of his followers exclaimed; one shook his fist at the northwest, toward Mashiz. "It is to be thought on," Shenuta admitted, his features under control again.

Arigh pressed the advantage. "We have done nothing to

Qatif save drink there. Send men to see if you care to. And in exchange for its water I have a gift for you." He gave the Nufud chief his spare bow. "See the backing of horn and sinew, here and here? It will easily outrange the best you have. Make more; use them against the Yezda."

"You are the oddest-looking man I have ever seen, but you have the ways of a prince," Shenuta said. "Have you a daughter I might marry, to seal our friendship?"

"I am sorry, I do not; and if I did, the journey from my land, which lies far to the north, would not be easy." Arigh spread his hands in regret.

Shenuta bowed in the saddle. "Then let the thought be taken for the deed. I give you and yours leave to use Qatif as if it were your own. This privilege you share with but three caravan masters: Stryphnos the Videssian, who taught me this speech in return; Jandal, whose mother is of the Nufud; and Tahmasp, who won the right to all my oases from me at dice."

"Sounds like him," Gaius Philippus said with a laugh.

For the first time, Shenuta swung his gaze toward the Romans. "You know Tahmasp?" He paid particular attention to Scaurus. "I have seen yellow-haired ones in his company once or twice."

"They are of a people different from mine," the tribune answered. "My comrade here and I served only one tour as guards with him, when he was on the road to Mashiz earlier this year. This is the fastest route we know to Videssos, which is why we told our friend Arigh of it. As he said, we meant no harm to what is yours."

"That is well spoken," Shenuta said. "If I had to choose between Videssos and Yezd, I think I would choose Videssos. But I do not have to choose; neither of them will ever master the desert. Perhaps one day they will destroy each other. Then the Nufud and the other tribes of free men shall come into their own."

"Maybe so," Marcus said politely, though his thought was that the desert nomads, for all their dignified ways, were no less barbarians than the Khamorth or Arshaum. Still, the Khamorth had conquered much of Videssos once.

The Nufud leader and Arigh exchanged oaths; Shenuta swore by sun, moon, and sand. Scaurus thought the encounter was done, but as Arigh was wheeling his pony to return to the oasis, Shenuta said, "When you catch up to Tahmasp, tell him I still think his dice were flats."

"Tahmasp is still in Mashiz gathering a cargo, we thought," Gaius Philippus said. "He told us he'd be months at it."

Shenuta shrugged. "He watered his animals at the Fadak water hole south of here day before yesterday." Marcus did not know that oasis. The desert nomad went on, "He said, though, that he planned to swing more north once he was further east. Your horses look good and you are not burdened by wares; my guess would be that you will meet him soon. Do not forget my message." He bowed again to Arigh, nodded to the tribesmen with him, and rode back to the rest of the Nufud. At his shouted command, they trotted off to the south.

"Wonder what made Tahmasp pull out so quick," Gaius Philippus said. "It doesn't seem like him."

"Would you want to stay in a city Avshar had just seized?" Marcus asked.

The veteran considered, briefly. "Not a chance."

When the Arshaum left Qatif, they traveled with double patrols in case the Nufud took their oaths lightly. But, though a couple of desert nomads stayed in sight to keep a similar eye on the plainsmen, Shenuta proved a man of his word.

Marcus and Gaius Philippus gradually grew hardened to the saddle, undergoing the same toughening Viridovix, Gorgidas, and Goudeles had endured when they went to the steppe the year before. At every rest halt the senior centurion would rub his aching thighs. When the Arshaum snickered at him, he growled, "If you were on a forced march in the legions, you'd laugh from the other side of your faces, I promise you that." They paid no attention, which only annoyed him more.

After Scaurus got the plainsmen to the next oasis, he felt his confidence begin to return. And when they came upon the signs of a recently abandoned camp and a trail leading east, excitement coursed through him. "Tahmasp, sure enough!" he exclaimed, finding a scrap of yellow canvas impaled on a thornbush. Holes in the ground where pegs had been driven showed the size of the caravaneer's big tent.

Pacing it off, Arigh was impressed. "Not bad, for one not a nomad born. Few yurts are larger."

Viridovix gave Marcus a sly glance. "A good thing, I'm thinking. Once we're after having this trader to hand, now, we'll no more be at the mercy o' these Romans for directions, with them so confused and all."

So much for confidence, the tribune thought. He said, "It'll be a relief for me, too, let me tell you."

He was astonished when the mercurial Celt cried angrily, "Och, a bellyful o' these milksop answers I've had from the Greek already!" and stalked off. Viridovix stayed in his moody huff all night.

The desert wind had played with the caravan's trail, but the Arshaum clung to it. And as they gained, the signs grew clearer. The sun was sinking at their backs when they spotted Tahmasp's rear guard. They were spotted in turn; by the time they caught up with the caravan itself, it was drawn up for defense, with archers crouched behind hastily dumped bales of cloth. Merchants scrambled this way and that; Marcus heard Tahmasp's familiar bellow roaring out orders.

The tribune said to Arigh, "Let us talk with him."

"You'd better. I don't think he'd listen to me." The Arshaum chief allowed himself a dry laugh. His slanted eyes were gauging the caravan's preparations. "Looks like he knows his business. Go on, calm him down."

Unexpectedly, Pikridios Goudeles said, "If you don't mind, I'll accompany you. Perhaps I shall be able to render some assistance."

"Not with one of your long speeches," Gorgidas said in alarm, remembering the grandiloquent orations the pen-pusher had delivered on the steppe. "From what the Romans have said, I don't think this Tahmasp is one to appreciate rhetoric."

Goudeles sniffed. "Permit me to remind you that I know what I'm about. Where there's a will, there's a lawyer."

With that his comrades had to be content. Shrugging, Arigh said, "As you please." The tribune, centurion, and imperial bureaucrat urged their horses out from the Arshaum around them and walked the beasts forward until they were well within range of the caravan's bows.

No one shot at them. Scaurus called, "Tahmasp! Kamytzes!" Gaius Philippus echoed with the name of the lieutenant under whom he'd served: "Muzaffar!" They shouted their own names.

"You two, is it?" Tahmasp yelled back furiously. "Another step closer and you'll be buzzards' meat, the both of you. I told you what we do to spies."

"We weren't spies," the tribune returned. "Will you listen, or not?"

Goudeles spoke for the first time: "We'll make it worth your while." Marcus wondered at that; the Arshaum had little past horses, clothes and weapons. But the bureaucrat's self-assurance was unruffled.

Scaurus heard Kamytzes' voice raised in expostulation. Knowing the turn of the grim little Videssian's mind, he guessed Tahmasp's aide was arguing against a parley. But the numbers at Marcus' back had a logic of their own, and Tahmasp, beneath his bluster, was an eminently practical man. He yielded gruffly, but he yielded. "All right, I'm listening. Come ahead."

The Romans' former comrades-in-arms met them with icy glares as they entered the perimeter of the improvised camp. Tahmasp stumped forward, closing the last catch on a chain-mail shirt Scaurus and Gaius Philippus could both have fit into. A spiked Makuraner-style helmet sat slightly askew on his shaved head. Kamytzes hovered a couple of steps behind him, his hands near a brace of throwing-knives at his bejeweled belt.

The caravan master folded his arms across his massive chest. "Thought you'd be in Videssos by now," he accused the Romans. "Or is this more of what you call 'business'?"

"We thought you were still in Mashiz," Marcus returned. "Or couldn't you stomach Avshar?" He hoped his guess was right. When Tahmasp's eyes shifted, he knew it was. He said, "Neither could we," and tugged his tunic over his head.

At the sight of the scar, Tahmasp pursed his lips. Several troopers who had been friendly with the Romans swore in a handful of tongues. But Tahmasp's first concern, as always, was for his caravan. "So—we have reasons for disliking the same man. But what has that to do with those robbers out there?" He jabbed a thumb at the Arshaum, a vague but threatening mass in the deepening twilight.

"That's a long story," Gaius Philippus said. "Remember why you chose not to go through the Hundred Cities on your way west?"

"Some barbarian invasion or—" The caravaneer juggled facts as neatly as he did bills of lading. "Them, eh? Don't tell me you were mixed up in that."

"Not exactly." Marcus told the story quickly, finishing, "You're heading into Videssos and so are we, but you know all the short cuts and best roads. Show them to us and you'll have the biggest guard force any caravan ever dreamed of.

The Yezda won't dare come near you."

"And if I don't . . ." Tahmasp began. His voice trailed away. The answer there was obvious. He took off his helmet and kicked it as far as he could; it flew spinning into the darkness. "What can I say but yes? Maybe your bastards'll plunder me later, but you'll sure plunder me now for a no. The pox take you, outlanders. My old granddad always told me to run screaming from anything that smelled like politics, and here you're dragging me in up to my neck."

"Not all politics are evil," Goudeles said. "Nor will you suffer for aiding us."

In his Arshaum suede and leather, with his beard untrimmed and his hair long and not very clean, the pen-pusher cut an unprepossessing figure. Tahmasp rumbled, "Who are you to make such promises, little man?"

The bureaucrat had learned on the plains to make do with what he had. When he drew himself up and declared haughtily, "Sirrah, you have the privilege of addressing Pikridios Goudeles, minister and ambassador of his Imperial Majesty Thorisin Gavras, Avtokrator of the Videssians." It did not occur to Tahmasp to doubt him.

He was not, however, a man to be overawed for long. "Why is it such a privilege, eh?"

"Fetch me a parchment, pen and ink, and some sealing wax." At the caravan master's order, one of his men brought them. The bureaucrat wrote a few quick lines. "Now, have you fire?" he asked.

"Would I be without it?" Several of Tahmasp's men carried fire-safes, to keep hot coals alive while they traveled. One of them upended his over a pile of tinder. When a small blaze sprang up, Goudeles lit the red wax' wick and let several drops fall at the foot of his parchment. He jammed his seal ring into the wax while it was still soft and handed Tahmasp the finished document.

The caravaneer squatted by the little fire. His lips moved as he read. Suddenly a grin replaced the scowl he had been wearing since the Romans and Goudeles entered his encampment. He turned to his followers and shouted, "Exemption from imperial tolls for the next three years!"

The guardsmen and merchants burst into cheers. Tahmasp enfolded Goudeles in a beefy embrace and bussed him on both cheeks. "Little man, we have a deal!"

"How delightful." The pen-pusher disentangled himself as fast as he could.

While Marcus was waving to the Arshaum that agreement had been struck, Tahmasp dug an elbow into Goudeles' ribs. Goudeles yelped. The caravaneer said craftily, "You know, it's likely I could beat the tolls anyway. Even your damned inspectors can't be everywhere."

"I daresay." Goudeles held out his hand. "Shall I take the document back, then? The penalty for smuggling is, of course, confiscation of all illegal goods and a branding for the criminals involved."

Tahmasp hastily made the parchment disappear. "No, no, no need of that. It is, as I said, a bargain."

The rest of the Videssian party, Arigh, and a few of his commanders rode up to fraternize with the caravan master and his aides; bargain or no bargain, Tahmasp was nervous about letting too many of his new-found allies near his goods. He was politic enough, however, to send several skins of wine out to the plainsmen—enough to make them happy without turning them rowdy.

Having been drinking naught but water for some time, Scaurus enjoyed the wine all the more. He was in the middle of his second cup when he exclaimed, "I almost forgot!" He went over to Tahmasp, who was simultaneously asking questions of Viridovix—whose red hair fascinated him—and answering them from Gorgidas, who wanted to know everything there was to know about all the strange places the caravaneer had seen in his travels. Tahmasp chuckled when the tribune delivered Shenuta's message.

"So he thinks my dice are crooked, does he? He's wrong; I'd never do such a thing," the burly trader declared righteously. Then he winked. "But I'm surprised the old sand shark has a robe to call his own if he's still using the pair he had that night. Those were loaded, all right—the wrong way!"

His booming laughter filled the desert night.

XI

"THIS IS ALL MOST IRREGULAR," EVTYKHIOS KORYKOS SAID. The *hypasteos* of Serrhes had said that several times already. Irregular or not, it was plainly too much for him. Nothing ever happened in Serrhes, a small city at the junction of the desert and the imperial westlands' central plateau. Even the Yezda passed it by; their invasion routes ran further north. All the convulsions in Videssian affairs had left it untouched and nearly forgotten.

That suited Korykos, whose chief aim was to vegetate along with his town. He stared resentfully at the rough-looking strangers who packed his office. "Irregular," he repeated. "This document grants an unprecedented exemption, and I am not certain I possess the authority to countersign it."

"You tripe-faced idiot!" Tahmasp roared. "No one gives a frike whether you countersign it or not. Just obey it and go back to gathering dust."

"Though his phrasing is crude, the good caravan master has captured the essence of the matter. The authority in question here is my own," Goudeles said smoothly. He confused the *hypasteos* more than any of the others. He looked like a barbarian, but spoke like the great noble he claimed to be.

"I also approve," Marcus put in. He bothered Korykos almost as much as Goudeles did. His speech and appearance both proclaimed him an outlander, but if he was to be believed, he was not only a general but also Goudeles' superior in the imperial chancery. And he knew so much more than Korykos about doings at the capital that there was no way to make him out a liar.

"Give us supplies and some fresh horses and send us on our way to Gavras at Videssos," Arigh said. Normally he would have scared Korykos witless. Dealing with him now was something of a relief—he did not pretend he was anything but what he seemed.

He also gave the *hypasteos* a chance to vent his suspicions and a moment of petty triumph. "The Avtokrator is not *at* Videssos," Korykos said primly. "Why are allegedly high imperial officials ignorant of such a fact?"

He did not enjoy the discomfiture he created. "Well, where is he, you worthless cretin?" Gaius Philippus barked, leaning over Korykos' desk as if about to tear the answer from him by force. Arigh was right beside him. If Thorisin had gone east against the Namdaleni, the Arshaum's hopes were ruined. This time Goudeles did not try to hold them back. He was leaning forward himself, his right hand on the hilt of his sword, an unconscious measure of how much he had changed in the past year.

"Why, at Amorion, of course," Korykos got out through white lips.

"Impossible!" Scaurus, Gaius Philippus, and Tahmasp said it together. The trader's caravan had left the place one step ahead of the Yezda.

"Oh, is it?" Korykos fumbled through the parchments on his desk. Serrhes being as slow as it was, there weren't many of them. Marcus recognized the sunburst of the imperial seal as the *hypasteos* finally found the document he was after. Holding it at arm's length, he read: "'. . . and so it is required that you send a contingent numbering one third of the garrison of your city to join ourself and our armies at Amorion. No excuse will be tolerated for failure to obey this our command.'" He looked up. "I sent off the nine men, as ordered."

"Wonderful," Gaius Philippus said. "I'm sure the Yezda thank you for the snack." Korykos blinked, wondering what he meant. The veteran sighed and gave it up.

"That definitely is Gavras—no mistaking the blunt, ugly style," Goudeles said. Skylitzes made a noise at the back of his throat, but let the bureaucrat's sneer slide.

"What's he doing in Amorion?" Marcus persisted. Aside from the Yezda, the town had been Zemarkhos', and not under imperial control at all.

The tribune had not intended the question for Korykos, but it seemed to push the harassed official over the edge. "I nei-

ther know, nor care!" he shrilled. "Go find out and leave me at
peace!" With one of the spasms of energy weak men show, he
grappled the toll exemption from a startled Tahmasp, scrawled
his signature in large letters under Goudeles', and threw the
document in the caravaneer's face. "Go on, get out, before I
call the guards on you!"

Tahmasp tapped his forehead. "All eighteen you have left,
eh?" Marcus said in his politest tones. Arigh sputtered laughter, adding, "Bring 'em on! The roomful of us'll clean 'em
out, the three that aren't hiding already."

"Get out! Get out!" Korykos purpled with impotent fury.
Skylitzes stiffened to attention and threw him an ironic salute.
The *hypasteos* was still blustering when his unwelcome guests
filed out, but Marcus did not miss the relief on his face as they
left.

"Troglodytes!" Gorgidas exclaimed a couple of days out of
Serrhes. Instead of raising houses from the soft gray stone of
the area, the locals carved their homes, even their temples to
Phos, into the living rock. The Greek scribbled observations
whenever he passed through a village: "Because even its users
do not view the technique as natural, they imitate more usual
styles of construction as closely as they can. Thus one sees
brickwork, shutters, lintels, even balustrades, all executed in
relief to fool the eye into thinking them actually present."

The people of the rock villages reacted to the arrival of the
Arshaum much as had those of Serrhes. Most slammed their
doors tight and, Marcus was sure, piled their heaviest furniture behind them. The adventurous few came out to the town
marketplaces to trade with Tahmasp's merchants.

The caravan master was unhappy at how slow business
was. "What good does it do me to be tax-free if no one is
buying?"

"What good would it do you to be rich when the Yezda
swoop down on you?" Marcus retorted.

"I can't say you're wrong," Tahmasp admitted, "but I'd
like it better if it didn't look so much like they already had."

His complaint held justice. As the Arshaum traveled east
toward Amorion, to the eye they might have been just one
more nomadic band drifting into Videssos in the wake of the
imperial defenses' collapse after Maragha. At a distance, even
the Yezda took them for countrymen. Small parties of horsemen passed them several times without a second glance. And

to the Videssians, they seemed as frightful as the rest of the nomads. Even Goudeles' formidable eloquence was not always enough to win the locals' confidence.

"Can't hardly trust nobody these days," one grizzled village elder said when finally coaxed out of his home, a building whose fresh stonework showed an eye for defense. He hawked and spat. He spat very well, being without front teeth in his upper jaw. He went on, "We would have had trouble ourselves last year, but for dumb luck."

"How's that?" Tahmasp asked. He seemed a bit less morose than he had; the villagers were coming out to buy, once they saw nothing had happened to their leader. Women exclaimed over lengths of cloth dyed Makuraner-style in colorful stripes and argued with merchants about the quality of their bay leaves while their husbands fingered the edges of daggers and tried to get the most in exchange for debased goldpieces.

The old man spat again. "We was holding a wedding feast —my granddaughter's, in fact. Next morning when we go out to tend our herds, what do we find? Tracks to show a Yezda war party had come right close to the edge of town, then turned round and rode like Skotos was after 'em. Must've been the singing and dancing and carrying on fooled 'em into thinking we had soldiers here, and they lit out."

"A genuine use for marriage," Goudeles murmured, "something I had not previously believed possible." Having met the bureaucrat's wife, a rawboned harridan who only stopped talking to sleep, Marcus knew what prompted the remark.

The elder took it for a joke and laughed till he had to hug his skinny sides. "Hee, hee! Tell that to my missus, I will. I'll sleep in the barn for a week, but worth it, gentlemen, worth it."

"Be thankful you're after having one to rail at ye, now," Viridovix said, which perplexed the Videssian but failed to dampen his mirth, leaving both of them dissatisfied with the exchange.

The journey across the plateau country put all of Tahmasp's gifts on display. He always knew which stream bed would be dry and which had water in it, which band of herdsmen would sell or trade a few head of cattle and which run them deep into the badlands at first sight of strangers.

He also had a knack for knowing which routes would have

Yezda on them and which would be clear. The Arshaum only had to fight once, and then briefly. A band of Yezda collided with Arigh's vanguard and skirmished until the rest of the plainsmen came up to help their comrades, at which point their foes abruptly lost interest in the encounter and withdrew.

Along with his other talents, the swashbuckling caravaneer was soon fluently profane in the Arshaum tongue. His huge voice and swaggering manner made the plainsmen smile, but before long they were obeying him as readily as they did Arigh, who shook his head in bemused respect. "This once I wish I could write like you do," he remarked to Gorgidas one day. "I'd take notes, I really would."

For all Tahmasp's skills, though, there was no escaping the fact the invaders were loose in the westlands. Broken bridges, the burned-out shell of a noble's estate, unplanted cropland all told the same story. And once the Arshaum traversed a battlefield where, by the wreckage still lying about, both sides had been Yezda.

As was his way, Gorgidas looked for larger meanings in what he saw. "That field shows Videssos' hope," he said when they camped for the evening. "It is the nature of evil to divide against itself, and that is its greatest weakness. Think of how Wulghash and Avshar fell out with each other instead of working together against their common enemy."

"Well said!" Lankinos Skylitzes exclaimed. "At the last great test, Phos will surely triumph."

"I didn't say that," Gorgidas answered tartly. Skylitzes' generalizations were not the sort he was after.

Gaius Philippus irritated both the Greek and the Videssian by objecting. "I wouldn't lump Avshar and Wulghash together. You ask me, they're different."

"How, when they both seek to destroy the Empire?" Skylitzes said.

"So did the Namdaleni last year—and would again if they saw the chance. Wulghash, from what I saw of him, is more like that—an enemy, aye, but not wicked for wickedness' sake, if you take my meaning. Avshar, now. . ." The senior centurion paused, shaking his head. "Avshar is something else again."

No one argued that.

Marcus said, "I think there's something wrong with your whole scheme, Gorgidas, not just with the detail of how evil Wulghash is—though I read him the same way Gaius does."

"Go on." The prospect of a lively argument drew Gordigas more than criticism bothered him.

Scaurus picked his words with care. "It strikes me that faction and mistrust are part of the nature of mankind, not of evil alone. Otherwise how would you explain the strife Videssos has seen the last few years, or for that matter, Rome, before we came here?"

When the Greek hesitated, Skylitzes gave his own people's answer: "It is Skotos, of course, seducing men toward the wrong."

That smug "of course" annoyed Gorgidas enough to make him forget for a moment how deeply the Videssians believed in their faith. He snapped, "Utter nonsense. The responsibility for evil lies in every man, not at the hand of some outside force. There would be no evil, unless men made it."

That Greek confidence in the importance of the individual was something Marcus also took for granted, but it shocked Skylitzes. Viridovix had been sitting quietly by without joining the discussion, but when he saw the imperial officer's face grow stern he tossed in one of the mordant comments that came easily to his lips these days: "Have a care there, Gordigas dear; can you no see the pile o' fagots he's building for you in his mind?"

On the steppe Skylitzes would have managed a sour smile and passed it off. Now he was back in his native land. His expression did not change. The discussion faltered and died. Sometimes, Marcus thought, the imperials were almost as uncomfortable to be around as their enemies—another argument against Gorgidas' first thesis.

The little spring bubbled out from between two rocks; a streamlet trickled away eastward. "Believe it or not, it's the rising of the Ithome," Tahmasp said. "You can follow it straight into Amorion from here."

"You're not for town with us, then?" Viridovix asked disappointedly; the flamboyant caravaneer was a man after his own heart. "Where's the sense in that, to be after coming so far and sheering off at the very end?"

"You'd starve as a merchant," Tahmasp answered. "No trader in his right mind will hit the same city twice in one year. I've kept the bargain I had forced on me; now it's time to think of my own profit again. A *panegyris* is coming up in Doxon in about two weeks. If I push, I'll make it."

Nothing anyone said would make him change his mind. When Arigh, who admired his resourcefulness, pressed him hard, he said, "Another thing is, I want out from under soldiers. Aye, your plainsmen have treated me better than I thought they would, but there'll be a big army at Amorion, and I want no part of it. To a trader, soldiers are worse than bandits, because they have the law behind 'em. Why do you think I got out of Mashiz?" The Arshaum had no reply to that.

Tahmasp pounded Gaius Philippus on the shoulder. "You're all right." He turned to Scaurus, saying, "As for you, I'm glad I don't have to bargain against you—a high muckymuck and never let on! Well, now that I'm shut of you, I wish you luck. I have the feeling you'll need it."

"So do I," the tribune said.

He did not think Tahmasp even heard him. The caravan master was shouting orders to his guardsmen and the merchants with him. The guards, under the capable direction of Kamytzes and Muzaffar, smoothly took their places. When the merchants dawdled, Tahmasp bellowed, "Last one in line is my present to the Arshaum!" That got them moving. His big shaved head gleaming in the sun, Tahmasp burst into bawdy song as his caravan pulled away from the plainsmen, and never looked back.

"There goes a free man," Gaius Philippus said, following him with his eyes.

"Maybe so, but how long will he stay that way if Avshar wins? It's our job to keep him free," Marcus answered.

"Plenty of worse work, comes to that."

The Arshaum followed the Ithome east. It swiftly grew greater as one small tributary after another added their waters to it. By the end of their first day of travel, it was a river of respectable size, and the land through which it passed was beginning to seem familiar to the Romans.

"At this rate, we'll make Amorion in a couple of days," Scaurus remarked as they camped by the side of the stream.

"Aye, and Gavras bloody well better be glad to see us, too," Gaius Philippus said. "Seeing as how he's sitting there, he'll have a time saying we didn't get it back for him."

"I wonder." Now that their goal was so close, the tribune found himself more and more apprehensive. Had the Avtokrator pledged him only nobility, he would have felt sure of his reward. But there had been more in the bargain than that. . . . He wondered how Alypia was.

Viridovix did nothing to help his self-assurance, saying, "Sure and a king's a bad one for keeping promises, for who's to make him if he doesna care to?" Despite having heard from the Romans that Thorisin had put Komitta aside, he was also uncertain of the welcome the Emperor had waiting for him. Fretting over that took his mind off other concerns.

Morning twilight roused the Arshaum with a jolt when their sentries caught sight of a squad of strange horsemen. "Careless buggers," Gaius Philippus said, bolting down a wheatcake. "They stand out like whores at a wedding, silhouetted against the dawn that way. From any other direction, they'd be invisible."

The riders showed no sign of pulling back after they were discovered. "The cheek o' them now, looking us over bold as you please," Viridovix said. He set his Gallic helmet firmly on his head; its crest, a seven-spoked bronze wheel, glinted red as his hair in the light of the just-risen sun.

Marcus shielded his eyes with his hand to study the horsemen, who still had not moved. "I don't think that's cheek," he said at last. "I think it's confidence. They have a big force somewhere behind them, unless I miss my guess."

Gorgidas was also squinting into the sun. As he was a bit farsighted while Scaurus was the reverse, he saw more than the tribune. "They're nomads," he said worriedly. "What are the Yezda doing in strength so close to a big imperial army?"

Speculation ceased as they ran for their horses; most of the Arshaum were already mounted and hooted at them for their slowness. "Took you long enough," Arigh sniffed when they were finally in the saddle. "Let's find out what's going on."

He led a hundred riders toward the strangers: in line, not column, but advancing slowly so as not to seem an open threat. Marcus could see the horsemen ahead reaching over their shoulders for arrows, but none of them raised a bow. Two or three were in corselets of boiled leather like those of the Arshaum, but most wore chain-mail shirts.

With a raised hand, Arigh halted his men at the extreme edge of arrow range. He rode forward alone. After a few seconds, one of the waiting riders matched the gesture. When they were about eighty yards apart, the Arshaum chief shouted a Khamorth phrase he had memorized: "Who are you?" By his looks, the approaching horseman could have been a Yezda or off the Pardrayan plain.

"Who are *you*?" The answer came back in oddly accented Videssian.

Marcus had heard that lilt before. He dug his heels into his pony's sides and rode toward Arigh at a fast trot. Several Arshaum shouted for him to get back in his place. His own shout, though, was louder than theirs: "Ho, Khatrisher! Where's Pakhymer?"

The stranger had set a hand to his saber when the Roman came toward him, but snatched it away at the hail. "He's right where he belongs and nowhere else," he yelled back. "Who wants to know?" The flip answer did not bother Scaurus; most Khatrishers were like that.

"They're friends," he called to Arigh, then shouted his own name to the Khatrisher.

"Why, you lying whoreson! He's dead!"

"Dead, am I?" The tribune rode past Arigh until he was close enough to see the Khatrisher clearly. As he'd hoped, the fellow was one of Laon Pakhymer's minor officers. "Look me over—" What was the name? he had it! "—look me over, Konyos, and tell me I'm dead."

Konyos did, carefully. "Well, throw me in the chamberpot," he said. "It is you. Is that other duck still with you, the ornery one?"

"Gaius?" Marcus hid a smile. "He's back there."

"He would be," Konyos said darkly. He waved at the Arshaum. "Who are those beggars, anyway? If you're with 'em, I don't suppose they're Yezda."

"No." As Scaurus began to explain, the Arshaum and Khatrishers, seeing there would be no fighting, moved toward each other.

Konyos eyed the men from Shaumkhiil with lively interest; their wide, almost beardless faces, snub noses, and slanted eyes were all new to him. "Funny-looking bastards," he remarked without malice. "Can they fight?"

"They've come through Pardraya and Yezd."

"They can fight."

The tribune introduced Konyos to Arigh, then nearly shouted the question that was burning in him: "What is Gavras doing in Amorion?"

"You ought to know," the Kharisher said. "It's your fault."

"Huh?" That was the last answer Scaurus expected.

"What else? When Senpat and Nevrat Sviodo gave Minucius the word you'd been shipped off to give Zemarkhos what for, wild horses couldn't have held him back from piling in to help. Naturally, Pakhymer brought us along for the ride."

A lump rose in Marcus' throat, despite Konyos' breezy way with the story. More than anything else, it showed what his troops—and the Khatrishers, too—felt about him. "The legionaries are at Amorion, then?"

"I just said so, didn't I? Everything by the numbers, one-two—damn boring, if you ask me. Not that you did."

"Hmmp." That was Gaius Philippus, crowding up with Viridovix and Gorgidas to hear the news.

Konyos backtracked for them, then went on, grinning. "We had a rare old time, punching up the Arandos. We moved so hard and fast Yavlak still doesn't know what hit him."

Gaius Philippus jabbed an accusing finger at the Khatrisher. "It was your bloody army—our own bloody army!—moving on Amorion all the time?"

"Of course. Who did you think it was?"

"Never mind," the veteran said. "Oh, my aching head." Marcus wanted to cry and laugh at the same time. He and Gaius Philippus had only gone west with Tahmasp's caravan —had only ended up in Mashiz, and the tunnels under it— because they were sure that army had to be Yezda.

Konyos turned to the tribune. "Oh, one more thing— Gagik Bagratouni has a bone to pick with you."

"Me? Why? I got rid of Zemarkhos for him."

"That's just why. He wanted to do it himself, a little at a time, over days. Can't say I blame him much, either, after things I've heard. But seeing as the bugger's dead, I expect Bagratouni'll forgive you this once." The Khatrisher sobered for a moment. "We thought the two of you'd gone into a hole you'd never come out of, too. We tore Amorion apart looking for you and never found a trace." He sounded a little indignant they had survived.

"A hole we'd never come out of?" Scaurus said with a shudder of memory. "That's too close to being true—there are worse places than Amorion."

The orderly rows of eight-man leather tents behind the square, palisaded earthwork made a striking contrast with the irregular arrangements all around them: here a noble's silk pavilion; there a clump of yurts; further over, a whole forest of shelters clumped together at random, lean-to next to three or four small cotton tents next to a huge canvas arrangement that could have held a platoon.

The sentry at the entrenched gate was a dark, stocky man wearing a sleeveless mail shirt. He peered over the edge of his big semicylindrical shield at the four approaching horsemen in nomad leathers. Hefting his heavy javelin, he called, "Halt and state your business."

"Hello, Pinarius. That's not much of a good day," Marcus said in Latin, and watched the Roman legionary drop his *pilum*.

"Will you look at the puir gowk of a man, now?" Viridovix said, shaking his head sadly. "If he canna put names to the lot of us, sure and he'll be useless for telling friend from foe."

Pinarius had been about to dash away into the camp, but when he recognized Gaius Philippus he did not dare break discipline by leaving his post. Instead he shouted, "By the gods, the tribune's back, and everybody with him!" Snatching up his spear and reversing it with a flourish, he stood aside to let the newcomers enter.

Discipline did suffer then, as Romans tumbled from their tents and came rushing from their drills with sword and spear. Marcus and his comrades scrambled down from their ponies before they were pulled off. The legionaries swarmed round them, reaching over each other to embrace them, clasp their hands, pound them on the back, simply touch them.

"Och, ye didna gi' me such a thrashing back in Gaul," Viridovix complained in mock anger. The Romans hooted at him.

For Gorgidas, who was particular about whom he touched, the tumultuous welcome was something of an ordeal. He was surprised to find Rakio at his side; the Yrmido had followed him when he left Arigh's band, but at a distance. Someone noticed the stranger. "Who's this?"

"A friend," the Greek answered.

"Good enough." From then on Rakio was pummeled with as much enthusiasm as any of the others. Unlike Gorgidas, he relished it.

"Way there! Clear aside!" Sextus Minucius came pushing through the legionaries. He made slow going of it, for the crush was very tight, but at last he stood in front of the tribune. Months of command had matured the young soldier; there was a finished look to his broad, handsome face that Scaurus had not seen before.

He snapped off a precise salute. "Returning your command to you, sir!"

Marcus shook his head. "It's not mine to take back. Gavras stripped me of it before he sent me out against Zemarkhos."

The legionaries cried out angrily. Minucius said, "We heard about that, sir. All I have to say is, we choose who leads us, and nobody else." He saluted again.

The Romans shouted again, this time in vociferous agreement. "Damn right!" "We don't tell Gavras his business; let him stay out of ours!" "Weren't for us, he'd still be sitting back in Videssos. We punched a hole in the Yezda a blind man could've walked through." And a rising chorus: "Scaurus, Scaurus, Scaurus!" Moved past words, the tribune returned the salute.

The cheers were deafening. Viridovix nudged Gaius Philippus. "You'll be noticing there's none of 'em making the welkin ring for you," he chuckled.

"There'd be something wrong if they were," the veteran replied evenly. "I'm supposed to be the cantankerous blackguard who makes the boss look good."

Fed up with soft answers, the Gaul snapped, "Aye, well, you're right for it," and felt better for earning a scowl from the senior centurion.

The non-Romans among the legionaries hung back at first to let Marcus' countrymen greet him, but they soon joined the celebration, too. Burly Vaspurakaners folded him into bear hugs, shouting a welcome in vile Latin and almost equally thick Videssian.

"So, you are safe after all," Gagik Bagratouni boomed, crushing the breath from the tribune. With his proud, heavy-boned features, thick wavy hair, and black mat of beard, the nakharar always reminded Scaurus of a lion. "For all we tried, we did not get here enough quickly, and thought the cursed priest had killed you."

"I'm amazed you came so close," Marcus said.

"Good information," Bagratouni said smugly. He turned, looked around, pointed. "Senpat, Nevrat—to me!"

The two shoved their way up to the nakharar and Scaurus. Senpat Sviodo was the only man the tribune knew who could bring off wearing the Vaspurakaners' traditional three-crowned tasseled cap; his good looks and zestful character let him get away with whatever he chose. He stamped a booted foot and shouted out the first three notes of a war song. "Hai,

hai, *hai!* We thought we'd see you sooner, but rather late than not at all, as the old saw goes."

His grin was infectious; Marcus felt one stretch across his own face. He turned to Nevrat. Even if she was not his, she deserved attention. The Vaspurakaners' features were too strong for beauty in most women, but she was a fortunate exception—as with Senpat, part of that was her own nature shining through.

She would not listen to the tribune's thanks. "This was nothing—a few days' ride through friendly country to Garsavra. Not worth thinking about. What of the time we were fighting Drax' men in the first civil war, and you killed that Namdalener who had me down?"

"Oh, that. Do you remember how you paid me back?"

Howls went up from the legionaries around them. Something in Nevrat's eyes said she remembered other things as well, but mischief also sparked there. "Quite well," she said boldly.

"I'll settle this the same way, then," Marcus said. The howls got louder. The tribune said to Bagratouni, "Watch close—I'm about to kiss a married woman." He gathered Nevrat in.

"Is it well with you?" she whispered against his ear. At his nod, she murmured, "All right, then," and made the kiss a more thorough, unhurried one than he had intended. Her lips were firm and sweet against his. "If you do something, do it properly," she said when they separated.

'Maybe we should have stayed in Videssos," Senpat growled, but he was laughing, too. A tiny headshake from Nevrat told Scaurus he did not know—not, really, that there was much to know.

Bagratouni dug an elbow into the tribune's ribs. "What was I supposed to watch? That much I knew when I was twelve."

The commotion in the Roman camp sent other imperial troops—Videssians, Khatrishers, Halogai, Khamorth, a few Namdaleni—rushing up to the rampart to see what had got into the usually staid legionaries. Troopers shouted the news to friends or to the world at large.

"So much for keeping our arrival quiet," Gorgidas said.

Scaurus understood what he meant as well as what he said. "It doesn't matter," he said. "With Goudeles and Skylitzes reporting to the Emperor, he already knows who came in with the Arshaum." Before long, he was sure, a summons would be on its way.

That did not seem to have occurred to Viridovix. "At least you're after having a pledge from himself," he told Marcus. "Me he'll chop into catmeat, belike, for playing 'tween the sheets with his ladylove."

Nothing the Romans had said had convinced him that Thorisin was not only rid of Komitta Rhangavve, but heartily glad she was gone. And the tribune was wondering how much the Avtokrator's promises to him were worth. He knew Gavras as a man of his word, but he also knew how great the temptation to break it would be.

No help for that. And no matter what Thorisin intended doing, Avshar had plans, too, that were all too likely to shatter everyone else's. "We need to know more of what's going on here," the tribune said to Gaius Philippus.

"Minucius and Bagratouni are right beside you," the veteran replied. "And I've already sent a runner after Pakhymer."

"Good."

Minucius led them to the commander's tent, which stood at the center of the *via principalis,* the chief street of the camp. He stood aside to let Scaurus enter first, saying, "Looks like I'll have to get used to smaller quarters again."

The inside of the tent belied his words. But for a bedroll, a few mats, and his kit, it was bare. The kit was an ordinary legionary's; Minucius had risen from the ranks over the last couple of years. Viridovix looked around, shook his head, and said, "What do you care what space y'have? You could live in a barrel, I'm thinking, wi' room to spare."

"I don't think Erene would like that," Minucius said. "She's expecting again."

"She's back in Garsavra?" Marcus asked.

"Yes. All the women are, but for Nevrat, and she's a story to herself. We came west in a tearing hurry. We didn't drive the Yezda away, we just pushed through them. So did Gavras; the buggers are still swarming between Garsavra and here."

"That answers one thing," Gaius Philippus said. "It's not what I wanted to hear, but it's what I expected."

Laon Pakhymer arrived just as they were settling down onto the mats. He sat, too, and nodded to Scaurus and Gaius Philippus as casually as if he had seen them a couple of hours before.

"That was quick," the senior centurion said grudgingly. It

was hard to be sure whether Pakhymer's slapdash style or effectiveness annoyed him more.

The Khatrisher leader knew he irritated the veteran and played on it. "We have our ways," he said airily.

"He talked with Konyos before the Roman runner got to him," Gorgidas said.

Pakhymer assumed an injured expression. "Why do I bother with my tricks, if you're going to shine a lantern on them?"

"Let's get on with it," Marcus said. The Khatrisher leaned forward, abruptly as businesslike as anyone in the tent.

Scaurus got the same picture from him as he had from the others: the legionaries and Khatrishers had made the thrust from Garsavra on their own, and when it looked like a success Thorisin had followed with the rest of the forces now at Amorion. He had not gained control of the Arandos valley, but the tribune learned that he had sent a detachment north to Nakoleia on the coast of the Videssian Sea. "Sensible," he said. "We aren't altogether cut off from the rest of the Empire here, then."

After that the talk shifted to questions of provisions, the readiness of the troops, and Gavras' plans. Sextus Minucius said, "At first I don't think he had any when he followed us here, past making sure we didn't keep Amorion for ourselves. But now there's a report Avshar's pushing through Vaspurakan toward us. If that's so, then this makes a good base to use against him."

The newly returned men exchanged glances. "Damned perambulating corpse moves too fast to suit me," Gaius Philippus said, but that was the only comment. None of them doubted the wizard-prince aimed to crush Videssos once and for all. They had seen his preparations with their own eyes; the tribune and senior centurion had his boasts and threats straight from his fleshless lips.

Pakhymer said, "There's more to the Emperor coming after us than Minucius spoke of, I think." He waited to let Scaurus and his friends supply the answer for themselves."

"Politics?" Gorgidas ventured.

The Khatrisher leader scratched his head. His version of the faith differed from the Videssians', but he was part and parcel of their world in a way the Greek, the Romans, and Viridovix could never be. He said, "Sometimes I think you people were born half-blind. See now, if you can: these past couple of years, Amorion has been in schism against the capital and its clergy, thanks to Zemarkhos. You Romans are most of you heathen, while the imperials reckon my folk one kind of heretic and Bagratouni's another. Thorisin couldn't trust any of us to set things right here; why else would he fetch Balsamon along, but to bring the schismatics back to the fold?"

"Did he?" Marcus pricked up his ears. "I hadn't heard that."

"He certainly did. The old baldhead's been preaching up a storm, too. I've listened once or twice myself; he's a lively one. Truth to tell, a few more like him and I'd think of converting to the imperials' way of looking at things—he makes you believe in the good."

"I listen, too," Bagratouni said. "Better than Zemarkhos? Yes, a thousand times. Convert? No, never. Too much the 'princes' suffer from Videssos for me ever to change the Empire's belief."

The conference limped after that. Marcus did not think even the pious Skylitzes would have dared urge his faith on the *nakharar* then. As for himself, though he did not follow Phos at all, he felt more apprehension about Videssos' ruler than all its ecclesiastics rolled together.

The next morning two Haloga guardsmen were waiting for Scaurus at the *porta praetoria*. They had learned something of legionary customs, he thought as he went out to them; the *porta praetoria* was the closest of the camp's four gates to the commander's tent. He tried to keep his mind on such trivia. The Halogai had only summoned him, not Gaius Philippus, Gordigas, or Virdovix. He was not sure that was any kind of good sign.

The northern mercenaries were sweating in the Videssian summer heat. They were big blond men, as tall as the tribune and wider through the shoulders. One wore his hair shoulder length; the other tied it back in a thick braid that fell to the small of his back. Both had swords belted at their hips, but relied more on their nation's characteristic weapon, a stout, long-handled war axe.

They nodded when they recognized him. The one with the braid said, "Ve are charged to bring you before t'Avtokrahtor." The Haloga accent was thick, but the tribune understood. He fell in between the guardsmen, who shouldered their axes and marched him away.

Several of Thorisin Gavras' officers enjoyed pavilions more impressive than his. He did not seek luxury for its own sake and in the field always lived simply. The blue pennant with the golden imperial sunburst in front of his tent said everything about his status that needed saying.

Another pair of Halogai paced in front of the tent's entranceway. They drew themselves up alertly as Marcus and his escort neared. The northerner with the queue spoke in a formal voice: "It is t'captain of t'Romans." The sentries stood aside.

Ducking under the tent flap, Scaurus fought to keep surprise off his face. Thorisin had taken his rank from him—was it his again? He got no time to wonder; up ahead the Emperor was saying impatiently, "All right, go see to it, then. I have other business to attend to now."

"Yes, sir." The officer who saluted had his back to Scaurus, but the tribune stiffened at the sound of his voice. And when Provhos Mourtzouphlos turned to leave, he stopped in his tracks, disbelief and rage chasing each other across his regular features. "You!" he cried, and went for his sword.

Marcus' hand flashed downward. One of the Halogai leaped between Mourtzouphlos and the Roman; the other seized Scaurus' wrist in an iron grasp. "Leave it in t'sheat'," he ordered, and the tribune could only obey.

Thorisin had not moved from behind the parchment-strewn folding table at which he was sitting. "Carry out your orders, Provhos," he said. "I assure you I shall deal with this one as he deserves."

The sound of that did not appeal to Scaurus, but it suited Mourtzouphlos no better. "Yes, sir," he repeated, but this time he had to choke it out. He flourished his cloak with aristocratic disdain and stalked past Marcus, snarling, "This is not done between us, you ass in a lion's skin."

All that kept the Roman from throwing himself at Mourtzouphlos was the guardsman's unbreakable grip on his arm. His fury astonished him, and the reason for it even more. He was not angry over what he had gone through himself; that was over and done. But Mourtzouphlos was also responsible for everything that had happened to Alypia these past months, and for that the tribune could not forgive him. She had already suffered too much to deserve more.

Perhaps the sight of the Emperor helped provoke Scaurus by reminding him of Alypia. Thorisin's oval face was longer than hers, and craggier, his eyes dark rather than green, but at a glance anyone would have known them for close kin.

"Take yourselves off, Bjorgolf, Harek," Gavras said to the Halogai flanking the tribune. "Eyvind and Skallagrim are outside to see to it this one doesn't try murdering me. He won't —he needs me alive. Isn't that right, outlander?" He gave Marcus a cynical stare. Nor sure if he was being baited, the tribune stood mute.

The Halogai saluted and left; they had no intention of arguing with their paymaster. Thorisin turned to a servant who was polishing a pair of boots. He flipped the man a piece of silver. "That will keep, Glykas. Go on; spend it on something." With effusive thanks, the Videssian followed the mercenaries out.

When he was gone, the Emperor grunted in satisfaction. "Now you've no one to scandalize but me by ignoring the *proskynesis*." Marcus stayed silent. He had seen Thorisin in this playful mood once or twice before. It made him nervous; he could not read him in it. Gavras raised an eyebrow. "If you won't go on your belly, you may as well take a chair."

The tribune obeyed. Steepling his fingers, Thorisin studied him for a good minute before he spoke again. "What am I to do with you, Roman? You're like a counterfeit copper; you keep turning up."

Marcus was suddenly sick of this oblique approach; Gavras would have been more direct before he became Avtokrator. He said, "Seems to me you have two choices. Either keep our bargain or execute me."

The Emperor smiled thinly. "Are you trying to persuade me? There have been enough times I'd have liked to see your head go up on the Milestone. But I won't be the one to settle your fate now."

"Avshar." It was not a question.

"Aye." Military matters turned Thorisin serious again. "Here, see for yourself." Scaurus hitched his chair forward; Gavras turned a map of the Videssian westlands around so it was right-side up for the Roman. He pointed to the Rhamnos River at the eastern edge of Vaspurakan. "I have word by fire-beacon that the Yezda army crossed just north of Soli yesterday."

The tribune gauged distances. The wizard-prince had moved faster than he thought possible. "A week away, then.

Maybe a day or two more; there's rugged country in their way as they turn southeast. Or will you meet them somewhere halfway between?"

"No; I aim to stand on the defensive." Gavras bared his teeth in a grimace of frustration; his instinct was to attack. But he went on, "After Maragha, after these rounds of civil war, this is the last army I can scrape together. If I throw it away, I—and Videssos—have nothing left. Which is another reason to keep you healthy—I can't afford a mutiny from your troops."

Marcus let the Emperor's concession of his command go as casually as Thorisin had made it. He asked, "How many men does Avshar have with him?"

"I was hoping you could tell me. It's a bigger force than mine, I think, but you know what long-distance scouting reports are worth. And the Yezda travel with all those spare horses, which makes them seem more than they are. But you were in Mashiz; Skotos' hell, from what Goudeles says, you were in Wulghash's throne room when Avshar stole the throne out from under him. That was the first news I'd had of the usurpation. You should know more of what went on in Yezd than anyone."

"Only if you're after the view from the tunnels. I can tell you something of Avshar, if you care to hear that."

Thorisin shook his head impatiently. "I know more than I want already. Whether it's been him or Wulghash with the title of Khagan of Yezd, he's been behind things for years."

"Having met Wulghash, I'm not so sure," the tribune said. "Here's something you didn't learn from Goudeles: Wulghash isn't dead, though Avshar thinks he is." He told how the khagan and the Romans had met far below the palace.

"A good story, but what of it?" Gavras said. "Dead or fled, he's out of play, and I miss him even less if he's sharp as you say."

Marcus shrugged. "You have my news, then. If you want to hear about the Yezda, talk with Arigh. He's been fighting them all summer and he watched them build up around Mashiz."

"I'll do that. There was something solid you did, Scaurus, bringing him and his plainsmen in." The Emperor stopped, looked at the Roman with annoyance and grudged respect. "May you rot, you son of a whore, you've turned out too bloody useful to shorten. If we live, maybe we'll have to chaffer after all."

The tribune nodded. "Is Alypia well?" he asked quietly.

Thorisin's mouth tightened. "You don't make it easy for me, do you?"

"I may as well find out the worst now. What good does it do me to catch you cheerful today if you turn sour again tomorrow?"

"Mmp. Sometimes I think Mavrikios should have curbed your insolence from the start; it would have saved us trouble." The Emperor drummed his fingers on the tabletop. At last he said, "Aye, she's in fine feather. She had half the young nobles—and all the ambitious ones—dancing attendance on her at my wedding. Not that she paid heed to them."

Scaurus was not worried about her fidelity, but the rest of Gavras' sentence made him goggle like a fool. "At your what?"

"Wedding," Thorisin repeated. "High time, too; your diddling reminded me how much I need a real heir. And I'll have one, too—four days ago I got word she'd pregnant."

"Congratulations," Marcus said sincerely. If Thorisin bred a successor, he might be less hindersome where Alypia was concerned. The tribune hesitated, then asked, "Er—who is she?"

"That's right, how could you know? She's Alania Vourtze —ah, you've heard of the family, I see. Aye, they're penpushers, right enough. It'll help put the buggers in my camp, or at least divide 'em amongst themselves. She's a quiet little thing—one of the reasons I chose her, after a few years of that shrieking jade of mine. Dear Komitta—Phos help the convent I shipped her to."

The Emperor smiled lopsidedly. "You're still closemouthed, aren't you? You've heard a good deal more from me than you've said, that's certain." The tribune started to protest that Gavras had not wanted to listen to his news, but Thorisin brushed that aside. "Never mind. Take yourself out. And if there's one of my eparchs out there, tell him it's his turn."

Blinking in the bright sun after the dimness of the tent, Scaurus found a bureaucrat shifting from foot to foot outside the entrance. He held it open in invitation. The eparch went through with a singular lack of eagerness. Marcus heard Thorisin roar, "You blithering, bungling, incompetent ass, where's the fifty wagons of wheat you said would be here day before yesterday?"

"He hasn't mellowed altogether, I see," the tribune whispered to one of the Halogai. The guardsman rolled his eyes.

When Marcus got back to the Roman camp, he found it in an uproar, with a large crowd of legionaries gathered in front of one tent. He could see Viridovix in front of the tent, a head taller than most of them. "What's this in aid of?" he demanded. The soldiers separated to let him through.

The Gaul had driven two tent poles into the ground, then sharpened their upper ends. Each impaled a dripping head. One still bore a snarl of defiance; the expression of the other was impossible to read, as a sword stroke had sheared away most of one side of its face.

"Trophies?" Scaurus asked dryly.

Viridovix looked up. "Och, hullo, Roman darling. So they are. Set on me, the spalpeens did, without so much as a by-your-leave. Begging your pardon for the mess and all, but I'm not after having a doorway to nail 'em to."

"Or even a Milestone," the tribune said, remembering his recent conversation. He looked at the heads again. Both had belonged to swarthy men with long, unkempt beards, now soaked with blood. "Yezda."

"I'm thinking you're right, though I didna stop to ask."

"How did they get into camp?" Marcus asked.

The commotion had drawn Gaius Philippus. He turned to the onlookers. "You, you, you, and you!" he said, telling off four. "One to each gate—relieve the sentries and send them back here to be questioned. They'll take their posts back as soon as we're through with them." The senior centurion had been back only a day, but his authority was unquestioned. The legionaries saluted and hurried away.

The Roman who had admitted the would-be assassins stared in horror at Viridovix's handiwork. "I, I never thought twice about it," he stammered in response to Marcus' question. "They asked for you or the Gaul by name. It was all over camp that the Emperor had summoned you, so I told them where to find him. I thought they were friends the two of you had picked up on your travels."

"Not your fault, Vectilianus," Scaurus reassured him. He did not need to ask how the Yezda had followed Viridovix and him across the miles, but did spare a moment to wish again that he had managed to persuade Wulghash to throw his sorcerous veil over the Celt's sword—then Avshar would have had less by which to track them.

"It turned out right enough," Viridovix said, wiping his blade clean. "Here's two less o' the omadhauns to be taking the blackheart's side come the day, and he's not likely to try flunkies again with his own self so close and all."

"Closer than we thought." Marcus relayed what Thorisin had told him.

"Good. It'll soon be over then, one way or t'other." With a faint scrape of metal against metal, Viridovix ran his sword into its sheath.

It was not yet dawn the next morning when a Vaspurakaner legionary stuck his head into the tribune's tent and woke him. "There a messenger is for you outside the *porta principalis dextra*," he said, mangling his Videssian and Latin about equally. "After what happens yesterday, I no want him to let into camp."

"You did right," Scaurus mumbled. He groped for tunic and trousers. Under his breath he complained, "At least Gavras gave me a whole night's sleep." He slid the tunic over his head, splashed water on his face. Through splutters, he asked the sentry, "Whose messenger is it?"

"He say he from the imperials'—how you say?—chief priest." The Vaspurakaner spat; after Zemarkhos, he had no liking for anyone in the Videssian clerical hierarchy. "You ask me, he can wait forever."

Marcus pushed past him. A summons from Balsamon carried almost as much weight as one from the Emperor.

The *porta principalis dextra* got its name from its position as seen by the encamped legionaries. But the commander's tent was on the other side of the *via principalis*; Scaurus turned left into the camp's main way and hurried to the gate.

He recognized the blue-robed priest waiting for him, though not with any pleasure. His voice came out as a growl: "What do you want with me, Saborios?"

Balsamon's attendant priest, despite his tonsured pate, bore himself like the soldier he had been. "To bring you to my master, of course," he replied crisply. He looked Scaurus straight in the face. "Hold whatever grudge you care to. My first concern is for his Imperial Majesty."

"Bah," Marcus said, but the wind was gone from his sails.

His own strong sense of duty answered too readily to that of Saborios.

The sun rose as they marched into Amorion. The town had suffered since the tribune last saw it. Many buildings bore the scars of fighting, whether in the riots Scaurus had touched off or later, when Zemarkhos' remaining fanatics had been rash enough to oppose the professional skill of the legionaries and Khatrishers.

Other buildings were simply deserted, weeds growing up at the base of walls, courtyard gates opening onto forlorn emptiness. Some of the city's finest houses stood thus. "The owners are long fled," Saborios said, following Marcus's gaze. "Some ran from your troopers, others for fear of the Yezda— or of the Emperor's justice."

A few homes had been reoccupied, by one squatter family or six. More newcomers crowded the town marketplace, which was half filled by a squalid collection of tents and crackerbox shacks. "Refugees from the tender mercy of the Yezda," Saborios explained unnecessarily.

"More will come in front of Avshar," Marcus predicted.

"I know. We have trouble feeding the ones here now. Of course, some of those will run again and even the balance a bit." Saborios spoke with the certainty of a man who had seen such things before.

Balsamon was dwelling in the cottage that had been Zemarkhos', close by the main temple of Amorion. Like most chief shrines in provincial towns, that was a smaller, clumsier copy of Phos' High Temple in Videssos. Marcus and Saborios walked in the shadow of its dome as they came up to the little building behind it. The tribune saw old bloodstains on its whitewashed walls.

Balsamon himself opened the door to greet them. "Welcome, welcome!" he said, beaming at Scaurus. "An unlooked-for guest is worth a dozen of the ordinary kind." He wore a look the tribune knew well, as if inviting him to share some secret joke.

But that droll expression was almost all that was left of the prelate Marcus had known in the capital. He had wondered at Balsamon's health then; now the patriarch was visibly failing. He had lost a great deal of flesh, so that his beloved threadbare old robe was draped in loose folds around him. His skin sagged unhealthily at his cheeks and jowls; he had to support himself by leaning against the doorpost.

Ill or not, he missed very little. He laughed at the dismay Marcus could not hide. "I'm not dead yet, my friend," he said. "I'll last as long as need be, never fear. Come in, come in. We have much to talk about, you and I."

For the life of him, Marcus could not see what that "much" was, but he stepped forward. Then he stopped and turned. As Saborios had before, he met the tribune's eye without flinching. "The Emperor knows you are here," he said steadily. "I shan't be listening at the keyhole."

Scaurus had to be satisfied with that. Balsamon moved aside to let him come in. Walking slowly and painfully, the patriarch made his way to the closest one of the three stiff-backed chairs that, but for a small table, were the only furnishings in the little room. The ascetic barrenness had to be a legacy of Zemarkhos.

Balsamon sat with a soft grunt of relief. Marcus said angrily, "What right did Thorisin have to drag you away from Videssos like this?"

"The best right of all: he is the Avtokrator, Phos' vicegent on earth," the patriarch replied. He surprised Scaurus by speaking in perfect seriousness; to the Videssians, the Emperor's power was very real. Balsamon went on, "To be exact, he ordered me here to preside over the dissolution of Zemarkhos' schism. I have attended to that with pleasure—you saw for yourself the hatred he preached."

"Yes," the tribune admitted. "But why you? Is it regular practice to send the patriarch out of the city to attend to such things?"

"The last one to leave Videssos, to my knowledge, was Pothos, three hundred fifty years ago. He was sent to Imbros to help uproot an outbreak of the Balancer heresy." Balsamon's tired eyes managed a twinkle. "I think I managed to provoke my Emperor quite a bit more than Pothos did his."

Knowing what had roused Gavras' wrath, Marcus lowered his head in embarrassment. Balsamon laughed out loud. "Phos preserve me, I've abashed the man of stone." That only served to fluster the tribune worse. The patriarch continued, "By the bye, man of stone, I have a message for you—a trifle late, as you were not in Amorion when you were expected to be, but perhaps of interest all the same."

"Go on," Scaurus said. He knew from whom he wanted the message to be, but after Balsamon's sly teasing he was not about to give the patriarch the satisfaction of showing anxiety or eagerness.

His studied composure seemed to amuse the prelate about as much as excitement would have. "I was speaking of stones, wasn't I?" Balsamon said in the allusive, elusive Videssian style. "Well, there is someone who would have me tell you that there are certain stones with which you may be familiar which that person has worn continuously since the last time you two saw each other, and that person will continue to do so until your next meeting, whenever that may be."

Let Saborios make something of that, Marcus thought; he assumed Balsamon's attendant had his ways of knowing what was going on with his nominal master, whether he listened at keyholes or not. But the tribune only wasted a moment on Saborios. Alypia's making a token of the necklace he had given her warmed him clear through.

Seeing that Balsamon knew he understood, all he said was, "My thanks. I hope I'll be able to answer that myself."

"So does the person who entrusted it to me." The patriarch paused, as if not sure how to change the subject. Then he said, "You traveled much further than Amorion."

"I hadn't planned to, and I didn't need to," Scaurus said, still chagrined at fleeing west with Tahmasp at the very moment his men were pounding to his rescue.

"Never be certain of that too soon," Balsamon said. "One of the things I've seen, both as a priest and, before that, as a scholar seeking the world's wisdom, is that the web of affairs is always bigger than it seems to the fly struggling in one corner."

"There's a pretty picture."

"Is it not?" the patriarch said blandly. He gave that odd hesitation again, before going on, "I am given to understand that you, ah, had considerable to do with the leaders of Yezd."

"Yes. " Marcus was not surprised that Balsamon had his sources of information; knowing the Videssians, he would have been startled if the prelate did not. He spoke of his encounter with Wulghash. Balsamon listened politely, but without much interest.

Once Scaurus mentioned Avshar, though, the patriarch's attitude changed. His eyes bored into the Roman's; his expression and bearing grew so intense that he and Marcus both forgot his infirmity. He snapped questions at Scaurus as he might have at some none-too-bright student in a classroom at the Videssian Academy.

When the tribune somehow dredged the name Skopentzana from his memory, Balsamon sagged back against his unyielding chair. Then Marcus could see how old and sick and tired he was. The patriarch sat still and silent so long that Scaurus thought he had fallen asleep with his eyes open, but at last he said, "Much is now explained."

"Not to me," the tribune said pointedly.

"No?" Balsamon quirked a tufted eyebrow. "Avshar was ours once, long centuries ago. Why else would he loathe Videssos so, and mock our every creation with his own?"

Marcus slowly nodded. Both the skill with which the sorcerer-prince used the language of the Empire and his antique turn of phrase argued for Videssian as his birth tongue. And thinking of the temple to Skotos in Mashiz, and of the dark-god's red-robed priesthood, Scaurus saw what the patriarch meant.

"How did Skopentzana tell you that?" he asked. "What is it, anyhow? I've never heard of it, save that once in Avshar's mouth."

"These days, Skopentzana means nothing," Balsamon said. "All that remains of it is ruins, hovels, and, in season, nomads' tents. It lies in what is now Thatagush. But when Avshar had only a man's years, the province was Bratzista, and Skopentzana the third city of the Empire, or maybe the second. Of golden sandstone it was built, and the river Algos ran singing to the gray sea, or so an ancient poet says."

"And Avshar?"

"Was its prelate. Does that really surprise you so much? It shouldn't. He was truly a prince as well, a distant cousin of the Avtokrator in the glorious days when Videssos held sway from the borders of Makuran in a grand sweep all the way to the frozen Bay of Haloga. He was highborn, he was able— one day he expected to be patriarch, and he might have been a great one."

"Ruins, Thatagush—" Marcus made a connection. "That was when the Khamorth invaded the Empire, wasn't it?"

"So it was." From the way Balsamon eyed him, perhaps he had some hope as a student after all. "A civil war weakened the frontier, and in they poured. They cast down in a decade three hundred years of patient growth and civilization. Along with so many other lesser towns, Skopentzana fell. In a way,

Avshar was lucky. He lived. He made his way down the Algos to the sea, eventually he came home to Videssos the city. But the horrors he had seen and endured twisted his thoughts into a new path."

The tribune remembered what Avshar had said, that dreadful day in the courtroom at Mashiz. "He turned from Phos to Skotos then?"

His mark had just gone up again, he saw. Balsamon said, "Just so. For he reasoned that good could have no power in a world where such evil dwelt, and that the dark god was its true master. And when he reached the capital, he saw it as his duty to convert all the hierarchy to his views."

A Videssian indeed, Scaurus thought. But he said, "They're stupid views. If your house burns down, do you go live in the bushes forever after? More sensible to make the best of whatever comes and rebuild as you can."

"So say you; so say I. But Skotos' cult is like poisoned wine, sweet till the dregs. For without good, don't you see, there is no guilt; why not kill a man, force a woman, do anything for pleasure or power?"

The ultimate egotism—a heady wine indeed. In a way, it reminded Marcus of the Bacchic rites the Roman senate had banned a century before his birth. But at their wildest, the Bacchic rituals were a temporary, constrained release from the real world. Avshar would have made lawlessness a way of life.

The tribune said so, adding, "Didn't people realize that? Without rule and custom, everyone is at the mercy of the strongest and most cunning."

"So declared the synod that condemned Avshar," Balsamon said. "I have looked at the acts of that synod; they are the most frightening thing I ever read. Even after he turned toward the false he was brilliant and terrible, like a thunderbolt. His arguments against deposition are preserved. They have a vicious clarity that chills the blood to this day.

"And if," the patriarch mused, "in worshipping the dark he found a means to preserve himself to our own time and to seek to lay low the Empire that first gave him favor and then damned him—"

"Not to lay it low, but to conquer it, and rule it as he would," Scaurus broke in.

"That is worse. But it being so, much of what has passed in the intervening centuries makes better sense—just as one example, the savage behavior of the Haloga mercenary troop that crossed the Astris in the reign of Anthimos III five hundred years ago—though I would still say Anthimos' antics had much to do with the success they enjoyed until Krispos gained the throne a few years later."

"I'm afraid I don't know those names," Marcus said. The admission saddened him. Even after so long in Videssos, he was ignorant of so much about it.

He started to say something more, but Balsamon was paying no attention. The patriarch's eyes had the distant, slightly glazed stare Scaurus had seen once before, back in Videssos. The back of the tribune's neck tingled as his hair tried to stand on end. He recognized that light trance and what it meant.

Caught up in his prophetic vision, Balsamon seemed a man trapped by nightmare. "The same," he said, voice thick with anguished protest, "it is ever the same."

He repeated that several times before he came back to himself. Marcus could not bring himself to question the patriarch; he took his leave as soon as he decently could. The day was warm, but he shivered all the way back to the legionary camp. He remembered too well what Alypia had said of the patriarch's visions: that he was cursed only to see disaster ahead. With Avshar getting closer day by day, the tribune was afraid he knew the direction it was coming from.

XII

THORISIN'S SCOUTING REPORT WAS GOOD, MARCUS THOUGHT; by the campfires winking at the far edge of the plain, the Yezda had a bigger army than the one standing in their way. The westerly breeze carried their endless harsh chant to the tribune: "Avshar! Avshar! Avshar!" Deep-toned drums beat out an unceasing accompaniment, *boom*-boom, *boom*-boom, *boom*-boom.

It was a sound to raise the hackles of anyone who had fought at Maragha, bringing back memories of the terrible night when the Yezda had surrounded the imperial camp. Now, though, Gaius Philippus gave an ostentatious snort of contempt. "Let 'em pound," he said. "They'll ruin their own sleep long before mine."

Scaurus nodded. "Gavras may not like the defensive, but he knows how to use it when he has to." The Emperor had moved north and west from Amorion until he found the exact battlefield he wanted; the sloping plain whose high ground the Videssians held formed the only sizeable opening in a chain of rough hills. A few companies and a couple of light catapults plugged the smaller gaps.

Avshar had not even tried to force them. He made straight for the main imperial force. Unlike Thorisin, he sought battle.

Scouts were already skirmishing in the space between the two armies. The squeal of a wounded horse cut through the Yezda chant.

"Tomorrow," Gaius Philippus said, fiddling with the cheekpiece of the legionary helmet he had borrowed. When it suited him, he turned his back to the fire by which he had

been sitting and peered into the darkness, trying to see who
had won the clash. There was no way to tell.

He turned his attention to the imperial forces. After a while
he sat again, a puzzled expression on his face. "Near as I can
see, Gavras is doing everything right. Why don't I like it?"

"The sitting around, it is," Viridovix said at once. Even
more than Thorisin's, his temper demanded action.

"That wouldn't matter, in a confident army," Gorgidas half
disagreed. "With this one, though . . ." He let his voice trail
away.

Marcus knew what he meant. Some units of the heteroge-
neous force were confident enough. The legionaries had
always given the Yezda all they wanted, as had the Khatrishers who fought beside them. The Emperor's Haloga bodyguards feared no man living. And to the Arshaum, the Yezda
were so many more Khamorth, to be beaten with ease. Arigh's
men formed a big part of the army's cavalry screen.

But the Videssians who made up the bulk of Thorisin's
men were of variable quality. Some veteran units were as good
as any of the professionals who served beside them. Others,
though, were garrison troops from places like Serrhes, or mi-
litiamen facing real combat for the first time. How well they
would do was anyone's guess.

And in the background, unmentioned but always there,
lurked the question of what deviltry Avshar had waiting. It
preyed on the minds and sapped the spirits of veterans and
new soldiers alike.

"Tomorrow," Scaurus muttered, and wondered if it was
prayer or curse.

Cookfires flared with the dawn, giving the troops a hot
meal before they took their places. Having chosen the field,
the Emperor had settled his order of battle well in advance. He
and the Halogai of the Imperial Guard anchored the center of
his line. As the northerners marched forward, their axeheads
gave back bloody reflections from the rising sun.

The legionaries were on their right, drawn up maniple by
maniple, each behind its own *signum*; the wreath-encircled
hands topping the standards had been freshly gilded and made
a brave show in the morning light. The points of the legionaries' *pila* were like a moving forest as they advanced.

Here and there a man clung to the weapons he was used to,
instead of adopting Roman-style javelins and shortsword. Vir-

idovix, of course, kept his Gallic blade. And Zeprin the Red, shouldering his axe, might have been one with his countrymen in the Emperor's guard. But the Haloga still did not think himself worthy of serving in their ranks and tramped instead with the rest of the legionaries.

To the left of the Imperial Guard were a couple of hundred Namdalener knights, men who still had Thorisin's trust in spite of the strife between the Duchy and Videssos. They wore conical helms with bar nasals and mail shirts that reached to their knees, and carried long lances, slashing swords, and brightly painted kite-shaped shields. The stout horses they rode were also armored, with canvas and leather and metal.

Rakio, in his own full caparison, rode over from the Roman camp to join them as the imperial force moved out. "No fear for me have," he said to Gorgidas. "I will be best fighting with men who fight as I do." He leaned down from the saddle to kiss the Greek good-bye.

The legionaries howled. Rakio straightened. "Jealous, the lot of you," he said, which raised a fresh chorus of whoops. They did not disturb the Yrmido at all; he was comfortable within his own people's standards. He waved and trotted off.

Gorgidas wished for his lover's innocent openness. Back among the legionaries, he found himself automatically falling into the old pattern of concealment. But when he looked around, he saw the grinning Romans were not so malicious after all. Maybe Rakio's nonchalance reached them, too. The Greek didn't know, or care. He accepted it gratefully.

"Pass me a whetstone, will you, someone?" he said, wanting to hone his *gladius* one last time.

Two or three legionaries offered stones; one chuckled, "The horseman thinks your blade is sharp enough." Gorgidas flinched, but it came out as camp banter, not the vicious mockery Quintus Glabrio had been forced to face a few years before. He gave back a rude gesture. The trooper laughed out loud.

Laon Pakhymer made his pony rear as he led his Khatrishers out to flank the legionaries. Marcus doffed his helmet to return the salute. "They're all right, that bunch, sloppy or no," Gaius Philippus said, echoing his thoughts.

Videssian troops, lighter-armed but more mobile than the men of Gavras' center, took their stations to either side. Some were horse-archers, others bore javelins or sabers. One of their officers brought his mount up on its hind legs, too, for no reason Scaurus could see other than high spirits. The imperials did not usually act like that; few of them gloried in war. Then he recognized Provhos Mourtzouphlos. He scowled. He did not want to grant his enemy any virtues, even courage.

Thorisin had stationed nomads at either wing of his army, outside his native soldiers. On the left were Khamorth, hired off the Pardrayan steppe. Marcus wondered if they were men who lived near the Astris, Videssos' river-boundary with the plains, or if his friends' friend Batbaian had sent them to the Empire's aid by way of Prista.

He had no such questions about the warriors on the other flank. Arigh was posted there. The Roman could hear the *naccara*-drum, at once deeper and sharper than the ones the Yezda used, through the horns and pipes that signaled the imperial force forward.

Avshar's army was moving, too, guided by the will of its chieftain. It looked to be all cavalry. The wizard-prince's tokens were at the center, opposite Videssos' gold sunburst on blue. Avshar had two huge banners. The smaller was Yezd's flag, a springing panther on a field the color of drying blood. The other's ground was of the same hue, but it took a while to recognize the device. When the imperials finally did, many of them sketched a quick circle over their hearts; it was Skotos's twin lightning bolts.

Around the wizard-prince came regiments of Makuraner lancers; their gear was between that of the Videssians and Namdaleni in weight and protective strength. A lot of them wore plumes atop their spiked helmets to make themselves seem taller.

The greater part of Avshar's power, though, resided in the Yezda proper. Scaurus had seen them in action too often to despise them for the poor order they kept trotting into battle; they combined barbarous spirit with the refined cruelty they had learned from their master. The emblems of many clans—here a green banner, there a wolf's skull, or a man's, on a pole—were held on high at irregular intervals up and down their line.

Avshar had taught them something of obedience, too; they drew to a ragged halt when Skotos' flag wagged back and forth three times. The armies were still several bowshots apart. Suspecting some sorcerous trap, Thorisin drew up his own forces. His mission was to hold, not to attack; let Avshar come to him.

A horseman emerged from the ranks of the Yezda and rode slowly into the no man's land between the two armies. Mutters ran up and down the imperial line as he grew close enough to be recognized; that terrible face could only belong to the wizard-prince himself.

He used a sorcery then, a small one, to let all the Emperor's troops hear his voice as if he stood beside them: "Curs! Swine! Last scrapings of outworn misbelief! Breathes there any among you whose blood flows hot enough to dare face me in single combat?"

"I dare!" roared Zeprin the Red, his face dark with the flush that gave him his byname. His axe upraised and his heavy chain-mail shirt jingling about him, he pushed out of the Roman line and began a lumbering rush at the wizard-prince, the object of his supreme hatred since Maragha.

"Stop him!" Marcus snapped, and several legionaires sprang after the Haloga. Alone and afoot, he stood small chance against Avshar in a fair fight, and the tribune did not think he would get one.

Avshar ignored Zeprin in any case. A Videssian horseman spurred toward the wizard-prince, crying, "Phos with me!" He drew his bow to the ear and fired.

Laughing his terrible laugh, Avshar made a quick, derisive pass. The arrow blazed for an instant, then vanished. "Summon your lying god again," the wizard-prince said. "See how much he heeds you." He gestured once more, this time in a complex series of motions. A beam of orange-red light shot from his skeletal fingers at the charging Videssian, who was now only yards away.

The soldier and his mount jerked and twisted like moths in a flame. Their charred, blackened bodies crashed to the ground at the feet of Avshar's stallion, which side-stepped daintily. The wind was thick with the smell of burned meat.

"Are there more?" Avshar said into vast silence. By then the Romans had managed to wrestle Zeprin back into their ranks. The overlord of Yezd laughed again, a sound full of doom.

Viridovix caught Scaurus' eye. The tribune nodded. If Avshar would meet them, they would never have a better chance. And at its worst, the match would be more even than the one the wizard-prince had given the brave, rash Videssian.

"Are there more?" Avshar said again. Plainly he expected no response. Scaurus filled his lungs to shout. Before he

could, though, there was a stir in the very center of the Videssian army. The ranks of the Halogai divided to let a single
rider through.

The tribune's throat clogged with dread. He had not
thought Thorisin could be madman enough to dare his
enemy's challange. He was a fine soldier, but Avshar's might
was more than a man's.

But it was not the Avtokrator who advanced to face the
wizard-prince, but an old man in a threadbare blue robe, riding a flop-eared mule. And from him Avshar recoiled as he
would have from no living warrior. "Go back," Balsamon
said; the same minor magic that let Avshar's voice ring wide
was his as well. "The synod cast thee into the outer darkness
of anathema an age ago. Get thee gone; Videssos has no room
for thee and thy works."

Marcus stared in awe at the patriarch's back. He had seen
how Balsamon, so casual and merry in private, could instantly
assume the dignity his priestly office demanded. This, though,
surpassed the one as much as that outdid the other. Balsamon
seemed strong and stern in judgment as the great mosaic
image of Phos in the dome of the High Temple in Videssos the
city.

But Avshar quickly rallied. "Thou art a fool, thou dotard,
to stand before me and prate of anathemas. Even aside from
thy presumption here, in a year thou wouldst be dead, dead as
all those purblind witlings who would not see the truth I
brought them. Yet I faced them then and I face thee now.
Who, then, cleaves to the more potent god?"

"One day thy span will end. Soon or late, what does it
matter? Thou'lt be called to account for thy deeds and spend
eternity immured in Skotos' ice with the rest of his creatures."

The wizard-prince's grim eyes burned with scorn. "Thou
showest thyself as deluded as thy forefathers. We are all of us
Skotos' creatures, thou, and I, and the headstrong bumpkin
who sits the throne that is mine by right, and everyone else as
well. Aye, in sooth man is Skotos' finest work. Of all living
beings, only he truly knows evil for what it is and works it of
his own free will."

He spoke as though he and Balsamon were alone, and indeed in a way they were, both being products, no matter how
different, of the rigors of the Videssian theological tradition.
Balsamon replied in the same fashion, seeming to seek to
bring an erring colleague back to sound doctrine rather than to

confront the deadliest enemy of his faith and nation.

He said, "As well argue all food is corrupt on account of a piece of bad fish. Or art thou so blind thou'dst forget there is great good as well as wickedness in the soul of every man?"

The patriarch might have meant the question as rhetorical, but Marcus thought it reached the heart of the matter. The older a man gets, the more fully he becomes himself. Avshar had been no more evil than any other man, before he read in the Khamorth invasions and the collapse of Videssos the sign of Skotos' triumph on earth and turned to the dark god. But through his magic he had gained centuries to live with his choice and grow into it, and now...

Now he cursed Balsamon with a savagery worse than any his Yezda could aspire to, for the outcast always hates more fiercely than the mere enemy. His voice rose until he was screaming: "Die, then, and see what thy goodness gets thee!"

His hands twisted through the same set of passes he had used against the Videssian cavalryman. As the fiery light stabbed at Balsamon, Marcus cried out and sprang forward, Viridovix at his side. The patriarch deserved better than to fall unavenged to Avshar's sorcery.

But Balsamon did not fall, though he slumped in the saddle as if suddenly bearing up under a heavy weight. "I deny thee and all thy works," he said; his voice was strained but full of purpose. "While I live, thy foul sorceries shall hold no more sway on this field."

"So thou sayest." Avshar loosed another enchantment against the patriarch. This one had no visible emanation, but Scaurus heard Balsamon groan. Then the prelate dropped as inessential the small magic that projected his voice over the plain.

The wizard-prince rained spell after spell on him. Balsamon was not, could not be, the sorcerer to match his opponent. He lurched several times, almost toppled once. He did not try to strike back. But in defense, his will was indomitable. Like an outclassed warrior seeking only to hold his foe at bay as long as he could, he withstood or beat aside wizardry that would have devastated a stronger but less purposeful magician.

Seeing him survive in the maelstrom of sorcery, the Videssian army took up his name as a war cry, shouting it again and again until the distant hills echoed with it: "Balsamon! Balsa-

mon! Balsamon!" And, as Marcus had seen before, the patriarch drew strength from his admirers. He straightened on his
mule, his arms wide-flung, his blunt hands darting now this
way, now that, as he deflected every blow Avshar aimed at
him or at the imperial army as a whole.

"Och, a good fairy has hold of him," Viridovix whispered
beside Scaurus. Gorgidas, well away from them, murmured a
Greek word to himself: *"Enthousiasmós."* It meant exactly
the same thing.

Finally, screaming in thwarted fury, Avshar gave up the
assault, wheeled his horse with a brutal jerk of the reins, and
stormed back to his own lines. A chorus of jeers and insults
rose from the imperials. Everyone cheered as a Haloga ran out
to take the reins of Balsamon's mule and lead him back to
safety within the Videssian army. Exhausted but unbeaten, the
patriarch waved to the soldiers around him. But Marcus could
see his face. He looked like a man who had staved off defeat,
not won a victory.

There was a brief lull. All along both lines, officers harangued their men, trying to whip them to fever pitch. Marcus
looked inside himself for inspiring words. He did not find
many. Whatever illusions he had of the glory of the battlefield
were long since dust, as were those of the legionaries.

At last he raised his voice and said, "It's very simple. If we
lose this one, we're ruined. There's nothing left to fall back on
any more. Hang together, do what your officers order you,
and don't let those bastards out there through. That's all, I
guess."

He heard a few voices translating what he said into throaty
Vaspurakaner for those "princes" who had never picked up
Latin. He got no great applause; the legionaries had given
Balsamon the cheers they had in them. He did not care. His
men seemed ready and unafraid. Past that, nothing mattered.

Scaurus thought he heard thunder from a clear sky and
wondered what new spellcraft Avshar was essaying. But it was
not thunder. "Here we go," Gaius Philippus said as the Yezda
urged their horses at Thorisin Gavras' line. The pounding of
their hooves was the noise that filled the world.

Laon Pakhymer bawled an order. The Khatrishers galloped
out to screen the infantry on their flank, to keep the legionaries and Halogai from having to stand against a barrage of
arrows to which they could not reply. Pakhymer's troopers
traded shots with the Yezda, slowing the momentum of their

charge. Marcus watched horses and men fall on both sides.

The Khatrishers were gallant but outnumbered. Having done as much as he could, Pakhymer waved his disreputable hat in the air. His men, those who survived, fell back into their place in the line.

"Avshar! Avshar!" The shouts of the Yezda filled Scaurus' ears. Arrows began falling on the Romans. Somewhere behind the tribune, there was a curse and a clatter of metal as a legionary went down. Another swore as he was hit.

Thock! An arrow smacked against Marcus' *scutum*. He staggered and was glad for the multiple thicknesses of wood and leather and metal. The shaft would have torn through the light target he had carried with the Arshaum.

Pushed on by the mass behind them, the first ranks of Yezda were very close. "*Pila* at the ready!" the tribune shouted, gauging distances. He swung his sword arm high and caught the eyes of the buccinators, who raised their cornets to their lips. "Loose!" he cried; the horns blared out the command to the legionaries.

Hundreds of heavy javelins flew as one. Wounded Yezda roared; their horses screamed. The cries of dismay went on as onrushing ponies stumbled over the fallen.

Some riders blocked flung *pila* with their shields. That saved them for the moment, but when they tried to tear the spears out and throw them back, they found that the weapons' soft iron shanks had bent at impact, fouling their shields and making the *pila* useless. With guttural oaths, they discarded their suddenly worthless protection.

"Loose!" Another volley tore into the Yezda. Then the legionaries' shortswords came rasping out. Whether the Yezda fought from fear of their master or raw blood lust, they did not shrink from combat. They crashed into the Romans.

The dust their horses kicked up rolled over the legionaries in a choking cloud. Marcus sneezed and coughed. His eyes streaming, he hacked blindly at the rider in front of him. He felt the soft resistance that meant flesh. Warm wetness splashed him. He heard a groan. Whether it was man or beast he never knew.

He swiped at his face with the back of his forearm to clear his vision and quickly looked about. Here and there the Yezda had driven deep wedges into the legionaries' line, but he saw no breakthroughs. By squads and maniples, the Romans moved up to cover the points of greatest pressure. At close quarters they had the advantage, despite the horses of the Yezda. Their armor, shields, and disciplined flexibility counted for more than their foes' added reach and ability to strike from above.

Marcus saw Titus Pullo engage a Yezda, yelling and taunting and turning slash after slash with his *scutum*. While the underofficer's furious enemy thought of nothing but slaying him, one of Pullo's troopers ducked down unseen and plunged his sword into the belly of the Yezda's pony. It foundered with a coughing squeal; Pullo killed the man who had ridden it.

"That's right, get him when he's down," Lucius Vorenus laughed. He dueled with an unhorsed Yezda; his *gladius* flicked out in the short stabs the Roman fencing masters taught. Mere ferocity could not withstand such deadly science for long. The Yezda reeled away, clutching at himself; Scaurus smelled the latrine odor that meant a punctured gut.

Pullo was already battling another horseman. He and Vorenus might have buried their feud, but he was not about to let his comrade get ahead of him.

A Yezda thrust his lance at Zeprin the Red, who twisted aside with a supple ease that belied the thickness of his body. He sent his axe crashing down between the eyes of the barbarian's pony. Brains spattered everyone nearby, and the horse collapsed as if it had rammed a stone wall. A second stroke dealt with its rider.

Axes rose and fell continuously on the legionaries' left, where Thorisin's Haloga guardsmen were taking a heavy toll of Avshar's finest troops. But the Makuraner lancers who opposed them fought with dash and courage themselves, and fresh northerners had to keep pressing forward to take the places of those who had fallen.

"Tighten up there!" Marcus yelled. "Help them out!" He led a maniple leftward to make sure no gap opened between the Halogai and his own troops. In an army made up of units fighting nation by nation, that danger was always there. Drax' Namdaleni had taught him that, to his cost, at the Sangarios.

Though under no man's order, Viridovix moved with the tribune. He was glad to go to the aid of the Halogai. They were more somber by nature than his own Celtic folk, but came closer to reminding him of them than any other people of this world.

A Makuraner tried to hit him over the head with a broken spearshaft. He ducked and countered; the horseman's dama-

scened corselet kept the edge from his vitals. His mount
kicked at the Gaul, who nimbly skipped away.

The two men looked at each other for a moment, both
breathing hard. Under the Makuraner's plumed helm, his
swarthy face was greasy with sweat, though his mustaches,
waxed stiff, still swept out fiercely like horns. Viridovix' own
whiskers were limp and sodden. Warily, his eye on the Gaul,
the Makuraner swigged from a wineskin. He raised it in salute
to Viridovix, then turned his horse in another direction.

"May you come through safe," Viridovix called after him.
He had no idea whether the Makuraner heard him, or understood Videssian if he did.

A fresh Yezda surge almost sent Marcus hurrying back
with his maniple to relieve the pressure on the rest of the
legionaries, but Gaius Philippus and Gagik Bagratouni battled
the nomads to a standstill. Bagratouni's Vaspurakaners, men
driven from their homeland by the Yezda, fought the invaders
now with a dour ferocity and a disregard for consequences that
horrified Gaius Philippus.

The senior centurion had to wince, watching one of the
"princes" and Yezda stab each other and fall together, locked
in a death embrace. "Idiots!" he shouted, though Bagratouni's
men showed no sign of listening. "Don't waste yourselves!
One for one's no bargain with these buggers!"

"You!" he rasped, spotting a foot soldier who seemed not
to know where his place was. The fellow turned his head.
"Oh, you," Gaius Philippus said in a different tone.

Gorgidas did not answer. Just then a Roman lurched by,
clutching at a slash on the inside of his arm that was spurting
bright blood. "Stop!" the physician shouted, and the legionary, trained to obedience, stood still. Gorgidas tore a long strip
of cloth from the hem of the soldier's tunic, pressed the edges
of the wound together, and bound it tightly. "Go to the rear,"
he said. "You can't fight any more with that."

When the legionary tried to protest, the Greek argued him
down. "Do as I tell you; as you are now, you're more trouble
protecting than you're worth. The Yezda won't come pouring
through because you've gone." The soldier stumbled away.
Gorgidas hoped the bandage would hold the bleeding; that arm
had been cut to the bone.

He unsheathed his *gladius*, which he had put away to tend
to the injured Roman. Then he jerked in alarm as someone
twisted it out of his hand. "Steady, there," Gaius Philippus

said. "I think I want this back after all."

"Fine time," Gorgidas said indignantly. "What am I supposed to defend myself with?"

"Let us worry about that," the veteran answered, grunting in satisfaction at the familiar heft of his old sword. "From what I've seen, you're more use to us as a doctor than you'd ever be as a legionary. It's not bad you know how and all, but stick to what you're best at."

The Greek considered, then dipped his head in agreement, saying, "Give me the blade you've been carrying, though. It's better than nothing."

Gaius Philippus had already turned away from him; the fight was picking up again. "Come on, Minucius!" he roared. "I need another two squads here!"

Even as he shouted, a couple of Yezda burst through the struggling line of soldiers. The centurion caught a saber slash on his *scutum*, then grappled with the nomad, tearing him from the saddle and hurling him to the ground. He sprang at the other warrior and drove his *gladius* into the small of the Yezda's back before his victim knew he was there.

But the first Yezda had only been slightly stunned. He scrambled up and leaped at Gaius Philippus. Gorgidas tackled him from behind. He seized the nomad's sword wrist in both hands and held his grip as they rolled on the ground. His wiry strength kept his foe from tearing free until Gaius Philippus, working carefully so as to miss him, thrust through the Yezda's throat.

"Bravely done," the senior centurion said, helping the Greek to his feet. "But why didn't you stab him with your dagger?"

"I forgot I had it," Gorgidas said in a small voice.

"Amateurs!" Gaius Philippus turned the word into a curse. "Try not to kill yourself with this, all right?" he said, handing Gorgidas the blade he had asked for. The Greek was spared further embarrassment when the veteran ordered the reinforcements from Minucius into the line to shore up the weak spot that had let the Yezda through.

The presence on the legionaries eased as deep-voiced horns brayed to the left of Thorisin Gavras' center. His Namdaleni rumbled forward, shouting what might be the only battle cry they could share with the Videssians: "Phos with us!" At first the weight of their armor and of the big horses they rode gave their advance an all but irresistible impetus. Avshar's Makuraners slowed but could not stop them; in tight fighting the Yezda, on ponies and lightly armed, went down like winnowed barley.

Had there been more Namdaleni, they might have torn the battle open. As it was, the Yezda swarmed round their flanks and poured arrows into them. Not even their mail coats or their horses' protective trappings were wholly proof against that withering fire. Their progress slowed.

But in bringing the knights to a standstill, the Yezda thinned their own line. Seeing an opening in front of him, Provhos Moutzouphlos stormed through it with the headlong dash that had first made Thorisin notice him. Shooting and chopping, he led a company of Videssian horsemen as reckless as himself clean into the enemy's rear.

Again, if the rest of the imperials had matched his troopers' quality, they could have split the Yezda in two and rolled up their right wing. The Yezda knew it, too; their cries grew frantic. The legionaries cheered, not knowing what had happened but sure it meant no good for their foes.

Yet despite the cheers, despite Mourtzouphlos' pleading and his oaths, the other Videssians hung back a few seconds too long. The Yezda repaired the breach, and then Mourtzouphlos was trapped, not they.

He turned his company straight for Avshar, but that way was blocked—too many Yezda and Makurani, all headed straight for him. His shout rose above the battlefield din: "Back to our own, lads!" Those who made it—maybe half the number who had plunged into the breach—burst out between the Namdaleni and Halogai, having hacked their way through a third of the Yezda army.

Along with the rest of Gavras' forces, Marcus was yelling himself hoarse at the exploit—until he recognized Mourtzouphlos. "I will be damned," he said to no one in particular. "Something to the popinjay after all." As it had before, the thought grated.

In the heart of the Yezda battle array, Avshar seethed with frustration. He felt all his designs, all his long-nursed plans tottering. For the hundredth time he gave Balsamon his curses, hurling another spell at the patriarch of Videssos.

It hurt; he could sense Balsamon's anguish. That was sweet, but not sweet enough. Eventually, he knew, he would shatter the patriarch like a dropped pot—but when? Ordinarily Balsamon could not have withstood the first blast of his sorcery, but this, worse luck, was no ordinary time. In his desperation he had somehow screwed himself up to such a pitch that he was still resisting. Even without Avshar's assaults, the effort that took would kill him in a couple of days, but the wizard-prince could not wait so long.

Being unable to use his magic frightened Avshar as nothing else had. Without it he was just another warlord, dependent on his wit and his soldiers to gain his triumph—or to lose. The imperials showed no sign of giving way; if anything, they seemed steadier than his barbarous levies. The Yezda were bold enough when they scented victory, but quick as any nomads to melt away if checked.

The wizard-prince ground his teeth. Why, he had almost been in the hand-to-hand himself, when that Videssian maniac sliced his men like cheese. He wished Mourtzouphlos *had* reached him; even without his sorceries, he would have given the wretch a bitter death for his daring.

Suddenly Avshar threw back his head and laughed. Several horses around him shied; he paid no notice. "What a dolt I am!" he exclaimed. "If the bridge has fallen into the stream, I can swim across just the same."

He stared over the grappling lines of soldiers, measuring what he had to do. Even for him it would not be easy, but it was within his power. Laughing again, he reached for a black-fletched arrow and set it to his bow.

The moan that went up from the Videssian center was so loud and deep that Marcus thought the Emperor had fallen. But Thorisin's sunburst standard still flew, and the tribune saw him under it on his bay charger, urging his troops on. In his gilded parade armor, coronet, cape, and red boots, he was unmistakable.

The Halogai were holding well, and the left wing, if anything, was still advancing. Where was the trouble, then? Scaurus used his inches to peer about. There was some confusion a bit behind the Avtokrator, several imperials huddled around a riderless mule—

The tribune did not realize he had groaned aloud until Viridovix said, "Where is it you're hit, man?"

"Not me," Scaurus said impatiently. "Balsamon's down."

"Och, a pox!"

Marcus grabbed one of his Romans by the arm. "Find Gorgidas and get him over there," he ordered, pointing. Almost certainly, Videssian healers were already tending to the patriarch, but he did not overlook the one-in-a-thousand chance that they were all dead or out of action. The legionary dashed away.

Gorgidas went to Balsamon's aid at the dead run. He did not know the patriarch as Scaurus did and cared nothing for him as a religious leader; Gorgidas was no Phos-worshiper. But any man with the spiritual strength and will to bring Avshar's sorcery to a standstill was too precious to lose to a chance-fired dart—for such the Greek assumed it was.

Scaurus had been right in thinking the healer-priests would be doing their best for the prelate. They stared suspiciously at Gorgidas as he came puffing up, then eased in manner as they recognized him for one who shared their skill, even if a foreigner. "The good god bless you for your concern," one said, sketching Phos' sun-circle over his heart, "but you are too late. You would have been too late the instant he was hit."

"Let me see him," the physician said. He pushed through the imperials; with their near-miraculous gift, they knew far less of simple medicine than he had learned. Perhaps the training he had scorned since coming to the Empire and finding the higher art would serve him now.

A glance at Balsamon, though, showed him the Videssian healer-priest was right. The patriarch lay awkwardly crumpled on his left side. His face wore an unsurprised expression, but his eyes were set and empty; a thin trickle of blood ran from the corner of his mouth and fouled his beard. His chest did not rise or fall. The shaft that had struck him down was buried almost to the feathers, a few digits to the left of his breastbone. Gorgidas knelt to take his wrist, but knew he would find no pulse.

The physician looked toward the battle line. He knew the power of nomad bows, but it would have taken a prodigious shot to reach this far. Then he stiffened. Viridovix had told tales of such archery—and of arrows feathered with black. Anyone who thought of Avshar as sorcerer alone made the fatal mistake of forgetting what a warrior he was.

The reverse also held . . . and now the imperials' shield had been snatched away. Springing to his feet in alarm, Gorgidas cried to the men around him, "Are any of you wizards as well as healers?"

Several nodded. The Greek had time to say, "Then look to yourself, for Avshar is—" He never got "unleashed" out of his mouth. All but one of the healer-priests who were also sorcerers toppled as if bludgeoned. Some got out gasps or choked screams; others simply fell, horror on their faces, their mouths twisted in agony.

The last healer, stronger than his fellows, stood swaying a good two minutes, a fox cub facing a dragon. Tears streamed down his cheeks; after a moment they were tears of blood. He pounded his temples with his fists, as if to relieve unbearable pressure inside his head. Then his eyes rolled up, and he dropped beside Balsamon's corpse.

Wizards went down one by one all along the Videssian line, broken under Avshar's savage onslaught. A couple of the mightiest held onto life and sanity, but that was as much as they could do; they had no strength to ward the army.

Gorgidas felt the tide of battle turning. Suddenly the imperials were uncertain and afraid, the Yezda full of fresh courage. The Greek drew the shortsword Gaius Philippus had given him and ran for the front line. The veteran had been wrong; it looked like he was going to have some fighting to do after all.

Had Avshar been a cat, he would have purred. He rested his bow on his knee, watching consternation spread through the Videssian army like ink through clear water or black clouds across the sun. He ground another sorcerer between the millstones of his wizardry and felt the man's spirit fade and die. It was easy, without Balsamon. He patted the bow affectionately.

"For thy gifts, Skotos, I give thee thanks," he whispered. He thought for a moment, considering what to do next. Magic could only win so much more for him now. As long as he kept up the killing pressure against the sorcerers who still opposed him, he was limited to minor spells on the side. But if he let them go to work some greater cantation, they might somehow find a way to block it. Battle magic, even his battle magic, was tricky.

Let it be the smaller sorceries, then, he decided. They would be enough to panic the imperials, who would surely see them as the forerunners of worse. And that would give his soldiers the battle; already they were pushing forward, sensing their enemies' discomfiture.

The wizard-prince put away his bow and drew his long, straight sword. He wanted no doubt about who was going to cut down Thorisin Gavras. With Emperor—two Emperors!— and patriarch fallen to his hand, Videssos would learn who its rightful master was. He briefly regretted not having Balsamon to sacrifice to his god on the altar of the High Temple in the capital, but no help for that.

His eyes gleamed. There would be plenty of victims.

Being at the forefront of the fighting, Marcus sensed the advantage slipping away from the imperials even before the shift became obvious to Gorgidas. The center held steady, and far off on the right wing Arigh was crumpling the Yezda facing him. But the Videssians themselves wavered as the news of Balsamon's fall spread; it was as though some of their heart had gone with him.

The tribune wished Mourtzouphlos was back where he belonged. Thanks to his own vainglory, the noble was not cast down by the loss of the patriarch, and could have inspired regiments of wobblers by his example. His reckless dash through the Yezda line, though, left him in the middle of troops who needed no incentive.

As he had at Maragha, Scaurus marveled at the steadfastness of the Halogai. They bore a burden worse than the legionaries', for the main force of Avshar's Makuraner lancers concentrated on them and on the Emperor they protected. Yet they stood firm against the armored horsemen, their axes working methodically, as if they were hewing timber rather than men. Whenever one went down, another tramped forward to take his place.

They sang as they fought, a slow chant in their own tongue that reminded the tribune of waves breaking on a rocky, windswept beach. The music had to be strong to reach him so; he was half baked in his cuirass, his face a dusty mask runneled by sweat. And this flat, hot plain had never known the touch of the ocean and never would.

Thinking such thoughts, Marcus was almost cut down by a Yezda's saber. He jerked his head away at the last possible instant. Viridovix clucked reproachfully. "There's better times nor this for smelling the pretty flowers, Roman dear."

"You're right," the tribune admitted. Then they both failed to give the battle their full attention; the druids' stamps on their blades came to flaming life at the same time. "Avshar!"

Marcus exclaimed. A couple of hundred yards to the rear, Gorgidas was yelling his futile warning.

Cries of fright rose from the imperials as the wizard-prince smashed their magicians like worms under his feet. Through the alarm and the din of battle, Scaurus heard Thorisin Gavras shouting, "Stand fast! Stand fast!" The Emperor did not sound panicked, or even much upset. From his voice, it might have been an order in a parade-ground drill.

His coolness helped bring the army back to itself. Seeing their leader unfazed, the soldiers borrowed courage from him and fought back. Again the Yezda were checked.

Viridovix glanced at his sword. The druids' marks were still glowing, and getting brighter. He shook his head gloomily. "Let 'em be brave whilst they can, puir sods. There's worse coming, sure and there is."

At first Marcus thought the buzzing that filled his head was a product of his exhaustion. Then the Haloga next to him broke off his song to growl something foul and slap at himself. A moment later another did the same, and a legionary, and yet another Haloga.

The imperial guard wiped his hand on his tunic. He noticed Scaurus looking at him. "Damned flies," he said with a sour grin. "Vorse t'an arrows, I t'ink sometimes."

The tribune nodded; bugs were always one of the small torments of the field. He had not been bitten himself, but he could see the big black flies droning around as they darted from one victim to the next.

Their bites were almost impossible to ignore, as a Roman found to his misfortune. Stung unexpectedly in a tender spot, he could not stop the reflex that made him clap his hand to it. The Yezda he was facing, untroubled by the cloud of insects, sworded him down.

Since the flies did not harass Scaurus, he took some time to realize how rare his protection was. Hardly an imperial was not swatting frantically or trying with all his might not to because he was locked in a fight for his life. And all their opponents shared the immunity that one nomad had enjoyed.

When the tribune recognized that, he knew with grim clarity where the blame lay. Avshar had worked grander magics, he thought, but hardly a more devilish one. The flies were hard enough for Thorisin's men to take; they robbed them of their concentration and gave their Yezda foes an edge. That first legionary was far from the only soldier to pay dearly for a second's involuntary lapse.

But the effect on the Videssian army's animals was ten times worse. There is no way to school a horse against a pain striking out of nowhere. Beast after beast squealed and reared or ran wild, leaving its rider, even if unstung himself, easy meat for a Yezda on a pony under control.

Thrown into sudden confusion, the imperials began to waver again. This time Thorisin had trouble steadying them. It was all he could do to keep his seat; his bay was bucking and plunging like any other fly-tormented beast.

He would not let himself be tossed. As he forced the stallion to yield to his will, he kept up the shouts of encouragement he had been giving all along: "Come on, you bastards, will you let a few bugs bugger you? Tomorrow you can scratch; today's for fighting!"

His cheers and similar words from a score of stubborn officers here and there along the line helped, but it was as if the Videssians were battling in the midst of a sandstorm blowing full in their faces. Each Yezda thrust was harder to contain, and those thrusts came ever more often.

Belong long, Scaurus thought as he cut at a nomad, the Yezda would find a gap or force one, and that would end everything.

But Avshar did not see anything that looked like victory. He had thought to sweep everything before him, and he was not succeeding in that aim. True, the imperials were giving ground on the wings, but not much, and their center remained unbudged. In that part of the field his plague of flies was failing. Gavras' infantry had the resolve to fight on despite them, and the horses of the Namdaleni were so heavily caparisoned that the biting insects could hardly reach their hides.

The wizard-prince clenched his jagged teeth as he watched his foes hold yet another attack. He had labored more than half a century to forge this latest weapon; he would *not* let it turn in his hand. His war on Videssos had cost too many years, too many defeats, for him to bear another. If for once his magic was stretched too thin, raw force would have to serve.

He turned to the messenger beside him. "Fetch me Nogruz and Kaykaus." The Makuraner generals came quickly. Nogruz, had things gone differently in his grandfather's time, might have been King of Kings of Makuran, but he bowed his head to Avshar. He was proud, able, and ruthless, a better servant even than Varatesh, the wizard-prince thought, and Kaykaus almost his match.

Avshar pointed at the sunburst standard still proudly flying to mark Thorisin Gavras' station. "Gather your men together —you see your target. We will shatter their best." He drew his sword. "I shall head the charge myself."

A slow smile lit Nogruz's lean, aquiline features. "I will guard your side," he said.

"And I." That was Kaykaus, though ragged bandages wrapped his shoulder and thigh. The great nobles of Makuran had a tradition of enmity with the Empire older than Avshar's vendetta. Any tool that came to hand, the wizard-prince thought, and made his preparations.

The Halogai roared in derision when the horsemen they had been fighting all day drew back, but they were too battle-wise to go lumbering in pursuit. Foot soldiers who chased cavalry asked to be cut off and slaughtered. Instead they leaned on their axes and rested, crushing flies, gulping wine or water from canteens, binding up wounds, and fanning at themselves to cool down before the battle began again.

Marcus stood with them, panting and wishing he could shed his mail shirt. As often happened in hard fighting, he had picked up several small wounds without knowing it: his cheek, his right forearm—cutting across an old scar—and on his right thigh just above his knee. When he noticed them, they began to hurt. He also realized that he stank.

Viridovix looked out at the enemy. "Bad cess for us, they're not through at all, at all," he sighed, wiping sweat from his face. Sunburn and exertion combined to make him as florid as Zeprin the Red.

He rubbed dirt in the palm of his hand, spat, rubbed again, then tested his sword grip. "Och, better."

The Makurani formed themselves into a great wedge aimed straight at the heart of Thorisin's army. There were more of them than Scaurus had thought. He mouthed an oath that was part prayer, part curse, when he saw the double lightning-bolt banner move to the point of the wedge.

The Emperor's standard came forward, too, and Gavras with it. This fight he would lead from the front. "The last throw of the dice," Marcus said to no one in particular.

A trumpet wailed in a minor key. The Makuraners shouted Avshar's name. Those who still had unshattered lances swung them down. The rest brandished sabers or shook their fists.

The Halogai and legionaries tensed to receive the charge. Far to the right, Scaurus heard Gaius Philippus bellowing orders and had a moment to feel glad the veteran was still in action. Then that mournful trumpet cried again, and Avshar's horsemen thundered toward the imperial army's center.

Scaurus' mouth went drier even than the day's thirsty work called for. He had faced cavalry charges before, and never wanted to see another. The greatest and most frightening difference between the Roman and Videssian arts of war was the stirrup and what it did for cavalry. Here the horse was the killing force, not the foot.

Brave as a terrier, Laon Pakhymer tried to lead his light-armed Khatrishers in a spoiling attack on the wedge, but the Yezda with whom they were already hotly engaged would not be shaken off. Pakhymer had to pull back quickly to keep his regiment from getting surrounded.

The Namdalener countercharge was something else again. The islanders' commander, a big burly man named Hovsa whom Scaurus barely knew, had no intention of receiving Avshar's assault with his own knights motionless; the momentum of their chargers was as important a weapon as their lanceheads. They slammed through the Yezda who darted out to bar their path and crashed into the right side of the Makuraner wedge close to its apex.

The noise of the collision was like an earthquake in an ironmonger's shop. The Namdaleni drove deep into the ranks of their opponents, thrusting Makurani from the saddle, overbearing their horses, and hewing them down with great, sweeping swordstrokes.

Provhos Mourtzouphlos unhesitatingly threw the survivors of his daredevil band after the knights from the Duchy. He despised and distrusted them, but he was too good a soldier not to see what needing doing.

The islanders and Videssians staggered the wedge and shoved it leftward. But the Makurani, no matter the leader they served, were warriors in their own right. They fought back ferociously, using their greater numbers to contain the imperial horse while their attack went home near the join of the legionaries and Halogai.

The first few ranks of infantry tumbled like ninepins, spitted on lances or ridden down by the Makurani, a fate Marcus barely escaped. He was spun off his feet; an iron-shod hoof thudded into the ground an inch from his face, flinging dirt in his eyes. He stabbed blindly upward. His blade pierced flesh, though it was almost ripped from his fingers. The wounded horse squealed. Its rider cried out in alarm and then in pain as the beast fell on top of him.

The tribune gained his feet, slashing wildly in all directions. He was not the only one to have got a blow in; there were horses with empty saddles and unhorsed lancers trying to rise and to keep from being trampled by their own comrades.

A few feet from him, a legionary was using a hoarded *pilum* to fend off a Makuraner. With his last strength, a dying Haloga hamstrung the lancer's horse. As it toppled, the Roman trooper drove his spear through the Makuraner's neck.

It could not have been more than twenty paces back to where the imperial foot was fighting to hold a battered line, but it seemed as many miles. Scaurus and the legionary fought back to back as they worked their way through the press. A Makuraner raked the tribune with a spurred heel. He yelped and hit the man in the face with the crossguard of his blade, being too nearly crushed for anything else.

A stone, thrown or perhaps kicked up by a horse, rang off the side of his helmet. He lurched and almost went down again, but then hard hands were pulling him and his companion away from the enemy and inside the imperials' shield-wall.

Though the Romans and Halogai were still being pushed back, they did not give way to panic. They knew they were done for if they broke. *Gladii* and *pila* thrust out between big *scuta* with drilled precision. The Halogai were not singing any more, but they kept chopping away with axes and broadswords, overhand now to get the most benefit from their round wooden shields. Where the fighting was fiercest, they and the Romans were inextricably mixed—any man standing after the Makuraner charge helped his mates without looking to see if they were blond or swarthy.

They had blunted the point of Avshar's wedge, but were no more able than the Namdaleni and Videssians to stop it. The wizard-prince cut down trooper after trooper. The sight of his

eyes blazing in that ancient face chilled the blood of the bold-
est and left them easy meat, but he would have been deadly
without the fear he created. His charger, a trained war-horse,
shattered shields and bones with its hooves, while he swung
his long heavy sword like a schoolmaster's switch.

His men followed him from fear, not affection, but they
followed. The distance between Skotos' bloody banner and
the imperial sunburst narrowed. Little by little, the wizard-
prince forced his attack back in the direction from which it
had been pushed. "First thy brother, Gavras, then thy priest—
now thee, and Videssos with thee!" he cried.

The Emperor brandished his lance in defiance and urged
his mount toward Avshar, but the big bay could not get
through the tight-packed, struggling foot soldiers ahead.

He was not the only one seeking the wizard-prince. Marcus
sidled along the line, now managing one step, now two or
three, now having to stand and fight. He bawled Avshar's
name over and over, but his voice was lost in the cries around
him.

Viridovix was not far away, though the impact of the
charge had swept him and the tribune apart. He had his own
war cry. It meant nothing to the troopers by him, but he did
not care. "Seirem!" he shouted. "For Seirem!"

A pair of Makurani who had lost their horses came at him.
He parried one saber cut, then turned the next with his shield.
The Makurani moved to take him from either side. His head
swiveled as he desperately looked for a way to deal with one
before the other could kill him.

Then one of them collapsed with a groan, hamstrung from
behind. Viridovix sprang at the other. They slashed at each
other, curved sword ringing against straight. The Gaul was
stronger and quicker. He beat down the Makuraner's guard
and felled him with a stroke that half severed his head.

He whirled to make sure of the other Makuraner, but that
one was down for good, the legionary who had dealt with him
already fighting someone else. He was in trouble, too, for he
had no shield. Viridovix rushed to his aid. Together they managed to force the enemy horseman back among his comrades.

"Indeed and I thank you," the Gaul said. " 'Twas a rare
nasty spot, that."

"Think nothing of it," answered his rescuer, a spare man of
about his own age with a beard going white. "Even Herakles
can't fight two, as the saying goes."

"Och, tha daft kern of a Greek, what're you doing here? Tend to your wounded."

"Someone else would be tending your corpse if I had been," Gorgidas retorted with a toss of his head.

Having no ready response, Viridovix ducked down to strip a fallen Makuraner of his shield, then handed it to Gorgidas. It was a horseman's target, small, round, and faced with boiled leather—not much for a foot soldier, but better than nothing. The Greek had a moment to grunt his thanks before the struggle picked up again.

Moving crab-fashion, Marcus had worked to within thirty feet or so of Avshar. In the crush, the wizard-prince gave no sign of knowing he was there; Wulghash's glamour still veiled his sword. It was all hard fighting now. The lancers at the thin end of the Makuraner wedge were the pick of the army; getting past each one was a fresh challenge, with finesse as important as brute strength.

Or so the tribune thought. But then, quite suddenly, several horses went crashing down. Makurani on Avshar's left, the opposite side from Scaurus, shouting in alarm. Above their cries he heard someone bellowing like a wild bull. Roaring in berserker fury, his axe hewing a swathe of death ahead of him, Zeprin the Red hurled himself toward Avshar.

Only one rider was left between him and the wizard-prince —a noble in silvered corselet and gilded helm. He cut at Zeprin. Marcus saw the blow land, but the Haloga took no notice of it. He swung his axe in a glittering arc. The noble stared in disbelieving horror at the spouting stump of his wrist. The next stroke caved in his cuirass and pitched him from his horse, dead.

"Kaykaus!" the Makurani cried; a name, the tribune thought.

Zeprin cared not at all. With another incoherent yell, he rushed on Avshar, his gore-splattered axe upraised.

It was too late for the wizard-prince to twist and meet him weapon to weapon, but Avshar was truly the greatest sorcerer of the age. Without letting go of any of his own spells, he flawlessly executed the complex magic that had slain the Videssian who met him in single combat. Fiery light stabbed again from his fingers.

But the Haloga, though he staggered, did not fall in flames. His battle-madness and thirst for vengeance proofed him against sorcery. He recovered; his axe rose and fell. Avshar met the blow with his sword, but could do no more than turn it slightly. Instead of splitting his skull, it fell square on his charger's neck.

The beast was dead before its legs went out from under it. Seeing it go down, the imperials raised a mighty cheer. "Avshar is fallen!" a legionary bleeding from a slashed cheek screamed in Scaurus' ear.

The tribune shouted too, hoarsely. The cry stuck in his throat when the wizard-prince kicked free of the stirrups, lit rolling, and gained his feet before Zeprin could finish him.

The Haloga rushed at him. Marcus scrambled to help, but they were already fighting before he could get close. Zeprin's first wild stroke met only air. Full of insane strength, he sent his axe whistling in another deadly arc. Avshar parried, though the force of the cut nearly tore his blade from his hand.

Yet he was laughing, in spite of his fearful plight. "If thou'dst kill a man, wilting," he mocked, "it should be done so—and so—and so!" Each slash went home almost faster than the eye could follow. Blood spurted after every one. Any of them would have dropped a normal warrior, especially the last, a frightful cut to the side of Zeprin's neck.

In his berserker rage, the Haloga did not seem to feel them. He waded ahead once more, and this time Avshar bellowed in pain and fury as the axe lopped the little finger from his left hand as neatly as if it had been on the block. He bunched the hand into a fist to stanch the flow of blood.

After that he fought silently, but with no less ferocity. He dealt three blows for every slash of Zeprin's, and most of his landed; the Haloga had forgotten defense. His arm drawn back for another chop at the wizard-prince, Zeprin paused in sudden confusion. A torrent of blood streamed from his mouth and nose. His madly staring eyes clouded; the axe slipped from his fingers. His armor clattering about him, he swayed and fell.

"Is there another?" Avshar cried, waving his sword on high and setting his booted foot on Zeprin's neck in token of victory. He strode forward, confident no imperial would dare face him. Then he halted in his tracks, his fleshless face contorted in angry surprise. "Thou!" he hissed.

"Me." Winded and afraid, Scaurus had breath but for the one word. He was so tired he could hardly hold up his shield. Unlike the time so long ago in the Hall of the Nineteen Couches, Avshar had no buckler. This time the Roman cared nothing for chivalry. He hefted his sword. "No farther," he said.

He thought with dread that Avshar would try to overwhelm him at the first onset, but the wizard-prince hung back, letting the tribune gather himself. Of course, Scaurus realized—he wonders where I've sprung from, for he didn't sense my blade. He risked turning his head to look for Viridovix, but could not find the Gaul.

Avshar's hesitation lasted no more than a handful of heart-beats. When he did advance on the Roman, he moved more warily then he had against Zeprin. Having crossed swords with Marcus before, he knew the tribune was no spitfire seek-ing only to attack—and he had a healthy respect for the Gallic longsword.

The first clash of arms showed Scaurus he was in over his head. He was close to exhaustion, while Avshar drew from a seemingly unending well of strength. The tribune took blow after blow on his *scutum*; Avshar's keen blade bit into the bronze facing of the shield and chewed at the wood beneath. The wizard-prince easily evaded or beat aside the thrusts he managed in reply.

They dueled alone. No Makurani came to Avshar's aid; had he been a different sort of commander, Marcus would not have lasted long. But the imperials as well as his own men feared the wizard-prince. None of them had the courage to join the Roman against him. As if the two sides were both reproaching themselves, they fought each other harder than ever.

To Gorgidas, who was directly in back of the tribune, Marcus seemed like Aias battling Hektor in the *Iliad*—out-matched, baffled, but too mulish to yield an inch except by dying. The Greek shoved Viridovix in the back. "By the gods, hurry! He can't hold him off forever."

"Ha' care, tha sot!" Viridovix yelped, wriggling like a snake to evade a Makuraner's slash. "Is it trying to get me killed y'are?" His backhand reply caught his foe in the right shoulder. The Makuraner dropped his saber and started to run. A Haloga guardsman cut him nearly in half from behind.

"Hurry!" Gorgidas insisted again. He stabbed at the lancer who loomed in front of him, pinked the rider's horse. Its flail-ing hooves proved as dangerous as the Makuraner's long spear. The Greek skipped back just in time.

Up ahead, Marcus was still on his feet, though he blearily wondered how. Avshar played with him as a kitten toys with a mouse, giving torment but holding off the blow that would end it. Every so often he would inflict another gash and smile his carnivore smile. "Escape me now, an thou canst!" he gloated in high good humor. He relished victory over the tribune almost as much as if it had been Gavras and was in no hurry to end his pleasure.

Not all the blood on his robes and cuirass came from his amputated finger; even a mouse can have fangs. But his injuries were of no importance, while Marcus bled in a score of places.

After some endless time the wizard-prince exclaimed, "Let the farce be done at last," and leaped at Scaurus. His armored shoulder slammed against the Roman's shield and bowled him over.

As he had been trained, Marcus kept the *scutum* between his enemy and himself. Avshar's sword came smashing down. The tribune felt boards split under that crushing impact. The next stroke, he knew, would be aimed with cunning, not blind blood lust. He waited for the steel to enter his flesh.

Then he heard the wizard-prince cry out in wrath and turn from him to meet a new foe. At the same time, the druids' stamps on the tribune's sword flashed so brilliantly that he screwed his eyes shut, dazzled by the explosion of light. Above him, Viridovix' blade was another brand of flame. The Gaul roared, "Here, you murthering omadhaun, use your sword on an upright man."

He traded savage cuts with Avshar, driving the wizard-prince from Scaurus. That was not what the tribune had intended. "Wait!" he shouted, getting to one knee and then to his feet.

But Viridovix would not wait. With Avshar in front of him at last, his rage consumed him, just as Zeprin's had. The plans he and Scaurus had made for this moment were swept away by a red torrent of fury. To wound, to maim, to kill . . . had Avshar been unarmed, Viridovix would have thrown his sword aside to rend him with his hands.

If Gaius Philippus had taught Marcus anything, it was to keep his wits about him in combat. He rushed after the Gaul, whose wild onslaught had forced Avshar back a dozen paces. At every step he took, his sword and Viridovix' glowed brighter. The magic raging in his blade seemed to lend him fresh vigor, as if he was becoming a conduit through which some force larger than himself might flow.

The hammerstrokes Viridovix aimed at the wizard-prince bespoke the same sudden rush of strength. But Avshar, indomitable as a mountain, was yielding ground no more. His bodily power and swordsmanship matched the Gaul's, and in force of will he was superior.

Nor did his spells falter as he fought. He maintained his hold over the wizards in the imperial army, and his plague of flies still tormented his foes and their horses. Thorisin Gavras' beast, maddened by scores of bites, squealed and bucked and would advance no further in spite of the Emperor's curses and his spurs.

At last Avshar's men began to move to help him. One closed with Scaurus, a solidly built warrior who cut at the Roman's legs. To Marcus he was an obstacle, no more. The tribune parried, countered in a similar low line. His point tore open the Makuraner's thigh just below his mail shirt. The man gasped, stumbled, and fell, grabbing at his leg. Marcus raced past him.

Avshar's deadly eyes flicked to the tribune. "Come ahead, then," he said, shifting his stance slightly. "Both of you together do not suffice against me."

Marcus stopped short. The wizard-prince's withering laugh flayed him. The tribune's sword darted forth. Avshar's moved to beat it aside, but Scaurus had not thrust at him. Instead, quite gently, his blade touched Viridovix'.

The fabric of the world seemed to stretch very tight. The pounding of the tribune's heart was louder than all the Yezda drums. Never since the Celtic blades brought the Romans to Videssos had he hazarded the ultimate magic in them. Viridovix' sea-green eyes were wide and staring. He had agreed to Scaurus' plan, but it daunted him now. Who could tell to what strange land the druids' magic would sweep them next?

The same thought screamed in Scaurus' mind, but if he took Avshar with him he did not care. His greatest fear was that the spells which had been woven to ward Gaul would not protect Videssos. Yet the Empire was now truly his homeland, and Viridovix' long service for it argued that he, too, held it dear.

The wait between hope and dread could only have lasted

for an instant. Avshar was still twisting to redirect his lunge when a torrent of golden flame leaped from his opponents' swords. Feeling the power of the unleashed sorcery, he sprang backward, throwing his own blade aside to shape passes with both hands. His mouth worked soundlessly as he raced through a spell to defend himself against the druids' charms.

Scaurus looked for the flame to form a great glowing dome, as it had in the blood-soaked Gallic clearing four years before—a dome to carry away Avshar, the flower of his army, and, all too likely, the tribune and Viridovix as well. But in Gaul no opposing magic had been operating. Here the power released from the two swords was hardly enough to contain the chiefest of Videssos' enemies; their sorcerous fire surrounded him in light but went no further.

The wizard-prince gave a trapped wolf's howl. Determined to the end, he hurled his strongest magics one after the other against the force that held him, striving to break free. The barrier heaved and billowed like a ship's sail in contrary winds. Two or three times it faded almost to transparency, but when Avshar tried to step through it back into his own world he found he was still restrained.

Men from both armies cried out in terror at the sudden outburst of sorcery. Many averted their eyes, either from the fierce glare or out of awe and fear of the unknown.

That was not Gorgidas' way. He wished he could take notes as he watched the flickering ring of light slowly tighten around Avshar. When the wizard-prince's desperate spells left him visible, he seemed surrounded by a swirling gray mist. Then the light flared to an intolerable peak of brilliance and abruptly winked out. Peering through green-purple after-images, the Greek saw it had taken Avshar with it.

"I wonder where he went," he muttered to himself, and tossed his head in annoyance at another question he would never have answered.

He had been some yards away; Scaurus saw and heard much more, though he never spoke of it afterward, not even to Viridovix. That was no mist inside the barrier, it was snow, not falling but driven horizontally by a roaring gale whose sound was enough to freeze the heart. The wizard-prince's feet skidded on ice, a flat, black, glistening sheet; somehow Marcus was sure it was miles thick.

Avshar's voice rose to a frightened wail, as if he recognized where he was. And in the instant when the ring of light flashed brightest, Scaurus thought he heard another voice, slow, deep, and eternally hungry, begin to speak. He was forever glad he had not caught enough to be certain.

He wished the wizard-prince joy of the master he had chosen.

XIII

A GREAT SILENCE HELD THE CENTER OF THE FIELD. MEN ON both sides stood with lowered weapons, stunned at what they had seen. The din of combat on either flank seemed irrelevant. Marcus and Viridovix looked at each other, dazed by the force they had called up and finding it hard to believe they had not been swept away with Avshar.

Then one of the wizard-prince's flies bit Scaurus on the back of the neck. Now that they were no longer under sorcerous control, his sword did not protect against them. The sudden pain and his automatic slap made victory real to him.

Across the line, the Makuraners began swatting at themselves, too. One of them caught the tribune's eye: a lanky, blade-nosed warrior who sat his horse with the inborn arrogance of a great noble. He smiled and nodded, as if to a friend. "We are all well rid of that one," he said, only a faint guttural rasp flavoring his Videssian.

Trumpets blared behind Scaurus. He heard Thorisin Gavras cry, "Drive them now, drive them! They'll be quaking in their corselets without the stinking he-witch to do their dirty work for 'em!"

The tribune's hand tightened on his sword. A last push against a demoralized enemy. . .

The Makuraner's smile grew wider and less pleasant, and Marcus felt a chill of foreboding. "Do you think we will run off?" the fellow said. "We are taking this fight; now it will be for ourselves instead of for a master who ruled us only because of his might."

He called to his lancers in their own language. They yelled

back eagerly, clapping their hands and clashing swords and shields together. Their cry became a swelling chorus: "Nogruz! Nogruz!"

"Och, it's another round for the shindy, I'm thinking," Viridovix said softly.

"Come over to us," the Makuraner noble urged. "Neither of you is an imperial by blood. Would you not sooner serve the winners?"

Marcus could see the ambition blazing from him like fire. No wonder this Nogruz had followed Avshar—he would not shrink from anything that looked to be to his advantage. The tribune shook his head; Viridovix answered with a contemptuous snort.

"A pity," Nogruz said, shouting to make himself heard over the yells of his men. "Then I will kill you if I can."

He spurred his horse forward. He was too close to the Roman and Gaul to build up the full, terrifying momentum on which heavy cavalry depended, but so clever with his lance that he almost skewered Marcus as the tribune sprang away. Viridovix slashed from the other side, but Nogruz was as good with his shields as he was with his spear and turned the blow. More Makurani rumbled after him, and the battle began again.

"Out of my way!" Thorisin Gavras shouted impatiently, pushing his charger through the ranks of the Halogai. He nearly rode Gorgidas down when the Greek did not scramble out of his path quickly enough. Then he was face to face with Nogruz, his gilded armor and the Makuraner's silvered corselet both battered and grimy. "I'd sooner have killed the wizard, but you'll do," he said.

Both master horsemen, they probed at each other with their lances. Thorisin closed first, ducking under a thrust and booting his big bay at Nogruz. He threw his lance aside and yanked out his saber, sent it whistling down in a vicious stroke. Nogruz dropped his own lance and took the cut on his mailed sleeve. His mouth twisted in pain beneath his waxed mustaches, but he bought the time he needed to draw his sword as he twisted away from the Emperor's backhand pass.

Marcus only got glimpses of their single combat, as he was battling for life himself. He did see the brief sequence when a Makuraner came storming at Gavras from the flank. One of the Emperor's Haloga guardsmen shattered his lance and cut him from his horse with two thunderous strokes of the axe. A moment later another of Nogruz' followers killed the north-erner, but did not interfere in the duel.

Nogruz's desperate use of his sword arm to meet Thorisin's attack left it numb and slow, and the noble found himself in constant danger. The imperials roared and the Makurani groaned when his sword flew from his hand.

The Emperor's next cut was meant to kill. Nogruz ducked away, not quite far enough. The blow laid his cheek open to the teeth. He reeled in the saddle. Then his men did rush up to protect him and bore him back into their ranks before Gavras could strike again.

"They *must* break now!" Thorisin cried, brandishing his red-smeared saber. He urged his foot soldiers to another push at their foes. The Makurani, though, were tough as steel. They had been fighting Videssos for fifty generations and did not need leadership to keep on; it was in their blood.

Marcus was listening to find out what was happening on either side of the deadlocked center, and misliking what he heard. The noise he had dismissed as unimportant in the after-math of Avshar's fall was vital again, and it showed a Yezda win in the making on the left. Even before Mourtzouphlos pulled out of line, that had been the weakest part of the impe-rial army; the Videssians there did not have enough plainsmen to screen them from the savage archery of the nomads who fought under Avshar's banner.

From the direction of the shouts, the Videssian left was already sagging badly. If it broke, or even if its flank was dislodged from the hill country that anchored it, the Yezda would have a free road to the imperials' rear. Scaurus' guts knotted at the thought. That was how Maragha turned into a catastrophe.

The tribune looked around for Viridovix. Having risked the unthinkable once made it less so in a second crisis. Were all the Makurani to vanish as Avshar had, the tide of battle would surely turn. . . .

But the Gaul was nowhere to be seen; a thicket of Makur-aners on horseback and tall Halogai had got between him and Marcus. The Roman set out toward where he thought Virido-vix had to be, but the going was as slow and hard as it had been when he was inching his way toward Avshar.

A mounted man pounded him on the shoulder from the side. He whirled and thrust, thinking he was under attack. Thorisin Gavras knocked his point away. The Emperor wore a fierce, harried expression. "I wish I'd put the damned Arshaum over there," he said, pointing with his saber.

"Then you'd only have the same problem on the other wing."

"Maybe so, but they're grinding us on the left, and there's nothing I can do about it—all the reserves are in." Gavras was clutching his sword hilt tight enough to whiten his knuckles. He scowled. "Phos, I thought they'd scatter once you did in the wizard. And if I know you, you've had it planned for weeks, too."

With what he hoped was a suitably modest shrug, the tribune answered, "It worked better than I expected. I was afraid I'd go with him."

A messenger on a lathered, blowing horse forced his way up to Thorisin before he could reply. Marcus and a Haloga drove away an enemy lancer; the tribune wounded the Makuraner's mount, but the fellow escaped anyhow. When the Roman turned back, Gavras' face was as set as if it had been carved from marble.

"Bad news?" Marcus asked. Like Nogruz, he had to shout to be heard over the clash of weapons; the panting, oaths, and war cries of the fighting men; the pounding of horses' hooves and the beasts' squeals; and the moans and shrieks of the hurt.

"You might say so," Gavras answered in a dead voice. He pointed over the Makuraner line. "The lookouts in the hills have spotted a dust cloud heading this way—cavalry, from the speed they're making. They aren't ours." He glanced at the sun, which had slipped startlingly far into the west. "We might have hung on till dark saved us. Now. . ."

Marcus finished the sentence for himself. If the Makurani and Yezda had reinforcements coming, everything was over. Thorisin could not hold against them and could not retreat without turning his own flank.

"Make them earn it," the tribune said.

"Aye. What else is there to do?" The Emperor's eyes still held bleak courage, but a rising despair lay under it. "All for nothing," he said, so softly Scaurus could hardly make out his words. "The Yezda gobble the westlands, fresh civil war over what's left to us . . . even though you routed him, Roman, it seems Avshar wins at last."

Still more quietly, he went on, "And Phos preserve Alania and my child, for no one else will."

He spoke, Marcus thought, like Cincinnatus or one of the

other heroes from the legendary days of the earliest Republic, putting the concerns of the state ahead of those of his family. But that spirit had not saved some of those heroes from disaster, and the tribune failed to see how it would here, either.

Hot fighting was an anodyne; he threw himself into it, to have no time to think of what was coming. He spied Viridovix for a moment and laughed bitterly—he was where the tribune had been not long before, probably searching for him as he had for the Celt. He struggled back in the direction he had come, but a knot of horsemen blocked his path.

"*Skhēsómetha?*" someone asked at his elbow: "Will we hold?"

His answer, to his surprise, also came out in Greek: "*Ou tón*—On my oath, no."

Gorgidas drew in a long, hissing breath of dismay. He was sadly draggled, his helmet jammed down over one ear; sweat, dust, and blood matted his beard; his cheeks were hollow with exhaustion. The target Viridovix had given him was all but hacked to flinders.

He nodded leftward and dropped into Latin to ask, "It's there, isn't it?" The noise from that part of the field was very bad. The Yezda had bent the imperials back a long way. They knew a building victory and whooped as if it were already won.

But Scaurus had to answer, "Worse than that." A head taller than the Greek, he could see over the fighting and make out that fatal onrushing cloud of dust himself. He told Gorgidas what it meant.

Too weary to curse, Gorgidas felt his shoulders sag as though someone had loaded him down with a sack of wet sand. "Not much sense in any of this after all, is there?" he said. The thought saddened him. As physician and historian, he searched for patterns to give meaning to what went on around him. All the events of the last several years, each of no great importance by itself, had come together to produce Avshar's downfall, unexpected but perfectly just. And now a relative handful of men from the west, thanks only to their untimely arrival, would rob that downfall of its significance and produce exactly the same result as if the wizard-prince still lived. Where was the right there? he wondered, and found no answer.

Yells of fear and dismay said that imperials up and down the line were spotting the approaching army. "Hold your ground!" Thorisin Gavras' shout was urgent, but he did not show his troops the hopelessness he had revealed to Scaurus. "Running won't help—you'll be caught from behind! The best chance we have is to stand fast!" The sensible advice, the kind an underofficer might give his squad, kept the soldiers steadier than any showy exhortations.

Marcus could see the banners of Yezd through the roiling dust. He felt no worse; he had known who those warriors were. Some of their countrymen spied them, too, and were waving them forward.

Lanceheads swung down as the newcomers went into a gallop. Makurani, the tribune thought dully—they would tear through the imperial line like a rockslide smashing a plank fence.

The noise of their impact was like the end of the world: the thud of body against body, horse against horse; the racket of weapons clashing and snapping; screams of terror, and others of pain. But the enemy was crying out, not the imperials; the attack crashed into their unprotected rear.

Marcus simply stood, rigid with astonishment. Then the new battle cry echoing over the field reached his ears, and he started yelling like one possessed. The newcomers were shouting, "Wulghash!"

Grinning a crazy man's grin, Gorgidas cried, "It fits! It fits!" He hugged Scaurus, danced three steps from an obscene dance, and leaped in the air in sheer high spirits. The tribune, bemused, drove off a dismounted warrior who made for the Greek while he was temporarily deranged.

If Gorgidas' pattern was completed, that of the men who had followed Avshar shattered into ruin. Chaos ripped through their ranks at the sound of the khagan's name. Some took up the cry themselves. Others, Yezda and Makurani both, had joined the wizard-prince in preference to Wulghash—or feared he would think so. They set upon men who had been their comrades until a moment before, hewing them down lest they be assailed in turn.

With fratricide loose among them, they could not hope to conquer the bewildered imperials, or even stand against them. Seeing the enemy's disarray, Thorisin Gavras went over to the attack. The Videssians' pipes and trumpets relayed his commands: "Press ahead, strike hard! This time they break!"

And break they did, unstrung at last. As nomads will, the Yezda galloped off in all directions, like spattered quicksilver.

Once they were seen to be running, the pursuit was not fierce; the imperials were at the end of their tether, and Thorisin only too aware of how readily the nomads could flock back together. He let them go.

Instead he swung his forces in against Nogruz' Makurani. Less able to flee than the Yezda, they had no choices but fighting or surrender—and, having been beset from behind out of the blue, few would risk the latter. Battling with reckless desperation, they hurled the imperials back time after time.

But the troops who shouted Wulghash's name fought with an anger that made them a match for the countrymen now their foes. The khagan headed them. Older than most of his men, he was still a formidable warrior, making up with experience the little he had lost in strength. Too, his own rage propelled him as he hammered through his opponents.

Nogruz met him in the center of his riven force. The Makuraner noble's head was bandaged, but he had his wits back, and the full use of his right arm. They availed him nothing. Wulghash rained blows on him with a heavy, six-flanged mace, smashing his shield and shattering the sword in his hand. A final stroke crushed his skull.

When Nogruz went down, his followers saw at last that their game was over. They began shedding their proud, plumed helmets and giving up, though a few chose to fight to the end. More yielded to the imperials than to Wulghash's followers. Accepting the surrender of a nobleman who kept his arrogance even in defeat, Marcus thought he, too, would sooner take his chances with an out-and-out enemy than with an overlord he had renounced.

The tribune did not see any mistreatment of the soldiers who had submitted to Wulghash. It was as if he had no time for them, for good or ill. He prowled through their disheartened ranks, his eyes darting this way and that.

He was so intent on his search that he reached the imperials' line without noticing it, only drawing up in surprise when he saw he was face to face with foot soldiers. The Halogai and legionaries paid him no special attention, except when one asked if he wanted to surrender. He angrily shook his head.

Scaurus called a greeting, his voice a dusty croak. Wulghash's head whipped around. His broad nostrils flared in surprise. "You!" he said. "You turn up in the oddest places."

"So, if your Highness will pardon me, do you." Talking hurt; the tribune reached for his canteen. To his disgust, it was dry.

The khagan of Yezd grunted. "No trouble raising men against Avshar, or following his tracks, though we had to forage like so many dogs for the scraps his army—my army!—left." Wulghash's scowl was black. "And for what?" he said bitterly. "Aye, he's beaten here, but what of it? He's escaped me. One way or another, he'll be back to start his blood-sucking all over again."

"Not this time." In as few words as he could, Marcus told Wulghash of the wizard-prince's annihilation. He had to work to convince the khagan that Avshar had not simply gotten away through his own magic. When Wulghash finally believed him, he dismounted and embraced the tribune. His forearms were thick and muscled, like a wrestler's.

Only scattered fighting was left; most of Nogruz' men were either prisoners or down. Scaurus looked around to take stock. He spotted Viridovix not far away; even coated with dust, his fiery locks were hard to miss. The Gaul was relieving a captive of his gold-chased saber and knife. He waved in reply to the tribune's hoarse shout.

"Where might you ha' been?" he asked, prodding the dejected Makuraner along ahead of him as he ambled over. "Sure and I thought there we'd have to be swording it again, and you off doing a skulk." The twinkle in his eye took any sting from his words.

He glanced curiously at Wulgash. "And who's this stone-faced spalpeen?"

"We've met," the khagan said coldly, looking him up and down. "I remember your loose tongue."

The Gaul bristled and hefted his captive's sword. Several of Wulghash's men growled; one pointed a lance at Viridovix. Wulghash did not move, but shifted his weight to be ready for whatever happened.

Marcus said quickly, "Let be." He told Viridovix who the khagan was, and Wulghash of the Celt's part in beating Avshar. "We've fought the same foe; we shouldn't quarrel among ourselves."

"All right," the two men said in the same grudging tone. Startled, they both smiled. Wulghash stuck out his hand. Viridovix put the saber in his belt and took it, though the result was as much a trial of strength as a clasp.

"Touching," Thorisin Gavras said dryly. He showed no concern at riding up to the very edge of the Makuraner line. A fly flew in front of his face. He stared at it cross-eyed, then waved it away. "Surely the priests would approve of making a late enemy into a friend."

There was no mistaking him; the setting sun shone dazzlingly off his corselet and the gold circlet on his brow. Wulghash licked his lips hungrily. He had a good many retainers behind him. . . . "If I gave the word," he murmured, "*you* would be the late enemy."

The Emperor's eyebrows came down like storm clouds. "Who's this arrogant bastard?" he demanded of Scaurus, unconsciously imitating Viridovix. Wulghash scowled back; he did not care for being insulted to his face twice running.

The tribune did not answer at once. Instead he said testily, "*Will* someone give me a drink of water?" Thorisin blinked. Viridovix was first with a canteen. It held wine, not water. Marcus drained it. "Thanks," he breathed, sounding like himself again. He turned back to the Avtokrator, who was barely holding his temper. "Your Majesty, I present Wulghash, khagen of Yezd."

Thorisin sat straighter on his horse. All at once, the Halogai behind him were alert again, instead of tiredly slapping one another on the back and exclaiming over what a hard fight it had been. Scaurus could read the Emperor's mind; Gavras was thinking what Wulghash had a moment before, what the tribune had in the throne room at Mashiz—one quick blow, *now.* . . .

"You wouldn't have won your battle without him," Marcus said.

"What has that to do with anything?" Thorisin replied, but he gave no order.

Wulghash had followed Gavras' thought as readily as the Roman. His guards were as loyal as Thorisin's; they had chosen him when he was a fugitive and followed him across hundreds of miles to restore him to his throne. He lifted his mace, not to attack but in plain warning. "Move on me and thou't not enjoy it long, even an thou slayest me," he promised the Emperor.

"Save your 'thous' for Avshar," Thorisin said. He was still taking the measure of the khagan's horsemen, weighing the chances.

"Avshar is gone," Marcus said. "Without him setting Yezd

against Videssos, can the two of you find a way to live in peace?"

Wulghash and Gavras both looked at him in surprise; the thought did not seem to have occurred to either of them. The moment for violence slipped away. Thorisin let out a harsh chuckle. "You hear the strangest notions from him," he said to Wulghash. "Something to it, maybe."

"Maybe," Wulghash said. He turned his back on the Emperor to remount his horse. Once he was aboard it, he went on, "We will camp for the night. If we are not assailed, we will not be the ones to start the fighting."

"Agreed." Thorisin spoke with abrupt decision. "I will send someone come morning, behind a shield of truce, to see what terms we can reach. Should we fail..." He stopped. Again the tribune could think along with him.

So could Wulghash. He grinned sourly. "You'll try to rip my gizzard out," he finished.

Thorisin laughed. Here, at least, was one who did not misunderstand him.

The khagan pointed at Scaurus. "Send *him*; no one else. No, I take that back—send his friend, too, the tough, stocky one. I can read a lie on him, where this one's too smooth by half." The tale Marcus had spun in Mashiz was not forgotten, then.

"Why them?" the Emperor said, not relishing Wulghash's demand. "I have real diplomats at hand—"

"Who sucked in tedium with their mothers' milk," Wulghash interrupted. "I haven't time to waste listening to their wind. Besides, that pair rescued me and let me go free out of their comrades' camp, knowing full well who I was. I trust them—somewhat—not to play me false." He gave Thorisin a measuring stare. "Can it be you do not feel the same?"

Challenged, Gavras yielded. "As you wish, then." Because he was at bottom a just man, he added, "All in all, they've served Videssos well—as has this outlander here." He nodded at Viridovix. "Ridding the world of Avshar outweighs anything else I can think of."

The Gaul had been unwontedly quiet since the Emperor came up, not wanting to draw notice to himself. At last he saw that Thorisin really did not hold a grudge against him. He beamed in relief, saying, "Sure and your honor is a fine gentleman."

"As may be. What I am is bloody tired." With that, no one

in earshot could disagree. Thorisin turned to Scaurus. "See me in the morning for your instructions. Between now and then I intend to sleep for a week."

"Aye, sir," the tribune said, saluting. "By your leave..." At the Emperor's nod, he and Viridovix took their leave. Along the way they picked up Gorgidas, who was doubly worn with fighting and healing. After waiting for him to help a last wounded Haloga, they steered him back toward the main body of legionaries, holding him upright when he stumbled from fatigue. He muttered incoherent thanks.

"Och, Scaurus, what'll you and himself do if Gaius Philippus is after getting himself killed?" Viridovix asked. "Wouldn't that bugger up your plans for fair?"

"Phos, yes," Marcus said, surprising himself by swearing by the Videssian god. He could not imagine Gaius Philippus dying in battle; the veteran seemed indestructible. Apprehension seized him.

His heart leaped when he heard the familiar parade-ground rasp: "Form up there, you jounce-brained lugs! You think this is a fornicating picnic, just because the scrap's over for a while? Form up, the gods curse your lazy good-for-nothing bungling!"

Gorgidas roused a bit from his stupor. "Some things don't change," he said.

Darkness was swiftly falling; the Roman, Greek, and Gaul were almost on top of Gaius Philippus before he recognized them. When he did, he shouted, "All right, let's have a cheer for our tribune now—beat Avshar singlehanded, he did!"

The roar went up. "I like that," Viridovix said indignantly. "There for my health, I suppose I was."

Marcus laid a hand on his shoulder. "We both know better."

So, in fact, did Gaius Philippus. He came up to the Gaul and said in some embarrassment, "I hope you understand that was for the sake of the troops. I know nothing would have worked without your having the backbone to go through with the scheme."

"Honh! A likely tale." Viridovix tried to sound gruff, but could not help being mollified by the rare apology from the senior centurion.

It seemed the legionaries had left camp weeks ago, not half a day. Great holes were torn in their ranks; Scaurus mourned each Italian face he would never see again. With Vorenus slain on the field, Titus Pullo trudged back to the Roman ditch and earthwork like a man stunned. Their rivalry was done at last. Pinarius, the trooper who had challenged Marcus and his friends when they returned to Amorion, was dead, too, and his brother beside him, along with so many more.

And Sextus Minucius was hobbling on a stick, his right thigh tightly bound up, his face set with pain and pale from loss of blood. Having seen more battlefield injuries than he liked to remember, Marcus was not sure the young Roman would walk straight again. Maybe Gorgidas' healing would help, he thought. Still, Minucius was luckier than not—his Erene was no widow.

If anything, the Videssians and Vaspurakaners who had joined the legionaries suffered worse than the Romans, being not quite so skilled at infantry fighting. Scaurus felt a stab of guilt walking past Phostis Apokavkos' corpse; had he left the Videssian in the city slum where he found him, Apokavkos might eventually have made a successful thief.

Gagik Bagratouni limped from a wound much like Minucius'. Two "princes" were dragging his second-in-command, Mesrop Anhoghin, in a litter close behind him. Perhaps mercifully, Anhoghin was unconscious; sticky redness soaked through the bandages wrapped round his belly.

Bagratouni gave Scaurus a grave nod. "We beat them," was all he said; the victory had been too narrow for exultation.

As the legionaries began filing into camp, Laon Pakhymer led the tattered remnant of his Khatrishers up to the palisade. "May we bivouac with you?" he called to Marcus. He looked from his own men to the Romans and sadly shook his head. "There's room for the lot of us."

"Too true," Marcus said. "Of course; come ahead." He made sure an adequate guard had been detailed to watch the legionaries' prisoners, then stumbled into his tent, started to undo his armor, and fell asleep still wearing one greave.

Seeing Gaius Philippus carrying a white-painted shield on a spearshaft, Pikridios Goudeles raised a sardonic eyebrow. "First Scaurus usurps my proper function, and now you?" he said.

The veteran grunted. "You're welcome to it. I'm no diplomat, with or without any damned olive branch."

Goudeles frowned at the Roman idiom, then caught it. "Blame your honest face," he chuckled. His own features were once more as they had been at the capital; he had trimmed his hair and beard, and also shed his Arshaum leathers for a short-sleeved green robe of brocaded silk. But he was wearing his saber and kept glancing proudly at the dressing that covered an arrow wound on his arm—penpusher or no, he had been in the previous day's fighting.

"Let's get on with it," Marcus said, hefting his own shield of truce. His head was buzzing with Thorisin's commands, and the most urgent of them had been to reach an agreement quickly.

Several Halogai and Videssians saluted the tribune as he walked out of the imperial camp; they knew what he had done. Provhos Mourtzouphlos, though, turned his back. Marcus sighed. "It's wrong to wish someone on your own side had been killed in action, but—"

"Why?" Gaius Philippus asked bluntly. "He's a worse enemy than a whole clan of Yezda."

Vultures and carrion crows flapped into the air, screeching harsh protests, as the Romans went through the battleground. Wild dogs and foxes scuttled out of their path. Flies, Avshar's and others, swarmed over the littered corpses. Those were already beginning to swell and stink under the late summer sun.

Makuraner sentries, apparently forewarned to expect Scaurus and Gaius Philippus, led them to Wulghash. On their way, they took them through the entire camp, which was even more sprawled and disorderly than the one they had left not long before.

The tribune caught his breath sharply when they rounded a last corner and approached Wulghash's pavilion. In front of it stood a long row of heads, sixty or seventy of them. Some still wore the gilded or silvered helms of high officers.

"I don't see Tabari," Marcus said.

"You were looking for him, too, eh? Let's hope he had sense or luck enough to stay in Mashiz."

One head still seemed to be trying to say something. Scaurus wondered uneasily if awareness could linger for a few seconds after the axe came down.

Gaius Philippus' thoughts went in another direction. He said, "I was wondering why we hadn't been shown any prisoners. Now I know. With the dangerous ones shortened, Wulghash drafted the rest to fill out his army."

Marcus smacked his fist into his palm, annoyed he had not

made the connection himself. It fit what he knew of Wulghash's bold, ruthless character. Following the logic a step further, he said, "Then he'll be looking to bring the scattered Yezda back under his command, too."

The words were hardly out of his mouth when a double handful of nomads rode by on their ponies. They scowled, recognizing the Romans' gear. Marcus was also frowning. "Something else we were meant to see, I think."

"Aye. Just what Gavras is afraid of, too."

The tribune's suspicion that the show had been planned grew sharper when the guides, who had disappeared into Wulghash's tent, chose that moment to emerge and beckon the Romans forward. One of the Makurani held the gray felt flap wide so they could enter.

The tent held no regal finery; its furnishings were an incongruous blend of the ornate Makuraner and spare Yezda styles —whatever had been easy to scrape up, Marcus guessed. The only exception was the large quantity of sorcerer's gear—codices, a cube of rose crystal, several elaborately sealed jars, an assortment of knives with handles that looked unpleasantly like flesh, and other oddments—now heaped carelessly in a corner.

Wulghash saw the tribune glance that way. "Useless preparations, as it turned out," he remarked.

"Like the performance you put on for us out there?" Marcus asked politely.

The khagan was unfazed. "It showed what I intended. I am not as weak as Gavras thinks—and I grow stronger by the hour."

"No doubt," Gaius Philippus nodded. He and Scaurus had agreed that he should deliver Thorisin's ultimatum. "That's why the Emperor gives you three days to begin withdrawing to Yezd. After that the truce is over, and he will attack without warning."

The senior centurion's bluntness made Wulghash's wide, fleshy nostrils flare with anger. "Does he? Will he?" he cried. "If that's what he meant by talking, let him come today, and I will speak a language he understands." He tugged his saber halfway out of its scabbard.

"You'd lose," Marcus said. "We were holding—barely, I grant, but holding—against the whole army Avshar had mustered, and you don't have much more than the core left. We'd trounce you. Why shouldn't you go home? This is not your country and never was. You have your own throne again—see to your land, and your hold on it."

The khagan looked so grim Marcus was afraid he would not be able to hold his temper. The trouble, he knew, was that Wulghash was as eager to conquer Videssos as Avshar had been. He had to be burning like vitriol inside because his charge, instead of ruining the wizard-prince, had only saved the imperial forces.

But he had been a ruler for many years, and learned realism. His bluster aside, Thorisin could crush him if willing to pay the butcher's bill. He breathed heavily for close to a minute, not trusting himself to speak, then finally ground out, "Has Gavras any other little, ah, requests for me?"

Again it was Gaius Philippus who answered. "Only one. Since all the nomads, not only from this latest invasion but from years gone by, too, have come to Videssos without his leave, he bids you order them back to Yezd and keep them there from now on."

Scaurus waited for Wulghash to explode again. Instead he threw back his head and laughed in the Romans' faces. "Then he may as well bid me tie all the winds up in a sack and keep them in the sky. The nomads in Videssos are beyond my control, or that of any other man. They go as they will; I cannot *make* them do anything."

As that was exactly what the tribune had thought when Thorisin gave him the instruction, he had no good answer ready. Wulghash went on, "For that matter, I would not recall the nomads if I could. Though they are of my blood, I have no use for them, save sometimes in battle. You've seen who backs me—Makurani. Civilized men.

"The nomads spread strife wherever they go. They plunder, they kill, they ruin farms, wreck trade, empty cities, and drain my coffers. When some of the clan chiefs wanted to harry the Empire instead of Yezd, I helped them on their way and sent more after them. Good riddance, I say. Had they all gone, my rule would have been ten times easier."

Marcus was suddenly reminded of the Romans after they had conquered Greece—captured by their captors in art, in literature, in luxury, in their entire way of life. Wulghash was much the same. His people had been barbarians, but he seized on the higher culture of Makuran with a convert's zeal.

The khagan had another reason to resent the folk from whom he had sprung. His hands bunched into fists, and he glowered down at the sleeping-mats on the ground as he paced between them. He said, "And the Yezda chose Avshar over me, followed him, worshiped him." That rankled yet, Scaurus thought. "It was not just his magic; he and they suited each other, with their taste for blood. So, since you serve Gavras, tell him he is welcome to the nomads he has. I do not want them back."

After his outburst, there did not seem to be much room for discussion. "We'll take your words back to the Emperor," Marcus promised in a formal voice, "and tell him of your determination."

"Can't say I blame you, either, looking at things from your side," Gaius Philippus added.

Wulghash softly pounded him on the shoulder in gratitude. "I said to Gavras' face you were an honest man."

"Won't stop me from cutting you up a few days from now, if I have to," the veteran answered stolidly. "Like your Makurani, I know which side I'm on."

"Be it so, then," the khagan said.

"He won't commit himself to getting the nomads out, eh?" Thorisin asked.

"No," Scaurus replied. "He disowns them. If anything, I think he hates them worse than you do. And in justice," he went on, and saw the Emperor roll his eyes at the phrase, "I don't see what he could do. Yavlak and the other clan-chiefs are their own law. They wouldn't heed his commands any more than yours, and he hasn't the power to compel them."

"I know that," Gavras said placidly. If he was angry at Wulghash's rejection of his demand, he hid it well. In fact, he looked pleased with himself, in a foxy way. "I wanted to hear them denied from his own lips."

Marcus tugged at his ear, not following whatever the Emperor had in mind. Beside him, Gaius Philippus shrugged almost invisibly.

"Never mind," Thorisin said. "Just make sure you see me tomorrow morning before you go off and haggle with him again. Now get out. I have more people to see than the two of you." He did sound in good spirits, Marcus thought.

The Romans bowed and left. Scaurus heard Thorisin shouting for his steward: "Glykas! Come here, damn it, I need you. Fetch me Mourtzouphlos and Arigh the Arshaum." A little pause. "No, you lazy lackwit, I don't know where they are. Find them, or find another job."

The Makuraner sentry spat at Marcus' feet when he and Gaius Philippus came up to Wulghash's encampment. The tribune thought he was about to be attacked in spite of the shield of truce he was carrying. He got ready to throw it away and go for his sword.

"Expected as much," Gaius Philippus said. He had also shifted into a fighting stance. Scaurus nodded.

But having relieved his feelings, the sentry haughtily turned his back and led the Romans to the khagan's tent. This time they went straight there. Wulghash's troopers shook fists as they passed. Someone threw a lump of horsedung. It smacked against Gaius Philippus' upraised truce shield, staining the smooth white paint.

Wulghash was outside the pavilion, talking with his bodyguards. One of them pointed to the Romans. The khagan rumbled something deep in his throat. He jerked his chin at Gaius Philippus' shield. "A fitting symbol for a broken peace," he growled.

"As far as Thorisin is concerned, the truce still holds," Marcus answered. "Have you been assailed here?"

"Spare me the protests of innocence, at least," Wulghash said. "I'd sooner believe in a virgin whore. You know as well as I what Gavras did in the dead of night—sent out his Videssians and those vicious savages from Shaumkhiil to harry my warriors in their scattered camps. Hundreds must have died."

"I repeat: Were you and yours attacked here?"

Scaurus' monotone made the khagan look up sharply. "No," he said, his own voice suddenly wary.

"Then I submit to you that the peace between you and the Emperor has not been breached. You told us yesterday that you had no use for the Yezda, that you could not force them to obey you, and that you did not want them. In that case, Thorisin has every right to deal with them as he sees fit. Or do you only claim them as yours when you gain some advantage from it?"

Wulghash flushed all the way up to the balding crown of his head. "I was speaking," he said tightly, "of the Yezda already in Videssos."

"That doesn't do it," Gaius Philippus said. "You were the

one complaining how the buggers with Avshar kissed his boot instead of yours. Now you want 'em back. All right. The way I see it, Gavras has the right to stop you if he can. They weren't part of the deal. And as for this," he glanced at the shield of truce, "your soldier flung the horseturd."

Marcus put in, "Thorisin could have attacked you here instead of the Yezda, but he held off. He isn't interested in destroying you—"

"Because it would cost him too dear."

"As may be. It would cost you more; he is stronger than you now. And while he is stronger, he intends to see you gone from Videssos. I warn you, he is deadly serious over his ultimatum. If he sees no movement from you come day after tomorrow, he'll move on you with everything he has. And there are fresh troops just in from Garsavra."

The last was bluff, but Thorisin had set the groundwork for it by lighting several hundred extra campfires the night before. Wulghash bit his lip, examining Gaius Philippus closely. But the senior centurion revealed nothing, for the khagan had slightly misread his man. Gaius Philippus would always say what he thought, but a team of fifty horses could not have dragged a stratagem from him.

Recalling what Wulghash had told him when they were just out of the tunnels below Mashiz, Marcus said, "I would also wish we were friends as well as what my people call guest-friends." Wulghash took his meaning, and he went on, "As a friend, I would say your best course lies in retiring. You cannot succeed against Thorisin here and you need to reestablish yourself in Yezd."

"I don't think the two of us will ever be friends, whatever we might want," the khagan answered steadily. "For now, worse luck, I fear you are right, but I am not done with Videssos yet. Defend it if you can, but it is old and worn. One good push—"

"I've heard Namdaleni talk the same way, but we survived them." Scaurus thought back to Drax the opportunist, and hotheaded Soteric. Remembering her brother reminded him of Helvis and how she had scorned him for calling the Videssians *we*. He shrugged, which made Wulghash scratch his head. He was content with his choice.

The Yezda khagan was not one to leave a point quickly. "If not in my day, then in my son's," he said.

"How is Khobin?" Marcus asked, dredging the name up

from Wulghash's use of it in the palace banquet hall.

"Alive and well, last I heard," Wulghash said gruffly. But his eyes narrowed, and his left eyebrow rose a fraction of an inch; the tribune knew he had gained a point. Wulghash's chuckle had a grim edge to it. "The hired killers Avshar sent out botched their job. They weren't his best; he must have thought Khobin not worth worrying about."

"I'm glad, and glad he was wrong."

"And I," the khagan answered. "He's a likely youngster."

"That's all very well, but it grows no barley," Gaius Philippus said, dragging them back to the issue at hand. "What do you propose doing about pulling out?"

Wulghash grunted, but Gaius Philippus' forthrightness had made him ask for the veteran. "If I had my choice, I would fight," the khagan said. "But the choice is not mine—and Gavras, it seems," he added wryly, "will not let me seize it. So . . . I will withdraw." He spat that out as if it tasted bad.

Scaurus could not help letting out a slow, quiet breath of relief. "The Emperor pledges that you will not be harassed as long as you are retiring in peace."

"Big of him," Wulghash muttered. He seemed surprised and not very happy to see the Romans still in front of him; he must have looked on them as symbols of his failure to hold his ground. "You have what you want, don't you? If you do, we're finished. Go away."

As they walked back to the imperial camp, Gaius Philippus said darkly, "I don't know about you, but I'm sick and tired of everyone telling me, 'Go.' Next time someone tries it, he'll know just where to go, I promise."

"You'd never make an ambassador," Marcus said.

"Good."

That evening, though, having heard their report, Pikridios Goudeles disagreed with the tribune. "You should be proud of yourselves," he told the Romans. "For amateurs, you did very well. Thorisin's unhappy because he can't slaughter Wulghash; Wulghash is disgusted because he has to go home. And after all, what is diplomacy," he paused to hone his epigram, "but the art of leaving everyone dissatisfied?"

Sullenly, Wulghash withdrew toward the west. Gavras sent out a company of Videssian horsemen to make sure he really was retreating, much as Shenuta had kept a close eye on the Arshaum when they were passing through his territory.

A couple of days later, after it became clear the khagan was pulling back, Gaius Philippus startled Marcus by requesting leave for the first time since the tribune had known him. "It's yours, of course," Marcus said at once. "Do you mind my asking why?"

The veteran, usually so direct, looked uncomfortable. "Thought I'd borrow a horse from the Khatrishers, do a bit of riding out. Sight-seeing, you might say."

"Sight-seeing?" Gaius Philippus made the most unlikely tourist Scaurus could imagine. "What on earth does this miserable plain have worth seeing?"

"Places we've been before," the senior centurion said vaguely. He shifted from foot to foot like a small boy who needs to be excused. "I might get up to Aptos, for instance."

"Why would anyone want to go to—" Marcus began, and then shut up with a snap. If Gaius Philippus had finally worked up the nerve to court Nerse Phorkaina, that was his business. The tribune did say, "Take care of yourself. There probably are still Yezda prowling the road."

"Stragglers I'm not afraid of, but Avshar's army went through there. That does worry me." The veteran rode out a couple of hours later, sitting his borrowed horse without grace but managing it with the same matter-of-fact competence he displayed in nearly everything he did.

"After his sweetling, is he?" Viridovix asked, watching the Roman trot past the burial parties busy at their noisome work.

"Yes, though I doubt he'd admit it on the rack."

Instead of laughing at the centurion, Viridovix sighed heavily and said, "Och, I hope he finds her hale and all to bring back. E'en a great gowk like him deserves a touch o' happiness, for all his face'd crack to show it."

Gorgidas spoke in Greek. Marcus translated for Viridovix: "'Count no man happy before his end,'" Solon's famous warning to Croesus the Lydian king. The physician continued tartly, "The mere presence of the object of one's infatuation does not guarantee delight, let me assure you."

The tribune and the Gaul carefully looked elsewhere. Rakio had not returned to the legionary camp after the battle, save to get his gear. Having taken up with one of the Namdalener knights, he left Gorgidas without a good-bye or a backward glance.

"Don't stand there mooning on my account," the Greek snapped. "I knew he was fickle when we started; to give him his due, he never pretended otherwise. My pride isn't badly stung, or my heart. It's the better matches that leave the lasting sorrow."

"Aye." That was Scaurus and Viridovix together, softly. For a few seconds each of the three men was lost in his thoughts, Gorgidas remembering Quintus Glabrio; Viridovix, Seirem; and Marcus, Alypia and Helvis both.

Where nothing else would have, the thought that his second love might go as the first had almost kept him from pressing Thorisin on their bargain. His combat injuries were healing. But when he touched it unexpectedly, the wound Helvis had dealt pained him as much as it had when it was fresh. He flinched from opening himself to the risk of such hurt again.

Well, what are you going to do, then? he asked himself angrily—hide under a rock the rest of your life so the rain can't find you?

The answer inside him was quiet, but very firm.

No.

The Emperor's Haloga guardsmen were used to the tribune asking for an audience with their master. They saluted with clenched fists over their hearts; one ducked into the imperial tent to find out how long a wait Scaurus would have. "Yust a few minutes," he promised as he reemerged.

Actually it was closer to half an hour. Marcus made small talk with the Halogai, swapping stories and comparing scabs. Apprehension tightened his belly like an ill-digested meal.

Glykas the steward stuck his head out and peered round, blinking in the bright sunshine, till he spied the Roman. "He'll see you now," he said. Scaurus walked forward on legs suddenly leaden.

Thorisin looked up from the stack of papers he so despised. With Videssos' enemies bested for the moment, he had to start paying attention to the business of running the Empire again. He shoved the parchments to one side with a grunt of relief, waited for Marcus to bow, and overlooked, as usual, the tribune's omitting the prostration. "What now?" he asked in a neutral voice.

"Perhaps—" Marcus began, and was mortified to have the word come out as a nervous croak. He steadied himself and tried again: "Perhaps it might be better if we talked under the rose." Gavras frowned; the tribune flushed, realizing he had rendered the Latin phrase literally. He explained.

"'Under the rose,' eh? I rather like that," the Emperor said. He dismissed Glykas, then turned back to Scaurus, his expression watchful now. "And so?" he prompted, folding his arms across his chest. Even in the ordinary linen tunic and baggy wool breeches he was wearing, he radiated authority. He'd had three years to grow into the imperial office, and it fit him.

Marcus felt his power, though he was not so intimidated as a Videssian would have been. He took a deep breath, then, as if to beat back his trepidation, and plunged straight ahead. "As we agreed in Videssos, I'd like you to think about me as a husband for your niece—if Alypia wishes it, of course."

The Emperor steepled his fingers, making Scaurus wait. "Did we have such an agreement?" he asked lazily. "As I recall, there were no witnesses."

"You know we did!" the tribune yelped, appalled. Denial was the last tack he had foreseen Gavras taking. "Phos heard you, if no one else."

"You win nothing with me for using the good god's name; I know you for a heathen," Thorisin jeered. But he went on musingly, "To be just, you never tried that trick, either. Don't tell me so stubborn a one as you has actually changed his mind?"

The squabbling among Phos' sects still struck Marcus as insane, and he had no idea how to pick the true creed—if there was one—from the baying pack. But after his experience on the field, he could no longer ignore the Empire's faith. "I may have," he said, as honest a reply as he could find.

"Hrmmp. Most men in your shoes would come see me festooned with enough icons to turn a lance, or singing hymns, if they had the voice for it."

The tribune shrugged.

"Hrmmp," Thorisin repeated. He pulled at his beard. "You don't make it easy, do you?" He gave a short snort of laughter. "I wonder how many times I've said that, eh, Roman?" He grinned as if they were conspirators.

Marcus shrugged again. The Emperor was drifting into that unfathomable sportive mood of his. Marcus realized that any response he made might be wrong. He cast about for arguments to prove to Gavras that he was no danger to him, but stood mute.

Gavras slammed the palms of his hands down, hard. His papers jumped; one rolled-up scroll fell off the desk. His voice came muffled from behind it as he leaned over to pick up the parchment. "Well, all right, go ahead and ask her."

Triggered by the silence breaking, Marcus gabbled, "As a foreigner, I'd be no threat to the throne because the people would never accept—" He was nearly through the sentence before his brain registered what his ears had heard. "Ask her?" he whispered. The Avtokrator had not invited him to sit, but he sank into the nearest chair. It was that or the floor; his knees would not hold him up.

Tossing the scroll back onto the desktop, Thorisin ignored the breach of protocol. "I said so, didn't I? After Zemarkhos, Avshar—Avshar!—and even a peace of sorts with Yezd, I could hardly refuse you. And besides—" He turned serious in an instant. "—if you know anything about me, you'd best know this: I keep my bargains."

"Then the argument was a sham, and you were going to say yes to me all along?"

The sly grin came back to Gavras' face. "What if I was?"

"Why, you miserable bastard!"

"Who's a bastard, you cross-eyed midwife's mistake?" Thorisin roared back. They were both laughing now, Marcus mostly in relief. The Emperor found a jug of wine, shook it to see how much it held—enough to suit him. He uncorked it, gulped, put the stopper back, and tossed it to Scaurus. As the tribune was drinking, he went on. "Admit it, your heart would've stopped if I'd told you aye straight out."

Marcus started to say something, swallowed wrong, and sputtered and choked, spraying wine every which way. Thorisin pounded him on the back. "Thanks," he wheezed.

He stood and clasped the Emperor's hand, which was as hard and callused as his own. "My heart?" he said. "This would be the first time you'd ever shown a counterfeit copper's worth of care for my health if that were true."

"So it would," Gavras said calmly, unashamed at being caught out. "Would it make you feel better if I admitted I was enjoying every second of the charade?"

Marcus took another drink, this time successfully. "Nothing," he said, "could make me feel better than I do now."

* * *

The imperial army was breaking camp, shaking itself into marching order for the return to the capital, and Gaius Philippus had not returned. "No need for you to come with us," Arigh told Scaurus. "My lads'll find him, never fear." He rode at the head of a company of Arshaum.

"Me, I'd bet on us," Laon Pakhymer said; he had a band of his own horsemen behind him. "The old hardcase's ghost would haunt us for spite if we didn't do everything we could for him." The Khatrisher would head into dangerous country after Gaius Philippus before letting on that he liked him.

Marcus paid no attention to either of them, but methodically saddled his horse. He mounted, then turned from one man to the other. "Let's go."

They trotted through the battlefield. The stench of the unburied horses and Yezda was beginning to fade; scavengers had reduced many of them to bare bones. Raw mounds of earth topped the mass graves of the fallen imperial soldiers. Broken weapons and bits of harness were starting to get dusty; whatever was worth looting had long since been taken.

Behind the search party, someone let out a yowl. Scaurus turned to see Viridovix galloping after them. "Why did ye no tell me you were for chasing down t'auld man?" he complained to the tribune once he had caught up. Mischief gleamed in his eyes. "Och, what a show—himself in love. Strange as a wolf growing cabbages, I warrant."

"Maybe so, but I'd be careful twitting him over it," Marcus advised.

"That I ken."

Stretches of ground pocked with hoofprints showed where Avshar's camp, and Wulghash's, had lain. Not far past them, a Khatrisher scout whooped and pointed. Marcus peered ahead, but his eyes were not good enough to pick out the rider the scout had spotted before the fellow went to earth, letting his horse run free. The search party hurried ahead, but short of firing the scrubby brush by the side of the road or sending in dogs, no one was going to find the suspicious traveler in a hurry.

But when he heard his name shouted, Gaius Philippus cautiously emerged from cover. Recognizing Scaurus, Viridovix, and then Pakhymer, he lowered his *gladius*.

"What's all this about?" he growled. "Where I come from, they don't send this many out after parricides."

"A vice of yours we hadn't known," Laon Pakhymer said, drawing a glare. It did not bother him, which only annoyed Gaius Philippus more. "And you'll pay for that pony if it's come to any harm," the Khatrisher added; three of his troopers and a couple of Arshaum were chasing the beast down.

Marcus cut through the senior centurion's obscenities to explain why they had gone searching for him. Gaius Philippus relaxed, a little. "It's nice of you, I'm sure, but sooner or later I'd have turned up."

"Not a bad brag," Arigh said, which touched him off all over again. Scaurus did not think he had been boasting. If anyone could travel the westlands alone, it was Gaius Philippus.

After his curses ran down, he reclaimed his horse and headed back with the search party, still grumbling that they had wasted their time. Both to distract him and out of curiosity, Marcus asked, "Did you manage to get all the way up to Aptos?"

"Said I was going to, didn't I?"

"And?"

"Not a whole lot left of the town," Gaius Philippus said, frowning. "The Yezda did go through with Avshar, and wrecked the place. The keep held out, though, and Nerse was able to save a lot of the townsfolk. Some others got away to the hills. If there's a calm spell, they can rebuild."

"Nerse, you say? Ho, now we come down to it," Viridovix exclaimed.

Gaius Philippus tensed; his face went hard and suspicious. Marcus wanted to kick the Celt and waited helplessly for him to come out with some crudity—here as nowhere else, Gaius Philippus was vulnerable.

But Viridovix, who had known loss of his own, was not out to wound. He asked only, "And will you be needing groomsmen, too, like Scaurus here?"

Even that simple, friendly question was almost too much. The senior centurion answered in a low-voiced growl. "No." He turned to Marcus. "Groomsmen, eh? Nice going—you pulled it off. I hope I'll be one of them."

"You'd better be." Gaius Philippus' smile was such an obvious false front that the tribune asked gently, "She turned you down?"

"What?" The veteran looked at him in surprise. "No. I never asked her."

That was too much for Viridovix. "You didna ask her?" he howled, clapping a hand to his forehead. "Are y'unhinged? You went gallivanting on up a couple days' ride, likely near got yoursel' killed a time or two..." He paused, but Gaius Philippus' bleak expression neither confirmed nor denied. "And you stopped in for a mug o' wine and a how-do-ye-do, then took off again? Och, the waste of it, man, the waste! If it were me, now—"

"Shut up," the senior centurion said with such cold anger that the Gaul actually did. "If it were you, you'd've talked her ear off and made her love every minute of it. Well, I haven't your tongue, loose at both ends, and I haven't anything much to offer her, either. She's a landed noble, and what am I? A mercenary who owns a sword and a mail shirt and precious little else." He glanced toward Pakhymer. "I had to hit up Laon here for a horse to make the trip."

Viridovix did not reply in words, merely pointed at Scaurus. Gaius Philippus turned brick red, but said stubbornly, "He's him; I'm me."

"Honh!" Viridovix said. Only the warning in Gaius Philipus' eyes kept him from going further.

The sad thing, Marcus thought, was that the veteran was right; he had grown too set in his ways to know how to change even when he wanted to. "You got there and back all right; that's what counts." He bobbed his head at Arigh. "Let's head back."

"Took you long enough," the Arshaum said. Like Pakhymer, he had waited halfway between boredom and irritation while the Romans and Viridovix talked, for they still favored Latin among themselves.

Everyone rode in silence for some time. They were nearly back to camp when Gaius Philippus said, "You know, Celt, you might have something after all. Maybe one of these days I'll get back to Aptos again and do the talking I should have done this time."

"Sure and you will," Viridovix said consolingly, but Marcus heard the melancholy edge to his voice. Gaius Philippus had no trouble making plans when he was moving directly away from his goal. Carrying them out was something else.

Thorisin Gavras had not known of the search party. Only a rear guard was left at the campsite, a garrison to hold the gap in the hills against Yezda raiders. But the main body of troops had hardly traveled a mile; Scaurus could still see companies of men and horses through the inevitable cloud of dust they kicked up.

"Let's race it!" Pakhymer shouted, spurring his pony ahead. "First one to the baggage train collects a silverpiece from everybody else!" He had given himself a head start, but his lead did not last long; an Arshaum shot past him almost before the wager was out of his mouth.

Galloping along in the middle of the laughing, shouting pack, Marcus knew he was going to lose his money. He did not care. Ahead lay Amorion, and beyond it Videssos the city. He was going home.

XIV

Last Night's Rain Still Dripped From Overhanging Eaves and trickled out of drainpipes, but the storm had finally blown through the capital. The day was clear and brisk, more like early spring than autumn.

"About time," Marcus said, eyeing the bright sunshine and crisp-edged shadows with relief. "If we'd had to put things off again, I think I would have screamed."

Taso Vones reached up to pat him on the shoulder. "Now, now," he said. "The people are entitled to their spectacle. A wedding procession isn't nearly as much fun if you have to get wet to watch it."

Nepos the priest shook a finger at the Khatrisher diplomat. "You have a cynical view of the world, friend Taso." He did his best to sound reproachful but his plump face was made for mirth, and he could not help smiling.

"I, cynical? Not at all, sir; merely realistic." Vones drew himself up, the caricature of affronted dignity. "If you want cynicism, look to this one." He pointed Scaurus' way. "Why else would he have chosen you for a groomsman, if not to get at least one Videssian into the party?"

"Oh, go howl, Taso," Marcus said, nettled. "I chose him because he's a friend. Besides, there's Goudeles over there, and Lemmokheir. And Skylitzes would be here, too, if he were up to it." Among other battle wounds, the dour imperial officer had suffered a broken thigh when his horse was killed and crushed him beneath it. He was mending, but could hardly hobble yet, even with two canes.

Still, as it did more often than not, Vones' sly needling

held a germ of truth. Almost all the men gathered together in the little antechamber off the Grand Courtroom were not Videssians. Their various versions of finery gave them a curiously mismatched look.

Gaius Philippus was in full military gear, from hobnailed *caligae* to crested helm; his scarlet cape of rank hung from his shoulders. Marcus wished he could remember everything the veteran had called some officious chamberlain who tried to persuade him to don Videssian ceremonial raiment.

Viridovix wore a burnished corselet. Below it, a pair of baggy Videssian trousers made a fair substitute for the tighter breeches his own nation favored. His head was bare, the better to display his ruddy locks, which he had washed with limewater until they stood up stiff as a lion's mane. "Gi' the lassies summat to look at," he was saying to Gorgidas.

For the occasion, the Greek had chosen his own people's garb, a knee-length chiton of white wool. Scaurus suspected the simple garment had originally been a blanket.

"Better than my skinny shanks, at least," Gorgidas said to Viridovix. He sighed. "You don't have to worry about drafts, either."

"You'd never get away with that thin sheet on the steppe," Arigh said. "Everything would freeze off at the first blizzard, and you'd sing soprano like any other eunuch." The Arshaum chief wore rawhide boots, leather trousers, a shirt of fine soft suede, and a wolfskin jacket. Marcus was gladder to have him in the wedding party than Arigh was to be there. He had hoped to sail for Prista with his men to start back to Shaumkhiil, but the onset of the stormy season had stooped shipping across the Videssian Sea until spring.

Senpat Sviodo was telling Gagik Bagratouni a joke in their own language. The *nakharar* threw back his head and bellowed laughter at the punch line. His wicker helmet, a traditional Vaspurakaner headgear, fell to the floor. He stooped to retrieve it, hardly favoring his injured leg. Senpat, as usual, preferred the three-crowned tasseled cap that looked dumpy on most of his countrymen.

Nepos, of course, was in the blue robe of the Videssian priesthood. Beside him stood Laon Pakhymer. The cavalry commander wore Videssian-style clothes, but not of a sort to gladden a protocol officer's heart. For reasons only he knew, he had chosen to dress like a street ruffian, with tights of a brilliant, bilious green surmounted by a linen shirt with enormous puffed sleeves tied tight at the wrists.

That left only Goudeles, Leimmokheir, and Taso Vones among the groomsmen in formal robes that reached to their ankles. And no one would have mistaken Taso for an imperial, not with his vast, bushy beard. Taron Leimmokheir was shaggy, too, but the admiral's thick gray hair and somber countenance were well-known in the city.

A eunuch steward stuck his head into the room. "Take your places, my lords, if you would be so kind. We are about to begin."

Marcus started to go to the head of the line that was forming and almost fell over. His own ceremonial robes were no lighter than Gaius Philippus' armor, and harder to move in. Gold and silver threads shot all through the maroon samite only added to its weight, as did the pearls and precious stones at the collar, over his breast, and running down along his sleeves. His wide gold belt, ornamented with more rubies, sapphires, amethysts, and delicate enamelwork, weighed more than the sword belt he was used to.

The steward sniffed at his slowness and paused to make sure everyone was in proper position. Turning his back, he said, "This way. Just as we rehearsed it," he added reassuringly.

No Videssian courtier in his right mind left anything to chance at an imperial function; the tribune had the plan of the procession down almost as thoroughly as Roman infantry drill. The thick, pleated silk of his robe rustled as he followed the eunuch.

He was glad of the weight of the material as soon as he stepped outside. The breeze had a raw edge to it. Behind him he heard teeth chattering, Arigh's chuckle, and Gorgidas' hissed retort: "Go ahead, amuse yourself. I hope you get heatstroke in the High Temple." Arigh laughed louder.

"Och, I ken this courtyard," Viridovix said. "We fought here to put Gavras on the throne and cast what-was-his-name, the young Sphrantzes, off it."

And rescued Alypia from Ortaias' uncle Vardanes, Marcus remembered, and drove Avshar out of the city. Had it really been more than two years ago? It seemed yesterday.

The bronze doors of the Grand Courtroom, which were covered with a profusion of magnificent reliefs, opened noiselessly. They had taken damage when the legionaries forced them that day, but the skilled Videssian artisans' repairs were all but unnoticeable.

First through the doors was another eunuch to direct traffic. Behind him came a dozen parasol bearers, markers of the presence of the Emperor. Thorisin Gavras wore a robe even more gorgeous than Scaurus'; only the toes of his red boots peeped from under its bejeweled hem. The imperial crown, a low dome encrusted with still more precious stones, gleamed golden on his head. Only the sword at the Emperor's belt detracted from his splendor; it was the much-battered saber he always carried.

A platoon of Videssian nobles followed Gavras, bureaucrats and soldiers together for once. Marcus spotted Provhos Mourtzouphlos, who looked as though he had an extraordinarily bad taste in his mouth. His robe was of a green that managed to outdo Pakhymer's tights.

The eye kept coming back to it, in disbelief and horrid fascination. Marcus heard Gaius Philippus mutter, "Now I know what color a hangover is." He wondered if Mourtzouphlos had chosen the dreadful thing as a silent protest against the wedding. If he was reduced to such petty gestures, his enmity was safe to ignore.

Under the watchful gaze of its chamberlain, the imperial party took its place some yards ahead of Scaurus and his comrades. He promptly forgot about it, for still another steward was leading Alypia Gavra and her attendant ladies into place between the two groups.

Her gown was of soft white silk, with silver threads running through it and snowy lace at the cuffs; it seemed spun from moonlight. A silver circlet confined her sleek brown hair.

She smiled and touched her throat as she walked by Marcus. The necklace she wore, of gold, emeralds, and mother-of-pearl, was not of a piece with the rest of her costume, but neither of them would have exchanged it for one that was.

He smiled back, wishing he could say something to her. Since returning to the city, he had only seen her once or twice, under the most formal circumstances. It had been easier when they were surreptitious lovers than properly affianced. But Thorisin had warned, "No more scandal," and they thought it wiser to obey. There was not much waiting left.

"Straighten your collar, will you, Pikridios!" shrilled Goudeles' wife, Tribonia. She was a tall, angular, sallow woman whose deep blue dress suited neither her figure nor her complexion. As the bureaucrat fumbled to fix the imaginary flaw, she complained to anyone who would listen, "Do you see how he takes no pains with himself? The most lazy, slovenly man . . ." The tribune, who knew Goudeles to be a fastidious dandy, wondered whether he had married her for money or position. It could hardly have been love.

Irrepressible, Nevrat Sviodo made a comic shrug behind Tribonia's back, then grinned triumphantly at Marcus. He nodded back, very glad his mistaken advances the year before had not cost him a friend, or rather, two.

Nevrat was the only non-Videssian in Alypia's party. Senpat said, "Some of the highborn ladies were scandalized when the princess chose her."

"I notice no one has withdrawn," Scaurus said.

An honor guard of Halogai and Romans fell in at the procession's head; another company took its place to the rear. Palace servitors formed a line on either side. Seeing everything ready at last, Thorisin's steward blew a sharp note on a pitch pipe. He strutted forward to set the pace, as if the day had been planned to celebrate him alone.

The wide pathways through the gardens of the palace compound had few spectators along them: a gardener, a cook, a mason and his wife and children, a squad of soldiers. As soon as the procession reached the forum of Palamas, all that changed. If twin sets of streamers had not kept the chosen path open, there would have been no pushing through the sea of humanity jamming the square.

Thorisin's iron-lunged herald cried out, "Rejoice in the wedding of the Princess Alypia Gavra and the Yposevastos Scaurus! Rejoice! Rejoice!" The herald's accent made the tribune's name come out as "Skavros," which did not sound too very alien to the ears of the city populace. The imposing title the Emperor had conferred on him—its significance, more or less, was "second minister," which could mean anything or nothing—also made him less obviously foreign.

One of the servants pressed a small but heavy sack into his hands. As he had been instructed, he tossed goldpieces into the crowd, now right, now left. Up ahead, the Emperor was doing the same. So were the servitors, but their sacks were filled with silver.

The sidewalks of Middle Street were also packed tight with

cheering onlookers. Marcus did not flatter himself that the hurrahs were for him. The city folk, fickle and restless, applauded any spectacle, and this one was doubly delightful because of the prospect of largesse.

"Rejoice! Rejoice!" At slow march, the procession passed the three-story red granite government office building. Marcus looked at it fondly, large and ugly though it was. Had he not happened to meet Alypia coming out of it last Midwinter's Day, he would not be here now.

"Rejoice!" The herald turned north about a quarter mile past the government offices. Once off Middle Street, the crowds were thinner. With every step, Phos' High Temple dominated more of the skyline; soon it *was* the skyline. The gilded globes topping its four spires shone bright as the sun they symbolized.

The walled courtyard around the High Temple was as crowded as the plaza of Palamas had been. The palace servitors threw out great handfuls of money; tradition required them to empty their sacks. The canny Videssians knew that perfectly well and thronged to where the pickings were best.

The honor guard deployed at the foot of the broad stairway leading up to the High Temple. Already waiting on the stairs were all the surviving Romans hale enough to stand. Their arms shot up in salute as Marcus approached.

The nobles and officials in Thorisin's party peeled away from the Avtokrator to take their places on the steps, forming an aisleway through which he, the bride, the groom, and their attendants could pass. "Step smartly now!" urged the chamberlain in charge of Scaurus and his companions. The tribune hurried forward. Alypia, her ladies, and Thorisin were waiting for him and the groomsmen to catch up. The Emperor between them, he and Alypia started up the stairs. Behind them, pair by pair, came the groomsmen with the princess' attendants on their arms.

At the top of the stairs, flanked by lesser priests on either side, stood the new patriarch of Videssos, his hands raised in benediction. Scaurus felt a small shock every time he saw the tall, middle-aged man wearing the robe of cloth-of-gold and blue. "It seems wrong, not having Balsamon up there," he said.

Alypia nodded. "He was as much a part of the city as the Silver Gate."

"This Sebeos will make a sound patriarch," Thorisin said,

a trifle irritably; the choice of Balsamon's successor had been in essence his. As custom demanded, he had submitted three names to a synod of high-ranking clerics, who selected the former prelate of Kypas, a port city in the westlands.

"Of course he's able," Alypia said at once. "He'll have trouble, though, making himself as loved as Balsamon—he was like a favorite uncle for all Videssos. And—" She stopped abruptly. To say what Balsamon had meant to her would only remind Thorisin of complications now past. She had too much sense for that.

They spoke in low voices, for they were approaching the High Temple. As they drew near, Marcus saw that Sebeos looked decidedly anxious himself. So he might, the tribune thought—hardly in place a month, he was conducting his first great ceremony under the Emperor's eye. Not all patriarchs reigned as long as Balsamon.

When Sebeos stayed frozen a few seconds longer than he should, one of his attendant priests leaned over to whisper in his ear. "Saborios knows his job," Scaurus murmured to Thorisin, who smiled. His clerical watchdog slid smoothly back into place.

Cued, Sebeos stepped forward to meet the wedding party, saying, "May the good god send his blessings down on this union, as his sun gives the whole world light and warmth." He had a mellow baritone, far more impressive than Balsamon's scratchy tenor—and far less interesting.

With Alypia, and Thorisin, Marcus followed the patriarch in sketching Phos' sun-sign. The ritual gesture still felt unnatural, but he performed it perfectly; he had practiced.

Sebeos bowed, turned, and led the way into the High Temple. The outside of the great building had a heavy impressiveness to it, with its walls of unadorned stucco, small windows, and massive buttresses to support the weight of the central dome and the smaller half-domes around it. For the interior Scaurus had his memories, as well as more recent ones of the shrine at Garsavra, which aped its greater model. He discovered how little they were worth the moment he set foot inside.

He could have overlooked the luxury of the seats that ranged out from the altar under the dome in each of the cardinal directions, their polished oak and sandalwood and ebony and glistening mother-of-pearl, the more easily because they were filled by notables not important enough to join the wedding party. The colonnades faced with moss agate were lovely, but the Grand Courtroom had their match in multicolored marble.

The interior walls reproduced the heavens, east and west mimicking sunrise and sunset with sheets of bloodstone, rose quartz, and rhodochrosite rising to meet the white marble and turquoise that covered the northern and southern walls down to their bases. They had their own splendor, but they also served to lead the eye up to the central dome; and before that all comparison failed.

The soft beams of light coming through the arched windows that pierced its base seemed to disembody it, to leave it floating above the High Temple. They reflected from gold and silver foil like shining milk and butter.

They also played off the golden tesserae in the dome mosaic itself; the sparkle shifted at every step Scaurus took. And that shifting field of gold was only the surround of the great image of Phos that looked down from on high on his worshipers, his long, bearded face stern in judgment. Beneath that awesome countenance, with its omniscient eyes that seemed to bore into his soul, the tribune could not help feeling the power of the Videssian faith and could only hope to be recorded as acceptable in the sealed book Phos bore in his left hand. The god depicted in the dome would give him justice, but no mercy.

He must have missed a step without noticing, for Alypia whispered, "It affects everyone so." That, he saw, was true. Even the imperials who worshipped in the High Temple daily kept glancing up at the dome, as if to reassure themselves that the Phos there was not singling them out for their sins.

A choir in a vestibule behind the northern seats burst into song, hymning Phos' praises in the archaic liturgical language Marcus still could only half follow. He thought how different Videssian marriage customs were from those of Rome. In Rome, while ceremonies, of course, usually accompanied a marriage, what made it valid was the intent of its partners to be married; the ceremonies themselves were not necessary. To the Videssians, the religious rites *were* the marriage.

As Scaurus, Alypia, and Thorisin passed the inmost row of seats, the Empress Alania stood and joined her husband. Because of her pregnancy, she had not walked in the wedding procession, but come ahead in a sedan chair. The Avtokrator would not risk her health, though in her flowing formal robes the child she was carrying did not show. She had olive skin and jet-black hair like Komitta Rhangavve's, but her face was round and kindly; her eyes, her best feature, were dark, calm pools. Thorisin, Marcus thought, had chosen wisely.

Then the tribune had no time for such trivial ruminations, for the wedding party had reached the holy table in front of the ivory patriarchal throne. The Emperor and Empress stepped back a pace. As he had been drilled, Marcus took Alypia's right hand in his left and laid them on the altartop; the polished silver was cool beneath his fingertips. Smiling, Alypia squeezed his hand. He gently returned the pressure.

From the other side of the holy table, Sebeos said softly, "Look at me." Marcus saw the patriarch take a deep breath. Until that moment he had held his own nerves under tight control, but suddenly he heard everything through the pounding of his heart.

The choir fell silent. Sebeos intoned the creed with which the Videssians began every religious service: "We bless thee, Phos, Lord with the right and good mind, by thy grace our protector, watchful beforehand that the great test of life may be decided in our favor."

Marcus and Alypia echoed the prayer together. He did not stumble. Having decided at last to acknowledge Phos' faith, he was determined to do so properly.

The High Temple filled with murmurs as the faithful also repeated the creed. A couple of high Namdalener officers ended it with their own nation's addition: "On this we stake our very souls." Their neighbors frowned at the heresy.

Sebeos also frowned, but carried on after a glance at the Emperor told him Thorisin did not want to make an issue of it. Again the prayers were in the old-fashioned liturgical tongue, as were Scaurus' memorized responses. He knew in a general way that he was asking Phos' blessing for himself, for his wife to be, and for the family they were founding.

He gave all the correct replies, though sometimes so quietly that only those closest to him could hear. Alypia squeezed his fingers again, encouraging him. Her own responses rang out firmly. Usually she was more outgoing in private than in large gatherings, but she was determined to make this day an exception.

Finishing the prayers, Sebeos returned to contemporary Videssian. He launched into a homily on the virtues that went into a successful marriage which was so perfectly conventional that Marcus found himself anticipating what the patriarch would say three sentences before it came. Respect, trust, affection, forbearance—everything was in its place, correct, orderly, and unmemorable.

In Latin, Viridovix whispered loudly, "Och, there's a man could make sex dull."

Marcus had all he could do not to explode. He wished for Balsamon, who would have taken the same theme and turned it into something worth hearing.

Eventually, Sebeos noticed the Emperor tapping his foot on the marble floor. He finished in haste: "These virtues, if diligently adhered to, are sure to guarantee domestic felicity."

Then, his manner changing, he asked Alypia and Scaurus, "Are the two of you prepared to cleave to these virtues together, and to each other, so long as you both may live?"

Marcus made his voice carry: "Yes."

This time Alypia's answer came soft: "Oh, yes."

As they spoke the binding words, Thorisin stepped forward to place a wreath of myrtle and roses on the tribune's head, while Alania did the same for Alypia.

"Behold them decked in the crowns of marriage!" Sebeos cried. "It is accomplished!"

While the spectators burst into applause, Scaurus slipped a ring onto the index finger of Alypia's left hand. That again followed the Videssian way; the Romans preferred the third finger of the same hand, believing a nerve connected it directly to the heart. The ring, however, was of his own choosing—gold, with an emerald set in a circle of mother-of-pearl. Alypia had not seen it before. She threw her arms around his neck.

"Kiss her, tha twit!" Viridovix whooped.

That had not been part of the ceremony as rehearsed; the tribune glanced at Thorisin to see if it fell within the bounds of custom. The Emperor was grinning. Marcus took that for permission. The cheers got louder. There were bawdy shouts of advice, of the same sort he had heard—and called—at weddings back in Mediolanum. Human nature did not change, and a good thing, too, he thought.

He felt Alypia tense slightly; some of the shouts must have touched memories she would sooner have left buried. Shaking her head in annoyance, she made a brave face of it. "This is us, as it should be," she said when he tried to comfort her. "It's all right now."

The crowds had thinned when the wedding party emerged

from the High Temple for the return procession to the feast laid out in the Hall of the Nineteen Couches. The palace servitors bore freshly filled bags, bigger than the ones from which they had thrown coins on the way to the High Temple, but the city folk were much less interested in these; they held only nuts and figs, symbols of fertility.

Full circle, Marcus thought as he walked through the smoothly polished bronze doors of the Hall of the Nineteen Couches. He had met Alypia here the Romans' first evening in Videssos the city, along with so many others. He was lucky Avshar had not killed him that very night.

As tradition decreed, he and Alypia shared a single cup of wine; a serving maid hovered near them with a silver ewer to make sure it never emptied. Others were quite able to take care of such matters on their own—Gawtruz, the fat, bald ambassador from Thatagush, had somehow managed to filch an ewer for himself. "Haw! Congratulations I you give!" he shouted in broken Videssian. He found it useful to play the drunken barbarian, but in fact he was no one's fool and could use the imperial tongue without accent and with great polish when he chose.

A fried prawn in one hand, Thorisin Gavras used the other to pound on a tabletop until he had everyone's attention. He pointed to another table, in a corner close to the kitchen doors, which was piled high with gifts. "My turn to add to those," he said.

There was a polite spatter of applause and a few raucous cheers from celebrants already tipsy. Gavras waited for quiet to return. "I've already honored the groom with the rank of yposevastos, but you can't eat rank, though I sometimes think that in the city we breathe it." Inevitably, a joke from the Emperor won laughter.

Thorisin went on, "To live on, I grant him the estates in the westlands forfeited to the crown by the traitor and rebel Baanes Onomagoulos and grant him leave to settle on those estates the men of his command, so he and they may have the means to defend Videssos in the future as they have in the past."

In the near future, Marcus thought; Onomagoulos' lands were near Garsavra, on the edge of Yezda-infested territory. A rich gift but a dangerous one—Thorisin's style through and through. And the Emperor had also granted him what every Roman general sought, land for his troops.

Filled with pride, he bowed nearly double. He whispered to Alypia, "You put him up to that last part." Having studied Videssos' past, she had seen that the Empire's troubles began when it weakened the population of farmer-soldiers settled on the countryside.

She shook her head. "My uncle makes his own decisions, always." Her eyes sparkled. "I think this was a very good one."

So, apparently, did most of the Videssians, who crowded up to Scaurus to congratulate him all over again—and perhaps to reappraise one grown suddenly powerful among them. If they thought less of him because he was not of their blood, they were careful not to show it.

But Provhos Mourtzouphlos was bold enough to shout, "This accursed foreigner doesn't deserve the honors you're giving him!"

Thorisin's voice grew cold. "When your services match his, Provhos, you may question me. Until then, hold your tongue." The hotheaded young noble, true to his own principles, stamped out of the Hall.

That was the only incident marring the day's festivities, though Marcus had an anxious moment when Thorisin steered him over to the gifts table and said, "I suppose you can explain this."

"This" was an exquisite ivory statuette of a standing warrior, perhaps a foot tall, carved in the ebullient, rococo style of Makuran. The sword the warrior brandished was of gold; his eyes were twin sapphires. "It's from Wulghash," the tribune said lamely.

"I know that. First damned wedding present ever delivered behind shield of truce, I'd wager." The Emperor seemed more amused than anything else; Scaurus relaxed.

"Here's fine silk," Gavras said, running an appreciative hand along a bolt of the smooth lustrous fabric, which was dyed a deep purple-red. "A rich gift. May I ask who it came from?"

"Tahmasp," Marcus said.

Thorisin raised an eyebrow at the exotic name, then placed it. "Oh, that caravaneer you traveled with. How did he find out you were getting harnessed?"

"No idea," the tribune said, but nothing Tahmasp did could surprise him any more. The surprise was the throwing knife next to the silk. That was from Kamytzes, and Marcus had thought the caravan guard captain utterly without sentiment.

After the Emperor let him go, Marcus returned to Alypia's side. A clavier on a little raised platform tinkled away, accompanied by flutes and a couple of men sawing away at viols of different sizes. The music was soft and innocuous; the tribune, who cared little for such things, hardly noticed it.

It mightily annoyed Senpat Sviodo, though. He slipped a servant a few coppers and gave him the password to the legionary barracks so the sentries would not take him for a thief. The man trotted away, coming back shortly with the Vaspurakaner's pandoura. "Ha! Well done," Senpat said, and tipped him again.

He sprang onto the platform. Startled, the musicians came to a ragged halt. "Enough of this pap!" Senpat cried. "My lords and ladies, here's a tune to suit a celebration!" His fingers struck a ringing chord. Heads turned, as if drawn by a lodestone. He sang in a clear, strong tenor, stamping out the rhythm with a booted foot.

Not many could follow the song, which was in the Vaspurakaner tongue, but no one could stand still with that wild music ringing through the Hall. Before long, the feasters were spinning in several concentric rings, one going one way, the next the other. They raised their hands to clap out the beat with Senpat.

Alpia's foot was tapping. "Come on," she said, touching Marcus' sleeve. He hung back, having no taste or skill for dancing. But he yielded to her disappointed look and let himself be steered into the outer ring.

"You don't get away that easy!" Gaius Philippus said. The treacherous senior centurion was in the next ring in; when he whirled past the tribune, he reached out and tugged him and Alypia toward the center.

Other dancers, laughing and clapping, pulled them further in, at last shoving them into the open space in the center of the rings, where Viridovix had been dancing alone. "Sure and it's yours," the Gaul said, easing back into the inner ring.

Scaurus felt like a man condemned to speak after Balsamon. Viridovix' Celtic dance, performed with gusto, had drawn every man's—and woman's—eye. It was nothing like the dances of the Empire, for he held his upper body motionless and kept his hands always on his hips. But his steps and leaps were at the same time so intricate and so athletic that they vividly displayed his skill.

The tribune kicked and capered, sometimes with the tune but more often not. Even with Alypia slim and graceful beside him, he knew he was cutting a sorry figure. But he soon realized it did not matter. As the bridegroom, he was supposed to be in the center. Past that, no one cared.

Senpat Sviodo finished with a virtuoso flourish, shouted "Hai!" and leaped off the platform to a storm of applause, his pandoura high over his head. Panting a little, Marcus made his escape.

Senpat's talent and his striking good looks drew a flock of admiring ladies to him. He flirted outrageously with all his new conquests and went no further with any; Scaurus saw him tip his wife a wink. Nevrat stood back easily, watching him enjoy himself.

Viridovix, Marcus thought, should also be getting some attention after his exhibition. The Gaul, though, was nowhere to be seen.

He came back through a side door a few minutes later, followed not quite discreetly enough by a noblewoman adjusting her gown. The tribune frowned; come to think of it, this was not the first time Viridovix had disappeared.

The Gaul must have caught Scaurus' expression from across the Hall. He weaved toward him. "Sure and you're right," he said in Latin as he drew near. "I'm a pig, no mistake." Only then did Marcus notice how drunk he was.

Viridovix' eyes filled with tears. "Here my sweet Seirem is dead, and me rutting like a stoat wi' Evdoxia and—och, the shame of it, I never found out t'other one's name!"

"Easy, there." Marcus set his hand on the Gaul's shoulder.

"Aye, tha can speak so, having a fine lass to wife and all. Me, I ken how lucky y'are. This hole-and-corner friking is a cruel mock, but what other way is there o' finding again what I lost?"

"What troubles him?" Alypia asked. She had not been able to follow the conversation, but the Celt's woe was plain without words. At Viridovix' nod, Scaurus quickly explained.

She considered the problem seriously, as if it were some historical dilemma. Finally she said, "The trouble, I think, is the confusion between what's called lovemaking and actual love. There's no faster road to a woman's heart than the one that starts between her legs, but many surer ones."

"Summat o' wisdom in that," Viridovix said after owlish

pondering. He turned to Marcus, drunkenly serious. "A treasure she is. Do be caring for her."

"Shall I put him to bed, Scaurus?" Gorgidas appeared at the tribune's elbow, as usual where he was needed.

"Aye, I'll go with ye." Viridovix spoke for himself, then bowed to Alypia with great dignity. "My lady, I'll take myself off the now, and bad cess to me for being such an oaf as to put a gloom on your wedding day."

"Nonsense," she said crisply. "Lightening sorrows should always be in season, and too seldom is. I remember." Her voice went soft, her eyes far away. Marcus slipped an arm around her.

She shivered and came back to herself. "Don't fret over me. I'm fine, truly." She spoke quietly, but with something of the same briskness she had used toward Viridovix. When Scaurus still hesitated, she went on, "If you must have it, one proof we're right for each other is that you noticed I was low. And here's another." She kissed him, which brought a huzza from the feasters. "There. Do you believe me now?"

The best answer he could find was kissing her back. It seemed to be the right one.

Some wedding guests were still singing raucously in the darkness outside the secluded palace building the imperial family used as its own. No one followed Marcus and Alypia in, though, but Thorisin and Alania, and they went off to their own rooms at once.

The tribune swung open the door to the suite he and Alypia would live in until they left the city to take up the estate the Emperor had granted him. Servants had already come and gone, only minutes before; a sweating silver wine jar rested in a basin of crushed ice, with the customary one cup beside it. The bedcovers, silken sheets and soft furs, were turned down. A single lamp burned on the table by the bed.

Alypia suddenly let out a squeak. "What are you doing? Put me down!"

Marcus did, inside the chamber. Grinning, he said, "I've followed Videssian ways all through this wedding. No complaints—it's only fitting. But that was one of mine. A bride should be carried across the threshold."

"Oh. Well, all right. You might have warned me."

"Sorry." He looked and sounded so contrite that Alypia burst out laughing.

Relieved, Marcus shut and barred the door. He started to laugh, too. "What is it, husband?" Alypia asked. She used the word with the proud possessiveness new brides have. "Or should I say, proved husband?" she asked mischievously, pantomiming him lifting her.

"Not proved by that," he answered. "I was just thinking, though, that that was the first time I've locked a door behind us without worrying that someone was going to kick it down."

"For which Phos be praised," Alypia said at once. Her laugh was a little nervous. "It's also, you will note, a stouter door."

"So it is, though I hadn't planned to talk about it all night."

"Nor I." She glanced at the ewer of wine. "Do you want much more of that? It's a kindly notion, but I think another cup would only put me to sleep."

"Can't have that," Marcus agreed gravely. "I drank enough at the feast, too, I think."

He took off the fragrant wedding-wreath and started to toss it to one side. "Don't do that!" Alypia exclaimed. "They go on the headposts of the bed, for luck." She took his marriage-crown from him and hung it on the nearer post, then removed hers and climbed onto the bed to set it on the other.

The tribune stepped forward and joined her. She hugged him fiercely, whispering, "Oh, Marcus, we came through everything! I love you."

He had time to say, "And I you," before their lips met.

The thick ceremonial robes hampered their embrace nearly as much as armor would have, but the fastenings were easier for Scaurus to undo. "Hurry," Alypia said as he began to pay attention to his own robe. "It's chilly here alone."

But she frowned when he shrugged the robe back from his shoulders. "That one is new," she said, running her finger down the long scar on his chest.

"It's the one I took in Mashiz. It would be worse, but Gorgidas healed it."

"Yes, I remember your saying so. It's in front, like any honorable wound. But it surprised me, and I want to get used to you again."

"There'll be years for that now." He gathered her in.

She held him tightly. "Yes. Oh, yes."

He blew out the lamp.

* * *

Gaius Philippus splashed through a puddle in the forum of Palamas. "Getting on toward spring. These last three storms only dropped rain, no new snow for a while now."

Marcus nodded. He bought a little fried squid, ate it, and licked his fingers clean. "I wish I could talk you into going to the westlands."

"How many times have we been through that?" the senior centurion said patiently. "You want to go live on a farm, fine, go' ahead. Me, I was raised on one—and I got out just as fast as I could."

"It wouldn't be like that," Scaurus protested. "You'd have the land to do what you want with, not some tiny plot you couldn't help starving on."

"So I'd bore myself to death instead. Is that better? No, I'm happy with the slot Gavras offered me. At least as infantry drillmaster I'll know what I'm doing. Don't worry over me; I won't forget my Latin. A good solid Roman cadre'll be staying in the city with me." That was true; while most of the legionaries eagerly accepted farms on the estate the Emperor had granted Marcus, a couple of dozen preferred more active duty. Thorisin was glad to keep them on so they could train Videssian foot soldiers up to their standard.

"The job counts for something," Gaius Philippus insisted. "The lot of you will lose your edge out there, too busy with the crops and the beasts and the brats to bother with drill. You won't hand it down to your sons, and it'll be lost for good unless the imperials remember—and with me teaching, they will. I'm no scribbler like Gorgidas; what better monument can I leave behind?"

"Anyone who lives through your exercises remembers them forever," Marcus assured him. He grunted, mostly in pleasure. The tribune went on, "All right, you've argued me down again. But we won't stop being soldiers ourselves, either, not with the Yezda for neighbors. Still, the main thing is that I'm selfish. I'll miss having you at my right hand—and plain miss you, come to that."

"Well, by the gods—" The veteran had no truck with Phos —"it's not as if we'll never see each other again. Come trouble, first thing Thorisin'll do is call up the Romans. And if the Yezda give *you* trouble, we'll come down from the capital to hold the line or push Yavlak further up the plateau.

"Besides, not wanting to farm doesn't mean I won't visit.

I'll be by every so often, guzzling your wine and pinching your wenches for as long as you can stand me. And who knows? One of these days I may get over to Aptos again, and you'd be the perfect jumping-off point for that."

"Of course." Over the winter, Gaius Philippus had talked repeatedly of courting Nerse Phorkaina. Scaurus did not believe he would ever get around to it on his own. He frowned a little. From the friendly reception she had given the veteran the previous fall, he thought she might be interested. Maybe a message telling her to make a discreet first move might help. He filed the idea away, to act on when he found the time.

Here and there green leaf buds were appearing on the trees in the palace compound. The first hopeful new grass had begun to poke through the dead, muddy, yellow-brown growth of the previous year.

Gaius Philippus left to argue with an armorer over the proper balance of a dagger. Marcus went on to the imperial family's private residence. The cherry trees surrounding the brick building were still bare-branched; soon they would be full of fragrant pink blossoms.

Rather absently, Scaurus returned the salute of the guardsmen at the door. His eyes were on the crates and boxes and bundles piled outside: furnishings and household goods ready to ship to his new home when the dirt roads in the westlands dried enough. Years of army life had got him used to making do with very little; the thought of owning so much was daunting.

The hallway smelled faintly of sour milk. The midwives had ushered Pharos Gavras into the world a month early, but he was strong and healthy, even if he did look like a bald, pink, wizened monkey. Marcus cringed, remembering the hangover he'd had after Thorisin celebrated the birth of his heir.

Alypia's voice was raised in exasperation. "What exactly do you mean by that, then?" she demanded.

"Not what you're reading into it, that's certain!" The reply was equally bad-tempered.

The tribune looked in at the open study door. Like the rest of the suite, the room was sparsely furnished; bare, in fact, but for a couch and a writing table in front of it. The rest had already been packed.

"Softly, softly. The two of you will have the eunuchs running for cover, or more likely the sentries running this way to pry you from each other's throats."

Alypia and Gorgidas looked simultaneously shamefaced and defiant. The secretary sitting between them looked harassed. Scaurus saw he had written only a few lines, and scratched out several of those. Gorgidas said, "Now I understand the myth of Sisyphos. The rock he had to push up the hill was a translation, and I'm surprised it didn't crush him when it fell back."

Then the Greek had to explain Sisyphos to Alypia, who scribbled a note that might appear one day in her own history. "Though who can tell when that will be done?" she said to Marcus. "Another reason for coming back to Videssos often —how am I to write without the documents to check, the people to ask questions of?"

Before he could answer, she had turned back to Gorgidas. Scaurus was used to that; the long labor of turning the Greek's work into something a Videssian audience might want to read had left them thick as thieves. Alypia sighed. "It's a fine line we walk. If we're too literal, what you've written makes no sense in my language, but when we stray too far the other way, we lose the essence of what you've said. *Eis kórakas*," she added: "To the crows with it," a Greek curse that made both the tribune and Gorgidas laugh in surprise.

The physician's irritability collapsed. "What business do I have grumbling? When I started writing, I thought I would be the only one ever to read this mess, save maybe Marcus. Who else could? To have it published—"

"It deserves to be," Alypia said firmly. "First as an eyewitness account, and second because it's history as history should be done—you see past events to the causes behind them."

"I try," Gorgidas said. "The part we're fighting through now, you understand, I didn't see for myself; I have it from Viridovix. Here, Scaurus, be useful." He thrust a parchment at the Roman. "How would *you* render this bit into Videssian?"

"Me?" Marcus said, alarmed; most of his efforts in that direction had not been well received. "Which part?" Gorgidas showed him the disputed passage. Hoping he remembered what a couple of Greek verbs meant, he said, "How about, 'Some clans backed Varatesh because they hated Targitaus, more because they feared Avshar'?"

"That's not bad," Gorgidas said. "It keeps the contrast I was drawing." Alypia pursed her lips judiciously and nodded.

"Let me have it again, please," the secretary said, and wrote it down.

Gorgidas and Alypia combined to tear Scaurus' next suggestion to pieces.

A little later, after more wrangling, Gorgidas said, "Enough for now. Maybe it'll go better, looked at fresh." His nod to Alypia was close to a seated bow. He told her, "If you like, I'd count it a privilege to search out the manuscripts you need and send them on to you at your new home. That can't take the place of your own inquiries, of course, but it might help some."

"A bargain," she said with the same quick decisiveness Thorisin might have shown. A warm smile and a word of thanks softened the resemblance.

The Greek rose to take his leave. "You'll be busy, doing your research, and some for Alypia, and healing, too," Marcus remarked as he walked to the entranceway with him.

"Physicians are supposed to be busy. As for running down the odd book for your wife, that's the least I can do, wouldn't you say? Not only for the favor she's shown me, but also because I've learned a great deal from her."

Scaurus thought the Greek could give no greater praise, but Gorgidas amazed him by murmuring, "Pity she has no sister." He barked laughter at the tribune's expression. "Not everything that happened on the steppe got written down. I can manage, after a fashion, and I'd like a son one day." As if on cue, a thin cry floated down the hall from the nursery.

One of the sentries outside must have told a dirty story. Scaurus heard chuckles, and then Viridovix saying, "Get on wi' your bragging, now. You're after reminding me o' the flea that humped the she-wolf and told her, 'Sure and I hope I've not hurt you, my dear.'"

More laughter; beside the tribune, Gorgidas let out a strangled snort. The guardsman said, "Did you come here to insult me, or do you have some honest reason?"

"Och, I like that," the Gaul exclaimed, as if cut to the quick. "But aye, I'm for Scaurus, if he's to home."

"I'm here." Marcus stepped out of the hallway into the watery sunshine.

"It's himself himself," Viridovix cried. He waved at the piled boxes and chests. "Sure and you must've emptied out all the palaces, and the High Temple, too. Me, I could carry what I'll bring with me on my back."

"Remember, though, mules carry an uncommon lot," Gorgidas said. "And if Thorisin hadn't set you up on your own estate, half the nobles in town would have clubbed together to buy you one and get you away from their wives."

The Gaul shrugged. "T'other half married ugly lasses, puir spalpeens." Gorgidas threw his hands in the air, defeated. The guards laughed so hard they had to hold each other up. Viridovix had not been able to take Alypia's advice to heart; his philanderings were notorious all over the city. But he was so good-natured through them that he had somehow kept from making any mortal enemies, male or female.

Marcus said, "Did you come here to insult me, or do you have some honest reason?"

"What an unco wicked man y'are, t'stand in there and spy on me. But you're right, I do." To the sentries' disappointment, he dropped into Latin. "Now we're for it and about to be going and all, I'd fain thank you for talking the Gavras into granting me land for my own self, and not just a chunk I'd have from you."

"Oh, that," Marcus said in the same tongue. "Forget it; the other way embarrassed me as much as it did you. Thorisin just sees all of us as one band and, since he's mostly dealt with me, he didn't think to do otherwise this time. Not," he added, "that you ever took orders from me."

"Forbye, you never tried to give 'em, and I'll thank you for that, too." Viridovix drew himself up with lonely pride. "Still and all, I'm not sorry to be on my own. I wouldna have Gaius Philippus say he was right all along, and the only Celt here a Roman gillie."

"Are you still fighting that idiot war?" Gorgidas said in disgust. "Haven't you found enough new ways here to satisfy your barbarian craving for gore?"

"Let him be," Marcus said. "We all remember, as best we can. It helps us hang together."

"Aye," Viridovix said. "You Romans now, you're the lucky ones, wi' sic a mort o' ye here. Belike even your grandsons'll recall a word or two o' Latin. And the Greek has his histories for keepsake. So I'll remember, too, and a pox on anyone for saying I shouldna bother." He looked pointedly at Gorgidas.

"Oh, very well," the physician said with bad grace. He fumed for a few seconds, then smiled lopsidedly. "I'm always annoyed when you outargue me. Those droopy red whiskers make me forget the brain behind them." Shaking his head, he strode off.

"Here, wait!" Viridovix shouted. "We'll hash it out further over a stoup o' the grape." He trotted after Gorgidas.

The guardsmen might not have been able to follow the conversation, but they recognized the tone. "Remind me of my dog and cat, they do," one said to Scaurus.

"You have it," the tribune said.

He went back into the imperial residence, walking past the portrait of the ancient Emperor Laskaris, whose harsh peasant face gave him more the look of a veteran underofficer than a ruler. The bloodstain marring the lower part of the picture was one of the few reminders of the desperate fighting against Onomagoulos' assassins two years before. Most of the damage had been made good, but Laskaris' image was impossible to clean and too precious to throw away.

The secretary came out of Scaurus' doorway. Alypia's voice pursued him: "I'd like a fair copy of that tomorrow, Artanas, if you can have it by then."

Artanas' shoulders heaved in a silent sigh. "I'll do my best, your Highness." He sighed again, bowed to the tribune, and hurried off, tucking his case of pens into his tunic.

"I shouldn't drive him so hard," Alypia said when Marcus joined her inside. "But I want to do as much as I can before we leave for the westlands." She gave a rueful laugh. "Not that I can accomplish much, with three quarters of my things stowed away where I can't get at them."

The tribune had learned she complained only over minor upsets; she did not let frets get in the way of dealing with real problems. Knowing that, he should have changed the subject. Because he was still adjusting to her, though, he said anxiously, "I hope it won't be too strange for you, away from Videssos the city."

She looked at him with mixed fondness and exasperation. "Strange? It'll be more like going home. Have you forgotten I grew up on a country holding not very far from the one we're taking? I never thought I'd see the city until my father led the revolt that cast out Strobilos Sphrantzes. No, you needn't fear for me on that score."

Flustered because he *had* forgotten, Marcus said, "All right," so unconvincingly that Alypia could not help laughing.

"It really is all right," she assured him. "This is the happy ending the romances write about, the one we all know doesn't happen in real life. But we have it, you and I—the villain overthrown, you with the acclaim you deserve, and the two of us together, as we should be. Is any of that bad?"

He laughed himself. "No," he said, "especially the last," and kissed her. He was telling the truth; his previous experience reminded him how lucky he was. One sign was the absence of the grinding fights that had punctuated his time with Helvis. But that was only the most obvious mark of a greater tranquility. Not the least reason for it, he knew, was his learning from earlier mistakes.

Yet there was no denying the part Alypia played in their contentment together. By not trying to make him over, he thought, she left him free to change for himself instead of being frozen behind a defensive shell.

The proof of her success—and perhaps of his own—was that they cared for each other more as time went by, where before happiness had steadily leaked away once passion cooled.

That was not to say he and Alypia did not have differences. She had just shown one, with her talk of happy endings. He thought the imperial religion, with its emphasis on the battles between good and evil, had much to do with that.

Scaurus had come to terms with Phos himself, but he still felt the influence of his Stoic upbringing. Endings *were* for romances, which did not have to worry about what came after them. In the real world trouble followed trouble without cease; there was only one ending, and that predetermined.

But many roads led toward it. "Call this a good beginning," he said, and Alypia did not argue.

(1967)
1979–1983
(1985)

ABOUT THE AUTHOR

Harry Turtledove is that rarity, a lifelong southern Californian. He is married and has two young daughters. After flunking out of Caltech, he earned a degree in Byzantine history and has taught at UCLA and Cal State Fullerton. Academic jobs being few and precarious, however, his primary work since leaving school has been as a technical writer. He has had fantasy and science fiction published in *Isaac Asimov's, Amazing, Analog, Fantasy Book,* and *Playboy.* His hobbies include baseball, chess, and beer.